"DON'T *EVER* KISS A MAN LIKE THAT, ABBY. NOT UNLESS YOU MEAN IT."

Startled at both his odd words and his hoarse tone, she reluctantly lifted her gaze to meet his once more. "Unless I mean it? What do you—oh!" She drew a sharp breath, forgetting to be embarrassed. "Do you think I *didn't* mean it? That I kiss just *any* man that way?"

She tried to jerk out of his grasp, for she was both hurt and angered by his unfair assumption about her. But Tanner's fingers tightened on her, an iron hold she could not shake off.

"I know you haven't," he replied, not rising at all to her anger.

The meaning of his words sank in. . . . He knew she had never kissed anyone that way before because she had done it so ineptly. Hot and painful, her cheeks again burned scarlet.

"I . . . I'm sorry," she mumbled. "I'll do better next time—" Then her eyes widened when she realized the implication of what she had said.

"If you do much better, Abigail Morgan, you'll probably kill me." He swept his hat off his head and raked one hand through his long, disheveled hair. "And think twice about kissing me again, because I don't know if I'll have the willpower to stop at just one kiss."

When Lightning Strikes

A Dell Book

Published by
Dell Publishing
a division of
Bantam Doubleday Dell Publishing Group, Inc.
1540 Broadway
New York, New York 10036

The trademark Dell® is registered in the U.S. Patent and Trademark Office.

ISBN: 0-440-21568-4

Printed in the United States of America

Published simultaneously in Canada

March 1995

10 9 8 7 6 5 4 3 2 1

RAD

*In 1855 Nathaniel Hawthorne
complained to his publisher, "America
is now wholly given over to a damned
mob of scribbling women and I should
have no chance of success."*

*To scribbling women everywhere,
I fondly dedicate this book.*

1

St. Joseph, Missouri
April 19, 1855

Morgan. How she hated having to go by the last name Morgan.

Abigail Bliss stared gloomily across the brown, churning waters of the Missouri River and beyond, to the rolling plains of the Kansas Territory. Everything was brown. The dried grasses, the few trees, the mud. The water. Even the sky, cold and heavy, threatening rain—or maybe sleet—was dark and muddy-looking. Until the wild prairie grasses began to grow, providing forage for the animals, the wagon train was going nowhere.

Maybe this year the grass wouldn't turn green at all and they wouldn't be able to go. But Abby knew that was a foolish hope. With a resigned sigh she moved nearer the bluff, braving the icy wind that raced across the endless, unobstructed plains. She clutched her blue broadcloth skirt and muslin apron with one hand as she peered down at the activity below. Wagons lined up along the banks of the rushing water, a long ribbon of white canvas covers, waiting to be ferried across.

The entire world appeared to be waiting on the banks of the Missouri River. People from Iowa and Illinois, from Missouri and Indiana, and even farther east. Everyone was waiting for the river to go down, the muddy ground to firm up, and the prairies to turn green. Only then would they swim the stock and ferry the wagons across. And so everyone in St. Joe just had to bide their time.

Abby turned her back on the river and the biting wind —and the territory beyond. She'd grudgingly reconciled herself to the fact that they were making the long trek to the Oregon Territory, but she didn't pretend to like it, nor to understand one thing about her father's desperate urge to get going. His insistence that they go by the name Morgan made absolutely no sense to her; at times she thought he was crazy. Today especially she was hard-pressed to be charitable toward him, for he'd sold her beloved pet, Becky, this morning, the pony he'd given her on her tenth birthday. He'd sold the pony to get an extra brace of oxen, as the wagon master had advised.

If it weren't for Tillie and Snitch, she would be completely alone.

Abby removed her precious paper tablet from her apron pocket, then found a protected spot and sat down. She pulled out one of her two graphite pencils and absently checked the point.

Tillie and Snitch. She'd decided to make this story longer than her previous ones, aimed at slightly older children. Perhaps an adventure. She opened the tablet to the first page, where she'd drawn her two mouse characters. Tillie was delicate with tiny gray paws and pink-tinged nose and ears. Snitch was always trying to protect her, even when she didn't need it. He was big and strong, and sometimes clumsy. But he looked out for her.

A shout wafted up from the river below, but Abby deliberately shut it out and pursed her lips in concentration. Then she smiled, caught up as always in one of the fanciful tales she'd been spinning since she was a child. What if Tillie and Snitch decided to go west? What if the family Tillie lived with decided to leave Rose Hill Farm? Maybe Tillie decided to go, too, and Snitch . . . Snitch couldn't bear to say good-bye to her. The big lug. When was he going to realize that he loved her?

"Where have you been?"

Abby winced at her father's sharp tone. Although Robert Bliss had always been stern, he'd tempered it with love. Lately, though, his patience had grown short and his tone curt. More often then not, his ill humor was directed at her.

"Abigail. I asked you a question."

"Yes, Papa. I'm sorry. I should have told you that I planned to take a walk. See the sights."

"Alone? You wandered the streets of this uncouth town alone?"

When her father used that tone of offended morality, Abby inevitably felt like an errant child. Though she very nearly matched him in height, it was all she could do to remind herself that she was twenty now, not twelve.

"I went up to the bluffs," she explained, burying her resentment beneath the mien of a dutiful daughter. "I was alone and completely safe—"

"This is not Lebanon, Missouri." Then her father sighed and rubbed his balding pate. "You're young. You do not comprehend how immoral this world can be. How godless and truly diabolical some people are."

"Nothing happened, Papa." Abby put a hand on his arm, searching for the father who used not to scold so severely, for the man he was before her mother—his beloved Margaret—had died. "I went up to the bluffs— you know the spot. I looked west across the Missouri and the prairies toward Oregon."

He stared at her with eyes just like her own, change-able eyes that veered from green to hazel to brown. Now they were a dark, indistinct color. "You went up there to write, no doubt."

Abby smiled a little. He was softening. "Yes. I admit I did. I've decided that Tillie and Snitch are going to take a trip on a wagon train."

He snorted as if in disgust. But beneath his newly grown mustache, his lips curved in the beginning of a smile. "You'd do better to read from the Scriptures. Or at least the classics." He gestured with the book in his hand, a well-read copy of *The Odyssey*, and shook his head. "Two mice."

"I study my Bible every night, Papa. You know that. And when have you *ever* needed to encourage me to read?"

"Yes, but *what* you read. Frivolous stories." He cocked one bushy gray brow at her. But then he patted her arm. "You're a good daughter, Abigail."

They made a peaceful meal and evening of it after that. In the two and a half months since they'd left their home in Lebanon, Abby had become quite adept at cooking from the back of a wagon. Her father always built the fire while she set up the plank table that swung out from the side of the wagon. While water heated in a cast-iron pot propped up in the fire, she made biscuits, sliced potatoes, carrots, onions, and ham for a soup; and ground a handful of coffee beans.

"Captain Peters announced that our company leaves within the week," Robert said once Abby had cleared his emptied plate from the table. He took out his pipe, packed it with tobacco, then waited as Abby lit a twisted straw switch and brought it to him. He puffed three times before the tobacco caught. While he leaned back to enjoy his evening smoke, she scraped the plates clean, gathered the utensils, cups, and pots, then folded the table back.

"Sit down a minute before you attend to the dishes," he said, gesturing to the chair opposite his.

Abby didn't wait to be told twice. She was tired through and through. Living out of a wagon was hard, though she knew that wasn't the entire reason. She'd cooked and cleaned and done laundry and all the other household chores ever since she'd been old enough to be of any help. And for the past three years she'd taught school as well. No, it wasn't the work that made her so weary. It was her father and his secrecy. The not knowing.

From the day her mother had taken ill, her father had changed. For all his sternness—his schoolmaster's demeanor—Robert Bliss had loved his wife completely. Only now did Abby recognize how her mother had softened him and brought out the gentleness in him. But when Margaret Bliss had died last fall, he'd begun to change. Still, it hadn't gotten bad until four months ago. He'd received a letter. That's all she knew. Ever since then he'd been obsessed with moving west. First California. Now Oregon.

He'd uprooted them from their cozy little cottage behind the schoolhouse in Lebanon. He'd sold everything in order to stock their wagon for the lengthy trip. But he'd refused to explain a thing to her. It was that fixed silence that wore at her the most. That and the fact that he insisted they go by the name Morgan.

The last time she'd questioned him had been the worst. He'd brought the new wagon home and told her to begin packing. "But why? Why?" she'd asked, consumed by an unaccustomed anger. "Why must we leave our home?"

When he'd remained silently obstinate on the subject, her anger had dissolved into a bitter grief. "If we have to leave here, must we go so far? Surely there are relatives somewhere? I know you have none, but surely Mama must have *someone*. Distant cousins. Uncles or aunts."

"There is no one. No one!" he'd shouted, going from determined silence to a raging fury in the blink of an eye. Abby had been cowed by the intensity of his reaction. Since then she'd been careful of her words, fearful of rousing him to that frightening pitch of anger.

But tonight he was more mellow than he'd been in weeks, and she resolved to enjoy it.

"There was a lot of activity along the riverbank today," she said. "Dozens of wagons are already lining up to cross."

"Captain Peters informed me that our company shall make the crossing upstream from here. We'll assemble tomorrow at daybreak, seventy-two wagons strong. We'll camp at a spot he has selected, then begin the actual crossing—perhaps as soon as Monday. He expects it will take several days for the entire company of wagons and stock to make their way across."

He puffed a few minutes and the fragrant tobacco smoke reminded Abby of the peaceful evenings they used to share at home. In the cold spring night a hundred campfires glowed around them, spread out in the dark fields that surrounded the village of St. Joe. Lumped together, the several wagon-train companies were very like a small city, she thought. A gathering of people set to move their entire community, lock, stock, and barrel, to the other end of the continent. When she thought of it like that, it seemed a glorious sort of adventure, one she anticipated gladly.

"The good Reverend Harrison has wisely elected to join with our company."

Abby paused in the process of unwinding two thick plaits that formed a gleaming coronet at the back of her head. "How nice," she murmured. "I'm sure the Oregon Territory can use as many preachers as possible. Sarah Lewis tells me it's a rough and rowdy place."

Her father removed the pipe from his mouth. "He's taken quite a fancy to you, Abigail. He was prepared to travel with Captain Smythe's company to California. But he's altered his plans, strictly on account of you."

Abby shot her father a wary look. She had been afraid of this, but she forced herself to continue combing her fingers through the dark chestnut length of her hair. "Did he actually say that? Or did you surmise it?"

"He respectfully requested my permission to call on you. What else should I surmise?"

She stared across the softly hissing embers to where

her father sat, dimly outlined by the faint firelight. "And how did you answer him?"

"I granted him my permission of course—unless you have some very strenuous reason to object. But he's a proper gentleman, Abigail. Pious. Well read. Just the sort to make you a good husband." When she didn't respond right away, he leaned forward, his elbows on his knees. "Well, daughter? Have you nothing to say?"

Abby pushed her heavy hair behind her shoulders, then rubbed her cold, chapped hands together, trying vainly to get them warm. She picked her words carefully. "While I am sure the Reverend Harrison will make someone a very good husband, I just don't think it will be me."

Her father straightened. "And why is that?" he demanded in a belligerent tone.

"Well." Abby thought a moment. "He is pleasant and well spoken but . . . but he simply does not appeal to me in that way."

He snorted contemptuously. "I take that to mean he doesn't make your heart pound faster every time you see him."

She averted her eyes, hiding behind the long fringe of her sable lashes. How embarrassing to discuss such things with her father. "Well, I suppose that's one way to describe it."

He took a few silent puffs on his pipe. When he spoke again, his voice was gentler. "You hardly know the man."

That was true. Yet somehow Abby was certain that made no difference. Getting to know him would not change things at all.

"You're past the age when most girls marry," he continued in a reasonable tone.

"I thought you wanted me to be a teacher. I thought you wanted me to help you establish a school in Oregon. If I marry, I'll hardly have time to teach."

He didn't answer that, and Abby felt a little better. It wasn't that she was opposed to marriage. Quite the opposite. But her parents had loved each other. It had been obvious to everyone who knew them. She wanted that sort of marriage too.

"I think I'll tend to these dishes, then turn in," she said, wanting to end this conversation. She rose to her feet and reached for the water bucket.

"Yes, you do that. But Abigail," he added, halting her before she could leave, "I would like you to consider Reverend Harrison just the same. He's a fine, upstanding young man. As a reverend's wife you'd be well respected."

"Papa." She hesitated, then decided just to plunge in. "Mama told me once that she loved you from the first moment she laid eyes on you."

He went rigid at her words, and she instantly regretted bringing up the subject of her mother. But whatever emotions he felt, he hid behind a stern tone. "Mrs. Bliss may have loved me from the first, but my initial impression of her was of a prissy, useless young thing."

Abby's mouth gaped open, so shocked was she by his disclosure. "Mama? Prissy? How could you have ever thought that of her?"

"Because I didn't know her then," he bit out. "Because I made a hasty judgment about her. I have thanked the Lord every day of my life since then that He thrust us together again and granted me the opportunity to know her better. To love her."

His point was painfully clear, and anyway Abby was too dumbfounded by his revelation to speak. Her mother had revealed very little of her early life. Her father had revealed even less. To hear now that their first meeting had not been magical . . .

"Will you consent to see him, Abigail?"

Though it was termed as a question, Abby knew his words were more a command. She was not in the habit of ignoring his commands.

"Yes, Papa," she answered softly. "I will see the Reverend Harrison."

Robert Bliss's heart filled with misgivings as he watched his daughter walk away. The trek to Oregon was not enough, he'd come to realize. No, marriage to the right sort of man was the best insurance he had. The best way to protect his Abby girl. And who better than a young and idealistic preacher?

He returned his pipe to his lips, then sighed when he sucked and the bowl was cold. Every joint in his body seemed to protest when he squatted beside the dying campfire to light a bit of kindling.

Their journey to the Oregon Territory would be a test of his endurance, but he was resolved not to fail. He would cross the burning sands barefoot if necessary, anything to save Abigail from his father-in-law, Willard Hogan. Twenty-one years and the man had not changed at all. Still arrogant. Still greedy. Still determined to control the lives of his family. Well, he'd not controlled Margaret. Robert had seen to that. And he would not control his granddaughter either.

Robert sat back with his relit pipe and puffed until the tobacco was well caught. Willard Hogan had opposed the marriage of his only child to a pious schoolteacher. A *poor* schoolteacher. In truth Robert had thought Margaret Hogan just a bit of pretty fluff, without a thought in her head beyond expensive clothes, late-night dances, and endless socializing. Willard Hogan had seen his beautiful daughter as a prize to be awarded to the man who could most help Willard further his business interests. But Margaret had possessed a pure soul and a sharp mind. Once Robert had realized that, there'd been nothing for him to do but marry her.

But Hogan had tried to stop them. He'd taken Margaret to New York, Boston, and Philadelphia, shown her a glamorous time, and hoped thereby to discourage her affections for Robert. Ah, but the man had never appreciated what a jewel he'd had in Margaret, Robert smiled to remember. Margaret had come back to Chicago, more sure than ever that she wished to marry her poor-schoolteacher beau. That was when Willard Hogan had made his mistake. In a rage he'd threatened to disinherit Margaret. He'd been so sure that would make her back down. But he'd underestimated her, as always.

Robert and Margaret had wed in secret. When she'd written her father a week later, hoping to make amends, her letter had been returned unopened. Sweet Margaret had been heartbroken by her father's cruel insistence on always having his own way.

Robert pulled the pipestem from between his clenched teeth. The gall of the man to write now and ask that his grandchild be allowed to live with them in Chicago! The problem was, Hogan would never give up that easily. He'd have come to Missouri soon enough. No doubt he'd send his hired men to track them down once he found them gone. But Robert would go to his grave fighting to keep Abigail safe from the selfishness of Willard Hogan, and Reverend Harrison seemed the answer to his prayers. As wife to a preacher, Abigail could not be influenced by the wealth her grandfather flung around so confidently. It would be impossible for Hogan to lure her to Chicago. For even if the man did find her, by then Reverend Harrison would have set up his church in Oregon. The most Willard Hogan would be able to do, should he ever locate Abigail, was to make a donation to the church.

Robert snorted in derision. How appropriately fitting that would be. Hogan could donate the money and Reverend and Mrs. Harrison could build a magnificent house of worship. But no amount of money would buy Willard Hogan a place in heaven. Nor would it entice Abigail to Chicago.

He would make certain of that.

2

The pattern had been set. Abby recognized it within a week and resigned herself to it—at least for the next four or five months.

The most tedious factor of the traveling was the constant packing and unpacking of the wagon. Cross a river —unpack everything and let it dry. Stop for the night— unpack food, clothes, bedding, and cooking utensils. And with every unpacking there followed, naturally, a repacking. When she finally had a stationary home once more, she knew she'd never again complain of any household task. One day living out of a wagon was filled with more work than an entire week at home had been.

Worse, the very nature of traveling presented a completely new set of problems. The western territories were alternately dusty or muddy. Everything was always dirty. Thank goodness she'd listened to what her new friend, Sarah, had said. Only wear dark clothes. They didn't look as filthy as they actually became. The fact was, nothing stayed white for long, no matter how hard you scrubbed. Besides, she'd been told water would not always be available for washing clothes as they continued farther on their journey west.

Then there was the ordinary daily routine. Up before dawn. The men prepared the animals. The women packed up and got breakfast on. Moving west all day. At first she and her father either walked or rode together in the wagon. But that soon grew monotonous. Though she

loved her father dearly, he tended to be rather humorless
—and even more so lately. So she'd taken to walking
alongside the train, away from the rutted road, talking
with Sarah and the other women.

She and Sarah helped several young mothers mind
their younger children. Sarah looked forward to the day
she would have her own brood; Abby just missed teaching. Already she'd accumulated a faithful little band of
followers, who clamored daily for another of her whimsi-
cal tales about Tillie and Snitch. She made them up by
day as they walked, and tried to write them down in the
evenings after dinner. It nurtured her secret hope that
someday she might actually publish her stories in books
for children.

This was their eighth day out of St. Joe. Abby had
noted it in her diary as they'd waited for the morning call
to break camp. She'd also noted that they'd passed two
graves the day before, and that there was a brand-new
grave in a pretty spot near the river. But she didn't dwell
on the graves. Better to look forward than back. That
was her new philosophy. Besides, it was a beautiful,
cloudless morning with a breathtaking sunrise. She
watched enthralled as a flock of large birds—she didn't
know what kind—rose in a graceful gray cloud from a
grove of willows on the bank of the Little Blue River.

Tillie would be thrilled by such a sight, Abby thought
as she made her way through the budding spring grasses.
Tillie would simply enjoy the beauty of the magnificent
birds in flight, wishing it were also possible for little mice
to fly. Snitch, on the other hand, would worry about
what had startled them into flight in the first place. Indians. A wild dog. Or worse, a hunting cat.

Maybe she should give Tillie a bird friend who could
take the little mouse soaring above the land. Oh,
wouldn't the dour Snitch be beside himself?

Abby laughed out loud at the thought and snatched at
a tall, dry seed stalk, a remnant of last year's waist-high
prairie grasses.

"What's so funny?"

Abby glanced over at Sarah. "Oh, nothing, really. I was just . . . just daydreaming."

"Anyone I know?"

Abby rolled her eyes. "No, Sarah. Nobody you know."

It was Sarah's turn to laugh. "My, aren't you the testy one? What's the matter, didn't poor Reverend Harrison come calling again last night?"

Abby let out a great sigh. She swatted the wiry seed stalk against her brown calico skirt in an agitated rhythm. "Unfortunately he did. The thing is," she hurried to add. "He's a very nice man."

"Yes. And handsome too. Or hadn't you noticed?"

Abby shot her new friend an exasperated glance. They'd been over this subject before. But Sarah was too newly wed—and too much in love with her shy husband, Victor—to really understand Abby's position. When she spoke of Victor, Sarah's freckled cheeks glowed with color, and her brown eyes grew dreamy.

"Are you telling me, Sarah Lewis, that you married Mr. Lewis because of his looks and nothing else?"

"Of course not. It's just that . . . well, the good reverend is so clearly smitten with you. If you would just give him a chance."

Abby gazed off to the left, at the wagons that rolled along so ponderously. Reverend Harrison now shared a wagon with an older couple and their teenage son. If not for Abby's vehement protests, the Reverend Dexter Harrison would have been assigned to *their* wagon. If she hadn't prevailed upon her father's well-developed sense of propriety, she would have been thrown together with the man every day of the entire journey. But a single woman and a single man, even with her father as chaperon, would raise some eyebrows. Her father, thank the Lord, had been unable to counter that argument.

As it was, however, the reverend found more than enough excuses to visit their campsite. Like last night.

She'd already cooked him enough meals to feel like his wife.

All the duties but none of the pleasures. Then her cheeks burned scarlet at such an unseemly thought.

"You're blushing," Sarah pointed out with a giggle. "Care to tell me why?"

"No."

"Oh, c'mon, Abby. I won't tell a soul. Cross my heart."

"Are you keeping secrets from your husband so soon, then?" she replied tartly.

"Honoring a confidence could hardly be construed as keeping a secret from my husband," Sarah retorted, undeterred in the least by Abby's reticence. They walked a few moments without speaking, with only the sounds of the wagons and distant voices to mar the prairie silence. Then Sarah spoke again. "Is it the man or the fact of marriage that scares you? The *act* of marriage," she added more slyly.

Abby's flaming cheeks gave her away, and as Sarah's pealing laughter rang out, Abby knew it was pointless to pretend. She gave a frustrated sigh.

"The thing is, though I'm not the least bit interested in Reverend Harrison as a husband, I am . . . well . . . I am rather curious about things. Marriage things," she finished lamely.

"Do you fancy some other fellow?"

"No. No one in particular," Abby confessed. "But I do wonder about . . . about what it's like." She chanced a quick sidelong glance at her friend and was relieved by the becoming blush that Sarah now wore. Encouraged, she went on. "Do you . . . you know . . . like it? Being married, that is."

It was Sarah's turn to hesitate. "Um . . . well. I do like it now. But at first . . ." She sighed, then let out a nervous giggle. "Looking back on it, I think Victor was just as naive and innocent as I was. It was rather uncomfortable the first time. And we were awkward for a while.

But once we got the hang of it . . ." She trailed off with another giggle.

"So. You like it."

Sarah met Abby's earnest look. "Oh, yes. I like it very much."

Abby digested that for a few seconds. "Tell me this, then. Did you love Victor before or after . . . it."

"It?" Sarah laughed again, but when she spied Abby's hot cheeks, she managed to control her mirth. "All right. I'll tell you the whole truth. I loved Victor before I married him. After that first night, well, I wasn't so sure that I hadn't made a terrible mistake. But after a few more days we were back to rights. There. Does that help any?"

Abby smiled at Sarah and reached for her hand. "Yes, very much. But it means you must stop trying to push me on the good reverend. And him on me."

With an exaggerated sigh Sarah conceded. "You know, Abby Morgan, you've just spoiled all my fun for this trip. I was so looking forward to playing the matchmaker. Are you sure there's no one else you have an eye for?"

"No. No one at all," Abby vowed as her good humor fled. Abby Morgan. She still had not grown used to the name her father forced the two of them to use. They'd been around and around about it on the long journey to St. Joe. Or at least *she'd* gone around and around it. Her father had remained firmly and unreasonably silent on the subject. They would be the Morgans from now on, he'd sworn—or at least until they were settled in the Oregon Territory. No matter how she had pleaded, he'd absolutely refused to explain.

Despite her angry urge to rebel, or at least to threaten to do so in order to force him to explain, Abby nonetheless couldn't quite bring herself to be that openly disobedient. Her father had always been a logical, hardworking man. If he was pursuing such strange behavior, it must be for a very good reason.

Yet she couldn't help wondering if this was all con-

nected to her mother's death and the depression he still
suffered. The move. The name change. The secrecy. It
made no sense at all.

No one named Bliss had joined any of the wagon trains
that had crossed the Missouri River this year. Tanner
McKnight flung his saddlebags across his tall gelding's
back and tied them down. There was no one named
Bliss, but there were at least seven men traveling without
wives but with daughters.

He settled his wide-brimmed hat securely on his head
and squinted back at the St. Joe Palace Hotel. There
would be no soft feather beds for a while. But hell, once
he found the girl and delivered her to Hogan, he could
buy himself the biggest feather bed Chicago had to offer.
The biggest feather bed anyone in the Kansas Territory
had ever seen.

"Do you have to go so soon?"

Tanner glanced past his packhorse to the woman
standing on the hotel's wooden porch. Fancy Francie,
her name was, and she'd known a few fancy moves even
he had never seen before. Right now, though, with her
face scrubbed of all makeup and her pretty blond hair
loose on her shoulders, she looked more a schoolgirl
than the highest priced working girl in St. Joseph. Re-
calling the night they'd just spent together, he was hard-
pressed to remember what he'd even come to Missouri
for.

"I've got to go," he replied. "But the next time I'm in
town, I'll look you up."

When she only smiled, then shrugged and went back
inside, Tanner let out a frustrated oath. It had been a
long, hard ride from Chicago. It would be an even longer
ride across the vast prairies searching for Willard Hogan's grandchild. He could be on the trail for weeks, in
the company of pioneer families, every one of them
fiercely protective of their womenfolk. Last night's ener-
getic diversion might have to sustain him for a long time.

But even on the Oregon Trail there were bound to be some willing women. There always were. Still, he had no intention of spending even one more day on this misbegotten search than he had to.

He frowned, concentrating once more on the task before him. Bliss was using another name, not that Tanner was surprised. Hogan described Bliss as an idealistic fool, a man who tilted at windmills. Still, Bliss had obviously tilted at Hogan's windmill and won: He'd married the man's daughter. Now Hogan was determined to get his grandchild away from Bliss. Only Bliss was hightailing it to California. Or so he said.

California. Tanner tugged the cinch belt snug on his dappled-gray gelding and patted the animal's flank. He'd almost bought it. But why would a man tell the very person he was trying to evade where he was going? Tanner had tracked down enough wily criminals in his day to know better than to assume the obvious. For whatever reason, Robert Bliss was running from his father-in-law. But if the man thought to throw Tanner McKnight off his trail that easily, he was a fool. The man was heading west, all right. But Tanner was convinced it was to the Oregon Territory, not to California.

Tanner mentally ticked off the few facts he had to go on. Robert Bliss was average height, probably close to fifty by now. His brown hair was probably going gray. Twenty years ago he'd been a humorless sort, a stern teacher, well read and well spoken but given to a preacher's style of discourse.

As for the girl who was the real focus of his search, he knew next to nothing about her. Not her age. Not even her first name.

It was that fact that had frustrated Hogan the most, Tanner recalled. After describing what he wanted Tanner to do, the normally decisive Hogan had paced his ostentatious office restlessly, caught midway between frustration and fury.

"I don't even know her name!" he'd ranted. "I don't even know my only grandchild's name!"

"Show me the letters."

While the older man continued to mutter, Tanner had scanned the first letter Robert Bliss had sent to Willard Hogan, informing the man that Margaret Hogan Bliss had passed on after a lengthy illness. One sentence only had revealed the existence of a granddaughter. "Our daughter was a great comfort to Margaret up to the very end."

"What did you say in your letters back to him?" Tanner had asked.

"I wired him—a long message saying that I wanted to meet the girl of course. Hell, I can give her everything she wants. And if we can't get it in Chicago, we'll go where we can get it!" the older man had boasted.

"I take it he turned you down."

"The bastard! The bastard," he began again, "told me in that same holier than thou way he has to basically go to hell. He said he was taking her to California—"

The door opened without warning. "Who's going to California?"

Hogan frowned at the man who'd entered so peremptorily. "I'm having a private meeting, dammit!" Then when the man only raised his brows mildly, Hogan swore again. "Tanner, this is Patrick Brady. He handles my East Coast ventures."

"And the foreign ones." Brady extended his hand to Tanner.

Tanner nodded and shook the man's hand. "Tanner McKnight."

"You're doing some work for us in California?" Brady asked, giving Tanner a quick once-over.

"For me," Hogan answered before Tanner could. "Family business."

"What kind of business?" Brady asked. Then his brows drew together in thought. "Are you the same Mc-

Knight that tracked down the gang that hit our First City Bank?"

"And found that weasel Lanford who embezzled three thousand dollars from that railroad venture," Hogan said. "We'll be finished in a few minutes. I'll find you in your office then," he added pointedly.

Brady shrugged, then turned and left. Only then did Hogan continue. "I haven't told anyone about Margaret's child," he explained to Tanner. He paused and poured himself a whiskey with shaking hands, then tossed it back. "There's no need to tell anyone, not until I know you've found her. So keep me posted, you hear? Send me a wire as soon as you learn anything."

The rest of their meeting had been brief. Though Hogan hadn't actually admitted to Tanner that he'd disowned his own daughter when she'd married Robert Bliss, it hadn't been hard to figure out. Now the aging business tycoon was desperate to make up for his mistake of all those years past.

The thought of dragging some child back to Chicago had not sat well with Tanner. It still didn't. But the extravagant amount of money the desperate Hogan had offered had been enough to assuage Tanner's doubts. He was to bring her back with or without her father's approval. With business and political connections such as Hogan had, he could guarantee that there would be no legal repercussions to Tanner.

Not that Tanner worried too much about the law. Once he had his payment from Hogan, he'd be gone. That money would buy all the breeding stock he needed —plus a huge feather bed. When he left Chicago the next time, it would be for good.

Tanner turned the collar of his jacket up against the sharp spring wind. He checked the bulky load on his packhorse, then pulled on his leather gloves and mounted his eager horse. There were four wagon companies ahead of him out of St. Joseph, the first almost two weeks gone. He had some hard riding ahead of him,

with delicate questioning to be done at each wagon train.
It was time to get going.

The wagon train reached Fort Kearney on the Platte
River on a Saturday afternoon, and Abby couldn't imagine, a more welcome sight. Almost three weeks on the
trail, and the thought of four more months of travel was
overwhelming.

"Why don't you go see if there's a newspaper to be
had," she encouraged her father once the wagons had
made their customary circle to form their camp. "I'll see
to the oxen."

Robert Bliss squinted straight ahead, his bushy brows
nearly hiding his eyes. "Tending to the oxen is men's
work."

"No, Papa. Really, I don't mind doing it tonight.
They've become like pets to me."

He swung his balding head around to peer at her.
"Like Becky was?" he asked, referring to her horse that
he had sold. "Have you transferred your affection for
Becky to the oxen now?"

Abby heard the edge of hopefulness in his voice, and
somehow it depressed her even more. "Yes, Papa," she
lied. "I suppose I have. So you go on. I'll tend to them
and start our supper. You go on up to the fort. Look for
whatever news there might be from Oregon. And from
the states."

It was wrong of her to want to be rid of her father,
Abby knew. But she would just have to pray on it because
the fact was, after three long, rainy days spent riding
beside him in the wagon, she simply needed a little solitude. Besides, it would do him good to mingle with other
people. He was becoming far too moody, veering from
boundless enthusiasm for the Oregon Territory to dark
moments of hopelessness. The enthusiasm brought out
his eloquence; the hopelessness, however, came with silence.

He'd always been moody, she realized. But now . . .

now without her mother's mediating presence, his emotions grew ever more extreme. There were times when even his books seemed unable to console him. She watched him walk away, his gait slow and heavy. He'd aged so since her mother had died.

With a sigh she set the brake, climbed down from the box seat, and discreetly rubbed her sore behind. At least here they would rest for the Sabbath. Her father would appreciate that. He could read in peace. And he always seemed to enjoy talking to Reverend Harrison. Unfortunately.

As for her, she could only hope that his moods lightened as time went on. If not . . . If not there was nothing she could do about it but continue on as best she could. Unable to escape that grim thought, she turned to tend the oxen.

But before she could get to that, she spied the earnest young preacher approaching her, his long-legged stride purposeful, his ever-serious expression even more so. She pasted a halfhearted smile on her face and braced herself.

"Miss Morgan." He doffed his plain felt hat and swallowed hard. Even beneath his rust-colored beard she could see his Adam's apple bob.

"Good evening, Reverend Harrison."

"I . . . uh . . . I just wanted to tell you—to invite you to attend Sunday services tomorrow. I'll be preaching a special sermon I wrote, about how our duty to God is tested and changed by this journey we have embarked upon."

He would have said more, preached the sermon to her then and there, she feared. But she cut him off.

"My father and I will certainly be there, and I thank you for coming to tell us. But I really do have to see to my team," she finished, edging toward the four oxen, who were beginning to stamp in impatience. They knew their day's work was done and they were ready for a long, cooling drink and the freedom of the pasture.

The reverend nodded his head and backed off a pace. "Well. I'll just be going, then."

As Abby watched him walk away, she tried to sort through her feelings. He was a very nice man. But all she felt for him was . . . was nothing. Somehow that just couldn't be the right way to feel about a man who wanted to make her his wife.

Grateful for a diversion from thoughts that were fast becoming depressing, she turned back to her team. For all their bulk, the four oxen were an amiable lot—though nothing approaching her beloved Becky. She'd named them Matthew, Mark, Luke, and John to satisfy her father's sensibilities. Privately, however, she called them Eenie, Meenie, Minie, and Moe.

After releasing them from their harness, she guided them toward the muddy riverbank, holding the willow whip high, though she knew only a touch was needed to keep them moving. Eenie was the clear leader of the quartet, so she had made a special pet of him. He minded her, and the others followed him.

She hung back as they waded into the deep muck that edged the shallow, meandering Platte River, but in the dull light of the overcast sunset she gazed longingly at the water beyond. How wonderful it would feel to take a full-fledged bath, not just a wipe-down. Clean hair. Clean skin. Clean clothes that were truly clean. And white.

She twirled the willow whip in her hand as her mind wandered. The very first thing she wanted to get when they arrived in Oregon was a brand-new hip bath. A big one, with a high back to rest her head against. She sighed and took a step nearer the sluggish water, then staggered when her foot sank past her ankle in the loose mud.

"Jerusalem!" she swore under her breath as she struggled to keep her balance. She leaned on the slender whip, but it, too, sank in the mire. "Botheration!" she cried, for she knew she was going to fall right on her face in the mess. "Eenie—come here, Eenie!"

Such a fruitless cry for help. As if an ox would come to her aid.

To Abby's surprise, however, a large animal did move right up beside her. Before she quite realized what was happening, a pair of hands reached down and plucked her effortlessly from the thick mud. To her complete amazement, instead of finding herself facedown in the slime, she was sitting crosswise on a tall gray horse, in the lap of a dusty man she'd never seen before.

"If you'd sunk any farther, ma'am, you'd have soon been in China."

And so she would have, Abby realized gratefully. But though the man had saved her from one predicament, finding herself now in such an intimate embrace, and with someone she did not know, presented her with another, even worse dilemma.

Self-consciously she stared up at him, preparing to thank him while wondering at the same time how she was to make a graceful retreat. But her frantic thoughts stilled when she met his amused gaze.

He had the face of an angel, was her very first thought. A dark, thoroughly male angel. Though grimy with trail dust and sporting a shadow of a beard, the strong lines of his face were unmistakable. Then he smiled at her, and she amended her original opinion. His was the smile of a fallen angel. Sure. Easy. Seductive.

Her stomach gave an odd sort of lurch. If only the good Reverend Harrison had such a smile—

Abby abruptly drew herself up, aghast at such an unseemly thought. "If you would put me down," she muttered, a bit too ungraciously considering the aid he'd extended her. She leaned away from him, readying herself to leap down from her high perch. But the horse swung around, its ears cocked forward in the direction of the water. Picking its way cautiously, it moved nearer the river, then lowered its head to drink.

"Be careful, miss. You might fall." So saying, the man

pulled her nearer, holding her altogether too boldly, with one large hand around her waist.

For a moment speech fled her. A pair of hard-muscled thighs pressed against her legs and buttocks, and the wide wall of his chest seemed to hug her back. With his arms circling her, she might as well have been in an intimate embrace with this stranger. Her face burned scarlet at the very idea.

"If you could just . . . just put me down," she choked the words out.

"Surely not here." He pushed his hat back on his head and peered at her more closely. "Anyway, what's a woman doing driving oxen? Where's your husband?"

"I don't—" She broke off as common sense finally set it. "My *father* had to go up to the fort. But he'll be back any moment. And he would be most outdone should he find me in this position," she finished a little breathlessly.

To her vast confusion he only laughed. "Well, we surely can't have him outdone, can we?" With a slight movement of his knee he turned the horse from its thirsty drink. Once they were on firm footing, she scrambled down from her seat and turned to face him.

"Thank you," she mumbled, though a part of her knew he'd taken advantage of her momentary distress. She backed away another pace, but her eyes never left him. Up close she'd been conscious of his hard body, pressed so familiarly against her own. Now, however, with a little distance between them, she saw so much more. He was a big man, on a big horse, dressed as any other rider on the trail might be. But there were subtle differences.

The slight tilt of his wide-brimmed slouch hat. The width of his shoulders beneath his shirt. The way the damp cotton outlined his chest and arms. Some instinctive warning signal started her heart to racing as her eyes swept over him. He wore a gun on his hip and two rifle scabbards on his saddle, and he sat his horse like one born to it.

He was no farmer, she decided on the instant.

Then his eyes slid slowly over her, the same sort of inspection she'd given him, and her breath caught in her chest.

She'd been looked at by men before. The trail was filled with men traveling alone. Hard men. Men her father took great pains to shield her from. When they stared too boldly, however, she felt nothing but distaste —and a faint feeling of uncleanliness.

But this man . . .

Though she had even more reason to be offended by his stare—after all, he'd clasped her against him in the most intimate manner—she felt more embarrassment than anything else. Her dress was filthy, her hair bedraggled. And her face and nails . . .

In the midst of her horrified cataloguing of her awful appearance, his grin widened. "May I escort you home?"

"That . . . that won't be necessary," Abby answered, struggling to regain her composure. "I've the oxen to tend."

He nodded slightly, but his gaze never wavered. "You and your father heading to the Oregon Territory?"

"Yes."

"Just the two of you?"

There was something in his eyes when he spoke, something that suddenly made her wary. "I've got to be going." She turned toward the oxen, and retrieving the willow whip, she carefully stepped nearer to them, just touching Eenie's shoulder.

"What's your name?" the man called from behind her. When she didn't respond, he laughed low in his throat. "I've been on the trail too long, it appears. I've forgotten my manners. I hope you'll accept my apology."

At that she chanced a sidelong glance at him. He swept his black slouch hat from his head and gave a good approximation of a bow from the saddle. "May I present myself. I'm Tanner McKnight. At your service, Miss . . . Miss . . ."

Abby straightened up when he removed his hat, and watched in fascination the dark fall of his hair across his brow. His hair was black, as were his eyes. No, his eyes were blue, only a very dark, midnight blue. His brows were a dark slash across a strong, tanned face, lean and square-jawed. His nose was straight, and his lips . . . the way his lips curved as he stared at her made her heart speed up. Only when he swept his hair back and replaced his hat on his head was she able to drag her eyes away.

"I'm Miss . . . Miss Morgan," she finally answered, remembering only at the last second not to give him her real name.

"Miss Morgan." He said the name slowly, huskily, as if testing it out. And all the while he continued to study her with his compelling midnight eyes.

Where their disturbing conversation might have led, she did not get to find out, for Victor Lewis arrived at that moment, driving his two mules and four oxen. He rode his saddle mount right up to Abby, placing himself between her and her disquieting rescuer. "Is everything all right here?" he muttered for her ears only.

"Oh, yes. Yes," she replied a little too brightly. A part of her was inordinately relieved by Victor's appearance. But another side of her was still curious about the man. About Tanner McKnight. "Be careful of all that mud," she added unnecessarily.

Victor nodded and edged past her toward the sluggish waters of the Platte. Abby touched Eenie again with her whip, starting him and the others in the direction of the wagon train's community grazing area. Only when she was what seemed a safe distance away did she look back for the stranger, but he was gone. She saw him in the distance cantering away. He was hard to miss, sitting so erect on his tall gray horse. He rode in the direction of the fort, toward the ramshackle assemblage of sod buildings that was the last outpost of civilization for at least the next month.

For a moment she saw once more that dark, sardonic

face, and she couldn't help feeling her initial reaction was right. His was the beautiful, knowing visage of one of the fallen angels, and she was both frightened and fascinated by him. She knew she should avoid him at all costs even as she wondered if she would ever see him again.

She drove Eenie forward, and the other three oxen followed. But Abby's mind was not concerned with the great, lumbering beasts. Instead she debated over and over whether the man was traveling east or west.

3

Abby's mind simply would not stay focused on Reverend Harrison's sermon.

". . . with us in our hour of greatest need. Most especially," he added, his voice dropping from its thundering roll to an imploring whisper. "Most especially address the needs of our sister in the faith, Rebecca Godwin, who was attacked so cruelly yesterday."

All around her, people nodded and leaned forward, clutching the prayer books they kept so well protected in waterproof caskets in their wagons. Her father sat beside her, concentrating on his prayers. But he must have noted her lack of focus, for he gave her a sharp but unobtrusive nudge.

Abby immediately bowed her head and concentrated on her own prayer book. How could she be so absentminded when tragedy lay all around them? Graves along the trail. Rumors abounding that cholera had broken out ahead of them. And now a young girl on their wagon train had been attacked. Had someone not come along and frightened the thug away, who knows what the villain might have done to the twelve-year-old girl.

But despite her best intentions at prayer, Abby's mind was completely uncooperative. The same inappropriate thought kept surfacing. Was the man from yesterday attending services also?

She managed to restrain herself from peering over her shoulder to see. As always her father had insisted on arriving early for Sunday-morning services and had seated them just below the pulpit.

Not that it was much of a pulpit. Reverend Harrison stood behind an upended crate, his Bible and notes laid out on a bedsheet that had been draped over the rough wood. The capricious wind constantly ruffled the pages of his book, and twice he'd lost his place. Yet all things considered, Abby thought today's place of worship the finest sort of church to be found. God's sweeping blue heavens above them; His living green carpet beneath their feet. The sweetest of His music—a mockingbird's trill—to serenade them.

Abby smiled to herself, forgetting for a moment the reverend, the tribulations of the trail, and even yesterday's stranger. How lovely this land was, green and rolling, with more varieties of birds than she'd ever seen. And yet Oregon was said to be even finer. Lush. Fertile. At times like these she truly relished the journey they'd so precipitously undertaken.

". . . exhort you to embrace your fellow travelers, your brothers and sisters. See to them and their needs, for they are the children of your Father, and His love will descend on you a hundredfold."

Abby joined in singing the final hymn, though an uncomfortable blush stained her cheeks when she recognized the selection. It was "Holy, Holy, Holy," her favorite hymn. She'd revealed as much to Reverend Harrison just the other day, and the fact that he had selected it for this morning's service, and moreover was staring straight at her as he sang, was not in the least lost on her.

She made a point, during the milling pleasantries after the services, to dodge both her father and the reverend. She was simply not in the mood. Not that it would do much good, she knew. Her father undoubtedly would invite the reverend to share the midday meal with them. At this rate he would soon have her washing the man's clothes! All the wifely chores and none of the—

Her mind veered away from that thought. What *was*

her perverse fascination these days with the dealings between husbands and wives? She frowned, and hurried away from the gathering, struggling to bury her untoward feelings in the comforting rote of prayer.

"Our Father who art in heaven . . ."

She hadn't gone even half the way toward their camp when all at once the oddest shiver coursed down her spine. She paused in her purposeful departure from the Sunday meeting, and it was then she spied him. He stood beside a small canvas tent, currying his horse. But he was staring straight at her.

At once all the inappropriate feelings she always managed to keep suppressed rose up inside her. Her heart thumped madly while the most disturbing knot curled up deep in her belly.

He smiled at her—that same smile, wicked and beckoning, as if they shared some secret—and Abby actually stopped breathing. The pleasures of marriage—once more that wanton thought popped into her mind. The reverend was good husband material, but this man . . . this man made a woman think the most sinful sorts of things.

Shocked by her thoughts, knowing an unmarried woman was wrong to think such things, Abby started to turn away. But his low, compelling voice halted her.

"Good morning, Miss Morgan."

She stood there, indecisive as she seldom ever was. Her father would not want her to speak to this man. She knew that for a certainty. But she seemed unable to resist. Slowly she turned.

"Good morning. Mr. McKnight." She added his name in a voice gone breathless.

Their eyes locked across the short stretch of dirt and grass between them. At least she looked presentable this time, she thought. Her hair was neatly coiffed. She had on her best bonnet, the one she'd just added new ruffles and ribbons to. She'd brushed her plain reefer jacket until it appeared almost as good as new, and wore it over her favorite blue gored skirt.

By contrast he wore neither hat nor coat. She'd known yesterday that he was a big man, but seeing him now—his legs long and lean beneath his black nankeen trousers, his shoulders so wide that his shirt pulled across them—she felt tiny and helpless, not at all her normal self.

His hair hung nearly to his shoulders, black as pitch, yet gleaming in the bright morning sunlight. It looked almost too silky to belong to a man.

Despite the brisk spring winds, he had his sleeves rolled up as he worked. How strong his forearms looked with their light sprinkling of dark hair. Was his chest also—

She squelched that thought with a gulp. Whatever was wrong with her these days? She clutched her prayer book as if it were her only hope. "Well. A good day to you, then."

"Wait. Wait, don't run off so fast." He tossed the brush down and gave his horse a pat on the neck. Then he grinned, and her composure slipped another notch. "Come say hello to Mac."

"Mac?"

"My horse. And over there." He gestured to another sturdy animal nosing around for the tenderest grass shoots. "That's Tulip."

"Tulip?"

"Actually, it's two-lip." He enunciated the words separately. "Look for yourself." He sauntered over to the sorrel and rubbed her neck affectionately, all the while shooting that angel's grin—or was it a devil's?—at Abby. "Her lower lip is huge and it has a ridge in it. Come over here and see. It looks like two lips."

She hadn't made a conscious decision to approach him, but Abby was not able to fight the urge either.

"Pull up some grass for her."

She did as he said, then had to laugh when Tulip

reached for it. Just as he'd said, the mare's lower lip was oversized and it tickled Abby's palm. The mare practically sucked up the twist of grass Abby offered her.

"Tulip," she murmured. "How appropriate."

"I thought so," he answered. Then his already low-pitched voice dropped to an intimate rumble. "And if I were to name you, I'd choose . . ." He paused and studied her face so intently, Abby swallowed, not once but three times. His eyes were the most intense shade of blue she'd ever seen, vivid and yet somehow a dark, smoky color too. "I'd call you Venus. She was the goddess of beauty in days of old."

Abby's eyes widened in shock. Venus. He thought she was as beautiful as Venus? And just as amazing, he actually knew who Venus was. She had to close her gaping mouth with an effort. Oh, but he had the devil's own smooth tongue, the rational part of her mind warned. But the irrational parts—those parts that daydreamed and made up stories and envisioned something more in her life than marriage to a pleasant but unimaginative minister—those parts overwhelmed and silenced that solitary warning voice. He thought she was beautiful.

"Shall I be forced to call you Venus, then?" he persisted in his velvet voice. He ran one slow, caressing hand up and down the curve of Tulip's neck. For one fanciful moment Abby felt as if he were stroking her neck that way, and a hot flood of color rose in her cheeks.

"I . . . I . . ." She pressed her lips together to stop her idiotic stammering. "That's not my name," she got out at last.

"No? Well, it should be." He looked away toward where the impromptu church gathering had been held, and Abby had a moment to compose herself. What in the world was she doing, all alone, speaking with a man her father didn't know, and of matters far too intimate to be proper?

But it wasn't the words that made their conversation so improper. It was the way he looked at her, and the way his warm gaze made her feel. As if she were melting on the inside, hot and shivery all at the same time.

She cleared her throat and glanced guiltily back at the dispersing group. "I'd best be going. Thank you for . . . for introducing me to Mac and Tulip."

"Which wagon outfit are you and your father traveling with?" he asked, ignoring her words.

Once more she hesitated to leave. "Captain Peters's. Bound for the Oregon Territory." Abby knew she was lingering when she shouldn't, yet she was loath to tear herself away. Was it really so wrong for her just to speak with him? It was broad daylight, after all, and they were in plain view of anyone who cared to look their way.

"Where are you headed?" she asked, deliberately stifling the knowledge that her father would not see her conversation with this man as innocently as she did. Not that it was truly innocent. The feelings he'd set off inside her might be completely unfamiliar to her, but she nonetheless knew they were not innocent. Still, she was not ready to pull herself away.

"I'm heading for Oregon as well."

Abby's heart began to pound. He was going to Oregon too!

"In fact," he continued, "I'm looking to hire on to one of the wagon trains. I've been this route before, and I'm good with a rifle."

When her eyes widened, he grinned. "Indians are occasionally a problem, but fresh meat is a constant need."

Abby clasped her prayer book tighter and made a silent wish. "Perhaps you should speak to Captain Peters," she suggested, her voice gone breathless.

"Perhaps I should," he echoed, his smoky-blue gaze holding with her own, silently saying things to her that no man had ever said before.

"Abigail!"

Abby froze at the familiar stern ring. Her father.

Tanner McKnight, however, only gave her a wink.

"So it's Abigail," he murmured before turning to face the two men hurrying up to them.

"Abigail. Get to the wagon," her father ordered, his face mottled with anger. Though Abby had known he'd be displeased to find her conversing with a strange man, his fury nevertheless seemed a vast overreaction. And in front of both Tanner and the Reverend Harrison.

"But Father—"

"Now!" he practically roared.

Tanner McKnight stepped toward her father and the trailing reverend. "You must be Mr. Morgan," he said before her father could address him directly. He stuck his hand out. "I'm Tanner McKnight. Pleased to make your acquaintance, sir."

Robert Bliss drew up, huffing hard from his exertions. He glared at Tanner, then sent his daughter a sharp look. Only when Abby stepped back as if to leave did he turn back to Tanner. "I'll thank you not to approach my daughter without my express permission."

Abby could have cried at her father's tone. Tanner's hand fell to his side and his face went very still. "I meant no disrespect to her, sir, as I'm sure she will verify. She was good enough to refer me to Captain Peters." Slowly —dismissively, Abby thought—he swung his glittering gaze to the reverend.

The younger man cleared his throat. "Reverend Dexter Harrison." To his credit the reverend extended his hand to Tanner, and after a moment they shook. Abby shot an angry look at her father, but he was not so easily placated. Then Dexter stepped over to her and took her elbow as if to guide her away.

Abby sent him a quelling look. How dare he try to imply that he had a claim on her. She shook off his grip with an impatient jerk just as her father spoke.

"You should not be making such queries to a young and unchaperoned girl. Your inquiry would be better directed to someone at the fort."

Tanner shrugged, but didn't concede a thing. Though

Abby realized that perhaps her father was right, especially given the recent incident with young Rebecca, she was too stung by his lack of faith in her—and his willingness to create a scene—to be sympathetic to his position. And as for Dexter . . . She raised her chin a notch and glared at her father, determined that he know just how angry she was with the both of them.

"I'm afraid dinner will be delayed. Reverend Harrison, I will understand, of course, if you wish to dine elsewhere," she added pointedly. And with that she turned with a swish of her full skirts and stormed off, furious with her father, Reverend Harrison, and the entire male species in general.

Except, of course, for Tanner McKnight.

She stayed at the Lewises' wagon until nearly dusk, though she declined anything but coffee. Her stomach was too knotted by anger and chagrin to allow her any appetite. But she'd been unable to discuss it, even with the sympathetic Sarah. Once Sarah had realized that Abby would be a relatively silent companion, she'd pulled out her sewing basket and they'd worked together on a set of embroidered pillow slips.

If she'd thought to bring her writing instruments, Abby would have spent the day writing. She wanted to finish that chapter with Tillie meeting a prairie dog—she decided to name the intimidating animal Rex. When Snitch found out about him, he would have a conniption fit, but Tillie was already fascinated. Unfortunately Abby hadn't brought her pencil and paper with her, and she refused to go back to her wagon to fetch them. Let her father fret. Let him know just how angry she was. She would just work Tillie's adventure out in her mind for now.

But as the afternoon wore on and the white, curving initials took shape beneath her deft needle, Abby's anger slowly subsided into a troubled resignation. When she finished the ornate *L*, she tucked the needle into a corner of the pillow slip. "Well, I suppose I'm cooled off enough to deal with my father."

Sarah paused, her needle in mid-air, and studied her friend. "Does this by chance have anything to do with Reverend Harrison?"

Abby shook her had. "No, not really. Well," she paused. "Perhaps in a way it does. I was . . . I was speaking to a man. Someone my father doesn't know—"

"Someone interesting?" Sarah broke in, leaning forward eagerly.

Abby felt her cheeks heat. "Well . . . as a matter of fact, he was. Interesting, I mean."

"Only your father didn't approve." Sarah sat back, nodding her head in commiseration when Abby didn't deny her words. "So. Who is he?"

Abby struggled to sound composed, though she was anything but. "Who he is is not the point. It's my father's inflexibility that troubles me, his complete disregard for my opinion or my feelings. His complete pigheadedness," she muttered after a moment's hesitation.

Sarah looked at her askance. "You *must* be smitten with this new fellow. But Abby," she added in a more cautionary tone, "your father wants only the best for you. Remember that. There are any number of unscrupulous men on the trail. That poor Rebecca is evidence enough of that. Her father is beside himself with worry over her. And even without that concern, it's only natural for your father to worry. My own father thought Victor a poor choice for me." She grinned then. "But he came around."

Abby gave her friend a wan smile. "Thank you, Sarah. I know what you say is so. It's just . . . " She trailed off, unable to reveal even to Sarah the true extremes of her father's odd behavior. The name change. The desperate urge to get to Oregon—or rather to leave Missouri, for that's what she had determined it actually was. She just didn't know why.

"I'd best be getting back to my own wagon. He probably hasn't even thought about preparing any supper for us."

Abby skirted the wide circle of wagons as she made her way back. Dusk was imminent. The western sky burned with red and gold streaks, made more vivid by the pale wisps of a few high-flying clouds. Though the air was crisp and cold, the scent of a hundred campfires made it seem warmer. How suggestible the human mind was, she pondered. The mere smell of fires burning gave her the illusion of warmth, just as the gurgling of a lively creek on a hot day in August always made a body feel cooler.

Was that the same sort of illusion that had been going on when Tanner McKnight had looked at her?

Abby kicked at a clump of dried mud as she considered that unpleasant possibility. Her reaction to him had been real enough. There was no point pretending otherwise. His dark, unwavering gaze. His slow smile. Even the sound of his voice.

And his touch.

She nearly tripped over a wagon shaft, then glanced around sheepishly.

His touch. Reverend Harrison's hand at her elbow today had not affected her so. Not even remotely. But just because she'd reacted that way to Tanner McKnight didn't necessarily mean anything. Any number of women might react the same way—no doubt plenty of them already had. The question was, how did he react to her? And more importantly, how could she possibly find out?

The wind gusted, buffeting her full skirts, and she automatically caught the excess fabric with one hand. But her attention focused on the white tent a little way outside the wagon circle. His two horses cropped grass beyond it, and a low fire glowed nearby. But he was not readily visible.

She paused, knowing she should not, but unable to prevent herself. Had he spoken to Captain Peters? Would he join up with their company? She forced herself to move on, to prepare herself to deal with her father. He would be angry and short-tempered, or else sullen and depressed. These days she could never predict his moods. But no matter his mood tonight, she had avoided him long enough.

To Abby's surprise her father had water going, the table down, and the basic kitchen utensils ready to go. He sat in his chair, one of the three they'd decided to carry west with them. It was plain he was waiting for her, sitting there with a book open in his lap. But he didn't speak as she put away her bonnet and her prayer book, and donned her apron. Only when she had her hands deep in a bowl, kneading the dough for pan biscuits, did he clear his throat.

"You risk the affections of a good and honorable man when you behave in a less than seemly manner."

Abby punched the dough, lifted it up and slapped it back into the white-enameled tin bowl. "Do you refer to yourself?" she replied, unable to completely contain her irritation.

"I refer to the Reverend Harrison!" he thundered, rising to his feet.

Abby lifted her face to him. She'd never spoken disrespectfully to her father. She'd never willfully disobeyed him—at least not on important matters. And she'd never tried to counter him when his voice took on that righteous timbre. But there was a first time for everything, she told herself, though her knees shook beneath her skirts.

"Since I do not seek Reverend Harrison's affections, there can be no risk for me."

For one long, terrible moment they stared at each other. She feared he would explode with fury, allowing the entire camp to hear what should be a private conversation, so she went on before he could speak. "I do not seek a husband, Father. I wish to be a teacher. And a writer," she added, deciding not to hold anything back. "You have uprooted me and forced me to this move, and so here I am. But you shall not force me into a union I cannot want. When we arrive in Oregon, I shall claim my half share of land as the Donation Act allows to women. I will be a good daughter and a good teacher, I hope. But I am twenty now, no longer a child. If you would but accept that . . ."

She trailed off as her emotions spent themselves. But she fully expected his words to rain down on her now, righteous and filled with fury. To her shock, however, his shoulders slumped. Then a sudden fit of coughing overtook him.

"Papa?" When his coughing did not abate, she hurried to his side, wiping her hands on her apron. "Papa, are you all right?"

He nodded his head and gestured her away with one hand as the last of his hacking coughs died down. "The dust—" He coughed again, then took the dipper of water she had hastily gotten. He drank deeply, coughed once, then cleared his throat and drank again. "It's this infernal dust," he finally said, wiping his face and mouth with his handkerchief. "Don't worry. I'm fine."

Despite his words Abby pressed the back of one hand to his brow. "I don't know," she began. "You could be a trifle warm—"

He shoved her hand away and stood up. "If I am warm, it's from worry over you, miss." But the righteous tone he strove for did not quite ring true, and even he knew it. With a sigh he shook his head, and his entire body seemed to droop.

"I only want to ensure the best future for you, Abby girl," he said, using his childhood name for her. "You need a husband. Every woman does. I just thought the reverend . . ."

He trailed off and they stared at each other across the width of their little campsite. Then he moved back to his chair and sat down, and she returned to her biscuit dough.

"I'll tell Reverend Harrison not to call on you again,"

he said curtly. "But you shall not take that to mean you are free to cavort with just any fellow who smiles your way. You're a beautiful woman, Abigail, the very image of your mother. The men you meet on the wagon trail will not be like the fellows you were accustomed to in Lebanon. We knew all of them, and their families as well. But these men heading west—some of them may be good enough sorts, but others . . . others of them will say anything to gain the confidence of a woman like you. You must promise me you'll not speak to any of them without my permission first. I would not have you hurt as that other young girl was hurt."

Abby rolled the dough out and with a glass began to cut it into biscuit rounds. Her father thought her as beautiful as her mother. His warning was forgotten as that surprising admission sank in. He thought she was as beautiful as her mother, and that knowledge warmed her as nothing else could.

She gave him a shy, self-conscious smile. "I'll be careful, Papa," she promised earnestly. "But I will not be rude to people either. You must begin to trust me a little more. I am *your* daughter, after all. I hope my father has not raised a fool," she finished, trying for a lighter tone.

Her father, however, did not smile. He only reached for his pipe and began to tap it, muttering, "I hope not as well."

4

The canteen inside the fort was probably cleaner, Tanner speculated. But the impromptu saloon that had been built outside the walls of Fort Kearney since his last trek west would provide him with a hell of a lot more information.

He leaned his back against the bar—probably the sturdiest part of the makeshift saloon, since it protected the liquor—and stared out at the noisy gathering. Farmers, most of them. Snatches of conversation—good rainfalls, deep topsoil, bumper crops—attested to their one overriding interest: the land.

There were others, too, though fewer in number. One burly fellow with arms as thick as tree trunks must be a smithy; another wearing spectacles and with well-manicured hands had the look of a solicitor. A graying older man and his son were both doctors.

One and all they were headed west, lured by the government's offering of land: a half portion—320 acres—to any man who built a home and put the land into cultivation. The other half portion to his woman.

Tanner downed the crude whiskey and shuddered as it burned its way down his throat to his stomach. Women. There were a lot more of them heading to Oregon since the Donation Act had passed. Proper women. Wives and mothers. The type of women that a man could stand by, and who would stand by their men. Women who made cooking an art. He grimaced as he set the squat glass down on the sticky bar. He was damned tired of eating his same old beans and hardtack everyday.

He was damned tired of this fruitless search too. He'd checked out three wagon companies already. This was the last. If he didn't find Hogan's granddaughter here, that meant he had outwitted himself: Bliss had taken the Santa Fe Trail to California after all.

He signaled for another whiskey, only this time he sipped it more slowly. He needed to be sharp if he was going to get any information about the motherless girls in this wagon company.

His eyes scanned the room, passing, then returning to a familiar face. A tall, lanky fellow, the one on horseback who'd spoken to that woman by the river.

Abigail Morgan was her name.

Tanner straightened, then sidestepping a pair of old men arguing about Stonewall Jackson's role in the Battle of New Orleans, he made his way toward the gangly young man.

Abigail Morgan was hardly the young grandchild Hogan envisioned. Still, it was possible that Hogan's grandchild was no child at all, but a fully grown woman. Abigail Morgan was a fully grown woman, he recalled with a slight twist of his lips. Very well grown indeed, and in all the right places.

He shouldered past a swarthy man punctuating his words with broad gestures, then gave his quarry a quick once-over. The man was a farmer—a married farmer, judging by the shiny new ring on his hand. Tanner's posture relaxed a little, and when he stuck his hand out in friendly greeting, it was not an altogether false gesture.

"You're with Captain Peters's company, aren't you?"

The man hesitated only a moment before taking Tanner's firm grasp. "I am."

"I've just joined up with your company today. Tanner McKnight. From Indiana," he added, sticking to the story he'd given Captain Peters.

"Victor Lewis. From Iowa." He motioned to a man next to him. "This is Bud Foley. He's on our train also."

Tanner shook hands with Foley, and the man murmured a greeting that was lost in the noisy atmosphere. When Tanner peered at him more closely, however, the man looked away. "I gotta get goin', Lewis." He nodded once at Tanner, giving him a hard, considering look, then sidled away and left.

Tanner watched him leave with a prickle of unease. There had been something odd in that stare, some edge of smugness. And animosity. Had they met before?

"So, you've joined up with us," Victor Lewis broke in on Tanner's musings.

"Yeah. Yeah, I'll be riding scout and hunting fresh game." He gave the younger man an assessing look. "Not everyone can provide for themselves on the trail. You hunt much?"

"Some," Victor admitted. Then with boyish pride he boasted, "I was the best squirrel shot in Muscatine County."

Tanner grinned. "That will surely come in handy. You have a lot of people to provide for?"

"Just me and the wife. Sarah," he added.

"Newlyweds, right? Was that your wife herding oxen by the river yesterday?" Tanner asked, looking for a reason to discuss Miss Abigail Morgan.

"I take care of my own stock," the young man countered. "That was my wife's friend, Abigail Morgan."

"Ah." Tanner nodded consideringly. "Fine-looking woman, that Abigail Morgan. Is she spoken for?"

Victor Lewis laughed and finished off his own whiskey. "Nah, though her father's trying hard to pair her up with Reverend Harrison."

Tanner had thought that might be the case, but he wisely did not say as much. "What does her mother think of a reverend for a son-in-law?"

"Her mother's dead, so I'm told. It's just Abby and

her father." Then Victor's eyes narrowed. "Are you, you know, interested in her?"

So her mother *was* dead. Tanner looked away, timing his reaction carefully. "That depends on how serious she and this reverend are." He grinned. "What's her father's name—just in case I need to speak with him?"

The younger man laughed again. "Robert Morgan, and he's a gruff old coot. As for the reverend, from what Sarah tells me, he's serious but Abby's not. 'Course with women you can never tell."

They talked a while longer, about the trail ahead and what they'd find in Oregon. By the time Tanner left, he'd had too much to drink on an empty stomach. But his stride was steady as he headed through the dark toward his solitary campsite.

His stomach growled in angry protest. He needed food. But despite his fuzzy head and burning gut, his thoughts kept veering back to Lewis's words. Robert Morgan *could* be Robert Bliss. But of even more interest to Tanner was the fact that Abigail Morgan wasn't interested in the devoted young reverend.

He should be more concerned that she could very well be the girl he was searching for—woman, that is. And he *was* concerned. Yet he couldn't help remembering how she'd felt sitting on his lap, her warm weight pressing against his loins, her slender waist easily encircled by his arm. She was hardly the type of woman he was used to—it was a safe bet that she was a virgin. But she'd smelled so good in a dusty, sweaty sort of way. Like dried rose petals. He'd wager half of what Hogan was paying him that she was a hell of a good cook.

He paused, sniffing the chill night air. Most everyone had turned in. Fires had been banked, and only the murmur of an occasional voice drifted across the flat camping area. But Tanner could swear he smelled ham frying. Ham and parsley potatoes with lots of butter. And snapbeans. His stomach groaned in longing, and for a moment he just stood there, swaying ever so slightly as he drew several deep breaths. But the mouthwatering scent was gone, and all he had for his troubles was an even dizzier head.

He shook his head, trying to sharpen his senses, when he heard a step behind him. Just the soft roll of a pebble beneath a boot, but it was enough to make him jerk to one side.

It was the only thing that saved him. The butt of a gun, aimed at his head, instead glanced off his shoulder. But the blow was hard enough to stun and deaden his entire right arm.

Tanner spun away from his silent attacker, grabbing at the same time for the knife in his left boot. But his heel caught on a rut in the dirt, and he stumbled back. He fully expected the man to be on him, but to his surprise— and disgust—the coward had already turned and run off. Tanner saw no more than a flash of white shirtsleeve. By the time he regained his balance and started after the man, he had disappeared.

"Dammit to hell!" he swore. Breathing hard, he stared around him. Tents. Wagons. Horses. Oxen. A chaotic village, temporary and changing shape daily, encircled the entire fort. It would be impossible to find the man in such surroundings.

He bent down to return the double-edged knife to its sheath, then winced at the movement. Damn, but the fool had practically ripped his arm off.

Had the blow landed as intended, though, Tanner knew he'd be lying in the dark, his blood and brains soaking into the prairie dirt. He rubbed his shoulder, feeling the hot swelling already. Gingerly he flexed his shoulder, then wriggled his arm. There would be no permanent damage, it seemed, only a painful reminder for a few days that someone wanted him dead—for he was sure that had been the bastard's intention. But why?

Tanner warily made his way back to his tent. No trace of his previous fuzzy-headedness remained. The unexpected attack in the very middle of the well-populated campsite had completely sobered him. He checked Mac and Tulip and made a cursory inspection of his belongings. No one had touched anything here. That left either an impulsive robbery attempt or a quite deliberate personal attack as the only choices.

He shrugged painfully out of his vest, then removed his gun belt, all the while turning the situation around and around in his mind. If it had not been some random act of violence, but a deliberate attack on him, did it have anything to do with his current assignment? Or was it maybe retaliation for some past job, vengeance from someone he'd hunted down before?

Bud Foley's face came disturbingly to mind, and Tanner tried to connect him to some incident in the past—to no avail. But no matter who or why, he knew now that he had to guard his back. Someone was watching him. It might take awhile, but eventually the man would make a mistake and reveal himself. And when he did, Tanner would mete out the only kind of justice that kind of man understood.

Someone was watching her.

Abby wiped a drooping lock of hair from her brow and glanced about. Everyone in sight was involved in packing up for the early-morning departure, yet she couldn't shake off the feeling that someone among them was observing her.

"Jerusalem!" she exclaimed under her breath. It was bad enough that no one had a bit of privacy on the trail. But did someone have to watch her wash her soiled undergarments? She'd brought plenty of rags for her time of the month. But with the constant traveling, the only place to dry the clothes was to hang them at the back of the wagon. She might as well run up a flag announcing her private business to the world.

"All right, Matthew. Get into the traces," her father mumbled to Eenie from the other side of the wagon. It was almost time to leave. Abby redoubled her efforts, scrubbing the soiled strips against the washboard with brutal efficiency. Washing clothes was the least favorite of her household chores. She'd chop wood before washing clothes, had she the choice. But she didn't have the choice, she reminded herself in rising irritation. She rarely had a choice in anything.

Lifting the cloths from the soapy water, she wrung them out with a sharp motion. Then she tossed them into the bucket of clean water, swished them around, and wrung them out once more. She dumped the water out, hung the two buckets next to the tar bucket and grease bucket, and put the scrub board in its place just inside the back gate. Just as she started the embarrassing task of stringing the wet cloths in the back opening of the wagon tent, where they could flutter and dry all day, the snorting of a horse alerted her.

"Good morning, Abigail."

Abby knew before she turned. Tanner McKnight. She'd recognize those low, stirring tones anywhere; that deep, vibrating rumble. And he'd called her by her given name.

Her heart was tripping double-time when she finally faced him. But when she realized she still held half the cloths in her hands, her face went scarlet. Of all times! Why did he have to come now?

She slapped the offending strips down behind her, not even caring if they soaked anything. Then she surreptitiously wiped her hands in her skirts.

"Why, hello." She gulped the words. "Good morning, Mr. McKnight."

"I'd prefer it if you called me Tanner." He gave her a slow, heart-stopping smile, a simple stretching of his lips across his teeth that logically should not have affected her in the least. But his lips curved in the most intriguing way, and those teeth were so white and strong.

Tanner. Abby swallowed hard. Why did she always act like such a ninny around him? But she didn't even try to look away from his mesmerizing gaze.

The saddle creaked as he shifted slightly, leaning toward her. "I've signed on with your company. I'll be riding ahead today, doing some hunting. I came to see how you were provisioned for fresh meat."

"I, ah . . . I'd be grateful for anything extra you have," she said, determinedly ignoring the wet strip of cloth danging just beside her head.

He nodded. "Well, I'll just have to see what I can do."

"Abigail?" Her father came up alongside the wagon, but before he could say anything, Abby spoke up.

"Father, Captain Peters has hired Tan—Mr. Mc-Knight. He . . . he'll be hunting today. He was just inquiring—"

"I'll be bringing fresh game in later," Tanner broke in on her babbling, facing her father. "I'll be certain you get your share."

Abby watched apprehensively as her father glared at Tanner. Why had he taken such a dislike to the man? But to her relief her father was, if not polite, at least not rude.

"Fresh meat." He nodded once, then, as if in dismissal, looked up at Abby. "Have you completed your chores? The call to leave will come any minute."

"Yes, Father." She gave him a fleeting smile, then turned back toward Tanner. "Good luck with your hunting."

He touched the brim of his hat with one hand, the most circumspect of gestures. But as he wheeled his eager horse around, Abby could have sworn that he winked at her.

She bent down to retrieve the remaining wet cloths, though every fiber in her being wanted to stare after him. To gape like some schoolgirl, she admitted to herself. But her father was there, and she was not about to give him any more fuel for the righteous fire that always burned inside him. Still, it was awfully hard. Tanner had winked at her. That was twice now, and both times her father was present.

Though she knew she should not read more into it

than was there, Abby couldn't prevent the rush of heightened color to her cheeks. It was that which must have alerted her father.

"Keep your distance from him, Abigail."

She looked up from her task, struggling to keep any show of resentment from her face.

"He works for the company, Father. It's his job to provide fresh meat for us."

"Yes, well, that may be so. But just you remember everything else that he is. He's a hired gun. While I'll not deny every wagon train requires such men, it still does not make him suitable for a young girl like you."

She couldn't help it. Abby slapped the last strip of cloth over the makeshift clothesline, then leaped down from the high wagon back, not mindful in the least of ladylike decorum.

"Just because he's not a preacher doesn't mean he's a terrible person. For your information he's read the classics."

His eyes narrowed until they were almost lost beneath his heavy brows. "The classics? Which classics? And how would you know that about him anyway?"

"The Roman classics. And the Greek," she added, though that was pure speculation. "We were discussing the mythological characters yesterday when you so rudely interrupted us."

If she hadn't stretched the truth so far, Abby would have taken more pleasure from the expression on her father's face. He was shocked, she saw. It was not often that she surprised him, and she knew he hated more than anything to be proven wrong. But he was also a fair man, and as she watched him, she could see that fairness struggle with his natural caution.

"The classics." The wind tugged at his hat, and he clamped it down tighter on his head. "Does he perchance also read his Bible?"

Abbly pursed her lips. "I'll ask him about that when he brings the meat," she replied tartly.

To Abby's relief the call to break camp came rolling up just then, a cry taken from wagon to wagon all the way around the circle of wagons. Her father passed it on, then coughed at the effort before turning to the team.

At that wracking sound Abby suddenly felt ashamed of herself. She hadn't meant to contradict her father. She hadn't meant to sound so flip either. She just wanted the chance to get to know Tanner McKnight, and that would be impossible if her father forbade it. But if they could just find some common ground. . . .

She lifted up the tailgate of the wagon and slid the two bolts home. Maybe she'd better find out just how much of the classics Tanner knew.

"What exactly did he do to her?" someone asked in a hushed tone.

Abby shot Sarah a wary look but kept on walking. They were a good-sized group of women this morning with a rowdy gang of little children loosely trailing them. But the women were not paying much mind to the children today. They were all straining to hear Doris Crenshaw's answer.

"Mr. Crenshaw had struck up a friendship with Mr. Godwin, you know. And being as how our own Charlotte is only a year younger than poor Rebecca, Mr. Crenshaw was practically distraught when he heard."

"But what exactly did he *hear*?" Martha McCurdle demanded in the loud, insensitive tones Abby had come to associate with the woman. A blowzy, overfed blonde, she was a vain, gossipy creature, and it hadn't taken Abby long to figure that out. But today at least, everyone was just as interested in Doris's answer, for no woman could feel safe if young women were being attacked.

"Well, I attended her myself, at Mr. Crenshaw's insistence. Not that I wouldn't have done it anyway, being a good Christian and all—"

"But what did he *do* to her?" Martha interrupted impatiently.

Doris sent her an irritated look. "Well." Her voice dropped a level, and everyone leaned in a little closer, even Abby. "It was very odd. He kept asking her name, like he wanted to be sure who she was, or something. But he didn't, you know, have his way with her—though God knows he tried. Her skirt was ripped—so was her petticoat. She's all scraped up on her knees and her thighs—"

"How can you be so sure he didn't do it?" Martha broke in again. "She wouldn't admit it if he did. I heard he hit her and knocked her out. How could she even remember what he did to her?"

Doris glared at the other woman, then indignantly drew herself up. "I was there when the doctor examined her, Martha McCurdle, and he said the brute did not ruin her, so don't you try to imply that he did."

Sarah smirked at Abby. Neither of them liked Martha and her malicious bent, and they enjoyed seeing her taken down a peg.

"Is she all right now?" Abby asked.

"Physically she will heal," Doris replied. "I saw her just this morning and persuaded her to take some oatmeal and coffee. But she's hurting inside. Afraid he'll come back. Afraid what people will think," she added, shooting Martha a warning look.

The group of women slowly drifted apart, breaking into twos and threes to wonder and worry about the new fear added to their burden. Bad enough that every day brought new dangers—accidents, illness. Snakes, Indian sightings. Did they now have to worry about some threat from within their own midst?

"It was probably some man at the fort," Sarah said, giving voice to Abby's own hopeful thoughts.

"Yes," Abby agreed. "But we still must be careful."

"Do you really think any of the men of our company would do such a thing?"

Abby shrugged. "I don't know them all. My father holds all the single men in suspicion, but there are also a few married ones that have the most unpleasant way of staring at a woman."

Sarah nodded, and the two of them walked in silence for a while. To the left the wagons rolled in a long, tedious line. To the right and a little ahead four children gamboled, happy and unaware of the worries that weighed so heavily on the adults around them.

Oh, to be that carefree again, Abby thought. She pulled her everyday shawl close against the biting wind. It was mid-May, yet with the overcast sky and the gusting wind it felt more like February. At least it wasn't raining.

"There's a new man on the train," Sarah said after a while.

"We seem to have gained a few and lost a few at Fort Kearney."

"Yes, but you'd remember this fellow if you saw him," Sarah replied, an odd note in her voice.

Abby sent her a sidelong glance, then when she spied Sarah's merry expression, began to redden.

"I knew it!" Sarah crowed. "It's the fellow you're so interested in."

"I'm not *interested* in anyone," Abby protested, albeit weakly.

"Not even a tall, dark, and handsome anybody?"

"You know, you're getting almost as nosy as Martha."

But Sarah only laughed. "Maybe if you knew what I know, you'd be nosy too."

"What is that supposed to mean?"

"Oh, nothing," Sarah answered nonchalantly. She turned toward the group of children. "Come over this way, Estelle! And bring the rest of the little ones closer to us."

"Sarah Lewis, don't you be that way. What is it you know that I don't?" Abby demanded, catching her friend by the sleeve. "Tell me right this minute."

Sarah sent her a triumphant grin. "We might not even be speaking of the same man. Let me see, what was his name? Tom. Tommy . . . Tommy McNeal . . ."

"Tanner McKnight. His name is Tanner McKnight and you know that just as well as I do."

"Oh, yes. Tanner McKnight. How could I forget?"

"Sarah, if you don't get to the point—"

"My, my. How impatient you are. But all right, I'll tell you." She gave Abby a conpiratorial grin. "It seems he was at that saloon last night. You know, that noisy place right outside the fort?"

"Yes, yes. So?"

"Well, Victor was there too."

"And?" Abby prodded. She was breathless with anticipation. Why was Sarah dragging it out so?

"And he asked Victor about you."

Abby stopped in her tracks. They'd been walking along, keeping a steady pace with the slow-moving wagons. But at Sarah's surprising words Abby was suddenly unable to do two things at once. She could not both walk and examine this astounding bit of news.

Sarah stopped also, turning to study her friend with a knowing smile. "Still not interested in anyone?"

"He . . . he inquired about *me*?" Abby asked, ignoring Sarah's friendly taunt.

"He did. He wanted to know how serious you and the Reverend Harrison were."

"We're not serious at all! I hope Victor told him that."

"He did," Sarah answered patiently.

After that the day passed in a bit of a blur. Abby positively brimmed with boundless energy. She could have flown all the way to Oregon on the sheer strength of her soaring emotions. Tanner McKnight was interested in her! Abigail Bliss, spinsterish schoolteacher, the object of such a man's attentions. It was too good to be true.

Though Sarah laughed knowingly at her foolish antics, Abby could not restrain herself. She played with the children, singing them songs, teaching them their letters and their numbers with the clever tunes she led them in.

"*A* my name is Abigail; I'm gonna marry Abraham; we're gonna raise apples and live in Alabama."

"*B* my name is Betty; I'm gonna marry Bobby; we're gonna raise bumblebees and live in . . . in Babylonia."

And so the day went. They stopped for the noon rest, and she prepared a substantial meal of biscuits and milk and leftover ham from last night's meal. Then they picked up the interminable trail. The day alternately dragged on, then seemed to fly by. By the time the sun neared the horizon before them, she was a bundle of nerves.

Where was he? Would he bring them a portion from today's hunt? Would it be too forward of her to invite him to sup with them?

She was still debating that subject when the call to make camp echoed down the line. Saying her good-byes to Sarah and the ragtag group of children, she turned toward the wagons, eager, for once, to begin the supper preparations. But first she would make herself presentable.

While her father unhitched the oxen, she rummaged in her box for her comb and a bit of ribbon. She should speak to her father about inviting Tanner, she told herself as with deft fingers she unwound her hair. But that would only give him the chance to say no. On the other hand, if she extended the invitation without her father's approval, he'd be extremely angry. He might even be rude to Tanner. Of course her father hadn't hesitated to invite Reverend Harrison without discussing it with her, she reminded herself. Still, it might be the most politic thing for her to extend the invitation in her father's presence. She could turn to him innocently and ask his permission.

Abby grimaced, then thrust the horn comb repeatedly down the long length of her hair. How devious she was becoming. First willful, now devious. What would her mother think?

She was just freeing the last of her tangles when the tattoo hoofbeat of an approaching horse alerted her.

"Not yet. I'm not ready," she muttered, grabbing up the ribbon. She hadn't rebraided her hair or anything. Panicked, she pulled the ribbon under her hair and tied it so that the thick mass at least stayed out of her face. Then, with heart pounding and palms sweating, she poked her head outside the back of the wagon.

5

As Tanner rode up to the Morgans' wagon, all he could think was that he didn't want her to be Willard Hogan's granddaughter. But the field was narrowing down. Today he'd learned enough to rule out the Hardwick girl—her father couldn't read or write. The Callahan girl and her father were Black Irish, not Bliss's coloring at all. That left a field of five, and Abby was at the top of the pack.

Only he didn't want it to be her.

That unsettling realization brought a frown to Tanner's brow. But he covered it by touching the wide brim of his felt hat with one hand. "I brought you a haunch of antelope."

"Antelope?"

He watched the expressions that flitted over Abby's face. Curiosity. Doubt. Then, when her long lashes lifted and she met his watchful gaze, embarrassment.

Embarrassment. That was an emotion he didn't usually associate with women. But then, she was not really his type of woman, as he'd told himself over and over again. He'd take a buxom blonde over a slender brunette, and a lady of the evening over a Sunday-go-to-meeting type any day of the week. Yet here he was, shifting uncomfortably in his saddle at the very sight of the proper Miss Abigail Morgan.

Then again, when had he ever had anything to do with proper women? His mother, despite her good heart, had still been a common whore. No use denying that fact. Except for a few youthful flings, every woman he'd had he'd paid well for her efforts. But this woman . . . this woman was the kind of woman you married and made a home with. He didn't have a home. At least not yet.

"You cook it like you would venison," he finally said, killing his confusing thoughts. "You can salt the extra. Or dry it for jerky."

She nodded, causing her heavy hair to fall in two shining arcs on either side of her face. God, but it was long, he thought, and it gleamed in the slanting light like the finest silk. Once more he shifted, but he hid it by sidling the weary Mac nearer the wagon gate. "Here." He untied the haunch from his saddle horn and thrust it toward her.

She stepped from beneath the wagon tent to take the hefty haunch. As she stood there clutching the crudely butchered piece of meat, Tanner was struck by incongruities of her appearance. She could have been a dark-haired Indian woman, receiving the bounty of her man's hunting trip. But her dress proclaimed her as straight-laced and proper as they came, covering her from chin to wrists to toes. Only her face and hands showed. And yet those were tanned to a warm color not typically seen on proper women. Then there was her hair. No matter how hard she tried to maintain a prim appearance, that hair was her undoing. It fairly cried out to be touched, and Tanner wanted to answer that cry in the worst way. Part lady, part Indian maiden, and part wanton, she appeared at the moment. The best of all three, he realized.

"Thank you," she murmured when the silence began awkwardly to stretch out.

He nodded his head curtly and with only the lightest move turned his horse. He didn't have to go. He'd saved her piece of meat to deliver last. But now he knew it had been a foolish idea. He had only one reason to linger around Abby Morgan, and that was to determine if she was Hogan's granddaughter. While he heartily hoped she wasn't, he knew that in either case it really didn't matter. If she was the girl he searched for, he'd take her back to Chicago then leave her there, never to see her again. If she wasn't his quarry, he'd still never see her again. She was heading to Oregon, and anyway she was the wrong kind of woman for him to be worrying about right now. Maybe one day, but not right now. She belonged with someone like that preacher.

"Wait. Don't go."

Tanner drew up at her soft call. He stared at her, conscious of the dust motes swirling red-gold between them in the afternoon sun. She pushed her hair behind her shoulders and took a deep breath, as if searching for courage. But what Tanner saw most was the fullness straining behind her bodice. She was not so slim as her narrow waist had indicated, at least not everywhere. His fingers tightened on the reins even to remember how she'd felt beneath his hands. Within his arms. On his lap.

"Will you stay to dinner with us? Please?" she added when he didn't immediately respond.

Tanner hesitated. A home-cooked meal and from the hands of a woman like her. Only a fool would turn down such an offer. And yet he could not bring himself to accept right away.

"What about your father?"

A slow flush crept into her cheeks. "He . . . ah . . . I'll speak to him. He'll . . . he'll agree."

"He doesn't like me," he persisted. "Doesn't approve of the likes of me. There's no use pretending otherwise, Abby." He smiled knowingly at the familiar use of her name, then perversely let his eyes slip over her in a way calculated to unsettle her even more. "He won't want to give me the chance to get to know his little girl."

"I'm not a little girl," she countered, despite the pretty blush that indicated otherwise. She might be a fully grown woman, he knew, but she was as innocent as any little girl.

Tanner pushed his hat back on his head and studied

her a moment. What was he doing anyway? Why was he toying with so unsuitable a woman? "No, you're no little girl. But I doubt your father sees it that way. Thanks for the invitation, Miss Morgan, but it would be better for you if I didn't accept."

Once more he moved as if to go, and once again she halted him.

"He's not as stiff-necked as you think." When Tanner only raised one brow and waited, she continued. "When I told him you read the classics, well, he softened a bit."

The classics. Tanner repressed any show of amusement. His references to Venus usually impressed only the ladies. How ironic that her father should be swayed by his handy line about Venus. Then his thoughts quickened. Did that mean the man had read the classics himself—that he could be the schoolteacher Bliss?

"He enjoys them also?" he asked with a careful show of nonchalance.

"Oh, yes," Abby replied. "Especially Homer. *The Iliad* and *The Odyssey* are great favorites of his. He's even read them in Greek."

Tanner knew he was onto something, though a part of him would have preferred otherwise. "I like the myths myself," he drawled. "Zeus. Venus."

She swallowed at his deliberate reference to the goddess of beauty and took an unsteady breath that tightened her bodice most becomingly around her high breasts. Though his conscience told him she was too easy a mark for his practiced lines, another part of him thanked the one teacher who'd spun stories of mythological beings and rousing adventures. He'd had but two years of schooling, and little enough to show for it. But good old Venus melted down even the coldest-hearted woman—and Abigail Morgan was far from cold, he suspected.

"Do you . . . do you read the Bible also?" she asked in a voice gone low and breathy.

That brought him up. "The Bible?" He shrugged,

debating how best to answer. "Not as much as I should. Not since I was a boy," he added, affecting a chagrined expression. After all, women loved to save a man from his wicked ways. Maybe this particular woman needed both the Roman gods and the Christian one to soften her up. "Is your father a preacher?"

She set the haunch on a crate, then leaped lightly to the ground. "No. No, not a preacher. He's a—" She broke off and straightened up a bit, lifting her face to stare up at him. "He's just a farmer. A farmer like most of the other men in the company."

Tanner nodded. She was a lousy liar, and that realization made him focus back on his task. If she was lying, it was for a reason, and if that reason was to hide from Willard Hogan, then he'd found his Chicago society heiress.

But he had to be sure.

He urged Mac nearer. Then with a creak of saddle leather, he leaned over and extended a hand to her. She hesitated, clearly confused by the gesture. But when he smiled encouragingly, she lifted her hand to take his. With the gentlest of tugs, he drew her closer, then bent down to skim her knuckles with his lips. Just a feather-light kiss, not so forward as to be deemed offensive. But his eyes promised more, and her wide-eyed gaze told him she'd received the message.

"I accept your offer, Abby. And I promise to be on my best behavior with your father."

Abby had to remind herself to breathe as she watched Tanner McKnight ride away. Lord, but had there ever been a more unsettling man? At the same time that he drew her like a magnet drew steel, he also managed to frighten her clean out of her wits. How could she want to be closer to him and yet also want to flee every time she saw him?

She pressed one shaking hand to her stomach and tried to calm her racing pulse. He was coming to dinner. Now what was she to do? She turned and hefted the generous portion of antelope in her hands. Good manners dictated that she cook his offering. But what if it came out awful? What if it was too chewy? Or tasteless? Then she remembered what Tanner had said. Cook it like venison.

Feeling a little better, she set the haunch down again, her mind whirling with thoughts. First she must do her hair and freshen up. She climbed back up into the wagon, and it was then that she spied the dried strips of cloth still dangling in broad view.

"Botheration!" she muttered, snatching them down from their conspicuous placement. Why hadn't she thought to remove them before he showed up?

She was still muttering to herself, whipping the comb through her tangled locks with brutal efficiency, when her father called out to her.

"Abigail? Where are you, girl?"

"Here, Papa. I'll be out directly."

She heard his footsteps near the tailgate. "And what is this?"

Nervous about what she had to tell him, Abby contented herself with fastening her hair into a single loose braid tied with a length of green ribbon. She made her way out of the tightly packed wagon.

"It's a haunch of antelope," she answered in what she hoped was an appropriately casual tone. "Mr. McKnight's hunt was successful, and this is our portion."

She leaped to the ground, then faced him, studying his suspicious expression. "It's the man's job," she added defensively.

"Well," her father finally replied. "We should all be pleased that he's so adept at it."

Abby covered her nervousness by lowering the plank table and propping the leg up. "Yes, we should. In fact I went so far as to invite him to share our dinner with us."

"You did what?"

"Just as you have frequently done with Reverend Harrison," she hurried on.

"You cannot begin to compare—"

"They are both men traveling alone. Both in need of a home-cooked meal."

Their gazes locked in silent battle, his eyes angry, hers determined.

"There is a considerable difference of circumstance, daughter. I had hoped you and the Reverend Harrison—" He broke off, and his heavy brows lowered even farther. "You cannot possibly be envisioning you and this hired hand—"

"We are all children of God," she said, throwing one of his favorite quotes back at him. "We should not judge, lest we be judged."

"Yes, but God the Father does not expect his children to behave like fools. Your heavenly Father looks after your spiritual well-being, while your earthly father—me —looks after your physical well-being. And I would hardly consider that sort of man—"

"Just what sort of man *is* he, Father? From everything I have observed, he is polite, well spoken. Well read," she emphasized. "And a hard worker. Surely adequate enough qualifications for a dinner guest."

Though she silenced him temporarily with her list of Tanner's attributes, Abby knew from his sharp scrutiny that his objections were far from assuaged. There was a dangerous quality about Tanner McKnight. She recognized it and so did her father. And while it both frightened and attracted her, it only worried her overprotective father.

Their eyes met and held, and in the silence a quick rush of understanding washed over Abby. Her father's life was changing too fast for him to deal with. He'd lost his wife and left his teaching position. Then their move. Now it must seem to him that his only child was ready to abandon him as well and find a new life of her own. What would he do then, alone in a strange land?

Her expression softened and she reached to take his hand. But he stepped back with a harrumphing sound.

"I'll suffer him at our fire this one time, Abigail. One time only. Then you will consider your Christian duty toward him sufficiently exercised."

As he turned and stalked off, Abby gritted her teeth in frustration. Why must he be so pigheaded? Her understanding of her father's position fled as she recounted all the ways he created his own misery. They hadn't needed to leave Lebanon. He wouldn't feel so alone in the world if they were still surrounded by their friends in Missouri. But he'd *had* to go, and still refused to tell her why. If he was depressed and lonely, it was all his own doing.

If only her mother hadn't died.

That sobering thought squelched her rising anger. It all went back to that. But although Abby would give anything to have her beloved mother back—and to know what had precipitated their sudden flight to Oregon— there nonetheless was a part of her that no longer regretted their move. Though difficult, their weeks on the trail were still an unfolding adventure, bringing something new to learn and experience every day.

And Tanner McKnight was the latest and most exciting part of that adventure.

Tanner presented himself shortly after dusk, freshly washed and in a clean blue chambray shirt, buttoned up to the throat. When he removed his hat and extended a hand to her father, Abby noted the damp tendrils curling at his neck. He'd gone to a lot of trouble, and she appreciated it. But would her father?

Robert grudgingly shook Tanner's hand, then retreated to his chair and his pipe.

"Sit down. Sit down." Abby fluttered around nervously, indicating a chair to Tanner. "Dinner is almost ready. I made the antelope. I hope it turns out all right."

"It smells delicious, Miss Morgan," Tanner replied.

At such a polite use of her name Abby sent him a grateful smile. The last thing she needed was for him to antagonize her father.

"Well, we'll soon see." She shot a speaking look at

her father. With Reverend Harrison he'd been swift to boast of Abby's cooking skills—and needlework and housework as well. But with Tanner he remained unremittingly silent.

"I hope you like corn bread," she said, beginning to feel awkward.

"Corn bread is one of my favorite dishes."

At that gallant answer her father cleared his throat. "Where are you from, McKnight?"

Tanner leaned back in his chair and turned his attention on her father. "From . . . Indiana," he answered after only the briefest hesitation. "But I hope to make Oregon my home."

Abby held her breath, hoping her father would relax his stern demeanor just a little. He always acted so suspicious of everyone these days. Only with Dexter did he ever appear trusting. But a quick glance at Tanner indicated that he was not in the least perturbed by her father's attitude. No doubt he'd expected this cool sort of reception after the men's two previous meetings. The fact that Tanner would brave her father's ill humor at all brought a heated glow to her heart. He did it for the pleasure of her company.

"What did you do in Indiana?" Robert asked, drawing out the last word until it almost sounded like a sneer. What in the world was he implying?

She could tell Tanner noticed, too, for his jaw flexed and his gaze grew sharp. "I worked for one of the railroad companies there, earning the money to buy breeding stock for the horse ranch I plan to build."

"The railroad." Robert puffed on his pipe a minute, a rapid, agitated rhythm that warned Abby of his simmering anger. But why should he be so angry?

"Where are you from?" Tanner threw right back at him.

Abby tensed. People seldom went on the offensive with Robert Bliss, for his stern appearance forbade it. But here was Tanner McKnight, jumping right in, unafraid. Nonchalant, even.

"Where am *I* from?" Her father straightened in his chair, glaring from one of them to the other. "Hasn't Abigail already answered that inquiry for you?"

In all honesty Abby could not recall if she'd told him or not. And if she'd done so, had it been the truth or the fabrication her father had demanded she use? She'd been so unnerved by Tanner.

She looked at him, suddenly afraid. But he was smiling at her, the easy, disarming grin she nonetheless knew was meant to turn her mind to mush. And it was working.

"If she did, I don't recall. Where did you say you were from, Abby?"

She cleared her throat and knotted her hands in the folds of her apron. What was the point of all this deception? "Arkansas. We had a farm there."

Tanner nodded, and his smile held firm, but whatever he thought of that was hidden behind the midnight blue of his eyes. "And now you plan to farm in Oregon."

"Yes." She nodded, then glanced imploringly at her father. But he was clearly determined not to help in the least, and it infuriated her no end.

All right, then. If he was already angry, she would lose nothing by angering him further. She would simply ignore her father—something she knew he could not bear.

"You know, Tan—Mr. McKnight, since you've read the classics, I'd be interested in your opinion of a little project of mine."

With a curious lift of his brows he turned his attention on her. "A project?" He smiled at her encouragingly.

"Yes. But let's eat, shall we? I'll explain it all to you over the meal."

"It's like this," she began as they each settled into a chair with a full plate in hand. "I write children's stories and I'm hoping someday to have them published."

"Children's stories?" Tanner echoed. She ignored her father's inelegant snort in the background.

"Yes. About this little mouse and all her adventures."

"What kind of adventures does a mouse have?" he asked as he cut into a generous slice of roasted antelope.

"Oh, all sorts," Abby replied, warming to her subject. She'd told no one but her father about her hopes to be published, and then only in anger. But Tanner . . . There was something about him that was unfettered by convention. Somehow she knew he would not be shocked by her unlikely aspirations.

"If you think about all the classics, they were one adventure after another. The Trojan horse with Helen of Troy and Paris. Jason and the Argonauts. And what about Pandora's Box? And . . . and Atlas. And Medusa. Why, if you think about it, we're on our own sort of odyssey right now. Venturing into the unknown. braving whatever might be thrown at us. Well, Tillie—that's my little mouse—she's on her own odyssey too. She's facing danger and making unlikely friends."

She broke off when a piece of meat flew off the fork she'd been gesturing with and landed with a sizzle in the campfire. "Oh!" Horrified at such undignified behavior, she glanced guiltily at her father. But although he clearly was displeased with her, there was also a glimmer of confusion in his eyes, as if he was only now beginning to really see her. Tanner had a bemused expression on his face, but the grin still remained, and he actually seemed to approve.

"So you plan to rewrite Greek and Roman myth through your little mouse character."

Abby nodded, then looked down at her plate and cut a new piece of meat. The meat. It was good, she noted vaguely. Thank goodness she hadn't made a fool of herself with her cooking. But flinging food off her fork . . .

"You read Greek and Roman mythology?"

Abby and Tanner both looked up at her father's grudging tone. But at least he'd spoken.

"It's been many years," Tanner conceded. "I haven't had the time recently—nor access to any books."

"We have books. Don't we, Father?" she added, prompting him to respond.

"A few," he replied after a long moment. "But everyone should at the very least keep a Bible at hand. There's many a stirring tale to be found within the Good Book—and they are all, without a doubt, more moral than the ancient myths," he added.

The pompous tone he used was not unfamiliar to Abby. Yet on this occasion it irritated her more than usual. Before she could prevent it, she blurted, "There are those biblical passages, however, that some might find almost immoral. The Song of Solomon, for instance. Have you ever read it?" She directed this last at Tanner.

Slowly he shook his head, but his gaze held steady with hers, as if he sensed that she meant to goad her father. "What's it about?"

That brought Abby to a halt. She knew the passage well, for she'd read it often, fascinated by its references to breasts and bellies and thighs, to desire and flourishing marriage beds. But she was hardly prepared to reveal that to Tanner. She was shocked at her unthinking boldness even to bring it up. And her father . . . She glanced at his stunned expression, then hastily looked away, swallowing hard and well aware of the hot color that rose in her cheeks.

"It's . . . it's about how he—the bridegroom, that is —loves his bride. He . . . he—"

"It's an allegory. An allegory," her father broke in tersely. "The bride and groom represent God and his chosen people. Do not read more into it than is meant, Abigail."

He glared at her furiously, and Abby knew she'd gone too far. What other response could she honestly expect from him?

"I don't recall the passage." Tanner spoke up, filling

the uncomfortable silence. "But then, I haven't read the Bible in a good while. Perhaps you will allow me to accompany the two of you to Reverend Harrison's next service."

"That would be nice," Abby managed in a meek tone. Then, seizing on an excuse to change the subject, she reached for the pan of corn bread. "Would you like more?"

By some sort of silent agreement Abby and Tanner kept the conversation on safer ground: their expectations of Oregon, what lay ahead on the trail. Her father remained silent, only handing her his empty plate, then accepting his pipe and tobacco pouch from her with a curt nod. The rest of the time he puffed silently, watching her from beneath his bushy brows.

Tanner, too, lit up, though he smoked a cheroot, which he deftly rolled as they spoke.

"What are the towns like?" Abby asked, leaning forward in her chair. Now that the meal was done and his smoke nearly over, her father was sure to stand up, signaling that it was time for Tanner to leave. But she wanted to hang on to every extra minute. "Are they like the towns in the States?"

Tanner blew a stream of smoke up into the night air. "They're raw places, and lack many of the amenities you may be used to. Churches are rare—although I suppose the good reverend plans to change that." He tossed the stub of his cheroot into the dying campfire. "Schools are needed too. Especially with so many new families each year."

Abby smiled at him. She was happy just to be in his presence, to hear his voice, to study the way he moved and the various expressions on his face. To hear now that her profession was in demand in Oregon completed her happiness. How could life be any better than it was this very minute?

He could kiss me.

She averted her face at that unseemly thought, yet it

would not go away. If somehow he could kiss her before the night was out, she would truly be the happiest, most grateful girl in the world—no, the most grateful woman. These restless feelings she'd been having—this curiosity —did not belong to a mere girl. And now Tanner had come along and provided the focus for that restlessness. She shifted in her chair, than raised her eyes to meet his unsettling gaze. What had they been speaking of? Oh, yes, Oregon. Schools.

"I . . . I hope to open a school in Oregon," she admitted, hoping he hadn't changed the subject while she'd been daydreaming about him.

His gaze sharpened and his lips lifted a fraction higher in a smile. "Are you a schoolteacher?"

"It's late." Her father stood up abruptly, cutting off any response from her.

Abby's face fell into a disappointed frown. Why did this have to end? But Tanner did not test her father's limits. He stood as well, but his eyes seemed to search hers with a new intensity, and Abby's entire being reacted to it. How she wished for just another minute or two with him. Alone.

"Thank you for the delicious meal, Abby. It was the finest I can ever remember eating," he added with a gallantry even her father would not be able to fault.

But when Tanner left, Abby swiftly learned how wrong she was.

"Stay away from him, Abigail. Do you understand me? Stay away from that man."

Abby followed her father's agitated movements around the fire with dismay. "But why?" she demanded as he lifted the chairs into the back of the wagon. "Why do you disapprove of him so?"

"Because he's not the right sort of man for a young woman like you."

Abby stiffened at such an implacable pronouncement. "Reverend Harrison is not the right sort of man for me.

But Tanner—he may very well be exactly the right sort. Only you—"

"Tanner, is it? Not Mr. McKnight, but Tanner." He shoved the wagon gate up, then drove the locking pin home. "He's a coarse man, too familiar when he has no right to be."

"How can you say that?" Abby pleaded, hardly able to keep her voice low-pitched enough that their neighbors would not hear.

"He was playing a part tonight, daughter. That's all. He made it his business to say all the right things, and he succeeded in impressing you with his act. But he did not fool me. Not for one minute did he fool me."

Although Abby knew she should have expected no more from him, she was nonetheless crushed by her father's disapproval. It took all her effort to suppress her anger at him. "You know, Sarah Lewis told me her father disapproved of Victor at first. But he eventually came around. Now you disapprove of Tanner McKnight, the first man whose interest I have returned—and you're right, he has succeeded in impressing me. But I don't believe it's an act." She took a shaky breath. "I wonder, though, do all fathers disapprove of their daughter's choices? Did Mama's father disapprove of you?"

He recoiled as if she'd struck him fully across the face. Had Abby not already been so upset, she would have wondered at such a reaction from him. But all that registered was the fury that stiffened his features into an unyielding mask, and the righteous thunder in his voice.

"Honor thy father and mother! Honor thy father and mother, Abigail Bliss. The Holy Book says it and it is a commandment of the Lord. Honor what I say, or risk the fires of hell!"

Then, shaking with his rage, he stormed off into the night, leaving her trembling with shame and wallowing in despair.

6

Hours passed before Abby heard her father return. She'd lain wide awake on her makeshift bed in the wagon after exhausting herself crying. They'd been tears of frustration mostly, but she was dry-eyed now, dry-eyed but heavy-hearted.

She listened as he crawled beneath the wagon onto the pallet she'd laid out for him. His head hit the wagon bed once and he muttered something unintelligible. But then all was quiet save for the gusting of the wind and the distant rumble of thunder.

Rain. How appropriate, she decided grimly. Rain made everything so much harder. Cooking. Packing. Slogging through an endless sea of mud. And the poor oxen. But everything else about this journey was depressingly hard, so why shouldn't it rain and make it even more so?

She rolled onto her side, seeking some comfort, knowing she needed to get her rest, for the day ahead would undoubtedly demand every bit of her strength. But her mind kept diverting back to her father—and to Tanner.

Thunder crackled again, and from a distance she heard a shout. The men guarding the animals would have a difficult time of it tonight, for foul weather made the animals nervous. Was Tanner among those riding herd?

With a sigh she abandoned any pretense of seeking sleep when all she really wanted was to think about Tanner. Where did he sleep at night—in his small tent? Where did he pitch it? And who would he take his meals with in the future?

She shoved down her quilted coverlet and breathed deeply of the rain-laden night air. Yet even that did not ease the warmth that radiated from the nether reaches of her stomach. She kicked the covers all the way down, baring her legs and feet. But a disturbing heat seemed to have overtaken her, and she knew the source of it. Though the Song of Solomon had often roused a vague and restless warmth in her, Tanner fanned that flame to fiery new proportions. Though she knew she should not, she couldn't prevent wondering just how Tanner's marriage bed would flourish—and who it would flourish with.

"Oh, stop it," she muttered out loud. But at the same time one of her hands moved down to press low against her belly. Thunder rolled across the open plains and it seemed to echo within her body. She burned somewhere deep inside, and yet she perversely did not want this fire to end.

She closed her eyes tightly, remembering how Tanner had lifted her so effortlessly from the mud up onto his lap. He was strong, but he'd also been gentle. He'd been polite, too, but there *was* that spark that he struck in her.

With a muffled curse she rolled over and buried her face against her feather pillow. Oh, dear God, what was wrong with her these days? She veered from exuberant to fearful. She wanted to dance barefoot and bare-legged through the prairie grasses, yet she also wanted to retreat to her old familiar life in Lebanon. She was hot at the thought of Tanner and his long, well-shaped hands touching her. But all the lessons of a lifetime turned her cold with fear at the thought.

She flopped over again. If it were light enough, she'd read from her Bible. Not the Song of Solomon, though. Not the way she was feeling right now.

A splat of rainfall hit the canvas tip, then another. In a

matter of seconds the lively sound of the rain drowned out every other of the camp's night sounds. Abby sat up, almost relieved to be drawn away from her inappropriate thoughts. She dutifully checked their belongings, making sure no box or barrel touched the canvas cover and thereby disturbed the watertightness of the cloth.

When she lay down again, however, it was to worry about Tanner and whether he was dry and, later, to dream of him and wonder if his lean fingers could ease the fires that burned her unceasingly.

The wagon train didn't break camp the next morning. The torrential rains made the trail an impassible quagmire, but more calamitous, a number of the draft animals had panicked and broken free during the night's violent storm, scattering to the four winds.

Abby awoke at dawn, though it was hard to discern day from night. In the dark, damp quarters she wriggled into her shortest skirt, oldest bodice, and closest-woven jacket. Then she donned her sturdiest boots and a large bonnet and tied a huge scarf around her head, bonnet and all. She would not stay dry for long; she knew that. But perhaps she could get the extra tarp positioned over her little table and then prepare breakfast in a modicum of comfort.

Her father crawled out from beneath the wagon once she had the tarp up.

"Have you wood—or chips?" he asked as he shrugged his suspenders onto his shoulders then reached for his jacket, all the while huddled beneath the meager shelter.

"I refilled the basket yesterday. Will you set up the fire tent, or shall I?"

He didn't answer, much to her frustration. He clearly meant to punish her with silence for her rebellious behavior last night. But once he donned his hat and boots, he did proceed to position the makeshift shelter that would prevent the rain from dousing the fire. Even so he was a long time in getting the chips to light. By the time the fire was marginally hot, Abby had the batter for hot-cakes ready and salt pork rinsed and ready to fry.

She squeezed both the coffeepot and the skillet onto the meager blaze, knowing she must work fast. Right now she had only a drizzle to contend with. But if another downpour came, they would be eating jerky and undercooked hotcakes. They ate in silence, waiting for the water to boil for coffee. When her father finished his meal, he handed her his plate, then climbed into the front of the wagon, still without speaking.

Abby sighed, and a huge weight seemed to settle over her, pressing her down with hopelessness. He would read the Bible all day, and she . . . she would go mad if she simply sat around waiting for him to relent.

Frustrated anew, she scrubbed the skillet, plates, and utensils, then thrust them still wet into the wagon. She tossed a handful of ground coffee into the boiling water, then carried the coffeepot to a hook beneath the wagon.

"Coffee's ready," she called, though she knew he expected her to deliver a brimming cup to him. But not today, she resolved. Let him sulk. She would visit with Sarah—or with poor Rebecca. Yes, she would call on young Rebecca Godwin and try to lift her spirits. She was certain to have more success with Rebecca than with her own father.

Sarah accompanied her, and Abby was especially relieved to have her company when they reached the Godwins' wagon. Rebecca sat huddled just inside the tailgate, staring morosely out across the endless rolling plains. When the two women approached her, however, the poor child flinched back, her eyes dark with sudden fear.

"Rebecca, dear," Sarah began cheerfully, though Abby could tell that her tone was forced. "You remember Abby Morgan, don't you?"

Rebecca shifted her hesitant gaze from Sarah to Abby, then gave a tiny nod. Abby forced herself to smile, but what she really wanted to do was to draw the tortured child into her protective embrace. What sort of monster would attack a young woman—any woman—in so vile a fashion?

"Hello," Rebecca murmured, fingering a lock of her long, tangled hair.

"Hello," Abby replied. Then drawing on her experience dealing with reluctant children in the classroom, she decided just to be forthright. "We've come to spend the morning with you, dear. Since the rain has eased, Sarah and I thought we'd help you straighten things up here. Why don't you come on down from there? And bring your hairbrush and a bit of cord or ribbon too," she added before the girl could protest.

While Sarah brushed Rebecca's neglected hair, Abby revived the dying campfire and put on coffee. Doris Crenshaw stopped by briefly, but when she saw Rebecca was in good hands, she didn't linger. By the time the sun rose to its watery zenith, the fragrance of hot corn bread and antelope stew scented the air. Between Sarah's deft ministrations and Abby's constant chatter, Rebecca slowly relaxed, and by the time her father appeared for the noonday meal, the girl was even contributing suggestions for Tillie's great adventure.

"What if she accidentally climbed into a buffalo's shaggy coat—you know, at night, when it was asleep. And then there was this stampede. She would be so scared. But she would be excited too."

"*I* wouldn't be excited," Sarah put in. "Once, this horse ran away with me. He took the bit in his teeth and simply took off for the hills."

"What did you do?" Rebecca asked, round-eyed with wonder.

"Why, I held on for dear life. What else could I do?" Sarah laughed. "The horrible beast eventually wore himself out. But it took me ten times as long to walk home, for I refused to ride the wretched creature."

Abby chuckled at Sarah's wry expression. "The two of you and your wild adventures would have poor Tillie stranded far away from the wagon train forever. But what about Snitch? He loves her in his own stubborn way."

"He would go searching for her of course." Rebecca smiled, a happy, innocent child again, at least for a while. "He could find her and save her. And they could live happily ever after."

"Actually I haven't decided yet whether the two of them should even make it all the way to Oregon," Abby replied. "There are so many lovely places along the way."

"Aye, there's that," Rebecca's father said, coming in from his work chasing after the missing stock. He nodded a greeting to each of the women. "But the land's free for the asking in Oregon."

"But Tillie and Snitch won't have to own the land," Rebecca responded animatedly.

The man stared at his daughter, his eyes slipping from her newly braided hair to her alert expression and neatly dressed figure. He swallowed once and sent a grateful look to Abby and Sarah. Then he faced his only child. "What's the point of anyone going to Oregon if not to claim their portion of land?"

Rebecca laughed out loud, a precious sound to hear. "Oh, Papa. Tillie and Snitch are Abby's mouse characters. She's writing a book all about their adventures."

When Abby and Sarah finally left the Godwin wagon, they were both in the best of moods. They'd accomplished something very good today, despite the dreadful weather and unfortunate reason the company had not broken camp. Each of them was uplifted by Rebecca's response.

"She'll be awhile recovering," Sarah said. "But she's on her way."

"Yes," Abby agreed. Then, spying her father up ahead, she added, "I only wish my father could recover as easily."

"You've never exactly explained what the trouble is with him."

Abby glanced at Sarah, then quickly looked away. She had strictly promised her father she would reveal absolutely nothing of their past, especially their real last name. Yet Abby knew that was somehow at the very center of her father's troubled mind. Some secret he was withholding, even from her.

Oh, how Abby longed to share her worries with someone else. But she knew she must not, so she only bottled up her feelings and pushed them back, closing them away in her heart, though it hurt her sorely to do so.

"He . . . he misses Mama so," she finally said. That was not a lie, but the truth went much deeper than that, she was certain.

"Maybe he needs to remarry."

Abby tilted her head sharply toward her friend. "Remarry? My father?"

Sarah shrugged. "Well, he might not fuss so about your romantic interests if he had one of his own."

There was a kernel of truth in that. Still, Abby could not see her father married to anyone but Mama. Most especially, she could not imagine him actually courting some woman. It would be nice if he would, she realized as they neared Sarah's wagon. But she didn't think it very likely.

Abby had just said her good-byes and started toward her own campsite, still deep in thought over Sarah's surprising suggestion, when a man crossed her path. She stumbled to a halt in the clinging mud, just avoiding colliding with him. But her quick anticipation rapidly disappeared. It was not Tanner, but another, far less savory-looking fellow.

"Good day, miss," he said, touching his hand to the brim of his hat.

"Good day," she murmured, sparing him the thinnest of smiles. Her father would not want her speaking to him, nor was she in the least inclined to do so. But as she

hurried on her way, she was uncomfortably aware that
his gaze followed her all the way.

Cracker O'Hara watched Abby's retreating figure. She
seemed kind of old, but she *could* be the one. Then again,
even though he had ruled out the Godwin girl, there
were still three other possibilities, three more girls traveling on the train with only their fathers. And though
none of the other three men admitted to having taught
school, it was still possible.

He pulled his hat from his head and wiped the sweat
from his brow with his forearm. He would lay low for a
while, just gather information and narrow it down until
he was sure he had the right one. But he'd need proof. If
he just killed her, he might never get paid. No, he needed
something. A picture of her mother. A letter. A family
Bible with a list of family members and important dates.

He jammed his hat back on and ambled toward his
raw-boned horse. He'd better get back to work. Bud was
trailing them in another wagon train. Bud had recognized McKnight as the bounty hunter they'd been
warned was after the girl. Ever since that bungled attack,
however, Bud didn't dare show his face in this company
in case McKnight recognized him. He would stay back
and investigate a different wagon company until Mc-
Knight was out of the way. But that was fine with
Cracker. He preferred to work alone.

Only he'd have to be even more careful now. He'd
almost ruined things with that Godwin girl. He should
never have followed her out into the prairie, especially
when he knew she wasn't the one. But it had been so dark
and she'd been so young. So young.

And she'd been so scared. Even now the memory of
her slender young body squirming in blind panic beneath
him made him hard.

He muttered a coarse oath. He'd had too much to
drink and his wits had been too dull to prevent her from
crying out in alarm. He'd had no choice but to run, and

he'd worried that the little slut would be able to identify him. But it was quickly apparent she could not. The fact that he could walk around in the same camp with her made his need for physical relief even stronger.

He rubbed his crotch, then swore and spit. He'd just have to forget about that for now. Business first.

Money first.

But once he did the job and collected his pay, he'd buy himself the youngest little girl he could find and vent his pent-up urges on her.

7

Her father coughed all night. Abby awoke in the middle of the night to his painful hacking and wheezing. When after a while it did not abate, she climbed down from the wagon to check on him.

"Come sleep inside the wagon. This cold ground is making you ill."

"No. I'll be fine right—" He broke off as another spasm of coughing gripped him.

"You're getting in the wagon," Abby stated, not about to back down. "It'll do us no good at all if you're ill. I can sleep here."

"That would not be proper," he protested, though he rolled over and sat up at her urgent tug on his arm.

"Proper be damned," she muttered to herself. But to him she said, "It's nearly dawn. I probably won't fall back to sleep anyway. I'll just start the fire and make coffee. Write a little," she added, for she'd been neglecting Tillie lately.

Once he was settled in her bed, Abby grabbed her shawl and wrapped it around her shoulders. She tied a belt around it to keep it out of her way as she worked, then slipped on her boots. What a sight she was, she thought, with her braid hanging over her shoulder and the skirt of her nightgown showing for the whole world to see. At home she would never have dreamed of stepping foot outside garbed thus. But life on a wagon train called for endless compromise, and in some areas at least, modesty must suffer. Thank goodness it was dark and no one else was around to see.

Once she had a small fire going, she heated water and made a small amount of strong tea with horehound, which she sweetened with a portion of their precious store of honey. Her father's coughing had not eased, but she was certain it would do so once the medicine had a chance to do its work.

He took the infusion without complaint, then fell back onto the pallet. He was exhausted, she realized. He was sick, both in body and in spirit. What if he got worse?

Abby had never considered losing her father. After her mother's death the very idea was inconceivable. Yet now, faced with his wracking cough and overwarm brow, she could not avoid it. What if he *did* only get worse? It had happened to others. Every day she noted the graves they passed. Little children, women and their newborn babes, and most of all men. That's what scared her. She knew logically that there simply were more men on the trail. But being logical didn't help.

She crouched in the back of the wagon, just staring into its cavelike blackness, listening to her father's labored breathing, and praying.

Spare him, dear God. Don't take my father too. Don't leave me all alone with no family. Please, God, I'll do whatever you ask of me. Only make him better.

After what seemed like forever, his coughing subsided, and after a while she knew he slept. His breathing came slow and regular, and Abby was finally able to relax. Her little fire was sputtering low, so she added a few chips to it and stirred it up to a respectable blaze. In the east just the first hint of the coming dawn showed. The false dawn. Before too long the morning buzz of activity would begin. They would probably break camp earlier than usual to make up for yesterday's delay. But for now all was quiet. Just the unique smells carried in on the prairie winds, and the sounds of birds and insects, so unlike those she was used to in Missouri.

She was sitting in her chair, her heels up on the top rung and her arms around her knees, staring into the fire as the coffee brewed, letting her mind wander wherever it would, when a low voice broke into her reverie.

"Can I invite myself for coffee?"

Tanner.

Abby drew a sharp breath as he stepped into the meager light cast by the fire. She'd just been thinking of him, or rather, trying not to think of him, and now here he was, conjured up as if by magic. Despite her every attempt to be unemotional, her heart began to pound like a drum.

She straightened at once into a more ladylike posture: feet on the ground, hands folded on her lap. But her hair . . . And her nightgown! She thrust the untidy plait behind her shoulder and tugged on the edges of her knitted shawl. "Coffee. Yes. It's . . . it's brewing." Only how was she to serve it without standing up in her nightgown before him?

Abby gestured weakly for him to sit in her father's chair, only barely remembering her manners. He always caught her at a disadvantage like this. Stuck in the mud. Hanging up her soiled rags. And now, sitting in her nightclothes, completely disheveled from her sleep. She watched his long-legged form step farther into the golden circle of flickering light, then take the seat she offered. He was so tall and strong and fit. Yet when he lowered himself into the sturdy rocker and stretched his legs out before him, he let out the smallest sigh. Only then did she noticed his unmistakable weariness.

"Why are you up so early?" she asked.

He smiled faintly. "Livestock are not known for their brains. The loose stock managed to scatter in every direction, and a couple of them got stuck in some mighty tight spots." He rolled his neck from side to side, then rubbed one of his shoulders. "I'm not up early, I'm up late. But what's your excuse? Why aren't you still curled up in your bed?"

Ther was no reason for the sudden rush of color to her cheeks. He'd referred to her bed in a purely innocent fashion. As usual her imagination was working overtime. Or was it?

Abby stared at him, conscious of how bold her gaze must appear, yet unable to stop herself. Did that glint in his eyes mean anything, or was it just a trick of the erratic firelight? She swallowed and rubbed her damp palms against the thin cotton gown. "My father is ill. I made something for his cough."

"And couldn't get back to sleep yourself."

She shrugged. "I don't mind. It's almost dawn anyway."

He met her eyes for a long, quiet moment. Despite the silence between them, however, her fertile imagination heard the most wonderfully intimate words conveyed in his gaze: that her eyes were like stars in the sky, that her skin was like silk. . . .

"A good time to think about your children's story."

Such an unlikely comment brought her back to reality, and without being conscious of it she leaned toward him. "Why, yes, I had been thinking about my little mouse characters." She smiled, both pleased and amazed that he remembered about her stories. At once any thoughts about how her eyes and skin appeared fled her mind. No one besides her young students had ever shown such an interest in her writing.

This time her blush had a completely different source. "Most people think my ideas about writing books are rather silly."

"If your stories make you happy—and the children who read them—then who's to say they're silly?" he reasoned, his voice a low, comforting rumble. In the cool night the weak circle of firelight gave their conversation an intimacy that belied the openness of the land around them. It was just she and Tanner. The rest of the world did not exist.

"I think so too. But most people, well, they read the Bible to their children and nothing else, even though they might enjoy penny novels themselves. I think of my stories as penny novels for children—or at least they will be if I can find someone who will publish them."

"That might be hard in the Oregon Territory."

Abby sighed. "Yes. I've thought about that. Most of the publishing houses are in big cities like New York."

"Chicago has a few as well, I've heard."

"Do they? Well, I suppose I can always write a letter to several of them once my manuscript is completed. Oh, I'm being a terrible hostess. The coffee's ready."

She fetched two cups, then crouched at the fire and, using the corner of her shawl to protect her hand, poured them each a generous portion. But when she looked up at him, she surprised the oddest look on his face. He had straightened in the chair, leaning forward with his elbows on his knees and his hat dangling from his hands. But it was the intensity of his gaze that took her aback, for he was almost frowning, he stared at her so hard.

"Sugar?" she asked, extending the tin cup to him with a hand that suddenly trembled.

"Don't need it," he muttered, more to himself than to her, it seemed. He put his hat on his knee, then took the steaming cup. Disconcerted, Abby returned to her chair with her own cup, then realized in further dismay that she'd forgotten about her nightgown. No wonder he'd looked at her so oddly! He was shocked at a woman who would sit around in her nightgown, completely unconcerned to be seen thus.

Cringing at what he must think of her, Abby took a nervous gulp of coffee, then nearly choked on the too-hot liquid. In an instant Tanner leaped to her aid, pounding her back as she sputtered and coughed. But that only added to her distress, for she feared he must now think her both foolish *and* improper. And she'd hoped to impress him!

Tanner was impressed, but not in the way Abby had hoped. Once she'd recovered sufficiently, he stepped back and reached for his cup, studying her anew.

She was the damnedest combination of innocence and seductive appeal. A churchgoing woman who wrote about mice. A flannel-clad beauty who sought to woo him with her domestic talents—for he was sure that was her intent. And it was working. But if she knew the turn his thoughts had taken when the wind had thrust the single layer of flannel against her hips. . . . There had been no drawers beneath the cloth, just sweet, smooth skin. He took a long sip of the strong coffee, then nearly choked himself on the scalding liquid.

"Maybe I should make a fresh pot," she murmured, clearly embarrassed and looking for a way to cover her discomfort.

"No, it's fine," he assured her. "Everything is fine."

And indeed it was, he realized. Ever since the other night when she'd revealed that she wanted to open a school in Oregon, he'd feared that she was Hogan's grandchild. But if she was, surely she'd know that the man lived in Chicago. Yet she hadn't so much as blinked an eye when he'd mentioned the town. Tanner didn't think she was devious enough to disguise her reaction that well. He had to conclude that she was not the girl he was searching for after all.

An enormous wave of relief poured over him. He didn't want her to be Hogan's granddaughter. Nor did he want to examine why it should matter to him one way or the other. But the relief was there nonetheless. He sipped his coffee, studying her with a new fascination. She was not the sort of woman he'd always known. And now that he was sure she was not Hogan's missing heiress, he couldn't help imagining exactly what lay beneath her plain nightgown. He didn't want to stifle the image of her pressed warmly against him. Naked. Willing.

"Abigail?" Robert Morgan's labored call was as effective as a bucket of icy mountain water in chilling Tanner's wayward thoughts. Abby, however, jumped as if burned. She cast Tanner a pleading look, one he understood at once. *Don't reveal to my father that you're here*, that look said.

Tanner stood up slowly. He was tired—damned tired—from the long day and night of riding. But somehow her father's impatient call made it worse. What was he doing nosing around a woman like her anyway? She was the kind of woman a man married. Only he wasn't the type of man fathers approved of for their daughters. Tanner might be attracted to her despite all the differences between them, but her father would never allow it to go any farther.

"Abigail!" the demanding voice came from the wagon tent.

"Yes, Father. I'm coming. I'm just fetching your medicine," she answered placatingly, though her gaze held with Tanner's.

It was Tanner who looked away first. He tipped his head back and finished the coffee in one long gulp, despite its stinging heat. Then he stood up, put on his still-damp hat, nodded curtly, and left.

He strode off, angry and aimless in his direction. If he weren't already so saddle-weary, he'd head for the hills, riding as hard and fast as he could until he and Mac were both soaked with sweat and trembling from the exertion. But Mac was done in from tonight, and anyway Tanner didn't think it would help. He was horny, plain and simple, and for a prim Papa's girl who dressed in plain calico and slept in flannel.

"Son of a bitch," he muttered out loud. Fifteen years he'd been on his own and never once had he been forced to deal with a woman's father. The women he knew didn't have fathers—at least not nearby. But along comes one little churchgoer with a beady-eyed father shadowing her every move, and he was sinking as surely as if he were in quicksand.

Quicksand. Mud. His mind quickly made the leap to the muddy, meandering river that pointed them west. What he needed was a cold dunking in the Platte River. Maybe that would kill the insane urge he had to steal a kiss—or more—from one Miss Abigail Morgan.

Once at the quagmire that was the riverbank he stripped off boots, jeans, vest, and shirt. Then with a careless shrug he yanked off his drawers as well. Only the first hint of light flirted on the eastern horizon, and even if someone saw him, what the hell. Though his skin prickled from the chilly breeze, and the mud and water were frigid on his bare feet, he forced himself into the water.

She was a pious innocent, better suited to the earnest young preacher than to someone who at fourteen had killed the man who'd murdered his mother, then celebrated by getting drunk and laid for the first time. It had been downhill for him ever since. No, she deserved someone high-minded and upstanding. Well educated. A man who'd give her the respectable place in society she deserved.

He flung himself forward into the shallow river, then gritted his teeth in a silent curse when he hit the bitterly cold water. The ocean couldn't be any colder! But it did accomplish what he wanted. As he set out in the sluggish current, swimming determinedly though his hands brushed the riverbed with every stroke, he concentrated on how cold he was and speculated how long he'd have to swim before his body forgot the cold.

And he forced himself to remember why he was here in the first place. He'd eliminated Abby and two others as Hogan's granddaughter, but there were four other possibilities. If he ever intended to collect his pay, he'd better apply himself to the job he'd been sent to do.

* * *

"Fetch me the Bible. The big family one."

Abby did as her father asked, though the big Bible was carefully tucked away in a trunk. Her mother had given it to him as a wedding gift, and he kept all their family records in it. But he only used it when his spirits were particularly low. When she handed it to him, she pressed one palm to his brow. Though he jerked away irritably, she was still able to determine that he was free of any fever.

"I'm fine," he grunted. But despite his best efforts to prevent it, he let out a harsh cough.

"You're better," Abby conceded, "but you're far from fine."

"I *am* fine," he countered. "Just let me read my Bible a few minutes and I'll be down to help you harness the oxen."

Abby took her father's breakfast plate. At least he'd eaten well; that was something. But he would not be pleased to hear what she must tell him.

"Eenie—I mean Matthew—is lame. Victor drove him and the others over, and the poor beast has hurt his leg."

Her father looked at her across the odd brightness beneath the double layer of white canvas. After the stormy skies of the past few days, this morning's brilliance seemed almost unearthly. But it showed every line in his face, and Abby fancied now that she could see the starch go right out of him at her news. His irritability and the forcefulness it lent him dissolved right before her eyes.

"Matthew is lame?" he echoed, his shoulders slumping disconsolately.

"His right hock is cut, probably when the stock scattered last night. But Victor has put a poultice on it, and we wrapped it well. In a few days he'll probably have healed enough to be back in the traces again. But till then the other three will have to pull the wagon alone."

She rubbed her hands nervously on her apron, not wanting to say the rest of what must be said, "We'll have to lighten the wagon." She hesitated. "We'll have to throw some things out."

He didn't respond, at least not in words. But Abby saw his hand tremble as he passed it restlessly over the worn leather cover of the Bible. "Throw things out?" He shook his head and clutched the Bible to his chest. "Throw out our meager possessions? Your *mother's* possessions?"

He frowned as if about to refuse. But then he paused and glanced helplessly around him, at the carefully stacked crates and barrels that filled the wagon near to overflowing. When he spoke again, his voice was low and wavering. "I'll have to pray on it. Just let me pray awhile, daughter."

Abby turned away from the wagon, shaken by his reaction. She'd known he wouldn't deal well with this setback, but anticipating it didn't make it any easier to witness. The strong, thundering father of her childhood was no more. Only now was she realizing how securely her gentle mother had propped him up.

But though she struggled to do the same for him, she was unable. She was the wrong person for the task.

Depressed, she made her way to the oxen, who nibbled aimlessly at the trodden-down grasses around the campsite. Maybe Sarah was right. If he were to remarry, he might be happier. He'd have a future to think about instead of only a past. Something to look forward to instead of only regrets.

She looped a lariat around Eenie and with only a little encouragement led him to the back of the wagon and tied him there. She paused a moment, stretching her back and flexing her knotted shoulders before heading back for the other draft animals. She was exhausted, drained both physically and emotionally, but it didn't matter. The call to depart would come any moment and they weren't ready to go. If she didn't harness the oxen, she wasn't sure her father would get to it in time. After that she would take up the dreary task of sorting out what must be discarded.

"Back, Moe. Back," she ordered, lending her weight to the force of her words. But both were inconsequential, no more than gnats buzzing around Moe's thick hide. He was the most stubborn of the four. And the stupidest, she decided with a grunt.

"Back up, blast you!"

"Can I give you a hand, miss?"

Abby looked around from her losing battle with Moe to see a man grinning at her. The man from yesterday, the unsavory one whose avid gaze had followed her to the wagon. He was looking at her with that same fascination now, his unshaven cheeks pulled up in a smug smile, showing tobacco-stained teeth, and his burly body strangely tensed, as if in anticipation.

But no matter how unappealing she found him, Abby knew she needed help. "Well, perhaps that is a good idea. He's just so—"

Before she could finish the statement, the man stepped up beside her and with a sharp movement jerked Moe's nose ring up, then back to the side.

With a startled bellow the docile animal lurched back, nearly stumbling into the wagon in its haste to avoid the pain in its sensitive snout.

"Gotta show him who's boss," the man boasted, turning now to face Abby directly. "He won't be so slow to move once he knows who's in charge."

Maybe so, Abby thought, stepping back from his unpleasant nearness. But she found his excessive cruelty distasteful. "Thank you," she muttered, hoping she didn't sound ungrateful but wanting to be rid of him just the same. Unfortunately it was not to be.

"Name's O'Hara. Cracker O'Hara." He yanked his battered hat from his head and thrust one beefy hand through his limp hair. "At your service, Miss Morgan."

Abby busied herself with attaching the chains to Moe.

How did he know her name? "Yes. Well, thank you, Mr. O'Hara."

"Can I get the other oxen for you?"

"No. No, that's quite unnecessary. They're both easier to manage than Moe."

But O'Hara seemed determined to help her. He backed Meenie and Minie into place, though with less display of cruelty, for both animals were content to follow where led.

"Thank you, Mr. O'Hara," she said again, as sweetly as she could manage. It was, after all, good of him to help her out. She should at least display good manners toward him.

"Anytime, miss. Don't you have anyone to help around here?"

"My father's a little under the weather today," she said, concentrating on Meenie's tracings. "But he's on the mend."

As if on cue her father stuck his head out of the wagon tent. "Abigail. I told you I would deal with the oxen. There was no need for you to undertake the task."

"It's all right, Mr. Morgan. I gave her a hand."

Her father nodded curtly at the man. "Thank you, Mr. O'Hara. But in the future that won't be necessary."

Abby sent the man an apologetic look at her father's curt tone of dismissal. If he minded, though, it didn't show. He only shrugged and turned to his waiting horse. But he sent her a parting glance. "You just call ol' Cracker if you need any help, missy. No matter what your Pa says."

Abby fervently hoped it would not come to that. With a tight smile she turned away. One unpleasant task done. Now to face an even worse one: sorting through and abandoning yet more of their past life.

8

Abby's hind end was numb by the time they stopped for the noon rest. She'd handled the reins all morning while her father had rested. No, he hadn't rested. He'd grieved. They'd left her mother's dresser behind, sitting crooked alongside the trail, near three fresh graves. It had been another wound to her heart, another blow she'd hardly been able to bear. But she had. Her father, however, had retreated to the wagon tent, coughing until his eyes teared up.

She'd followed him with another dose of medicine. After he'd taken it, however, she'd sat there, hurting, wanting to comfort him and be comforted in return but not knowing how to reach him.

"Papa," she'd finally begun, still clutching the spoon in her hand. "We can go back, you know. We don't have to go to Ore—"

"No!"

He'd cut her off with only that one harsh word, that and the stony silence that had followed. But it had been enough. He was beyond reasoning with, she knew. Whatever his initial incentive for this precipitous flight west, it was compounded now by his increasing depression.

She wondered if perhaps she should ask Reverend Harrison's aid.

Abby offered her father a simple lunch of bread and butter and left him drinking cold coffee. After watering the oxen she hurried down the line of wagons, searching for the reverend. She found Tanner instead.

He sat in the shade of a cottonwood tree, finishing his own meal while his horse—Tulip this time—swiped up long clumps of bunchgrass. Leaning back against the tree trunk, one arm resting on a bent knee, he looked as tired as she felt, and her heart went out to him. When he spied her, however, that weariness seemed to disappear. He took a last pull from his tin cup, then rose to his feet.

"Abby." He gave her a curious smile. "Is everything all right?"

Abby hesitated, for the urge to confide in him was strong. But he couldn't help her father with the hurt that dwelled in his soul. Only Reverend Harrison had any hope of doing that. "Have you seen the reverend today?"

His smile faded. "He's with the Godwin wagon."

Abby nodded. "Thank you." She started to go. Time was short and she need to find the man before the wagons pulled out again. But then she paused. "It's not . . . that is, it's my father. He needs to talk with someone. And the preacher, well, he'll be a comfort to him, I think."

Was it her imagination or did the tension in Tanner's shoulders ease at her explanation? He tossed the dregs in his cup aside. "You go on back to your father. I'll find Harrison and send him to you."

As Abby watched him mount the leggy mare and ride up the line, she was beset by the oddest mixture of emotions. A part of her wanted to cry while another part of her exulted. He was the man for her. A part of her knew it as surely as if it had been proclaimed out loud by the good Lord Himself. She could so easily fall in love with him; all the signs were there. But her father . . . Her father would never approve.

Disheartened, she turned back toward her own wagon. Bringing the reverend in would only strengthen her father's objections to Tanner, she feared. But if her father renewed his efforts to pair her with the other man,

Abby would just set him straight. Meanwhile she could only hope that Tanner could bring Reverend Harrison.

But she should not have feared, for she had no sooner returned to her father than Tanner rode up, the reverend mounted awkwardly behind him.

"Miss Morgan," the reverend began once he slid down from the mare, though his tone was more formal than it had previously been. "McKnight tells me you specifically requested my presence here."

"Oh, thank you for coming, Dexter. And thank you too." She sent Tanner a grateful smile, then turned back to the reverend. "Do you think you could ride with my father this afternoon? He's . . . he's been ill, both physically and emotionally," she added in a quieter tone. "He's so withdrawn. Perhaps he'd talk to you, though." She pressed her lips together, hoping he'd agree, but also that he would not read more into her request than there was.

He stared at her a long moment, then swallowed once. His neck bobbed convulsively before he glanced over at Tanner. Finally he sighed, and she knew a surge of pure gratitude.

"Mr. Morgan?" he called in his most preacherly tone. "Mr. Morgan, I've got a point of theology I'd like to discuss with you. May I ride the afternoon in your wagon?"

Abby watched him climb up over the front wheel and onto the seat. Her father's reply came, muffled and weary from inside. But she knew he'd feel better by nightfall. Dexter Harrison was exactly what her father needed right now.

Sighing her relief that for now at least another pair of shoulders would bear the burden she carried, she turned back toward Tanner. He sat his horse with a natural grace despite his apparent weariness. He could probably sleep in that saddle without tumbling off, she speculated, so at one with the horse was he. Though that was not a talent she'd ever thought to value, out on these vast prairies where a horse was such a precious commodity, it suddenly seemed critical. A man must be able to hunt and ride—to survive—if he were to protect his possessions and his family.

Did Tanner have a family?

That sudden and disquieting thought drew her brows together in a small frown.

"What exactly is wrong with your father?" Tanner asked, obviously misreading the look on her face.

Abby glanced distractedly at the wagon, then, following the thrust of the ever-present prairie winds, moved a little distance away. He dismounted, dropped Tulip's reins, and followed her as she'd hoped he would. Yet that only increased her confusion. What was it about this man that beguiled her and yet also unnerved her so?

She rubbed at an old stain on her apron. "It's not cholera," she stated firmly. "He's coughing, that's all. His fever was very mild, and the medicine I gave him took care of it. It's just a nasty cough that he's having a hard time shaking off. That's all," she finished insistently.

Though she stared out at the rolling countryside beyond them, she was acutely aware that he'd come up beside her. Then he took her arm and turned her so that they were face-to-face, and her heart began to race in an odd sort of panic.

"It's more than a cough, Abby. You wouldn't bring Harrison into this otherwise."

Staring up into the midnight blue of his eyes—eyes that urged her to confide in him, that promised her comfort—it was impossible for her to resist. "He's . . . sad. That's the only way I can describe it. He's just so sad."

"Why? What happened to make him sad?"

"Mother died," she replied, gulping past the quick rush of emotions that clogged her throat. "And he hasn't gotten over it. I don't know if he ever will."

Their eyes clung a long moment. Then he murmured, "And what about you? It must have been hard on you too."

Abby nodded, and to her enormous embarrassment her eyes misted with tears. Just as suddenly Tanner pulled her into his arms, and at the unexpected gesture she burst into tears.

The sensible part of her knew she was behaving foolishly. She was clinging to him like a frightened child and soaking his shirt with her weeping. But he held her there with arms that were so strong and comforting, and low, soothing words of understanding.

"I know, Abby. I know. My mother died when I was a boy, and it's not something easily put aside. But life goes on."

"But my father—" She caught her breath on a sob. "He can't get past it. He . . . he's so different now."

"The trail's a hard place to try to heal," he murmured against her hair.

She took a shaky breath and rubbed her cheek against the damp cotton on his chest. "It's been good for me," she admitted, relaxing into the strength of his embrace. "I didn't want to leave home, but now I'm glad we did. But Papa . . . This was his idea, only he's getting worse instead of better."

"Harrison will talk him out of his mood, sweetheart." He leaned a little back, then with one finger tilted her chin up so that their eyes could meet once more. "Harrison will see to your father's bleak moods." His voice grew husky. "And I'll see to yours."

Abby knew they were in plain view of anyone who cared to look their way. She knew she had already behaved scandalously by moving so easily into his arms. But as he lowered his head, she didn't care about any of that. He meant to kiss her. He was giving her enough time to back out of it if she wanted to, only she didn't want to. He meant to kiss her, and she meant to kiss him back.

Then their lips met and she realized how very little she knew of kissing. Dexter had kissed her just this gently the one time he'd attempted to kiss her. Caleb Dawson had done as much back in Lebanon at the county fair last year. But when Tanner did it . . .

His lips were firm, pressing lightly yet not at all tentatively against hers. He knew what he was doing as he slid his mouth sideways against hers, she realized, for he fit them better together. He knew also how the touch of his tongue along the seam of her mouth would affect her, for he was ready when she gasped in delight. His tongue surged into her mouth, and Abby nearly swooned. She clung to his wide shoulders as a torrent of new emotions poured over her like a violent summer storm. His tongue stroked her inner lips and it was like lightning striking her, spreading through her veins to every least portion of her body, so fast that she was utterly consumed.

Without conscious thought Abby arched nearer, pressing the entire length of her eager body against his hard masculine form. She heard him groan in response, heard it on her lips and caught it in her throat.

But as abruptly as the kiss had erupted, so did it end— almost brutally.

"Whoa, there. Slow down, Abby." He thrust her an arm's length away, holding her yet, with his hands on her shoulders. His chest heaved with his labored breathing. "Just slow down," he muttered once more.

The same wildfire that had surged through her body, now rushed in a burning wave of color to her cheeks. Dear God, what had she been thinking? Where had such unseemly—such wanton—behavior sprung from? Appalled at her lack of decorum, Abby tried to pull farther away from Tanner. But he held her firmly, not letting her go nor pulling her nearer. He just stared at her as if he might discover with his dark gaze every thought in her head. Every secret in her soul.

And indeed Abby felt as if he read her very mind. In an agony of confusion she averted her eyes from his.

"Don't *ever* kiss a man like that, Abby. Not unless you mean it."

Startled at both his odd words and his hoarse tone, she reluctantly lifted her gaze to meet his once more. "Unless I mean it? What do you—oh!" She drew a sharp breath, forgetting to be embarrassed. "Do you think I *didn't* mean it? That I kiss just *any* man that way?"

She tried to jerk out of his grasp, for she was both hurt and angered by his unfair assumption about her. But Tanner's fingers tightened on her, an iron hold she could not shake off.

"I know you haven't," he replied, not rising at all to her anger. He sounded patient even, the same way she often did with an errant student.

Then the meaning of his words sank in, and she was even more acutely chagrined. He knew she had never kissed anyone that way before because . . . because she had done it so ineptly. Hot and painful, her cheeks again burned scarlet.

"I . . . I'm sorry," she mumbled. "I'll do better next time—" Then her eyes widened when she realized the implication of what she had said. What if he didn't *want* there to be a next time?

He closed his eyes for a moment, as if drawing strength to let her down as easily as possible. To her surprise, however, a faint grin curved one side of his mouth. "If you do much better, Abigail Morgan, you'll probably kill me." He released her and expelled a great gust of a sigh, while she only gaped at him, completely baffled.

"Don't kiss anyone else like you just kissed me, all right?" He swept his hat off his head and raked one hand through his long, disheveled hair. "And think twice about kissing me again, because I don't know if I'll have the willpower to stop at just one kiss." He stared at her—*glared* would be a better word, she realized through her shock, for his grin had faded and he looked almost pained by what he said.

"I've got no time for a woman like you, Abby. Not

now, anyway. Maybe we'd better stay away from each other."

"Why?" Abby asked, bewildered by the vast array of emotions that tore through her. He'd come to her aid, then he'd kissed her until she was practically a helpless puddle at his feet. Now he told her that he didn't have time for a woman like her. "Why?" she repeated in a strangled tone.

He looked away into the wind so that it blew his hair back from his broad, furrowed brow. She saw the fan of creases at the corner of his eye. The strong profile. The movement of his throat when he swallowed.

"You're the kind of woman a man marries." He swung around abruptly to face her. He slapped his hat against his thigh once, and a cloud of dust lifted from it, then dispersed into the wind. "But I'm not looking for a wife."

There was no way for Abby to misunderstand his meaning this time. He was the sort of man her father had warned her about, even he knew that. And he was giving her the chance to get away before she did something she would regret for the rest of her life.

But at the moment it was impossible for her to be grateful.

She swallowed hard, trying to still the quivering in her voice. "I see." She knotted her fingers together, pressing her clutched hands to her stomach as she sought some words that might salvage the shreds of her pride. "Well, as it happens, I'm not looking for a husband."

He raised one brow in mocking acknowledgment of her bravado. "Don't say that too loud, Abby. A lot of horny men might take it the wrong way."

Horny? She didn't know precisely what that meant, but given their intense interchange, she could harbor a guess. His restored equanimity when she was still so shattered by his rejection stung even more.

"I am quite able to handle myself with any man who

has the wrong idea about me." *Except for you*, she realized with painful clarity.

But he seemed to read her thoughts. "I don't have the wrong idea about you. That's why I broke off our kiss. I know exactly what kind of woman you are. If you think about what kind of man I am, you'll know I'm right."

Maybe he was right, but pain lent a recklessness to Abby's words. "What if I don't care what kind of man you are?"

Tanner's jaw clenched and his lips thinned angrily. He jammed his hat on his head. "Then I'd say you're a damned fool."

She had no response to that. Indeed it was all she could do to keep her chin high and meet his stinging gaze. She *was* a fool, she admitted as she finally pivoted away from him. She was a complete and utter fool who should be thankful that he was gentleman enough to save her from the sure scandal she'd been headed for. Yet as she marched as resolutely as was possible through the knee-high grasses that pulled and tugged at her plain calico skirt, she could not muster even an ounce of gratitude toward him. Why *wasn't* he looking for a wife? Why wasn't he as enamored of her as she had become of him?

Why couldn't he be even a little bit in love with her?

Tanner watched Abby's retreat with a mixture of relief and dejection. Damn, but he was a fool. She'd been so ready, so prime for the taking in a way he never would have expected. Prim and proper like the churchgoer she was. But beneath that dutiful exterior lay an untapped fountain of passion. He'd tasted it in just that one kiss, and the very intensity of his response had shaken him. Even now his hard arousal was a painful reminder of how much he wanted her.

But she was going on to Oregon, and he had a job to do, one that precluded any involvement with a woman that lasted more than a night. Besides, he rationalized, there was no privacy to be had on the trail anyway. Between the flat open land and her father's watchful protection, there could have been no more between them than an occasional stolen kiss—and a lot of long, lonely, and restless nights for him.

He heard the rolling call to resume the trek, and with weary resignation he made his way back to Tulip and mounted. A hard afternoon still lay ahead of him, but that was good. He'd ride until every muscle ached and he was blind with fatigue. That way he'd be too exhausted to do anything but sleep. No tossing and turning for a shapely young body that he couldn't have beneath him. No keeping one eye open, watching for another attack like the one at Fort Kearney. He'd sleep. And with any luck he wouldn't dream about how good it would feel to wake up every day beside the same woman.

With only the lightest touch Tulip responded and swung into an easy canter alongside the rumbling wagon train. Like a dormant cloud, the dust stirred to life beneath a hundred wheels and a thousand hooves, rising up in dry, hazy waves. Tanner didn't notice the several pairs of eyes that watched him angle away from the company.

Abby watched him with eyes that burned and a heart that ached.

Martha McCurdle waved a handkerchief at him, then when he did not notice, shot the unaware Abby a jealous glare.

Cracker O'Hara rubbed his stubbly chin, then spat a fat brown stream into the tall grasses and smirked. McKnight was having as bad a time of it as he was, panting after women on the trail when he was supposed to be tracking one of them down. But he wouldn't get anywhere with that one. She was too stiff-necked to respond to anything but brute force. Then she'd be willing.

But McKnight, for all his dangerous reputation, wasn't tough enough for that. O'Hara laughed out loud, then kicked his weary bay into a gallop. That would be

McKnight's undoing: the man was smart but he had a soft middle. All O'Hara had to do was let the other man find the right girl. Then he would move in with Bud and have the pleasure of killing them both.

9

" . . . Tillie knew that Rex the prairie dog would never be reliable. He was basically good, but he was a wild creature and she, in her heart, was a domestic mouse. A house mouse," Abby explained for the youngest of her ragtag followers.

"Doesn't she like Rex anymore?" young Carl asked.

"Well, yes. Of course she likes him," Abby replied. "She just . . . she just knows they can only be friends."

"A mouse can't marry a prairie dog anyway," Estelle reasoned. "They're too different."

"Yes. Too different," Abby echoed, though her thoughts were not of Tillie and Rex.

Noticing her preoccupation, Sarah clapped her hands. "All right, children. Enough storytelling for now. Fan out alongside us and search for buffalo chips. If you want a good supper, your mothers will need fuel. So let's see who can find the most, shall we?"

The several children scattered with many good-natured boasts about who would find the most, but Sarah kept her gaze on Abby, much to Abby's discomfort. Sarah was a dear, but she was sometimes far too observant.

"Is your long face over your father, or is it over Tanner McKnight?" she began with her usual bluntness.

"My father is more depressed than ever," Abby answered, hoping to appease her with that subject.

"I guessed as much when I saw Reverend Harrison

driving your wagon. But I also heard that you and Tanner . . ." She hesitated as if selecting her words carefully.

Abby's heart sped up. "That we what?"

Sarah searched Abby's face. "So it's true."

Abby frowned and looked away. Someone had seen Tanner kiss her. How the gossips would love that bit of juicy news. "Don't beat around the bush, Sarah Lewis. Just ask me your question and let's get it over with."

They walked in silence a few moments, sidestepping prairie-dog holes and a dust wallow. "Martha McCurdle is a spiteful person, Abby. She's telling everyone that you threw yourself at Tanner earlier and that . . ." Again she hesitated.

Abby forced herself to face her friend. Why was she so unlucky? Why, of all people, had Martha been the one to witness her humiliation? "That what?" she softly prompted Sarah to finish.

Sarah sighed. "That you threw yourself at him and he would have nothing to do with you."

Abby laughed, though there was no trace of humor in the sound. She wasn't certain which was worse, the truth or Martha's skewed version of it.

"I suppose that's how it must have looked." Her throat constricted with emotion and she had to pause in her explanation. Sarah wisely kept her silence, so for a few minutes only the relentless wind and the quiet calls of the children surrounded them. The wagons were downwind, so even their creaking was muted.

Abby squinted beneath the shelter of her everyday straw hat, staring at the ground before her but seeing nothing. "I asked him to fetch Reverend Harrison for my father. And he did. Then he talked to me a little while and, well, I told him about my mother dying. And his mother had died too. Then . . . then I started crying and he . . . well, he kissed me."

Abby didn't look at Sarah, but she knew nonetheless the exact expression on her friend's face. "Why that's so very sweet," Sarah breathed, confirming Abby's speculation. "So very, very sweet."

"Yes, it was." Abby sighed and refocused her eyes. "The trouble is, he's not looking for a wife."

"Not looking for a wife? Why, that's nothing to concern yourself with. Men always say— Oh, no! He isn't already married, is he?"

A lump formed in Abby's chest. She wondered herself about that possibility. "Oh, Sarah, I don't know. I don't think so. He said . . . he said that he didn't have time for a woman like me." She heaved a great sigh. "And that he was the wrong kind of man for me."

More silence. Then Sarah caught Abby's hand in her own and squeezed. "Did he seem to like the kiss? Did you?"

Abby tightened her hand around Sarah's, holding on as if for dear life. "I— Yes. I liked it." At that understatement she finally met Sarah's concerned gaze. "I liked it so much that I practically melted into a puddle right at his feet."

Sarah chuckled knowingly. "It's the loveliest of feelings, isn't it?"

"While it's happening, yes. But afterward . . ."

"Did *he* like the kiss?"

That was harder to answer, and more embarrassing. "He told me not to kiss any other man that way. I thought he meant, you know, that I hadn't done it quite right. But then he said if I did it any better, it would probably kill him."

This time Sarah's laughter was full and unrestrained. "My dear girl. You've got nothing at all to worry about if he said that!" She released Abby's hand, then snatched up a handful of bunchgrass and began to fling the spiky leaves at Abby. "He's hooked if he said that."

Abby frowned at Sarah's antics. "He said we shouldn't see each other anymore."

"He's just a big old fish, Abby, a fish that's already taken the bait but now is fighting the line. I mean, think about it. He wants to kiss you, then he says you're killing him. Next he pushes you away and says he's the wrong kind of man for you. Only the right kind of man cares enough about a woman's reputation to push her away—especially when she's melting at his feet."

The way Sarah explained it made Abby almost believe it could be true. Almost. "He could be a decent sort of man and still know that I'm not right for him."

Sarah shook her head, laughing again. "Trust me, Abby. I know all about how difficult and evasive men can be."

"How could you? You said you loved Victor from the first—"

"So I did. But he was no easy case. Besides, I have four older sisters, all married before me, and two of them wed to the wildest pair of brothers in the whole county. But you should see them now. Good husbands. Good fathers." She rolled her merry eyes. "Mark my words. You just go on being sweet to him—cooking him dinner, sneaking peeks at him when you know he'll catch you doing it. But at the same time be sweet to every other nice fellow who comes around. Why, between wanting you and wanting nobody else to want you, he'll be crazy as an old bull on locoweed."

More than anything, Abby wanted to believe it was so, for every time she thought of not seeing Tanner, an emptiness seemed to well up in her, black and bottomless. Though her rational side told her that the feeling would ease in time, another side feared she would never be whole again. He'd taken a piece of her heart and she'd never have it back again.

Was this how her father still felt, empty and hollow? For the first time she thought she understood his endless mourning. It was worse for him, though, for he'd had her mother with him for over twenty years, while she'd only known Tanner a very short time. She resolved to be more patient with her father. More compassionate.

She turned to stare at the long line of wagons, picking

out their own sturdy outfit by the trailing Eenie tied behind. She could just see her father and Reverend Harrison seated side by side, involved in animated conversation if her father's gesturing hands were any indication.

"Speak of the devil." Sarah elbowed Abby in the side, drawing her attention. "Isn't that your young man?"

Sure enough, cantering from off to their left, Tanner McKnight angled toward the wagon train. He'd been hunting, it appeared, for an awkward bundle lay lashed behind him. If he recognized them, he gave no indication, and he was moving fast enough that he would cross their path some way ahead of them.

"Hurry up, Abby. Walk faster so's he'll see you."

"No. If he wants to speak to me, he knows very well where to find me." She ignored Sarah's mutterings— something about "lost opportunities" and "hard-headedness." But despite her best intentions to appear uninterested, Abby couldn't help following Tanner's progress toward the forward wagons of the convoy. He sat his horse so easily, as if Tulip were an extension of him, not a separate beast with a will of its own. His hat dipped low over his brow, shading his eyes, but in her mind she could picture every detail of his face. Sun-browned skin. The shadow of a beard. Blue eyes, so dark as to be mistaken for black. And lines of weariness bracketing his mouth.

"That's Martha McCurdle's wagon."

Abby squinted across the green-gold expanse of knee-high prairie grasses, trying to see past the ever-present clouds of dust that hung like a haze over the land. It *was* Martha's wagon. She'd lost a husband fording a river somewhere in Iowa and traveled now with her brother and his family, though she was very free about criticizing everything about them. It gave Abby no comfort to remind herself that, although Martha was looking for a husband, Tanner was not searching for a wife. She'd heard enough whispers about the widow and seen how her disposition changed so dramatically whenever a man was near. No doubt she would turn on all her charm for Tanner. But would he be as gallant with Martha as he'd been with her?

Abby's uncertainty grew tenfold when the buxom young widow waved to him, and his horse changed direction.

"She's after *your* man," Sarah muttered. "And you're not doing anything about it."

"And what precisely do you expect me to do?" Abby exclaimed. "Anyway he's not my man, as you put it." But she knew her anger was poorly directed at Sarah. It was Martha she resented. No, Tanner was an even more appropriate target. Why was he being so difficult?

Abby and Sarah walked on, drawing nearer until they were almost abreast of the pair. Tanner sat the patient Tulip, leaning slightly to one side as he spoke with Martha. Martha meanwhile was gazing up at him in clear fascination, bending a little forward, Abby noted sourly, in order to give Tanner the best possible view of her generous bosom.

So engrossed were Abby and Sarah in glowering at the oblivious pair that neither of them at first heard the startled cry.

"Carl! Don't move. Don't move!"

"Get help!"

By the time the panicked voices broke into Abby's awareness, four of the children came scrambling toward them.

"Snakes! A whole nest of 'em!"

"Carl's been bit!"

Without a moment's thought Abby took off running, holding her skirt high as she raced toward young Carl. She could barely see him—he was only six, and small for his age. Another child was there, too, his sister, Estelle.

"They're rattlers," the nine-year-old girl called in a strained tone when Abby neared.

"Carl. Are you all right?"

Carl's tearstained face turned toward her, but otherwise he didn't move a muscle.

"They bit his toe—but his boots are thick."

Abby stared at Estelle. How could she be so composed when Abby was petrified with fear? She could see one of the snakes, a small, poisonous coil between herself and Carl. But the rattling sound so common to these snakes came from beyond Carl. How many were there?

She untied her apron from her waist and unpinned it at the shoulders. Then, holding the sturdy fabric at arm's length, she slowly circled Carl.

Five feet from him she stopped. There were three small snakes together, not just one. All of them were too young to have rattles, but that made them no less dangerous. For a moment the rattler behind Carl quieted, and she saw the quick leap of hope in the boy's round eyes. It mirrored her own hope that the creature would just slither away. Then if she could just fling her apron over the others and grab Carl . . .

"Be careful, Abby," Sarah called in a hushed tone, still breathing hard from her run.

"Get back and take Estelle with you."

She heard their retreat, but her eyes stayed on the trembling little boy. "All right, Carl. Here's what we're going to do. You peek over your shoulder. See if you can spot any more snakes."

"There—there's a big one right behind me. I heard him."

"Yes, but look anyway. Is he still there?"

After a cautious peek the child shook his head. "He's gone."

"Don't move," Abby ordered when the boy looked ready to bolt. "He's moved, but we don't know where."

She took a step nearer him, reaching her hand out. "Now get ready. When I throw this apron on those little snakes, you grab my hand and I'll pull you away from there."

He nodded, willing to do anything she said, believing

she could save him. Abby, however, was not so sure. Still she knew she had to do something.

Somewhere in the distance she heard the vague sounds of the day: the hoofbeats of a horse, the erratic rush of the wind. But her concentration was on the tense nest of snakes. She must throw carefully, just a little this side of the snakes to distract them and block them should they strike.

"I'm scared," Carl whimpered pitifully.

"Me, too, sweetheart. So get ready. Now!" Abby flung the apron at the three small snakes, then snatched Carl's hand. She heard the dry rattling, the quick, deadly threat of it, but couldn't tell where it came from. But it was too late for her to change direction anyway. She jerked Carl so hard, she feard his arm would be pulled out of the socket. But once they stumbled back from the nest, he flung his arms around her, nearly crawling up into her embrace.

At once the shadow of a tall rider fell across them.

"Dammit, Abby! That was a foolhardy thing you did!" Tanner bellowed. With his eyes blazing and handgun drawn, he looked at once both wildly dangerous and like the most heavenly of saviors.

The rattle buzzed louder, a frightening warning that seemed to come from all around them. Tanner reached down to pluck her away from the danger. But before he could, Tulip squealed and lurched back. Already unbalanced, Tanner tried to right himself, but the mare twisted and started to fall. Before he could free himself from the stirrups, they were down, lost for a moment in the high grass and choking dust.

"Tanner!" Abby had scrambled away from the struggling horse. Now she thrust Carl toward Sarah and circled Tulip, afraid of the snakes, but even more afraid that Tanner was hurt.

Tulip squealed again, a harsh, guttural sound. Somewhere beneath the mare Tanner cursed. Abby made a mad grab at Tulip's reins. She knew the animal would run once she found her footing. If Tanner were caught in the stirrups he could be dragged. . . .

Suddenly Tulip was up, trembling and wild-eyed. Abby wrapped the reins around her hand. No way was she letting go until she was sure Tanner was safe.

Tulip reared, jerking Abby forward. "Get back!" Tanner's cry came from just behind the mare. "Get the hell back, Abby!"

But she couldn't. The mare bucked, squealing madly. The rattles hummed their deadly threat. Where was the snake? Where was it!

Then in the midst of the chaos a gun went off, a deafening crack of thunder that shook the very ground beneath her feet.

At once the rattling ceased. Once more Tulip reared, and Abby feared the panicked mare would trample Tanner. But he rose, gun smoking, and limped to her side.

With a firm grip on Tulip's bridle he calmed the terrified animal. But his eyes searched the trampled ground around them and he held his gun at the ready.

Then Abby spied it, the mangled body of a huge rattlesnake, its head just a bloody stump, shot off by Tanner. Not aware of what she did, she unwound the reins from her hand. But her eyes stayed on the dead snake. They'd come so close to disaster.

"There are more snakes—over there, under my apron." Was that her voice, so thin and wavering?

"Let's get out of here— Dammit to hell!"

Abby tore her eyes away from the dead snake. "You're hurt," she cried when he crossed to her. He nearly fell when he tried to put weight on his right leg. She met him halfway, not hesitating at all to put her arm around his waist for support.

"Son of a bitch," he muttered, clenching his teeth. "Son of a bitch."

Though she winced at the vulgarity, Abby couldn't fault Tanner for it. His face was closed in a painful grimace—in concentration—as he struggled not to fall and yet not lean too heavily on her.

"Sarah, go for help. He can't walk all the way to the wagons. Tell my father to bring our wagon here."

"Wait. Someone's got to take care of my horse first," Tanner insisted. "She may have been bit by that rattler."

Abby glanced at Tulip, who now stood with her head lowered and her flanks heaving. She held one of her forelegs gingerly off the ground, and Abby could already see the first indications of swelling.

Tanner, too, had seen it, for once more he swore, words that Abby had never heard before. Still, she was certain they were curses.

"Come on." He hobbled toward the mare, forcing Abby to edge forward also. "Hold her head. Use all your weight, because she's not going to like this."

"Tanner, I don't think this is a good—"

"Do it, Abby. Just do what I say." He put the reins in her hands then hopped over to Tulip's side and pulled a wicked-looking blade from a sheath strapped to his leg. "There's no time to waste arguing."

He meant what he said. While Abby held Tulip's big head down, Tanner grabbed the mare's leg and deftly sliced open the mare's bony knee.

"She'll need a poultice, or at least a mud pack. Can you get some mud?" He looked up at her.

Abby nodded. "I'll find something. But first I have to see to your leg. Is it broken?"

"My leg will keep," he barked. Then spying her concerned expression, he blew out a huge, exasperated breath. "My leg will keep," he repeated, but more gently. "If we don't get a poultice on her leg, though, she won't make it. We've got to draw as much of the venom out as possible."

"All right. All right," Abby conceded. She squinted toward the wagon train. She could see Sarah gesturing and barely make out her father—or was it Dexter—upon the seat. Another wagon had also pulled out of line. Little Carl and Estelle's family. It was that wagon that turned and began to rumble their way, followed—reluctantly, she thought—by her own.

"Sit down," she ordered Tanner. "I'll get water from the wagons and a rag to tie the poultice on. You just sit down and wait. Once Tulip is taken care of, though, I want to take a look at that leg. All right?"

Tanner lowered himself awkwardly to the ground, then looked up at her. Now that the immediate danger was over, he gave her an ironic look. "Once Tulip is taken care of, you can look at any part of me you damn well please."

10

"He stays with us!" Abby hissed, hoping Tanner would not hear this conversation, but afraid he could. "If not for him, I might have been killed. He's hurt because he saved my life—"

"You're making more of it than it was, Abigail—"

"You weren't there!" she burst back at her father. "You have no idea how terrifying it was. Just go take a look at that snake, why don't you?" She planted her fists on her hips and jutted her chin out. "He stays with us, Father, until he can get around on his own. He came to my rescue—mine and little Carl's. I intend to do everything I can to make sure he heals. It's my Christian duty," she added, daring him with her eyes to contradict that statement.

Her father glared at her for a long moment, then, as if he needed help in this argument, turned to Reverend Harrison. But the younger man only raised his fair brows slightly and gave a helpless shrug. Abby seized on that at once.

"Even the reverend knows I'm right. Mr. McKnight helped me when he did not have to—"

"It's his job to help everyone in the company," her father interrupted.

"And it's our job to do the same," Abby countered. "You have absolutely no reason to be so suspicious of him. He helped me, and now I shall help him. If you'll excuse me, I have work to do."

Abby made her way to the back of the wagon, still simmering at her father's bullheadedness. Then she paused and looked back at the two baffled men. "By the way, would you please fetch my apron? It's over there." She pointed toward the trampled area. "There may still be some baby rattlers under it, though. So use a stick and be careful."

When she climbed into the wagon, her haughty attitude fled at once. Tanner lay on her bed, staring up at the canvas wagon cover.

"Are you all right?" she inquired, her voice barely above a whisper. He lay so still. Perhaps his injuries were worse than she'd suspected.

"Are you?" His gaze shifted to her and his lips curved in a wry grin.

Smiling her relief, she replied, "If you're referring to my father, don't worry. He sounds stern, I know. But he's really a very good man." *Except that he's taken to suspecting everyone lately*, she silently added.

As if to underscore her words, her father's voice came to them, and the wagon lurched as he and Dexter climbed into the driver's box. "Don't know what's gotten into the girl lately."

Abby sighed at that. Yes, she was changing from the mild-tempered, dutiful daughter she'd always been. But what else could she do? Her father had changed too. She was just trying to make the best of what was often a very difficult situation.

Tanner must have sensed her mood, for his smile faded. "I appreciate what you're doing for me, Abby. But I'm sure I could ride in another wagon."

"No." She had only to think of how eager Martha would be to tend him to know that that possibility would never do. "No. You saved my life. It's the least I can do."

"Your Christian duty?"

Their eyes met and held a long, silent moment. It was more than that, and they both knew it. But her father was just a few feet away, and anyway, what could she actually say to Tanner? You do funny things to my insides? Every time I see you my heart speeds up and my mind goes blank?

No, better to say nothing at all.

She braced herself on one of the tent supports as the wagon lumbered forward, and stared down at her patient. Where was she to begin?

"Victor Lewis said he'd tie Tulip behind his wagon so he could keep an eye on her," she said, though she knew she was only avoiding what she knew she must do.

Tanner's face darkened. "If she can't stay up with us, I don't want her just left behind. I'll have to put her down."

"You mean shoot her? But why? Her leg's not broken."

"If she can't walk, she's easy prey for any animal that comes along. Even buzzards." He stared again up at the canvas ceiling. "Better for her to die fast and clean than slow and tortured."

Abby tried to swallow the large lump of guilt that had formed in her throat. "I should have been watching the children more closely. This would never have happened if I . . ." *If I hadn't been so consumed with jealousy when I spied you speaking with Martha.*

"They're not your children, Abby. They're not your responsibility."

She perched on a crate and pulled her rumpled skirts to the side. "We're all responsible for every child around us. As adults we always have to set the example. Always watch out for them. Even children we don't know."

"It's their parents' responsibility, not yours."

Abby eyed him sagely. "If that's your philosophy, how do you account for why you came to Carl's rescue? According to what you say, he's not your responsibility."

"I came to *your* rescue."

The tiny wagon enclosure seemed suddenly charged with tension, like the air before a violent thunderstorm. Abby's scalp prickled, and every square inch of her skin raised up in goose bumps. "I . . . I'm not your responsibility," she finally whispered.

He frowned, just a faint creasing of his brows at her words. "No," he agreed. But his eyes remained locked with hers, telling her otherwise. Had the wagon not lurched, throwing them both hard to the side and eliciting a groan from him, Abby was not sure how the moment would have played out.

"Are you all right?" She bent over him, not sure where to begin. "Where does it hurt?"

To her relief he kept his eyes shut. "My right knee," he grunted. "And my ribs."

"Well, we'd better get you comfortable first," she said, relieved to have something concrete to do. "Can you remove your boots and belt?" *And your trousers and shirt*, she silently added.

He must have been thinking the same thing, for he chuckled despite his pain. "Turn around. I'll take care of the undressing." But when he tried to sit up, he groaned again, and beads of sweat popped out on his brow. He fell back onto the bed with a grunt. "Maybe not."

His pained expression was all it took to stir Abby to action. What was wrong with her that she could be thinking improper thoughts about him when he was hurting so? Concentrating on her task, she moved to the foot of the bed.

First one boot, worn and dusty, followed by the other. Then his socks. They both had holes in the toes, but she could mend them. The sight of his bare feet, however, sent the oddest sort of quiver through her. Though she beat it down, she wondered at her own perversity. Did the Song of Solomon have anything to say about the allure of bare feet?

She dragged her eyes away from his feet. "I need to check your ribs. Can you help me to remove your shirt?"

He tugged his shirttail free of his trousers, then unbuttoned it. One button was missing, she noticed. She could mend that too.

"Can you roll onto your side?"

He complied, and one side of the shirt fell away from his chest. Tan skin. Dark, curling hair. That's all Abby glimpsed, but it was enough to make her want to look anywhere but at him. There was something far too intimate about this, something that had her heart beating a thunderous tattoo in her chest, flaming her cheeks a telltale scarlet.

In a vain effort to control her wayward thoughts, she concentrated on the faded chambray fabric, on the frayed stitching on the collar and the mended tear on one shoulder. The stitches were neat and even. His, or some woman's?

Stifling a groan of her own, Abby unfastened the button on the cuff and carefully pulled the sleeve free of his arm. The cloth was so warm, dusty and sweaty too. It needed to be washed. But for all her mental wrangling, she still could not stop herself from staring at this first full view she'd had of his chest. She swallowed hard. "Roll the other way," she muttered.

He did, but not without a muffled grunt of pain. Abby hurried as fast as she could, tugging the bunched cloth from beneath his side, then gently pulling it down his arm. When he rolled onto his back again, she could see he was hurting, and she felt even more guilty. He was suffering, and she was mired down in improper thoughts about the pattern of hair on his chest and the curve of muscles down his back. Even the lingering warmth in his shirt was causing her to behave like a fool. He needed someone to tend his injuries and all he was getting was a blithering idiot.

"Let me see your side," she said, forcing herself to focus on the matter at hand.

"What about my pants? How can you examine my knee if you leave my pants on me?"

Abby went beet red, and he started to laugh. But his laughter swiftly turned to a groan of pain.

"Damn, but that hurts."

"Don't curse in this wagon," she muttered, covering her humiliation with a show of affronted dignity.

He let out a slow sigh. "I'll try to remember that."

They didn't speak as she checked his side, running her fingers along the length of each rib. She tried to keep her touch light, but sometimes she had to probe harder in order to feel the bone beneath the hard ridges of muscles, and she knew she hurt him. But he lay still, eyes closed, his breathing shallow and regular—almost inhumanly so.

When at last she was justified in removing her hands from him, she let out a profound breath of relief. He'd been in their wagon less than ten minutes and already she regretted her impulsive insistence that she be the one to tend him. It was going to be awful—and wonderful, she knew. Torturous. Yet she would not give up this chance to be so near him for anything in the world.

"I don't think any bones are broken. But you *are* going to have a pretty bad bruise. Already I can feel some swelling." She rummaged in a cloth bag that hung from one of the spars. "I'm going to wrap your chest. You should leave it that way for a few days. But first . . . well, you might want to bathe. . . ." She bit her lip and stared at him uncertainly. "Can you manage alone?"

Tanner wanted to laugh, only he knew it would hurt like blazes. Besides, she would have been even more embarrassed than she already was. He had kept his eyes shut during her gentle exploration. He'd controlled his breathing, keeping it shallow and steady—mentally counting to maintain the rhythm. He had managed that, but only barely. The pain in his side had been a welcome diversion.

But he would never be able to manage if she tried to bathe him.

"I can bathe without your help," he muttered, still avoiding her anxious face.

"Well, all right. I'll . . . I'll get a pan of water for

you—it'll be cool, though, not hot. And a towel and soap."

"Fine," he retorted, knowing he sounded like an ungrateful jerk. But he couldn't help it. There was something about her sincere concern and tender ministrations that was getting to him. She was a fine-looking woman— for a slender brunette. But when she touched him with her fingertips . . . When she bent near and he caught the faintest scent of flowers that clung to her . . .

He'd teased her about helping him to remove his worn denim pants, but it was no joke, he realized. She was not the kind of woman to be jested with—at least not about sex.

He heard her rummaging about again, but he determinedly kept his eyes shut and his head turned to the wall of the wagon.

"I have to go get the water." She hesitated, then, when he only responded with another terse "Fine," made her way through the crowded wagon and leaped down.

Tanner heard the top of the water casket drop and dangle from its rope tether, bumping the side of the wagon as she dipped into the reservoir. The wagon rolled on, slow and steady. When he lifted his head, he could see one of the oxen—the one she called Eenie, lumbering behind, limping noticeably. Then Abby appeared back at the wagon gate and thrust the deep pot up onto the wagon bed. She gathered her skirts and made a light bound, to land sitting down. Then she swiveled around and rose to her feet, all the while oblivious to his scrutiny.

She was like a little girl in many ways, Tanner realized. A woman fully grown, yes. But she was innocent and incredibly naive. No wonder her father feared for her around a man like him. The women Tanner knew were world weary and cynical long before they reached their twenties. They struggled to survive, using the only things of value they possessed: their youth and their bodies. In his own way he did the same.

But Abby had lived a different sort of life, and though she was attracted to him—and he to her—they were like night and day. For brief moments, like dusk and at dawn, they might meet and connect, but the rest of the time they were on opposite sides of the earth.

"Can you manage?"

She had placed the bucket beside the bed and set a clean wash rag and round bar of soap on a wooden crate crammed beside it. Now she stared at him as if torn between wanting to stay and wanting to flee. He saw her eyes stray to his chest, then jerk back up to his face, and he had to stifle an insane urge to grab her hand and make her stay. Make her remove his pants and bathe his hard, sweaty body. Make her—

"I can manage," he bit out. To prove that, he swung his legs over the side of the bed and forced himself to sit up. The searing pain in his side and the throbbing in his knee were welcome alternatives to the intense desire that burned in his belly. "Go on. Get out of here."

Abby did not wait to be told twice. He was in a foul mood, although, she admitted, he had every right to be. But more, she was behaving like an absolute idiot. She needed a little time and space to get her haywire emotions under control.

She stood beside the slow line of wagons, letting them proceed without her as she slowly took stock of the situation.

All right. He would be staying with them for a few days. She could sleep beneath the wagon with her father. She could easily manage the extra cooking. She could wash his clothes and tend to his injuries.

But could she bear to spend so much time with him? Could she be so near him and still keep her composure?

The memory of the kiss they'd shared rushed over her, bringing with it the same confusion she'd felt then. Something inside her yearned for him, something that was intensely physical, for her belly burned and her very limbs trembled from the force of it. Yet it was more, for her heart was affected too.

The wind blew her hair in stinging disarray around her face, and she automatically put up a hand to hold it back. She'd left her bonnet in the wagon. Nor did she even have her apron anymore. She was bareheaded, standing alongside the trail in only her dress. Inadequately garbed both inside and out, the absurd thought struck her. The good folks of Lebanon would never recognize the proper Miss Abigail Bliss if they were to see her now. Her nails were scruffy and her hands rough. Whatever spare pounds she'd carried before had long been walked off, so that she was lean and firm where she'd once been softer. Her hair was a mess and her clothes, as usual, were dusty.

But those were nothing compared with the changes inside her. She lusted. It was as plain and simple as that. Abigail Bliss was—horny. The word Tanner had used suddenly came to mind. She was horny and all because of some rough-and-tumble trail hand. Passages from the Song of Solomon filled her head, and the most inappropriate feelings roiled around inside her.

The irony of it all, however, was that the man in question knew they were ill matched. Her father thought Tanner the blackguard, yet it was Tanner who'd had the good sense to put a stop to their kiss, not her.

She shook her head, letting her hair blow where it would. Her skirts belled out before her, catching in the grasses as she trudged forward.

"I wish you were here, Mama," she said out loud. *To tell me what to do. How to act.*

Her father had revealed that he'd not been particularly impressed with her mother on the occasion of their first meeting. But time had obviously changed his mind. Could Abby change Tanner's mind as well? Did she even dare to try? It was hard to know and might be even harder to do.

Abby heard a call but ignored it. She needed to think. But the call came again, and when she looked up, it was to find Martha McCurdle bearing down on her.

"Abby, wait."

Go away, Abby wanted to reply. But she didn't. She didn't slow down, though. By the time Martha caught up with her, the woman was panting from the effort.

"What . . . what happened back there? And how is poor Tanner?"

Tanner, was it? Abby's eyes narrowed resentfully.

"I'm afraid he's been quite crippled. Temporarily," she added, though ungraciously.

"Oh, my. I must bring him my special elixir, then. That'll help ease the poor man's pains," Martha boasted.

Her special elixir. Abby glared straight ahead at the undulating horizon, but instead saw in her mind the bounteous curves the widow McCurdle was so prepared to offer Tanner. "I have matters well in hand," she stated.

Martha laughed, a mirthless sound that made Abby turn her head back toward the shorter woman.

"You'd be better off holding on to your preacher, Abigail Morgan. Tanner's not the kind of man for someone like you."

Echoing as it did Tanner's own words, Martha's smug pronouncement destroyed the last of Abby's equanimity.

"And what sort of woman is that, Martha? One who cooks him meals that he raves about? One who tends his aches and pains? One he kisses—" She broke off, aghast almost as much by what she'd revealed as by the braggart's tone she'd used.

Martha's lips thinned and her nostrils flared, and Abby was reminded of the tense posture of a wild barncat, preparing for a territorial fight. If the woman had possessed a tail, Abby was certain it would be flicking back and forth in agitation, fluffed out in fury.

"Why, you common little slut," Martha spat, her face ugly with her anger. "You play the role of the little church mouse, while underneath those long skirts you're all wet for him."

Abby was not prepared for the pure venom in Martha's tone. But she knew to her chagrin exactly what Martha meant. All wet for him. She'd wondered about the physical changes she'd been going through. But the way Martha sneered the words made it seem like an awful, dirty thing.

"You may read anything you like into it, Martha McCurdle. I don't care. Everyone knows what you're like anyway."

"Oh, do they, now? Well, we'll soon see what they think you're like, won't we?"

If looks could strike a person dead, the parting glare Martha shot at Abby would have left her gasping for her last breath, fallen and hidden in the tall grasses of the endless prairie. As it was, Abby's pulse beat such a harsh rhythm in her ears that she would not have been surprised if she burst a blood vessel right then and there.

What a truly vile creature that woman was! A gossip. A liar. And . . . and a slut.

Abby took a harsh breath and blew it out, then repeated the action until she had her anger marginally under control. She was not the slut. Martha was.

Yet even in the midst of her emotional turmoil, Abby recognized the ugly kernel of truth in Martha's words. She did lust after Tanner. There was no use pretending otherwise. And she did become . . . *wet* was the only word to use. She became wet and hot and all stirred up inside whenever he was around—and even when he wasn't. Just the thought of him made her want to jump out of her skin with yearning.

Horny was the word he'd used, though he'd referred to men at the time. If it was possible for a woman to be horny, then that's what she was.

And now Martha was going to trumpet it to the whole world.

Abby trudged alongside the wagon train a long while,

well away from the dust plume that hung over the line of slow-moving vehicles. Despite her preoccupation, however, she was mindful of her path. No more tall grasses for her. She stuck to well-trampled areas where a lurking snake could more easily be spied. But today she could do little better than a dawdling pace, and as the sun arched behind a line of clouds to the west, she fell farther and farther behind her own wagon and the terribly conflicting problems it held for her.

Tanner fared no better. He managed to wash his face and neck and most of his upper body. Not that it would help him heal any faster, but he wanted to be presentable. For her.

"You're a fool," he muttered to himself as he rinsed the cloth in the cool water. *A fool asking for trouble*, he silently added.

From the front of the wagon he heard Abby's father. ". . . but the apostle Paul states in the Bible time and time again that a woman is more susceptible to temptation. And to sin. She must be guarded by her father and then by her husband."

Dexter Harrison responded in a tone far more calm than Robert Morgan's. "Our modern interpretation of the Bible must be carefully considered. As you well know, there are any number of passages that Abigail can quote back to you regarding charity and good deeds. The Good Samaritan is just one of many."

Tanner heard Abby's father harrumph in irritation. "The Good Samaritan was a man, not a woman. I'm certain he considered the consequences of his actions more thoroughly than my daughter did."

"If she'd asked you instead of demanding, would you have agreed?"

The answer to that never came, at least not in words that Tanner could hear. But he knew the answer. Robert Morgan wanted him as far away from Abby as possible.

A part of him understood. A part of him agreed that

he'd do the same if some hired gunslinger came nosing around a daughter of his.

Then he shook his head in amazement at the very idea. A daughter of his own. A son. He'd never really thought how he'd feel about having a child. He'd never imagined being a parent except in the most practical of considerations: they'd be a big help around the horse-breeding ranch he hoped one day to establish.

He unfastened his worn denim pants and braced himself against a barrel as he balanced on one foot while he shoved his pants down. His knee was already swelling, and after bathing the lower half of his body, he wrapped the damp cloth around the aching joint.

His saddlebag was shoved into a corner, and he found a relatively clean union suit in it. But as he dressed himself, he couldn't stop thinking about Abby. How would she react if a daughter of hers were enamored of a totally unsuitable man? A daughter of theirs . . .

His foolish imaginings were interrupted by a demanding yet most definitely feminine hail. "Yoo hoo! Mr. Morgan. Slow up. I want to climb aboard."

Once more the disdainful snort came from the driver's box. "Better her than my Abigail," Tanner heard Robert Morgan mutter. Then the Widow McCurdle clambered with surprising agility into the back of the high wagon bed. Tanner only had time to sit down on the bed and yank a sheet over his lap.

"Oh, Mr. McKnight—Tanner," she cooed. "I heard how you rescued that poor little boy. Are you all right?"

Tanner nodded, "Yes, ma'am. I'm fine. I'll just have to stay off my feet for a few days, that's all."

She moved nearer, staring at him with unblinking avidity. She was a cute little thing, just the voluptuous, aggressive sort of woman he usually favored. Were it possible for them to find a minute's privacy—away from the silently listening pair in the driver's box—he had no doubt she'd prove to be as eager and talented as that hot little number in St. Joseph.

But that knowledge gave him not the slightest pleasure. Nor could he muster even a polite interest in the generous Widow McCurdle. If he didn't know better, he would have thought that fall had damaged more than merely his ribs and knee. But it wasn't the fall. It was Abigail Morgan, curse his luck.

He forced a smile when Martha held up a brown bottle and shook it enticingly. "My special tonic," she revealed with a saucy grin. "I'm going to dose you with Martha's special remedy three times a day, and mark my words, I'll have you raring to go in no time at all. No time at all," she repeated more huskily, letting her hot gaze roam his body.

Once more a snort of disdain floated back from the driver's box. But Tanner knew that despite Robert Morgan's contempt, he would gladly suffer the Widow McCurdle's not-so-subtle attempts at seducing Tanner. The man saw it as his best chance to drive a wedge between Tanner and Abby.

"Actually, Abby already gave me something and it's made me a little drowsy. I was just about to take a nap." Tanner twisted on the bed, only wincing slightly at the sharp pain in his side. He pulled the sheet up to his waist, then rolled over to face the wall and closed his eyes.

There was a moment of silence, broken only by the everyday sounds of their traveling. The creak of wagons. The heavy tread of the draft animals. The distant sounds of voices and insects and the ever-present wind. But inside the Morgan wagon there was no sound at all.

Tanner knew that both Morgan and the reverend waited. Listening. Hoping that he would succumb to his baser instincts and accept what the saucy young widow so plainly wished to give him.

He yawned, then opened his eyes and peered back over his shoulder. "Sorry, Mrs. McCurdle. I just can't seem to be able to keep my eyes opened. I'm sure you understand."

He saw her face tighten. Her brows lowered and her

eyes narrowed. Her lips pursed as his rebuff became clear. With a sharp intake of breath she shoved the brown bottle into the pocket of her apron, then drew herself up.

"Oh, I understand, all right. I understand *very* well."

She left with a flurry of skirts and petticoats, and with a relieved sigh Tanner closed his eyes once more. She was insulted; Morgan was disappointed; and good old Dexter probably didn't know how he ought to feel. As for himself, though, Tanner suddenly wanted only to sleep. Abby would come back after a while and once she did, he'd figure out what he was going to do about his unlikely attraction to her.

He still had a job to do for Hogan. Until he settled his feelings for Abby, however, it appeared he would never be able to fully concentrate on finding the man's granddaughter.

His last semicoherent thought, though, was that once he found Hogan's missing heir, he would be free to concentrate on getting some heirs of his own. Though he'd never once imagined being part of a family, the idea held a growing fascination for him. A family. Children. A wife . . .

11

Cracker O'Hara didn't know whether to be glad McKnight had saved the woman or not. If she'd died before he'd had proof she was the one, that hotshot eastern bastard wouldn't fork over a damned penny. Then again, maybe it wasn't her.

He squinted at Abigail Morgan's solitary figure, slowly falling behind the rest of the group. Maybe he'd just go offer her a ride. Now that McKnight was out of commission for a while, maybe he would take advantage of the situation.

Before he could turn his mount toward her, however, he saw another woman heading her way. He muttered a foul string of curse words.

The Morgan woman looked over at a call from the other woman, and after a moment she picked up her pace and angled over to join her. Well, he'd just have to catch her alone some other time. And who knew? Settled as McKnight was in her wagon, the other man would have the perfect opportunity to find out if the Morgan woman was the one. Hell, the cagey bastard probably wasn't hurt at all. He could be using this as a way of getting to the truth—and of getting under her skirts.

He laughed coarsely. More power to him if he could breach that snooty little bitch's defenses. As for himself, he'd have to dig out a bottle of whiskey and do a little research somewhere else tonight. Maybe he'd offer a couple of shots to the skinny boy who'd been chasing one of the other young women who was traveling alone with her father. Maybe she'd told the boy something that might reveal whether *she* was the Bliss girl.

"Personally I think it's an ideal situation."

Abby glanced at Sarah. "On the surface, yes. But I get so mixed up around him. I feel like such a fool. I mean, I don't know what to say. I turn beet red, as if I were twelve instead of twenty." She sighed in exasperation. "And now there's Martha. . . ."

"What's *she* up to?"

"Oh, you know how she is. She sees everything in the worst light—or else she deliberately *casts* it in the worst light. Anyway she got me so furious that I—"

Abby broke off, not certain if she should reveal any more about her run-in with Martha. But the story was going to be spread around the entire company like wildfire—probably much elaborated, too, thanks to Martha and her malicious streak.

She shaded her eyes with one hand and peered intently toward the head of the wagon train, barely visible in the dusty distance as it disappeared over a hill. She took a deep breath.

"I more or less implied that Tanner and I were sort of a couple."

There was a little murmur of approval from Sarah. "And since she's been trying to lure him in ever since he joined up with us . . ."

"Right. She's jealous and she's mad."

They walked in silence for a few minutes, angling ever nearer the rumbling line of wagons. Finally Sarah caught Abby's hand in hers and gave it a reassuring squeeze. "Don't worry about Martha. Everyone knows by now what she's like. They may listen to what she says —after all, who can resist a bit of gossip? But they'll also consider the source. Besides, when they also hear how Tanner has been rebuffing her, they'll have a good laugh at her expense."

Abby smiled at her friend's merry countenance. Being with Sarah always made her feel better.

"How is Tanner doing, anyway?"

"Bruised," Abby admitted. "But he'll be all right. *I'm* the one who may never recover."

"In my considered opinion he's just as smitten as you are. I bet," she paused and laughed. "I bet the two of you are wed before we ever reach Oregon."

Abby laughed too. Then after getting the latest news about Tulip's condition, she waved her friend off to her own wagon. But her mind spun at the thought. Married to Tanner. Was that what she wanted?

The sun approached the low hills to the west. They would soon circle up for camp, and she could not put off seeing Tanner again. Perhaps this time she would be able to control her careening emotions a little better.

When she reached their wagon, her father and Dexter were walking alongside the oxen. The slight uphill grade they'd been following all day put a strain on the animals, and Captain Peters constantly encouraged people to keep their wagons light. That meant everyone walked as much as possible.

Keeping that in mind, Abby caught up to the back of the wagon but did not climb in.

"Tanner?"

"What?"

The impatient tone of his voice made her pause. "How are you doing?"

He gave a disgusted laugh. "I'm doing about as good as a lame steer in a stampede. How's Tulip?" he added, a little less irritation in his voice.

She peered into the wagon and saw him sit up and slowly swing his legs over the side of the bed. He was cleaned up with dampened hair combed back from his face, and his shirt now covered his chest.

Thank goodness.

"Tulip is limping pretty bad, according to Sarah. But

Victor is tending to her. I'm sure he'll do everything he can for her."

"Yeah, as much as he can."

Abby saw him rub his knee. "Are you in much pain?"

He gave her a halfhearted grin. "I'm fine, Abby. It's nothing that won't heal."

"I . . . I never really thanked you. For saving me—and little Carl from those snakes."

"No. You didn't."

At that unexpected response Abby tried to decipher his expression. Was he teasing her? But his face was serious and his eyes . . . his eyes held her enthralled. Mesmerized. Caught in a web of uncertain emotion.

"Thank you," she managed to whisper, though her mouth was suddenly as dry as the vast land that surrounded them, and every thought seemed to flee her head. "Thank you."

He frowned slightly. Was he in pain?

"Could you come in here?"

Abby was inside the cramped wagon in a moment. "What's wrong? Where does it hurt?"

He looked up at her from his seat on her bed. Their gazes held once more, and his glittering stare roused the most inappropriate feelings inside her. She felt a flame of color rise in her cheeks, but she could not look away.

"I hurt—I hurt deep inside," he said in a hoarse whisper.

"Your ribs?" Abby took a step nearer so that they were but inches apart.

Tanner's eyes moved down to her lips for one agonizingly long moment. When he again met her eyes, she knew he must see every one of her emotions clearly written in her face: how she yearned for him, how she wanted him to feel the same toward her. And for a moment she could believe he did, for the deep navy of his eyes seemed to burn with a hot blue fire. Those eyes seared her with their scorching intensity. Then he caught her hand in his, and with the faintest of pressure drew her so close, their knees bumped.

"Kiss away my pain," he ordered in a low, beguiling voice. "Kiss me, Abby."

She should not. Yet all the lessons of a lifetime disappeared at Tanner's softly worded request. Kiss him. Why not? She wanted to—oh, God, how she wanted to. And he wanted it also.

Abby bent to the tug of both his hand and her heart. She leaned forward, caught by his compelling gaze and the urgent needs of her own femininity. She'd been aching to kiss him again, ever since that first time.

Her eyes closed when their lips touched. So gentle. So light and fleeting. Merely the press of skin to skin. Yet it was infinitely more.

Then the wagon lurched—just another rut in the well-worn road west. But Abby almost lost her balance. She braced herself with a hand on his shoulder and he steadied her with a hand at her waist. Two more simple touches, yet they changed the tenor of the kiss entirely. This time he slid his lips back and forth along hers, and she responded from some wellspring of repressed emotions. She leaned into the kiss, and when he nipped at her lower lip, then soothed the same spot with his tongue, she opened to him on a long, welcoming sigh.

Abby heard a faint moan of passion. Did it come from her? But it didn't matter. Tanner's mouth took possession of hers and she melted against him. His tongue slid within her mouth, stroking boldly, stoking her hidden passions into a hungry fire. His hand slipped around her waist to pull her between his legs and up against his chest.

Relying solely on her feminine instincts, Abby's hands cupped his face as she bent down to kiss him. His other arm circled her, holding her most intimately just below her derriere.

"Tanner," she gasped, lifting her head from his. But her fingers remained entwined in his long, damp hair.

"I still hurt," he murmured, his voice husky, his eyes alive with passion. He slid one hand over her derriere, slowly, provocatively, until Abby thought she would burst into flames beneath his touch.

"Oh!" she breathed, unable to be any more coherent than that. No one had ever touched her derriere before. No one had ever told her how it would make her feel, not even Solomon in his many verses. Then Tanner's hand moved down again, and somehow she found herself sitting on his lap.

At his slight grunt of pain she tried to get up. What in heaven's name did he think he was doing? What did she think *she* was doing?

But Tanner held her there. "Kiss me. Quick," he added. "I'm hurting bad."

She did as he asked, though the sensible side of her knew her kiss would have no impact whatsoever on his physical ailments. But that sensible side of her, that rational, logical part of her, was fast disappearing. In its stead appeared some other emotional creature, some wanton, full of strange desires and foolish longings.

She kissed him, held close in their intimate embrace. She kissed him, opening her mouth to the exquisite assault of his tongue, meeting his probing shyly at first, then more boldly. Her arms wound around his shoulders and neck as he fitted their mouths together even better.

Abby noted only vaguely that every place he touched seemed to incite her raging emotions to ever higher peaks. Her arm. Her knee. When he leaned her back, then hovered over her, kissing her senseless, pressing her into her own familiar sheets and pillows, she clasped him to her with unfettered enthusiasm. Then his hand slid up her side to cup her right breast and the entire world seemed to stand still.

The entire world, that is, except for the wagon. At a sharp whistle the wagon began a slow turn. Then her father's shout, "Giddap, Mark. Giddap!" pierced her consciousness, and her eyes flew open in alarm.

Tanner's face was mere inches above hers. His hand still curved around her breast.

In the heated silence they stared at each other, both struggling with a passion that had almost gotten out of control.

Abby closed her eyes and groaned in dismay. *Almost* gotten out of control? *Almost!* Dear God, what had she done?

At once Tanner straightened up, though his hand was slow to leave her bodice front. They sat that way for a moment. Or rather, she lay, her legs across his thighs. Then with another small, embarrassed sound Abby swung her legs around and leaped up as if she'd just been scalded.

She nearly fell, her legs were so unsteady. But she held onto the tent bracing and stepped as far back from him as the crowded interior would allow. What was she to say now?

"Ah, damn. I'm sorry about that, Abby."

She glanced hesitantly at him, knowing her cheeks were aflame. *He* was sorry? "Why?" she blurted out without thinking.

Tanner raked both hands through his hair and shifted on the bed as if he were uncomfortable. Then he looked up at her. "I don't usually take advantage of innocents."

Abby swallowed hard. Should she be upset or relieved by his words? "Who *do* you usually take advantage of?"

Only when he laughed did she realize how awkwardly that had come out. "I try not to take advantage of any woman. But if you're asking who else I've . . . kissed like that," he finished after a brief hesitation. "It doesn't matter who they were. It didn't mean anything anyway."

Feeling like a fool already, Abby decided to complete the role. "Did this mean anything?"

At her softly worded question his eyes searched her face. Then the wagon came to an abrupt halt, and for a few seconds the canvas top swayed above them. Her father's bark broke in. "Abigail. Come along, daughter. Time to make camp."

Suddenly Abby was afraid to hear Tanner's answer. She turned toward the back of the wagon, but he caught her wrist before she could escape. For a long moment their gazes clung, and she fancied his was as fearful as her own.

"I don't know," he murmured. "I don't know." Then he let her wrist fall, and turned away.

Abby wanted to say something. That it had meant something to *her*. That it had meant everything. But she was afraid to appear too bold. He wasn't looking for a woman like her, he'd once told her. But if she could just be patient, just bide her time and not lose her head and perhaps drive him away. . . .

With quiet efficiency she smoothed her blouse and straightened her skirts before leaping down to the ground. She gave Eenie an affectionate pat, but her mind was preoccupied. She feared her father would be able to tell at once from her flustered expression what had just happened between her and Tanner.

To her surprise, however, it was Dexter she ran into first.

"How is your patient?" he asked, his expression noncommittal. He had a good face for a preacher, she realized. Nonjudgmental.

"He is . . . well, in some discomfort. But there doesn't appear to be anything broken." She pushed a loose curl back from her cheek and tucked it behind her ear. "How is my father?"

Dexter stared at her through dark, serious eyes. "His soul is in pain. Your mother," he added when her eyes widened in concern. "He mourns her, and yet . . ."

"And yet?"

He shrugged. "I feel sometimes that it's more than that. That he's keeping some secret, some pain he's not ready to share with anyone just yet."

"I've thought the same thing." For a moment Abby

was tempted to tell him about their use of the name
Morgan, when their real name was Bliss. Maybe Dexter
could get her father to open up to him if he knew about
that. But her father appeared from around the wagon and
she was prevented from acting on that idea.

"I've invited Reverend Harrison to sup with us," he
announced, challenging her with his lowered brows to
counter his words.

But Abby couldn't have been more pleased. "How
nice that will be." She smiled at her father and the lanky,
bearded reverend. How nice that she would not have to
keep the peace between her father and Tanner all alone.
How nice that she would have a less threatening person
to converse with, for she was not at all certain how she
would be able to face Tanner again. She smiled. "Well,
I'd better get started."

While Dexter helped her father unhitch the three
oxen, then lead them and the limping Eenie away, Abby
built the cooking fire. She folded down the table, fetched
water, and performed myriad other chores. But she
avoided any task that might require that she climb back
into the wagon. Though she knew she couldn't put it off
forever, she simply did not know what she was going to
say to him. How she should behave.

Then a thud and a muffled curse came from within
the wagon, and her heart began to pound. "Do you need
any help?" she called in a tentative tone.

"No."

Another thud sounded, and the wagon creaked with
his movements. "Son of a bitch!"

Abby pressed her lips together in panic. He was coming out. Despite her nervousness, however, she moved to
meet him. He would need a helping hand.

"You shouldn't be out of bed," she scolded when he
teetered at the tail of the wagon. His weight was all on
his good leg while he held one arm pressed to his bruised
side. Somehow he'd managed to put a clean pair of trousers on as well as his boots. But his shirt hung out of his

pants and he looked as if the effort to dress had cost him dearly. "I can bring you your supper inside the tent."

He snorted. "I might be able to eat in there, and sleep and bathe too. But there are some things better done elsewhere."

Once Abby caught his meaning, blood rushed scarlet to her cheeks. He needed . . . some privacy. She swallowed her embarrassment as best she could and moved nearer him. But she couldn't look at him.

"Lean on me. I'll help you get down."

Somehow they managed, though not without a few grunts of pain from him. Once on the ground he let out another muffled curse. One of his arms rested heavily over her shoulder, and her arm encircled his waist. As she disentangled herself from him, she couldn't help saying, "Please don't curse. If my father hears you . . ."

"He'll leave me sitting in the dirt, crippled or not," he finished for her.

"I don't think he'd go that far."

Tanner grimaced, then hobbled toward the thigh-high grasses beyond the rutted wagon track. "I'll try to remember," he called over his shoulder. He planted his hat on his head as he limped off, his broad shoulders dipping with every step.

As encounters went, Abby wasn't entirely disappointed. Better to have him grouchy than amorous, she supposed. But her eyes lingered on him, and even as she returned to her work, she couldn't help periodically sending searching glances for him. What would happen the next time they were truly alone? Should she avoid such a circumstance, or should she seek it out?

She added salt and pepper to the water heating over the fire, then the chopped onion grass she'd picked several days ago in a pretty valley just past Fort Kearney. But her mundane tasks left her mind free to wander, and her thoughts returned again and again to one subject alone. Tanner had kissed her and touched her—and thrilled her—in a way she'd not known was possible. The very idea that she could maneuver them into a situation where that could happen again . . .

A heated knot tightened in her belly at the thought.

She took a shaky breath and blew it out, then did it again. She knew she had to get these unseemly urges under control, but it was practically impossible. Tanner would be with them for several days. There would be so many opportunities for them to be alone.

"I don't want you alone with that man."

Abby jerked upright at her father's curt remark. Were her immodest thoughts so clearly written on her face? She might have argued with him, but one glance at his glowering expression told her that she would get no-where with him just now. "Yes, Papa," she murmured, though somewhat grudgingly.

He stared at her for several seconds, then nodded and moved to the wagon gate. Once he had their three chairs pulled out, he lowered himself into one of them. "He's too coarse a man for you, Abigail, no matter what you say about him having read the classics. The fact that he can read—if that is even the truth—doesn't make him suit-able."

"I don't want to talk about it," she replied. She thrust the heavy skillet onto the struggling fire and slapped a spoon of bacon grease into it. "You've made your opin-ion clear. What I don't understand is why you dislike him so. You disliked him from the minute you laid eyes on him. You've never given him a chance."

"He's a hired gun, daughter. A man who makes his living on the basis of how good he is with his weapons."

"But we all benefit from that. He hunts for all of us. And I bet you'd be mighty grateful for his hired gun if we were to be attacked by Indians."

"That's not the point," he thundered. "Do you hon-estly think that's all he's ever hunted? Did you ever won-der how he got so good with a gun? He excels at violence because he is a man of violence—" He broke off in a fit of coughing. But for the first few seconds Abby did not respond. Then as his face grew red and he doubled over, she leaped forward in chagrin.

"Oh, Papa. I'm sorry. I'm sorry." She pounded on his back, then when that didn't help, ran for a dipper of water.

After a few false starts he was able to swallow a mouthful. He leaned back in his chair, heaving for breath. As swiftly as his face had turned red, now it seemed to drain of all color.

Gray hair, gray mustache. Gray skin. With his eyes closed, only his rattled breathing saved him from looking like a corpse. That grim picture filled Abby with even more guilt than she already felt.

"I'll mix up more cough medicine," she murmured. But he caught her hand before she could go.

"Promise me, Abby girl." He coughed again, and his entire frame seemed to shudder with the effort. "Promise me that you'll turn your eyes away from him."

Abby squeezed his hand in response to his imploring grip. "Papa. For once won't you please explain to me what's really going on? If you would just trust me. Why are we running away from Missouri?"

But he ignored her pleading words. "We don't need the likes of him." He sank back in the chair and let his eyes close once more. "We'll do just fine. You'll see."

Only they weren't doing fine, Abby admitted as she returned to cooking. Her father's decline was beginning truly to alarm her. It didn't help that he was so fixed in his dislike of Tanner. But as she mixed flour and water to begin biscuits, Abby had to admit that her father was right in certain respects. Tanner *did* live by the gun. God only knew what acts of violence he'd engaged in over the years.

Still, there was a deep well of goodness in him. Of honor. He'd come to her aid twice now. And he'd even warned her away from himself. She knew he was a good man. If only there were some way to convince her father of it.

Robert Bliss worried the very same subject, only it was Abigail he felt needed the convincing. She had a perfectly good man ready and willing to marry her, yet she was blind to Reverend Harrison's sterling qualities. She was blind because she only had eyes for that gunslinger.

Robert rubbed one hand across his eyes. *Father in heaven, help me*, he silently prayed. For a moment he wondered if perhaps he should tell Abigail everything. About her grandfather and his letter. About the wealth the man was ready to cast before her. Perhaps if she knew, she would understand why marriage to Dexter made so much sense.

But no, that was far too risky, he realized. He watched her as she shook the heavy skillet back and forth to prevent the pan biscuits from scorching. There was no guarantee she would be as repulsed by Willard Hogan's vulgar offer as he was. After all, she'd never had any extra money available to her. Hogan's offer might sound awfully tempting to someone who'd lived so sheltered a life as Abigail.

No, they must simply go on as they were. Best for her not to know about her selfish grandfather. And as for Tanner McKnight . . . Robert let out a long, slow sigh. Whether the man was simply the gunslinger he appeared to be or some hireling of Hogan's, it hardly made any difference. Robert would just have to be on his guard whenever that man was near her. He would just have to always be on his guard.

12

The three men sat evenly spaced around the fire, her father studying his Bible by the last streaks of sunlight, Dexter mending a tear in a pair of his pants, and Tanner massaging his knee. Abby had thrown together a dinner of beans, pan biscuits, and a little gravy made from the last of the antelope. The false rush of energy her nervousness had generated was fast waning, and she was glad the food was nearly done. She wanted nothing more than to crawl beneath the bed linens and succumb to the mind-numbing weariness that already threatened to overwhelm her.

It was an exhaustion, she knew, not just of the body but also of the spirit. For as she'd worked, she'd tried to pray, and even her prayers had been muddled.

Help me to be patient with my father. Help me to stay strong, at least until journey's end. Help me to know what to do about Tanner.

But there had been no answers, no flashes of insight. No God speaking directly to her as He apparently did to her father.

What was she to do? she worried as she scooped a generous portion of beans onto each tin plate. Life had been so simple in Lebanon—a very long time ago, it seemed. But now she felt like the thick knotted rope her students used for tug-of-war during their lunch break, yanked back and forth, shredding apart on the inside.

"This is delicious," Dexter told her once they'd begun their otherwise silent meal. He even smiled at her, a tentative, hopeful smile. But after only a nod of acknowledgment she averted her eyes, concentrating on the beans. She didn't want to give him any ideas whatsoever, especially since she suspected her father might be encouraging his suit again.

She glanced at Tanner, then took a sharp breath when she found him already staring at her.

"Yes, delicious," he echoed in an innocuous tone. But the full meaning of his words started the most disquieting feelings reverberating throughout her body. His gaze held steady, telling her things she knew she should not want to hear. But she *did* want to hear them. She wanted to listen to every word, for the rest of her life.

Her father's hacking cough drew her eyes abruptly away from Tanner. She realized with relief that her father had not noticed the look that had passed between her and Tanner. But then she felt an awful guilt. Her father's physical strength was declining. His cough was getting worse, and yet her first reaction to it was relief for herself.

She set her plate down on the crate she sat on and crossed over to him. "No more sleeping on the ground," she told him once the spell had passed and he could catch his breath. "You sleep in the wagon. With Tanner," she added.

Her father shifted his dulled gaze to the man watching from across the fire. Abby expected him to object, to bluster and protest. When he did not—when his arm trembled beneath her hand—she knew a sudden, chilling fear. He was more ill than she'd suspected. All the terror she'd felt as she'd watched her mother's decline came back in excruciating detail. Every torturous minute. And then the bleak days after she'd died—

"No," she practically shouted, unnerved by the grim turn of her thoughts. "No reason for you to stay up any longer," she amended. "You need to rest. Come on, Papa. I'll help you."

He stood, though it took considerable effort for him to muster the strength. Tanner and Dexter watched the interchange between father and daughter. Then they both stood as well.

"May I be of any assistance?" Dexter asked.

"Fetch some water," Tanner answered. "I'd do it but for the obvious reasons. Two buckets," he added as he limped toward Abby and her father.

Dexter hesitated, but at a pleading look from Abby he turned to his task. Tanner meanwhile took Abby's place with one strong hand under her father's arm. "I'll take him off for a moment of privacy. You make whatever concoction you must so that he can get a good night's sleep."

Like Dexter, Abby did as she was told. Indeed, so shaken was she that she was incapable of thinking for herself. By the time they reassembled, however, and she put her father in bed with a strong dose of horehound and honey, she had her emotions better under control. The other two men puttered around, cleaning up the dinner mess while she sat beside her father in the darkly shadowed wagon.

"I want the big Bible," he whispered hoarsely. "The big Bible."

Once more Abby retrieved the old family Bible from the trunk where it lay with the other most precious of their mementos.

Though her hands trembled with fear, Abby swiftly laid the book beside him, then placed one of his hands on the familiar worn leather. His eyes were closed, and in the dark it would have been difficult to read anything. But Abby knew he did not need to see the Bible. His fingers moved lightly over it, tracing the embossed patterns on the cover and sliding up the well-creased spine. He was not a man who craved material goods beyond what was necessary for health and comfort. But he loved that Bible. Because her mother had given it to him it was his most prized possession.

"Whither thou goest," he murmured, so low that she had to bend down to hear. "That's what Margaret vowed to me, and she was true to her word." He coughed, but it was milder than before. "Perhaps it's my time to go with her."

"No, Papa. Don't say that." The anguish in Abby's voice must have registered, for he opened his eyes. Even in the dim wagon their gazes clung. "You have to get well, Papa. For me," she added, barely holding back her frightened tears.

His eyes closed again, and panic welled in her chest. But he patted her hand, and the faintest smile flitted across his lips. "You're a good daughter, Abigail." He took a slow, labored breath. "You would make a good preacher's wife."

If she thought it would make him well, she would willingly wed the Reverend Dexter Harrison, Abby decided as she sat beside him once he slept. If it would give her father the strength to carry on, she would promise him anything at all. She simply could not bear to lose him. To lose the last family she had.

"Abigail?"

Dexter's hushed call, coming so swiftly on the heels of Abby's desperate thoughts, seemed almost a sign from God. She pressed a light kiss to her father's brow, then pushed herself wearily to her feet. Both Dexter and Tanner waited in the pale moonlight for her, and her troubled gaze slid from one of them to the other.

"He's asleep now. I think . . . I think we'd best do the same."

Dexter helped her climb down from the wagon. "I'll bed down here, if you like."

She gave him a tight smile of gratitude. "Thank you. I know he would appreciate it."

The lanky preacher bobbed his head, then shot a wary glance toward Tanner. "I'll just go fetch my bedroll. Will you be all right?" he finished, taking her hand in his.

"I'll keep a watch on things," Tanner answered before Abby could.

At the sound of Tanner's voice all the mixed-up feelings inside her seemed to multiply a hundredfold. Abby extricated her hand from Dexter's warm grasp, but she did not look at Tanner.

"I'll be fine," she assured Dexter. "And I appreciate everything you've done for my father."

Dexter stared hard at her, his heart shining in his eyes. "I hope you know that I'd do anything for your father. And for you, Abigail."

She had no answer to give him. Every part of her that was sensible wanted to feel toward him as he obviously felt toward her. But she didn't feel that way. It was as simple—and as complicated—as that. Again she gave him that small forced smile. Once he left, however, she felt as if her face would crack under the pressure of maintaining that expression.

"Come here, Abby."

Before she even heard his approach, Tanner took her arms in his hands. "Come here, sweetheart, before you fall down from exhaustion."

Whatever remnants of logic she possessed fled as Tanner turned her to face him and enfolded her in his strong embrace. He was solid and warm, and he offered her the one comfort she truly needed. No demands. No pressure. Just someone to lean her head against and wrap her arms around.

For a long, quiet moment they stood that way, sheltered by the night, surrounded by the cool breeze and soft evening sounds. She could have stood that way forever, his heart beating a reassuring rhythm beneath her ear as she borrowed from his vast reserves of strength and will. But her father's cough, though nothing like the hacking of before, intruded on her momentary idyll.

Abby pulled back reluctantly. Then, when he would have tugged her into his arms once more, her sense of responsibility forced her to slip all the way free of his hold.

"I . . . I can't," she whispered.

"Can't what, sweetheart? Rest even a minute? If you don't rest soon, you're going to get sick yourself. Then what will you do?"

Abby shook her head and silently cursed the tears that stung her eyes. "I can't," she whispered brokenly, unable to explain any further.

She heard him expel a long breath. "Go wash up for bed. I'll sit with your father a few minutes. Go on," he prompted when she remained rooted in her tracks.

In the end it was easier for her to do as he said than to try to explain. He climbed into the wagon, favoring his injured knee, while she found one of the buckets of water. She bathed her face and neck, her hands and arms. Then she made a quick trip into the dark prairie surrounding them for a private moment.

She looked up when a faint light flared in the wagon. Had Tanner lit a candle, or the lantern? But after only a few seconds the light was snuffed out.

By the time she returned to the wagon, once more washed her hands, and checked to see that their camp was settled for the night, Tanner was perched near the back of the wagon, a cheroot glowing softly in the night.

"You'd best sleep in here beside him. He might need you in the night."

Abby nodded, though she knew he could not see her movement. She waited until he climbed down before she climbed up. He didn't speak again, and they didn't touch.

She was grateful for that, she told herself as she removed boots and stockings, her skirt and single petticoat. But when she slid her flannel gown over her head and let her hair down, she knew she was lying. She wanted to be with Tanner. Not in the carnal way. At least not tonight. But if she could have simply lain beside him in his arms, pressed up to his strong body, and still have retained her reputation, she would have done so without a qualm.

But she couldn't. She couldn't, and she would very likely mourn that fact every day of her life.

Tanner took a last pull on the cheroot, then tossed it down and viciously ground it out. Why her? He wanted to throw his head back and scream his frustration at the impassive night sky. Howl his anguish at the moon. Instead he settled for a low string of oaths, the foulest language he'd heard in a lifetime spent moving around in foul places and foul company.

Why the hell did it have to be her?

But it was her. She was Willard Hogan's missing granddaughter. He'd sat there in the wagon beside her sleeping father while she was gone, and for the longest time he'd just stared at the Bible in the man's hands. He'd known it would provide the proof he needed, one way or the other. But he hadn't wanted to look.

In the end, though, he'd done it. He'd slid the Bible from the man's slackened grasp and opened it, and he'd found all the evidence he needed. But instead of satisfaction he'd felt a disappointment so keen, it hurt, and a shame he'd never experienced before. All the men he'd hunted down, all the lousy things he'd done in his life, and it was this one simple act that made him feel like a low-life snake. For inside their family Bible had been listed every momentous date of the older man's life—including his real name, Robert Bliss, and that of his wife, Margaret Hogan. Abigail Morgan was Abigail Bliss—Willard Hogan's missing granddaughter and only heir.

Tanner yanked his hat off his head and wiped his brow with his sleeve. He needed a bath and a haircut. Then he swore again. Hell, who did he think he was kidding? It would take a lot more than soap and water and a visit to the barber to put him in her class. Bad enough when she was only a proper little church mouse. But now . . . now he had to take her back with him, back to become the toast of Chicago society.

He wished to God he'd never taken this job.

He turned sharply, then let out another blistering string of swear words. Damn, but his knee hurt! There was no way he could sleep, yet walking was a torture.

Still he limped on, heading toward the loosely guarded stock.

"This ain't no place for a man on foot, McKnight," one rider barked in friendly greeting.

Tanner did not reply but instead whistled, a long, low compelling note. A few horses looked up, then returned to their grazing. But across the darkness an answering whicker came. Tanner whistled again, and in a few seconds Mac ambled out of the herd.

Tanner rubbed the animal's muscular neck with true affection, then grabbing a handful of mane, flung himself up onto the animal's back.

"Son of a bitch," he muttered at the twin stabs of pain. His side or his knee—it was a toss-up which hurt worse. But once straddling his longtime companion, Tanner felt marginally better. People came and went, but a man could always rely on his horse.

With a nudge of his heels and only the slightest shifting of his weight, Tanner guided Mac away from the peaceful herd of horses and mules, milk cows and oxen. If he was going to deliver Abby Morgan—Abigail Bliss, he amended—to her grandfather, he'd need two horses. Since he was too keyed up to sleep, he might as well go check on Tulip.

Victor Lewis was working on Tulip's leg by the light of a tightly twisted grass torch. The mare stood, head down, her injured leg held up in obvious pain.

Tanner alighted gingerly and made his way to Victor's side. "How's she doing?"

Victor packed a fresh glob of mud on the swollen leg, then wound a wet cloth around it. "The walking hurt her bad. I stayed back with her as long as I could, walking her real slow. But even so, every step was a torture for her. She's hurting pretty bad right now."

"Will she make it?" Tanner asked, rubbing the mare's

ears. She had raised her head a little at his arrival and bumped her nose against his chest in greeting. But there was no mistaking that she was not well.

"If she hasn't gone down yet, I don't think she will. She could use a day of rest, though. It's the walking that aggravates her leg. But if she could favor it a day or two . . ." He trailed off with a shrug.

"Maybe I should stay back tomorrow with her," Tanner mused out loud. "She and Mac and I can make up the time once her leg's better."

Victor gave him a sidelong look. "I would have thought you'd want to take advantage of Abby's doctorin' skills."

Tanner didn't smile. "She's . . . she's already got her hands full with her father."

"That's not the point," Victor persisted. But when Tanner still didn't smile, he shrugged again. "Whatever. But it might take more than just one day for this leg to be ready for any serious traveling."

"I'll stay back with her as long as it takes."

And maybe while he waited with Tulip, he might figure out how to deal with Abigail Bliss. Her father had dragged her out here to avoid Hogan. That was clear. But he was beginning to suspect that Abby didn't know anything about it.

Tanner knew Robert Bliss would do everything in his power to keep Abby with him. But Tanner didn't have any idea how Abby would react to the news that she had a wealthy grandfather in Chicago, one who wanted to spread the world at her feet.

He was certain, however, that it would fall to *him* to break it to her, curse his unlucky hide.

13

Tanner came back very late. Abby heard his irregular step and occasional grunt of pain as he crept into the pallet she'd laid for him beneath the wagon. True to his word Dexter had made his bed just beyond the fire. Beside her her father slept fitfully, his breathing shallow and too often broken by his lingering cough.

If only they could take a reprieve, she thought longingly as Tanner settled down, so near and yet so far away. Between the heat, the choking dust, and the snakes, she was sick to death of traveling. A day spent in a shady grove of willows beside a clear running stream would lift everyone's spirits, even the draft animals'. Lord knew that Eenie and Tulip both could use the extra time to heal.

But there was no chance of that. Captain Peters pushed them all a little faster every day. Besides, the Platte was hardly a clear running stream. It was more a hot, shallow river of thin mud, moving at a snail's pace.

She shifted on her hard pallet, looking for a more comfortable position. Her father, Dexter, Tanner—the three of them were tearing her into little bitty pieces, shredding her emotions as well as her common sense. The level-headed, gentle Miss Abigail who taught school in Lebanon was gone, to be replaced by an irrational, often sharp-tongued woman who didn't know which way to turn anymore.

Her father was ill—declined into melancholia. He

needed her support more than ever. Yet she was so consumed with Tanner—by any standards a completely unsuitable man for her—that she turned a blind eye to her own father's needs. He was all she had in the way of family, yet she let Solomon's Song and all the inappropriate feelings it roused inside her distract her from that fact.

Abby reached out a hand to lightly touch her father's brow. No fever. Thank the good Lord for that. She lay back and stared up into the darkness of the wagon tent. The moon shone faintly through the canvas, very like the truth straining to shine through the murkiness of her many emotions, she thought morosely.

What would Tillie do? she wondered, though she knew that what she needed was logical thought, not fanciful imaginings. Still, she couldn't erase the thought. What *would* her little mouse character do if she found her innate sense of responsibility swayed by the inexorable pull of emotions?

Oh, just call a spade a spade, Abby. She was pulled by more than emotions. Lust was not just an emotion. It was like the rest of the seven deadly sins, a failing of her fickle mortal soul, something to be fought and resisted with every fiber of her being.

She closed her eyes and prayed. *Make me be an obedient daughter. Make me accept the life you've planned for me.* But even as she prayed, she knew her heart was not entirely in it. She should implore her heavenly Father's help, not demand it. God gave her a free will to make her own decisions, to do good or evil as she chose.

But longing for Tanner . . . was that such an evil thing? If they were to marry, to enter the holy sacrament of matrimony, surely that would be good.

Except that her father would never allow it. And anyway, Tanner wasn't looking for a wife. How could she have forgotten that fact?

First he'd saved her from her own wicked tendencies when he could so easily have ruined her. Then he'd saved her life from that horrible nest of snakes. But he didn't want to be bound to her for a lifetime.

She shut out the hopelessness of that fact the only way she knew how.

Once upon a time there was a little mouse named Tillie. She lived in such a big house that it supported a huge community of mice. In the dairy barn even more mice lived. But they were field mice, and the house mice kept strictly apart from their more common relatives. . . .

Abby awoke with a headache and a crick in her back. By the time she checked on her father, dressed and alighted, both Tanner and Dexter were moving about. While Dexter fed a small fire, however, Tanner stuffed his meager belongings into his saddlebags.

"Where are you going?" Abby blurted out as a sudden panic seized her.

He didn't respond at first, and in the awkward silence she heard Dexter's tentative "Good morning, Abigail."

"Good morning," she managed to reply, sending him only a brief glance. But her gaze returned at once to Tanner. "You should be resting, or your knee and side will never heal. See?" she added when he limped over to the fire to test the warmth of the water heating for coffee.

"I plan on getting plenty of rest the next few days," he retorted, though he did not look at her.

"What do you mean?"

"Stop mothering me, dammit. I can take care of myself just fine."

Abby gasped in dismay at his curt tone. Why was he angry with her?

"I'm not mothering you," she said quietly, mindful that Dexter had risen to his feet and watched them now in uneasy silence. "I'm just . . . I'm just concerned. After all, you wouldn't have been hurt except for me."

A swirling eddy of wind drove the smoke from the fire toward her, causing her eyes to sting with quick tears.

When Tanner finally met her gaze, however, she knew it was not entirely the smoke. He was doing the right thing, putting some distance between them. Only she couldn't bear it.

"Please stay," she whispered for his ears only.

For a long moment their eyes held. His were so dark that they looked more black than blue. Hers, she suspected, revealed everything she felt for him. That she had fallen in love with him. But if he read the truth, it did not prevent him from turning away from it. And from her.

"I've got to take care of my horse. I'll be back in a couple of days."

He didn't elaborate, and Abby did not have voice enough to question him further. Giving up on the coffee, he slung his saddle and saddlebag over one shoulder. As he limped away, a tall, solitary figure in the early-morning light, Abby could only watch him go—and her heart with him.

Dexter laid one hand on her shoulder, by way of comforting her, she supposed.

"It's for the best, Abigail. Truly it is."

Perhaps she would think so one day, Abby admitted, bending away from him to blindly tend the coffee. But she would be a very long time believing it.

Still, he'd said he'd be back in a few days. That was something to hold on to, wasn't it?

It was the longest, most miserable day of her life. Dexter drove the wagon; she walked. Her father lay abed the whole day, clutching his Bible both sleeping and waking.

Abby never strayed farther than hailing distance from the wagon. Her father might need her, and anyway she could not bear the thought of the other women's company today. She wished to be entirely alone in her misery.

And miserable she was. There was no sign of Tanner at all, no indication whose wagon he rode with. At the noon rest she prepared a substantial meal of bean soup and corn bread, but she couldn't eat. Nor did her father take much, but Dexter more than made up for their lack of appetite.

Their rest was cut short, however, when a heavy band of clouds was spied advancing over the horizon from the northwest. Rain would be a welcome reprieve from the June heat. But it would turn the little swales to rivers and the ever-rising hillocks before them to slippery mudbanks. Traveling would become that much more difficult, so Captain Peters wanted to make as much distance as they could before the storm struck.

Obligingly Abby hurried to repack the wagon, taking one last sip of tepid water to sustain her. If it rained, she would find a way to take a good bath, even if she had to drape sheets between two wagons for privacy. But as the long afternoon ensued and the clouds only hung far beyond them, thoughts of a refreshing bath waned. She trudged along in the sticky heat, patting at her perspiring brow with a stained handkerchief and wondering about Tanner.

Not until they camped beneath a grim and threatening sky did she get an answer. As she set up buckets and bowls to catch whatever rainfall she might, Sarah called out a friendly greeting.

"Abby. At last. I'd have found you sooner, but I had to drive our team today." With typical enthusiasm she positioned an enameled bowl so that runoff from the wagon tent would pour into it. "I had hoped you would come search me out. Or is your father too ill?" she added, concern coloring her voice.

"He's sleeping right now," Abby answered. She pulled her friend a little way from the wagon so as not to disturb him—and so that their conversation might not be overheard.

"Oh, Sarah. I don't know what to do anymore. Papa . . . Dexter is driving our team. And Tanner . . ." She wrung her hands together. "He left this morning and I don't know where he's gone. He's still injured from yesterday, and I've been so worried—"

"He's with his mare. Didn't he tell you?"

"Yes, but—" Abby broke off. She was behaving like a fool, she knew. But she seemed unable to stop herself.

"Victor stayed back with him this morning. He says Tulip—that's the horse—she should be much improved in two days' time."

"Stayed back with him? What do you mean?"

Sarah gave her a quizzical stare. "Didn't he explain— No, I can see he didn't." Sarah patted Abby's arm comfortingly. "Tulip could barely keep up yesterday afternoon. Tanner decided to camp a day or two with her so her leg could mend easier. He'll catch up afterward. And he'll have a chance to mend as well."

Abby nodded as if she understood, and part of her did. It made complete sense for him to stay back with his injured mare, and she found his loyalty to his poor horse commendable. But she didn't understand why he hadn't explained it to her. He'd behaved as if he was furious at her. And considering what had passed between them the day before . . .

Perhaps it was *because* of that. That and her pleading with him. "Please stay," she'd begged. But he'd gone, leaving her to torture herself about why he'd left, and where—and with whom—he was.

"He's with Tulip," she said, nodding once more. Well, if he'd wanted to punish her, he'd done a very good job of it, she decided as a spurt of restorative anger shot through her. A damned good job.

Oh, but she was getting just as bad as him, she realized, what with her cursing and all. But she was too outraged to care. She'd worried and fretted the livelong day, only to find that he was off with his horse, not with Martha McCurdle—though she had no real reason to think he'd be with her.

"It's so very good of Victor to help Tanner out."

Abby forced herself to sound civil, when she realized that Sarah was staring at her most curiously.

"Oh, my Victor has a way with animals. He likes nothing better than to mend some poor creature that's ailing. You just watch. He'll have Tulip right as rain."

As if mentioning the word summoned it, a rattle of thunder rolled over the circle of wagons, and the first fat raindrops splattered in the dusty soil. Both women looked up at the glowering sky.

"Well, we shall all have our baths and our clothes washed tonight, it seems. I'll be off, then. But, Abby, if you can get away, come walk with me tomorrow. It might do you good to talk with a woman. Why, you've been surrounded by nothing but men of late."

"So I have," Abby agreed. The company of women would be a welcome reprieve indeed.

She had the fire started before the rain began in earnest, and with the aid of the fire tent she was able to make a meal of beans and corn cakes. Beans. By the time they reached Oregon, she'd have eaten enough beans to last her a lifetime. But even the steady downpour and unappetizing meal could not entirely dampen her spirits. Tanner was with Tulip, doing the responsible thing for the mare. Though he was a hard man to pin down, he was extremely responsible. No one could deny that, not even her father.

She was still angry with him of course. He'd worried her so unnecessarily. But her anger was assuaged by her relief that he'd not abandoned her for someone like Martha. Where had this jealousy sprung from?

Besides, she was going to have a proper bath.

The sheets were in place. Every bucket, pan, and pot they owned was steadily filling with rainwater. Abby had already removed her boots, stockings, and petticoat. Her head was bared to the rain, and now she unpinned her hair and began to unwind the single braid and comb it out.

What was Tanner doing right now? Did he have shel-

ter from the rain? Was he cleaning himself of the trail
dirt as she was?

"Abigail? Are you there, daughter?"

She blinked at the sound of her father's voice and
wiped at the raindrops that clung to her lashes. "I'm just
outside, Father."

"You'll get wet," he complained. "Come in and read
the Bible with me."

"As soon as I finish bathing, I will," she promised.

With his demand hanging over her she felt compelled
to hurry at her ablutions. However, Abby was so pleased
at her father's strengthening voice that she could not
regret having to rush. She made certain there was no one
about, then pulled all the water containers inside her
makeshift bathhouse. Finally she removed her blouse and
skirt so that only her chemise covered her. As it met with
the rain, however, the thin muslin garment clung to her
skin so that every curve was revealed had anyone been
there to see.

Let him kiss me with the kiss of his mouth . . . the first
line from the Song of Solomon came to her. As when
she'd helped Tanner remove his clothes, she now had the
most improper thoughts. Though she'd feared the idea
of bathing his smooth tanned skin, she could now admit
that she would have loved to touch him that way. To rub
a cloth, slippery with soap, over every part of his body.
His shoulders. His chest.

She lifted her wet cloth and squeezed it so that sudsy
water ran down her chest and belly in rivulets. Did she
dare remove her chemise and scrub all the places on her
body that heated now to think of Tanner?

But that would be far too wicked. Instead she used a
dipper to pour water over her head. She then rubbed the
cake of soap down the long tangles of her hair and pro-
ceeded to scrub until the soap trickled onto her face and
stung her eyes. Only then did she rinse her thick hair
clear of the soap, blinking all the while from the soapy
burn.

It served her right for thinking such improper thoughts. Yet when she lifted her clinging chemise to swiftly wash beneath it, sliding the cloth over her belly and buttocks, she once more pictured Tanner. Only this time he was bathing her.

How different it would feel if it were his hand that wielded the soapy cloth, if he slid it across her stomach and down to the inside of her thighs. . . .

With a sodden plop the cloth fell from her nerveless hands. Abby stood there, her drenched chemise hiked up to the apex of her thighs, trembling from the force of the wicked feelings that consumed her.

The rain fell harder, stinging her with its needling power, and the wind whirled in rising crescendo. She should have shivered from the cold, but her shivering had another source, a hot, melting source that welled up from deep inside her belly.

If he ever touched her there, she suddenly understood, she would never recover. She would be his to command, to bend to his will, to use in whatever way he might wish to use her.

Once more she was consumed by the sin of lust. She released the hem of her chemise and with a low groan of frustration turned her face up to the dark, weeping sky. She was a sinner, but though she should despise the terrible feelings that burned within her, what she truly wanted was to see them exhausted, to seek out the culmination of how he made her feel and to revel in it.

Only Tanner was not there. Nor did she have any reason to think he would cooperate.

"Dear God in heaven," she mumbled on a shaky breath.

"Miss Morgan?"

She whirled around at the sound of a man's voice. Beyond her flimsy wall stood Cracker O'Hara, and above the soggy, drooping sheets he had a clear view of her.

"Beg pardon, ma'am," he murmured, but the smirk on his face didn't change, and he made no move to leave.

His eyes slipped over her, head to toe, before she grabbed a towel she'd hung in a dry spot beneath the wagon bed.

"If you don't mind," she muttered, furious and repulsed all at once. His smirk turned to an outright leer, and after a long, revolting moment he winked. Then he turned and sauntered away.

Whatever warmth she'd felt disappeared in the wake of O'Hara's appearance. Shivering now, Abby wrapped one towel around her body and another around her head. It was awkward dressing in the rain, but she managed to pull a loose blouse and an old skirt on, then put her father's rain slicker on over it all. Her hair she ignored for the time being. She was too humiliated by what had just occurred to care about the appearance of her hair. All she wanted was to escape to the inside of the wagon.

Once the pots, bowls, and buckets were emptied, rinsed, and set out to fill again, Abby found her boots, hung her abandoned clothes on a line until she could get to them, and climbed up into the wagon. O'Hara was nowhere to be seen, and for that she was inordinately grateful.

Inside, her father lay on his back, the big family Bible balanced on his chest. A small candle burned in a dish beside him—a luxury he didn't often allow himself. When he heard her, he opened his eyes and gave her a wan smile.

"You look a sight, daughter. Sit beside me while you comb your hair."

Relieved to have someone to concentrate on besides herself, Abby pressed the back of her hand to his brow. Cool. Thank the good Lord.

"Do I pass inspection?" he asked with an impatient shifting of his head on the pillow.

"You pass." Abby smiled at him, then perched on the side of his bed and rummaged in a basket for her comb. "But that doesn't mean you can't use another full day of rest tomorrow."

"Humph. You treat me like I'm the child, not the other way around."

"I do not. Besides, I'm not a child either. Not anymore." She stared at him in the golden light of the solitary candle. Inside the wagon tent the atmosphere was soft and intimate, made cozy by the darkness outside and the steady drizzle. If she squinted her eyes until they blurred, she could almost pretend they were back home on a rainy evening, before they'd set off for the western territories. Before her mother had died. It was precisely the comforting reminiscence she needed tonight.

"No, you're not a child," her father conceded. Their eyes met in understanding and he let out a slow sigh. For a quiet while he simply watched her work her mother's ivory comb through the wet tangles of her hair.

"You have your mother's hair," he murmured, more to himself, it seemed, than to her. "I always did enjoy watching her comb her hair in the evenings after all the chores were done. It was so long. So lovely."

Abby smiled. "When I was little, she used to let me comb it for her. Remember? That was always my favorite time of the day. Just she and I. Talking together. Laughing." Her smile faded a little at the bittersweet memory and she, too, sighed. "Would you tell me something, Papa?"

He arched one bushy brow fondly. He seemed as mellowed by the cozy atmosphere as she was. Encouraged, she continued. "Tell me about how you and Mama met. You told me a little bit before," she hurried on, hoping to head off any objections before he could raise them. "But I'd like to know more. Where you were living. Who introduced you. How you proposed to her."

She'd been concentrating on her hair as she spoke, working on the knotted ends. Perhaps she was a little afraid to face him with her request. But now she chanced a peek at him, to gauge his reaction to her inquiries, and when she did, her hands stilled at their task.

A tear glistened in his eye. He turned his head

slightly, and in the shadows she could no longer see it. But she knew she had not been mistaken.

A guilty lump rose in her throat and she put one hand over his and leaned forward. "I'm sorry, Papa. I'm sorry. I know that talking about Mama makes you sad. But . . . but I hate having to act as if she never existed at all. I *need* to remember her. I *need* to talk about her sometimes."

He turned his head slowly, as if it took a Herculean effort. "I know, Abby girl. I know you miss your mother. I miss her—"

He paused and passed one bony hand over his face. "We'll talk soon. But not tonight. I'm too tired tonight."

Abby nodded. Though disappointed, she was nonetheless encouraged. It was so hard for him. But it was hard for her too.

Still they'd made some progress. Eventually he'd be ready to talk about the past from which they fled. And when he did, she was convinced he'd finally find the comfort he so desperately needed.

She put down the comb and pushed her wet hair behind her shoulders. "Shall I read to you awhile?"

He gave her a small, grateful smile and handed her the Bible. "You pick the passage, daughter. Whatever you like."

Abby took the heavy tome, sliding her hands over the familiar bindings. No matter where this journey took them, so long as they had this book with them, they still had all the memories of their happy home in Lebanon. Her father's voice would thunder as he read the Good Book. He loved the passages about righteousness and retribution for sinners. Her mother's readings, however, always had been gentle—full of wonder, it sometimes seemed. She'd read the passages about love and forgiveness.

Abby opened the leather cover, then paused at all the family records inscribed so carefully in her father's neat hand: *Married, Robert Matthius Bliss to Margaret Adelaide*

Hogan, September 9, 1833. Born, Abigail Margaret Bliss, December 8, 1834.

There were more listings, of course. Her baptism. The date her father had become a deacon in the church.

The final entry was of her mother's death and the place of interment. Abby wondered with a sudden wave of heartsickness whether she would ever lay flowers on her mother's grave again.

With trembling hands she found the passage she wished to read, the passage she needed to read for her own comfort as well as her father's.

"The Lord is my shepherd," she began in a less than steady voice. "I shall not want. He maketh me to lie down in green pastures . . ."

Her father's breathing slowly relaxed, and as she recited the familiar words, not needing to read them at all, she prayed fervently that the Lord would shepherd both of them out of the darkness of their recent past and into a valley of love and happiness and fulfillment.

And for herself she prayed that Tanner McKnight would be beside her in that valley.

14

Her father was up the next day, though he was not strong enough to walk very long. He rode in the driver's box while she and Dexter walked alongside the wagon. Though she did not want to give the gentle reverend any false encouragement, Abby could not deny that she welcomed his company. He was a comfort to her father, and besides, he was congenial company for her.

He'd had a fire built when she arose, and she'd been conscious of his eyes following her. When she'd caught him staring, a faint blush had crept onto his bearded cheeks. She'd pretended not to notice. Why must all the wrong men be attracted to her? Dexter. O'Hara. She shivered to remember that unpleasant incident last night. Now as they toiled along the mud track formed by yesterday's deluge, she tried to forget by immersing herself in safe conversation. They spoke of Oregon, of the schools that would be needed, and of the church he planned to establish.

"When did you first hear the call to preach?" Abby asked him, breathless from a long, slippery rise they'd just topped.

"I've always known I was no farmer. Nor herdsman either." He pulled at his beard in an unconscious manner. "Fortunately for my father, he had other sons for those tasks. My talents seemed to lie in building things. Had I the funds, I would have studied architecture. There's nothing so remarkable as a Gothic cathedral, you know. I've a book that depicts the most magnificent structures in all of Europe."

He shrugged and smiled, and Abby was put in mind of a bewhiskered little boy. "I've built all sorts of things," he continued. "Birdhouses with arched windows and gabled roofs. A pigsty with a cupola on top. Our home near Lexington had a different style of window in every opening. But when my father died . . . When he died, you could say that I went through a rather bleak period."

Abby studied him. "You mean like my father is doing now?"

He nodded. "Prayer. Reading the Bible. Long talks with my minister. They are what saved my sanity. I turned to the church and became the minister you see before you now."

Abby smiled at his good and open countenance. "And shall your church in Oregon have a different style window in every opening?"

He laughed, then nearly slipped in a shallow puddle. "Unfortunately a church must be dignified. All the windows will be alike. But they shall be beautiful just the same."

From ahead of them a slight figure approached. Rebecca Godwin, Abby recognized, though the scarf covering her head and bonnet hid half her face. How wonderful that she had emerged from the seclusion of her wagon.

"Hello, Miss Abigail. Reverend Harrison," the girl added with a shy smile at Dexter.

"Good day to you, Rebecca." Dexter nodded a friendly greeting. "Have you come to keep us company, then?"

"If it's not an intrusion," she answered, a little timidly.

"Of course it's no intrusion," Abby replied. "I'm so glad to see you. How have you been?"

"Much better, thank you." The girl fell in step on the other side of Dexter, and her eyes darted back to him. "I read the passages you recommended. I especially like the one about Job." Rebecca's face grew serious, and Abby caught a glimpse of the woman she soon would become. "He suffered—terribly—but he rose beyond it and was better for it. I thought about that all night and . . . and I have decided to follow his example."

Abby listened as the two of them talked, and watched in amazement as the shadows fell away from Rebecca and the ebullience of youth once more colored her face. Dexter, in his own gentle way, was the exact sort of balm the brutalized girl needed, she realized. Not all men were cruel. Some were kind and careful and nurturing, like Dexter. And under his attention young Rebecca was healing.

Perhaps in a few years, if Dexter had not already taken a wife, he and Rebecca . . .

"If you two will excuse me." Abby made her way to where her father sat, nodding in the driver's box. "Papa. Papa!" she called. "Why don't you lie down? You'll rest much better that way."

She expected an argument, but he only gave her a somewhat confused look, then nodded and climbed over the seat back and into the wagon. Abby continued to walk alongside the oxen, keeping them moving by her presence. As she trudged along, she worried, though. Dexter had done wonders for the young Rebecca's melancholia. As time went on, he would do the same for her father; she was certain of it. If only her father didn't succumb to ill health before then.

But by evening Abby's worst fears threatened to overwhelm her. Two wagons ahead of them a child had died of cholera. When they circled up for camp, she heard from down the line that a man and his wife both lay in the final throes of that same violent illness.

She busied herself with preparing the meal, but as she worked, she watched in fear as a huddle of mourners cut a shallow grave for the child. It had started to drizzle again, and as Abby watched from a distance, she found the absence of human sound the saddest thing of all. The sky wept for the little boy, but his parents stood there, numb in their grief. Silent.

Blinking back her tears, she sent a prayer aloft for the innocent child stripped so abruptly of his life. Though she knew he now rested in the arms of his heavenly Father and that she should rejoice for his eternal soul, there was that part of her that could not see it as anything but unfair. A child deserved to live, to grow up and have a full life, to love and marry and have a family. But that was not to be for this little boy.

It was God's will, she tried to tell herself. God's will. But when she climbed into the wagon to check on her father, that sentiment was forgotten. Her father's brow was hot—clammy. And his color—

She drew back in horror. She wanted to run and hide from the terrible possibility that lay before her. Her father had been weak for days. And now he had all the symptoms of cholera.

Even as she tried to deny the awful reality, he groaned and turned on his side. Then he drew his knees up as a cramp tightened his stomach and an agonized moan filled the wagon tent.

"Abigail. Abby . . ." he weakly called out to her once he recovered enough to catch his breath. But he was caught just as quickly in another painful spasm.

"I'm here, Papa. I'm here." She knelt beside him and clutched his hands. "Try to relax—"

"Abby—" He broke off as his entire body strained against the wave of pain that rushed through him. His hands tightened so hard on hers that she cried out from the pain too. But his pain was so much worse, she would willingly take any part of it that she could.

"Dexter. Dexter!" she cried out for the reverend's help, though she knew he could do nothing.

"Abby? What's wrong?"

A man's face appeared at the back of the tent. Not Dexter, but Tanner.

Tanner.

"I think . . ." She stared helplessly at him, wanting him to tell her she was wrong. "I think he has the cholera."

He was beside her in an instant, testing her father's brow with a sure hand. When his sympathetic eyes met hers, however, confirming her diagnosis when what she wanted was for him to refute it, the bottom dropped out of her world.

"He's burning up."

Abby took her father's hand, wanting it not to be true. But the evidence was overwhelming. Her father's skin was unnaturally hot. In just the few minutes since the onset of his fever, it had risen dangerously high.

"Papa, no!" she futilely ordered. "Don't do this to me. Don't do it!"

His eyes opened and for a moment their gazes held, though his was filled with pain. But the whites of his eyes were bloodshot, and the fever lent a glassiness to his normally direct stare.

"I'll be with Margaret," he whispered in parched, cracking tones. "Margaret." He even smiled a little before another spasm rocked through him.

"What about me?" she whimpered, through a haze of stinging tears. "I need you, too, Papa."

Before she could completely dissolve in a panicked fit of weeping, Tanner took her by the shoulders. "Get water and rags. And whatever you have for pain. Whiskey will do."

When she only stared numbly up at him, though, he gave her a hard shake. "Don't give up on me now, Abby. Don't give up on him."

Choking back a sob, Abby nodded. Like a blind woman she stumbled from the wagon, found two buckets, and filled them from the water casket. In the distance she saw the small funeral party returning and she easily picked out Dexter among them. Would he be saying words over her father's grave next?

Abby tried to push that unthinkable fear away, but it lurked at the edges of her consciousness even as she shoved the buckets into the wagon and searched desperately for laudanum and a spoon.

Tanner bathed her father's arms and neck while Abby tried to get the medicine down him. But her father fought them, thrashing one moment, drawn up into a shivering ball of misery the next.

"Papa, please. Just open your mouth. You need this. You'll feel better."

But it would only mask the pain. It wouldn't make him better. Still, as his body convulsed in the illness's wracking spasms, masking the pain seemed worthwhile enough to Abby. She couldn't bear to see him suffer so.

It took Tanner's forcible effort to hold her father still enough for Abby to pour a triple dose of laudanum down his throat. By the time Dexter returned to their campsite, her father had just slumped back as the first effects of the laudanum set in.

"Abigail? Mr. Morgan?"

"Keep away, Harrison," Tanner ordered before Abby could respond.

"Is that you, McKnight? Where is Miss Morgan—?" Dexter broke off when he peered into the wagon and spied Abby and Tanner together. For an instant an expression of outrage lit his normally placid features. "What is going on here? It's bad enough the talk going around—" He broke off when he spied her father's prostrate form, and his vexation turned to concern. "Abigail, has your father taken a turn for the worse?"

Abby nodded, too fearful even to speak. Tanner answered the preacher. "It's cholera. There's no need for you to be exposed to it, however."

"Can I do anything to help?"

"Pray for him," Abby whispered. "Pray for him to survive."

"Make some coffee. Cook some beans," Tanner added.

Word spread quickly. Cholera was the biggest fear of the travelers, worse than floods, or stampedes, or even Indians. People stayed away from a stricken wagon, but Sarah came by with biscuits and gravy, and Rebecca sent word that she was praying for a miracle.

Yet as the evening progressed and darkness fell, damp and dismal, Abby was forced to accept the bitter truth. A miracle was unlikely. Her father had already been weak; now he would not even last the night. Though the laudanum eased his torture and occasionally he slept, it could not change the progress of the disease. Fever. Sweating. Then complete dehydration. Come morning they would bury him. Then the wagons would move on as before, and all that would remain of Robert Bliss would be a marker beside the muddy road west.

Abby simply could not bear the thought.

She sat beside her father in the close quarters of the wagon, holding his hands and silently praying. At the foot end of her father's bed Tanner shifted in the chair he'd positioned there and stretched his injured side. His eyes were on her, and when she met his gaze, some long, unspoken message passed between them. He was there for her, that look seemed to say. How could she ever convey to him how much that meant to her?

"I haven't asked how you're healing," she began quietly.

"I'm fine. Almost back to normal."

She smiled, though her eyes remained grave. "And Tulip?"

He leaned forward, resting his elbows on his knees. "She's going to be fine. Still limping. And I wouldn't try to ride her just yet. But the swelling's gone down, and the fever in her leg is gone."

"I'm so glad. I would hate for her to have died because of me."

A short silence fell between them. The rain came down fitfully now. An occasional voice carried on the sporadic wind. But for the most part they were all alone.

Even Dexter, concerned as much by the cholera as by propriety, had turned in elsewhere. He slept tonight near the Godwin wagon.

"Abby, we need to talk."

Abby looked up at Tanner's odd tone. His face appeared serious; his eyes were dark in the pale glow of the small oil lantern. She couldn't mistake the concern in his expression, and it touched her as nothing else could. Despite his words to the contrary, he *did* care about her future. Maybe there was some hope for them.

"I know, Tanner. I know he's going to . . ." She couldn't say the word, for quick tears clogged her throat and flooded her eyes.

"What will you do?"

She took a shaky breath and wiped her face with an old crumpled handkerchief. "I don't know. I . . . I can't think that far ahead."

"You don't have to go on to Oregon, you know. You could turn back."

At that surprising suggestion Abby straightened. "Turn back? What do you mean? Return to Lebanon?"

"Is that where you're from? I thought you said you were from Arkansas."

Abby's lower lip trembled. What was the point of lying anymore? But before she could begin to explain, Tanner spoke again.

"How about Chicago? There are publishers there."

Abby shook her head. "I can't think about that now. I can't."

He reached out and took her hand as fresh tears blurred her vision. "I'm sorry, sweetheart. I shouldn't have brought the subject up."

"Abby?"

Her father's wavering call drew both their attention. "Yes, Papa. I'm right here."

She took his burning hand in hers and felt the tremulous flutter of his pulse. How much more could he take of this torture?

"Bring me my Bible."

"It's here, Papa. Right beside you." She laid his hand upon it. "Would you like me to read something to you?"

"Later . . . maybe later." His eyes remained closed, and as the silence stretched out, Abby thought he'd drifted back to sleep again. Then his fingers tightened on hers, and she anxiously leaned forward.

"Make me a promise," he whispered. His eyelids lifted and his fever-bright eyes clung to her frightened stare.

"Anything," she choked out. "Anything."

His hand trembled in hers. "Promise me you'll marry Dexter."

Abby's shocked reaction must have been reflected on her face, for he repeated his words, more forcefully. "I need to know you'll be taken care of. He still wants to marry you, Abby. He told me so. Just say you will. It's my only request of you. Say you'll marry him."

His only request. His dying request. Abby was too horrified by his calm acceptance of his impending death to agree. "Don't talk that way, Papa. Not to me."

He subsided into the feather bed; his body seemed literally to shrink even as she watched, and his eyes fell closed. "If you knew . . . maybe I should tell you . . ." He trailed off, and Abby leaned forward, afraid for him but wanting to know what it was he should tell her. Then he rallied again.

"I need to know you will be all right, Abby girl. Say you'll marry him. For me." With an effort he opened his eyes again, and in them Abby saw not fear for himself but fear for her. It was that which was her final undoing.

"If that's what you want," she whispered. Then she flung her arms around him and began to cry. "But please don't leave me. Don't leave me."

Tanner sat in the back entrance to the wagon, watching Robert Bliss die in his daughter's arms. He heard the man exact the promise from Abby. He listened as she began to recite the Lord's Prayer with him, her father's voice hardly there, just a faint movement of his lips, and Abby's voice a soft, trembling thread of sound. Yet the prayer, broken and almost impossible to follow, touched him profoundly.

How must it be to find so much comfort in mere words, to find solace in a faith that went soul deep? To find joy even in the midst of pain and misery, just in one person's touch. One special person's presence.

He sat rooted to the chair, a voyeur to the most personal melding of two souls he'd ever witnessed. Abby loved her father, and her father loved her. It changed nothing of course. The one would die; the other would continue on. That was the way of the world.

But the love between them . . . That would never disappear, and as Abby struggled through the last words, "For thine is the power and the glory . . . ," he forced himself to look away.

He didn't belong here, in this wagon with the two of them. Abby had made her father a promise that Tanner knew he could not let her keep. There was no way he would let her go off to Oregon with that preacher. Yet he stayed, unable to leave her to face her loss alone.

When the end finally came, Tanner knew at once. Robert Bliss's struggles for breath ceased. Abby's soft flow of words came to an abrupt halt. Then she began to cry, a nearly silent weeping that shook her bowed frame and pierced Tanner's heart.

He crossed to her side and gently pulled her back from her father. When she turned her tear-streaked face up to his, and he saw the terrible pain—and fear—on it, he did the only thing he could. He pulled her into his arms and let her cry.

But with every violent shudder that wracked her slender body, he felt worse and worse. He was the vilest sort of lowlife, offering her comfort when he knew he could never let her fulfill that deathbed promise to her father.

The last thing he wanted was to hurt her, and yet he knew he was going to do just that.

He rubbed one hand up and down her back. Up and down as he steeled himself. Tomorrow, after they buried her father, he'd have to tell her everything.

15

"I cannot marry on the same day I bury my father," Abby told Dexter. She faced into the raw wind that blustered its way across the endless expanse of land. The four new graves stood out like a fresh wound upon the earth. The end of four lives, marked by four mounds of dirt, four piles of stone, and four crude markers.

She'd written her father's name in pencil, though the lead broke repeatedly on the rough board. She'd seen the question in Sarah's eyes when she'd written Bliss instead of Morgan. But she'd had no explanation to give her or anyone else.

Dexter had said words over the graves of the three new cholera victims, and a small group watched as they'd been lain to rest beside the grave of the little boy. But Abby hadn't watched. She'd stared instead into the wind, across the desolate miles that lay before them still. To the west.

She stared unblinkingly toward a future that loomed before her with frightening immediacy. She was alone now, utterly alone. Four oxen and the contents of one wagon. That summed up her life.

There was her half portion of land waiting to be claimed in Oregon, she reminded herself. But that was small comfort to her today. What was the point of continuing on to Oregon? What had ever been the reason? Her father had died without telling her.

She blinked as tears formed in her eyes, but she re-

fused to let them fall. She'd cried all her tears last night.
There was nothing left inside her anymore. She was an
empty, exhausted shell, and all she wanted was to sleep,
to crawl into her bed, pull the quilt over her head, and
sleep forever.

"Perhaps tomorrow *would* be better." Dexter spoke in
careful, solicitous tones from just behind her. He put a
hand beneath her arm and tried to steer her back toward
the wagons. The call to depart had come, and already the
line of wagons had started forward. But Abby shrugged
off his hand.

"I need to be alone. You go on with the wagon. I'll
catch up before very long." She sent him what she hoped
would pass for a reassuring smile. "Go along. I appreciate all you've done for me, Dexter. But for now I need to
be alone."

He didn't want to go; she could see it in his hesitant
expression. "Well, all right. But only if you promise not
to fall behind the last of the wagons."

"I promise," she conceded, though at that moment
she wished she could be rid of the wagon train forever.
Just let them disappear in their slow, ponderous line over
the edge of the horizon.

And then what?

She heard the few mourners leave. The dead couple's
children had witnessed their parents' interment in mute
shock. But now the youngest, a girl of about seven, began
to wail.

"I want my mama. I want my papa!"

Someone shushed her, and slowly her unhappy keen-
ing faded away. But Abby's heart had taken up the re-
frain.

I want my mother. I want my father. Only they were
gone from her for good. If she needed comfort now, she
must turn to Dexter.

He had promised his aid as soon as he'd heard the sad
news, and she, in her grief, had told him of her father's
deathbed request. He'd been so happy, though he'd

struggled to contain it behind an appropriately somber mien. But Abby could tell, and it had depressed her even more. Her parents were dead and she was to marry Dexter. It felt like the end of the world.

Pushed forward by the wind, a deep bank of clouds closed off the sky. Behind her, to the east, brief patches of blue sky still showed, but soon they would disappear and all would be gray. Rain threatened, but for now held back. When it came, however, she knew it would hamper their travel even further.

At least Eenie was well. He'd healed, as had Tulip. Her father was the only one who had not recovered.

"Abby?"

A shiver coursed up her spine at the sound of Tanner's low voice, muffled by the rising wind. He'd comforted her in those first cruel moments, then he'd stepped back and let Sarah and Dexter take over. How she'd wanted him to stay, to shelter her from her pain and fear. But he hadn't, and the practical side of her knew why. He didn't want to encourage her to turn to him. He wasn't the marrying kind. Whatever desire he felt for her was nonetheless tempered by the basically honorable side of him.

It would be so much easier, she thought sadly, if both of them could just throw caution to the wind.

He dismounted behind her, and she heard the high grasses part as he approached her. "Abby? Are you all right?"

She let out a long, pent-up sigh, and with it a large portion of her determination to keep her emotions under control. "Honestly? I don't feel like I'll ever be all right again. Not ever."

She turned her head and met his watchful gaze. He had his hat in his hands, and the strengthening wind lifted his dark hair back from his face.

"You're feeling all alone now. I know how that feels. But . . . it won't always hurt this bad. Your loss is fresh and painful. But time . . . time will help."

Abby shook her head. All of a sudden she was angry. At her father. At her mother. At Dexter. And especially at Tanner. "Time *won't* help." She turned her back on him and started to walk, not toward the wagons but out away from the trail and the river, into the vast emptiness that surrounded them.

To her surprise he fell into step beside her, easily keeping up with her angry strides. But that only fueled her anger. If he meant to comfort her, she didn't need it. His comfort only made it worse, for he would never offer her what she wanted most from him.

"Go away, Tanner. I need to be alone."

"Don't marry him."

At that startling request Abby stumbled to a halt. She faced him warily. "What did you say?"

He jammed his hat on his head before slowly meeting her gaze. But though she tried to read his face, he kept his expression deliberately blank.

"I said, don't marry him."

Abby drew a sharp breath. She was afraid to ask why, but she knew she must. "I promised my father. Why should I break my word to him?"

He hesitated and for a moment he looked past her into the distance, as if he gathered his thoughts—or perhaps his courage, she wondered with the tiniest flaring of hope.

"He exacted that promise from you under false pretenses."

Now she was really confused. "What do you mean? What are you saying?"

"Your name is Abigail Bliss."

Abby nodded. She'd put her father's true name on the pitiful marker. For whatever reason he'd adopted an alias, it no longer mattered. It wasn't a secret anymore.

"Your father dragged you west because your grandfather is searching for you."

"My grandfather?" Bewildered, she shook her head. "I don't have a grandfather."

"Yes, Abby. You do have a grandfather. You just were never told about him. And he wasn't told about you, either, not until your mother died."

Abby heard every word he said, yet it was impossible for her to comprehend them. She stared at him, aware that he was watching her closely.

What was he trying to do? Why was he hurting her this way?

She turned away from him as anger muddied her grief. Wasn't it bad enough that she'd just buried the last of her family? Must he provoke her this way, pretending she had more family when she knew she did not? "Go away, Tanner. Leave me alone."

But he came nearer. "I can't leave you alone, Abby. The fact is, your mother's father, Willard Hogan, has been searching for you. For whatever reason that they were estranged, you are still his grandchild—his *only* grandchild."

"But . . . No, this makes no sense. I don't believe you. And anyway how could you know any of this?"

"It's true. He hired me to find you and bring you back."

Shock followed upon shock as Abby tried to make sense of his words. This wasn't true. None of it. She didn't have a grandfather. Her father would have told her if she did. No, this was some fabrication of Tanner's, like some penny novel, a dreadful concoction of a plot that had absolutely no logic to it.

But Tanner's expression was so serious. . . .

She pressed one hand to her throat. Could it be true? Could she really have a grandfather? Could he have hired Tanner to find her—?

The sudden implication of that drew Abby up with a gasp. If Tanner had been hired to find her . . . Did that mean the attentions he'd paid her had just been a part of his search? A way to find out if Abigail Morgan was indeed Abigail Bliss?

That possibility was simply too hard for her to face

following upon her father's death and Tanner's far-fetched revelations. She searched instead for the holes in his story. "Why would he hire someone to find me—assuming he's my grandfather at all. Assuming you're not making all of this up."

His dark eyes—this morning more gray than blue—studied her intently, a trace of sympathy visible in their depths. "I've worked for your grandfather before. He's a very powerful, very wealthy man. But his only daughter —your mother—married against his wishes. Now that he's found out about you, he wants to provide for you. And he can provide well, Abby. He can *buy* you a publishing company, if that's what you want."

Abby shook her head in denial. She didn't want to believe it. A grandfather? No, she would have been told if that was true.

Battered by too many churning emotions, she turned away from him and once more headed into the wind, almost desperate in her flight now. A low rumble rolled over the land; the storm would be a bad one, she noted vaguely. But it could not begin to compare with the storm of emotions that raged now in her chest.

Her heart thudded with painful regularity. Her stomach clenched with both outrage and an all-consuming sense of loss. Had she been allowed the luxury of solitude, she would have succumbed to the scalding tears that welled up inside her. But she refused to do that and instead took refuge in her anger. She had lost her mother, been uprooted from her home, and had just buried her father. And now this unbelievable tale of Tanner's . . .

She stiffened, then turned her head just enough to see him still keeping pace beside her. "What reason do I have to believe this mad tale? What proof? It sounds to me that you would do better to publish *your* fanciful stories than I will mine. Mr. Charles Dickens should envy you your creative bent of mind," she finished sarcastically.

He did not rise to her taunt. Indeed, she realized, he probably did not know who Charles Dickens was. He was, after all, just as her father had said: a man who lived by his wits and his gun. He'd spoken of a few mythological characters, and she'd made it into something more, because she'd wanted it to be so. He was exactly what her father had warned her about, she was forced to admit, an opportunist who could not be trusted.

She fixed him with a cold stare. "Just as I thought, you have no proof."

"I have your father's letter to your grandfather."

Abby halted her angry progress, as all the starch went out of her. "My father's letter? To my . . . to my grandfather?"

He pulled a faded envelope from a pocket beneath his slicker. The paper was folded and creased, but even before she took it from him, Abby knew with a sinking despair that it was all true. She could see her father's strong, neat hand. He *had* hidden this truth from her.

She scanned the letter quickly; it was not long. Then she handed it back to Tanner with a hand that trembled. She had a grandfather. So many years she had wished for the large, extensive sort of family that other people had. But it had always been just the three of them, no one else. Now, however, she knew that there had been her grandfather.

But even though a part of her knew she should be relieved to find some remnant family, considering that she had just buried her father, it was impossible.

"Why does he look for me now?" she challenged Tanner, thrusting the letter back at him. "Where has he been these past twenty years?"

Tanner folded the letter back into its envelope and slid it into his pocket. A sharp crack of lightning split the sky, and behind them his horse Mac snorted in alarm. But Tanner kept his eyes steady on her.

"He didn't want his daughter—your mother—to marry a poor schoolteacher. Fathers are particular about who their daughters wed, it seems," he added in an ironic tone. "When she married him anyway, he was furious. By the time he recovered, though, your parents had left for parts unknown. Though he searched, he never found them. He'd given up until this letter came."

"He was furious," she repeated. "You mean, he disowned her, don't you?"

Tanner shook his head. "I don't know what happened between them, Abby. I wasn't there. But even if he did, he wants to make up for it now. He wants you to come live with him in Chicago."

Chicago. So that's why Tanner had brought up the subject of Chicago. Though she knew she had no reason to feel betrayed by him, that was nonetheless precisely how Abby felt. Betrayed. Tricked. Foolish.

Trying to salvage the tattered remnants of her pride, she sent him a quelling stare. "I'm afraid you've wasted your time if you think I'd return to Chicago with you just on the basis of this man's request. I'm going on to Oregon; nothing has changed on that score. I'm going there to claim my half portion of land. The only difference now is that I'll claim it with my husband, not my father."

If only she felt as pleased with that arrangement as she tried to pretend she was.

Tanner's brows lowered at her firm statement, but she did not flinch under his cool scrutiny.

"The trail gets a hell of a lot harder than this, you know. And even when you reach Oregon, you'll only be a poor preacher's wife. In Chicago you could be the toast of the town, at the top of society. You could get your book published too," he added calculatingly.

At that her anger boiled over. "Don't think to use that as enticement, for it will not work. I have no intentions of going to Chicago, so whatever fee he offered to you, well, you shall just have to do without it. I am marrying Dexter Harrison, and he and I shall build a fine church and a fine school in Oregon."

As if to punctuate her words, a huge bolt of lightning

streaked to earth, followed almost immediately by an ear-splitting crack of thunder. Abby jumped. So did Tanner.

He whistled sharply, and in an instant his raw-boned horse skittered to a halt before them, its eyes rolling in fear. The first few drops of rain splattered around them, and Abby drew her shawl tight over her shoulders. All her fortifying anger seemed to flee under the storm's onslaught, and, shivering, she turned dispiritedly toward the wagons. She would get soaked if she didn't seek shelter soon, and while she really was too numb to care whether she was wet or dry, cold or warm, she didn't want to become ill and chance weakening her resistance to something worse—such as cholera.

But before she'd progressed even three paces, the heavens opened up on them.

"Son of a bitch." She heard Tanner's muttered oath as Mac half reared in alarm. "Easy, Mac. Easy." Then he called out to her. "Abby, come here."

That was the last thing she would do.

She'd gone hatless to her father's funeral, and now the rain swiftly drenched her hair. Her shawl was no real protection either, and before she'd gone any distance at all, her best calico skirt was drenched and weighing her down. The rain stung her face and blinded her eyes, while beneath her feet the already soaked ground turned to a quagmire of mud and clinging vines. She stumbled once, then slipped, just catching herself with one knee and hand before she fell flat on her face.

She wanted to go home. That one thought repeated itself over and over in her mind. She wanted to go home. But she couldn't find her footing, nor could she see her way. And anyway she had no home anymore. Neither home nor family.

A sob broke free of her throat, hot and burning, then another, harsh, wrenching sobs that tore at the very fabric of her soul. *It's not fair*, she cried inside, as the rain poured over her, cold and uncaring. *Not fair*.

She pushed to her feet, hiking her ruined skirt up so that it would not hinder her. But just as she was about to struggle forward again, a hand wrapped around her upper arm, staying her progress.

"Ride with me," Tanner ordered, though the roar of the storm muffled his words.

"No!" Abby jerked her arm free, then nearly slipped again in the slick, matted grasses. But Tanner caught her before she could fall and, despite Mac's unsettled prancing, pulled her up and plopped her unceremoniously on the saddle before him.

"Ouch! Let me down!" she shouted when the saddlehorn dug painfully into the back of one of her thighs.

"Shut up, woman, before you bring this horse down too!" Tanner barked as Mac turned in a tight circle, scrambling for surer footing.

Afraid to fall—and afraid to cause another of his horses to be injured—Abby grabbed onto Tanner, holding tightly around his waist. It only took him a minute to calm the flustered animal. Once Mac was steady, however, Tanner pulled Abby up against his chest, settling her in a more comfortable position. Then he pulled his loose rain slicker around her for protection from the rain as he urged the animal forward.

Despite the warmth of Tanner's body against hers, a violent shiver coursed up Abby's spine. In just a matter of seconds the rain had completely drenched her. The weight of her wet hair had pulled her coiled braid loose, and now it lay like a cold, fat rope between her back and Tanner's chest.

She mopped at her face, though it was a useless effort. The rain was a blinding sheet of water, a gray curtain that masked every other sound and reduced their world to a small circle of visibility.

Abby had completely lost her sense of direction. Were the wagons straight ahead or to the left? But Tanner seemed to know where he was going. She felt the slight tensing of his thighs beneath her bottom and the subtle shifting of his arm muscles along her back as he guided the horse. How he located her wagon was beyond her. All she knew was that a moment more in such intimate proximity with him would surely have driven her to do something totally impulsive—something absolutely unforgivable.

Come with me to Oregon, she wanted to plead with him. *Forget about this man who says he's my grandfather. Forget about Dexter. What about us?*

Dexter stood in the back of the wagon as they rode up, squinting anxiously into the torrential downpour. The wagons had all stopped on the trail, just standing where they were, waiting for the worst of the storm to pass. The concern on Dexter's face, however, quickly turned to disapproval.

"Get inside. Quickly," he ordered, grasping her arm in a firm hold and pulling her into the meager shelter of the wagon tent.

A part of Abby was truly relieved to be away from Tanner. In another instant she would most certainly have behaved like an utter fool. But Dexter's proprietorial air irritated her. They weren't married yet.

With an angry jerk she moved out of his grasp. Just beyond the arched opening of the canvas tent, Tanner sat his horse, his hat pulled low as rain shunted off it, his slicker closed against the punishing storm. Abby stared at him, regret and anger and hopelessness merging to leave her too confused to speak.

But there was no mistaking the animosity that bristled between the two men. Dexter stood, a little stooped over, to peer out at Tanner. Tanner just sat there, unbowed and undeterred, it appeared to her.

Given a choice, which would she take? Abby shoved her clinging hair back from her face. One was an upstanding man, honest and hardworking. He would make a good husband and a fine father. The other was a rough-and-tumble hired thug with no future but the one he could carve out with his guns and his wits. He had nothing to commend him but the beguiling smile of a fallen angel and an unexpected sense of honor.

So why was she so drawn to him?

He saw her as a source of financial gain, a job to be completed for pay, nothing more. Why did she persist in this shameful longing for him?

Dexter jerked the canvas curtain across the opening, cutting off Abby's view of Tanner and shutting out the slanting rain. For a moment he stood stiff and angry, not speaking. Then he took a slow breath, blew it out, and turned to face her.

"You're soaked. You'd best change out of those wet clothes." His eyes moved down her body, over her wet, clinging blouse and the soaked and muddied skirt that hugged her hips and thighs. His bearded cheeks colored, but when he met her gaze again, he did not look away.

"Can we be wed tomorrow?" He took one step, bringing them face-to-face in the crowded quarters. "Say that you will wed me tomorrow, Abigail."

The answer lodged in Abby's throat. She wanted to say no, that she'd been too hasty to agree to her father's request. But her father'd had her best interests at heart, and in truth, marrying Dexter would solve so many of her problems. That was the only way Tanner would ever leave her alone about this man who claimed to be her grandfather. If Tanner was only interested in her because he'd been hired to find her, she didn't want ever to lay eyes on him again. It made everything much too hard.

But marriage to Dexter . . .

She braced herself and nodded her head before she could change her mind.

Dexter smiled then, and the tension seemed to ease from his lean body. "There's another minister in the train ahead of ours. We can send someone to fetch him." He placed a hand on each of her shoulders and urged her nearer. Only her palms pressed against his chest stopped him from taking her fully into an embrace.

"I'll make you happy, Abigail. I promise I'll make you

as happy as you've just made me." Then he lowered his face and kissed her.

Abby forced herself not to pull away. Tomorrow he would be her husband and he would be entitled to many more liberties than just a simple kiss. His mouth met hers, tentatively at first, then bolder. His lips were soft and dry, and in truth, the kiss was not unpleasant. But it was not particularly thrilling, either, and Abby knew a keen disappointment.

Tanner's every touch sent the most untoward sensations skittering along her nerve endings. His look, even, threw her into the most wonderful and unsettling sort of panic. But Dexter's kiss was merely pleasant, the way a pat of approval on the shoulder might also be pleasant.

How could that ever be enough for her now?

She drew away, trembling in misery as well as from the cold. Dexter stepped back at once, his cheeks even redder than before.

"I . . . I'll go see to the beasts," he stammered. "You change into something dry."

When he left, conscientiously refastening the curtain to protect her from the storm and prying eyes, Abby slumped onto the bed, unmindful of her soaked skirts and dripping hair. She'd never felt so defeated in her entire life, so empty and without hope.

She'd never had to worry about her future before, although many times she had wondered whom she might marry and whether she'd have sons or daughters or both. She'd wondered also if she would ever see any of her stories in print. But she'd been young and strong and capable, and it seemed that the future would take care of itself.

Now, though, the future was here and it *was* taking care of itself. She seemed to have no choice in the matter —or rather, two equally bleak choices. Marry a man she liked only in the most platonic fashion, or be dragged back to a grandfather she'd never known, by a man who saw her only as the means to secure a monetary reward.

Her father had done this to her, she bitterly admitted. He'd hidden the truth and then tried to push Dexter on her.

For one terrible, black moment she hated her father. Truly hated him and his righteous, unyielding ways. But hating him only made her feel worse.

"Why, Papa? Why?" she whispered to the dreary confines of the wagon tent. But there was no answer, no explanation, and she knew there never would be. Her parents were both lost to her now; it was too late for them to explain.

And now she feared she was about to lose what little she had left of herself: her heart to one man, her body to another.

16

Robert Bliss was dead. Cracker O'Hara kicked the crude cross marker once, then again, and in the rain-soaked earth it came free and tilted to one side, only catching on one of its outstretched arms.

Who would have guessed that it would be Morgan and his daughter? But though Cracker would have preferred the girl be younger—like that sweet Godwin girl—he would make do with this one. He needed some proof for his employer, though, before he killed her. An old photograph. A letter. The family-records page from their Bible. That Bible-toting Morgan—that is, Bliss—probably wrote everything down in his Bible. It shouldn't be any problem at all to find what he needed.

The big question was when to let Bud Foley in on it. Or perhaps, whether to let him in at all. He took off his wide-brimmed hat and slapped it against his left leg, sending an arc of droplets flying.

Damned rain. McKnight would be able to track him if he snatched the girl now. But chances were McKnight himself would be stealing the girl away, he thought craftily. He could just follow them and pick McKnight off. Then he'd celebrate with the girl—at least *he'd* celebrate. She'd learn a quick lesson about men. Then she'd have to die.

He'd have to ride back to the wagon train Bud was traveling with. Then he laughed out loud. He'd get Bud

to help him kill Tanner, but a bullet was the only share of
the reward Bud would ever get.

He cleared his throat noisily, then spat a glob at the
rock-strewn grave and mounted his half-wild pony. The
horse reared, but he spurred the animal into a harsh run
that quickly consumed all the beast's concentration.

Yep, there was no need for Bud to see even two bits of
the reward, he decided as he leaned low over the laboring
horse's neck. He hadn't done any of the work anyway.

Abby walked alone, struggling through mud that was
ankle-deep. It sucked at her boots and clung to the hem
of her skirt, but today she hardly noticed. Her legs
moved mechanically. Left, right; one after the other;
propelling her forward at a steady pace. The other
women made their way over to her, offering condolences
on the loss of her father. But death was a constant companion on the trail, and life must go on. Eventually they
all drifted back to their own wagons and their own re-
sponsibilities, leaving Abby to walk beside her oxen,
alone with her frozen thoughts.

Dexter was ministering to a man who'd broken his
hip. The man's family was staying behind today. It was
just too painful for the man to be bumped around in the
wagon, and besides he was not expected to live long. By
tomorrow a fifth grave would join the others, she feared.
But despite her sorrow for the hurt man and his family,
Abby was relieved not to suffer Dexter's constant presence this day. She simply did not think she could bear his
hovering nearness. As for Tanner—she didn't know what
to think.

She hadn't seen him since he'd confronted her this
morning with his shattering story, though the truth was,
she'd been very careful not to look for him. Still, several
times she'd felt as if someone was watching her.

No doubt he still thought he could convince her to
return with him to Chicago. But once she married Dexter, he would give up and go away.

So why did the thought of him leaving raise such an aching weariness in her chest?

The slurping sound of a rider approaching tightened every ending of her already overwrought nerves. When the rider slowed, however, and doffed his hat, it was not Tanner at all, and Abby knew a keen and undeniable disappointment.

"Miss Morgan—I mean, Miss Bliss." The man O'Hara sawed at the mouth of his wild-eyed horse. "Sorry to hear about your pa."

She swallowed her immediate revulsion of him and tried to ignore the unpleasant glint in his eyes. In his own way he was trying to be polite. She could at least respond in kind.

"Thank you, Mr. O'Hara."

"It's gonna be hard on you, what with you being alone and all."

Abby concentrated on the oxen, refusing to meet his narrow-eyed gaze. "I'm hardly alone." *I'm getting married tomorrow.* But she couldn't bring herself to boast about something that she dreaded so much.

After another long moment of silence he kicked the horse forward, then turned it in a tight circle, watching as she struggled along in the mud. "You're probably right. A woman who looks like you don't never have to be alone. Not if she don't want to." Then with a last leering grin he spurred the laboring animal into a dead run.

She shouldn't allow the insincere words of such an unsavory person to disturb her, she told herself as he disappeared in the drizzle. He was crude and ignorant. Yet Abby couldn't shake off the icy finger of misgiving that ran down her backbone. He was a man who would take advantage of her, or anyone else, if he thought he could get away with it. Her father had warned her that the trail would be filled with people like him. And like Tanner.

The only difference between Tanner McKnight and

Cracker O'Hara, she realized, was that the one at least possessed a veneer of manners to cover what was essentially a cold, unfeeling soul. They both saw people with a jaundiced eye, seeking out their weak spots, deciding how to use them to their own best advantage.

It would not surprise her if Cracker O'Hara had something to do with the attack on Rebecca Godwin.

Abby swallowed at that distasteful possibility, and the hairs stood up on the back of her neck. She had no proof, she realized, only instinct. But she was suddenly convinced of it. The man had the most degrading way of staring at a woman.

At least Tanner wasn't like that. The last thing she felt when he looked at her was degraded. Flustered, maybe. Thrilled. Breathless.

And stupid, she reminded herself, before she could become *too* caught up in her foolish fantasies. He muddled her mind and chased every bit of logic right out of her head. She should be grateful to have finally recognized his true nature. He was a duplicitous rogue. A liar. An opportunist.

If only she could chase him out of her every waking thought.

Trying to do just that, she turned her mind toward her father and his painful, tortured death. He was at peace now. She had to cling to that one truth or else fall apart from sheer loneliness. Her father and mother were both in heaven now, and they were praying for her. She must not disappoint them.

But what, she wondered, would her mother think of this? What did she think of her own father—Abby's grandfather—and his determined pursuit of her?

"Miss Abigail!" a childish call steered Abby's thoughts away from that troubling subject.

"Why, Carl, I haven't seen you in a couple of days. How have you been? How's your foot?"

"Oh, it's good. The snake just got my boot, not me."

He fell into step beside her, though he had to take two steps for every one of hers.

Abby affectionately stroked the wet felt of the hat he wore. "Where's Estelle?"

"She's sick." He sighed. "Mama said for me to leave her alone."

"Sick?" Abby sucked in a sharp, worried breath. "Sick how?"

He made a face. "Throwin' up and stuff. You know."

"Does she have a fever?" Abby asked, struggling to keep her fear for his sister from showing in her voice.

"Nope." He hopped and landed with both feet in a shallow puddle, then laughed at the spray he'd caused. "Mama made us pray a long time last night *and* again this morning that Estelle wouldn't catch a fever."

Abby sent up a quick, fervent prayer of her own. Thank God. At least it wasn't cholera.

"Can you tell me a story?"

Abby smiled down at the gap-toothed little boy. He'd survived the incident with the snakes well enough and had gone on daily to other adventures. But none had been nearly so dangerous. With God's help he'd make it to Oregon and grow to be a man with children of his own someday.

She caught his hand and gave him a fond smile. "You know, I was just wondering how Tillie and Snitch managed on wet, muddy days like today. What do you think?"

He grinned. "I bet Snitch catches on to an oxtail and rides there."

"And what about Tillie?"

"Hmmm." His face screwed up as he thought. "Does she ride in the wagon?"

"Under the wagon. On one of those braces between the wheels. See?" She pointed to her wagon, and Carl peered under it.

"That's a pretty good place to ride," he conceded. "But it's kinda boring. Not like being on an oxtail."

"You think so? Well," Abby mused, letting her mind spin with fanciful possibilities. "Did I ever tell you about the time Tillie and Snitch got caught in a raging flood?"

"A flood?" His eyes grew round. Then his face split in a wide grin. "I know. I know. I bet Snitch saves Tillie from drowning."

"Actually it happened just the other way around . . ."

By the time Captain Peters called for the noonday break, Abby was feeling calmer. Carl and his never-ending demands for more stories had forced her to put aside her own miseries for a while, and she'd spun all sorts of wild and dangerous tales of mouse escapades.

Now determined not to slide back into depressing thoughts just because the child left to get his midday meal, Abby busied herself with tending the oxen, mending a small tear in the canvas wagon tent, and checking the wheels for any sign of wear. At least with the wet weather there was no chance for the wooden wheels to dry and shrink and fall out of their steel rims, as they'd been warned could happen.

She ate a cold leftover potato with just a sprinkle of salt while she waited for the call to proceed. But it started to rain again, harder than ever, and soon the call to circle up came echoing down the line.

"Jerusalem," she swore. Walking was boring. But sitting was even more so. Still, she heeded the call, and when her turn came, she aligned her wagon with the rest.

By then the rain was a blinding torrent. Was any place in the world dry today? she wondered as she retreated into the damp recesses of the wagon. After donning her oilcloth rain slicker, she freed the oxen from their tracings. Victor Lewis rode up, though he was so covered against the rain that she could hardly identify him.

"I'll herd them to their grazing," he shouted over the steady roar of the storm. "You go keep Sarah company."

Abby nodded her acceptance of his suggestion. She didn't want to be alone with her sad thoughts today.

Young Carl's company had been a blessing. She knew now that she could not spend the rest of the day in her wagon, surrounded by so many reminders of her father and a life that was no more. And maybe Sarah's cheerful company and her unremitting joy in her marriage would help prepare Abby for her own forthcoming wedding.

She rummaged in the wagon for her needle and thread and a faded cotton blouse she'd torn beneath the arm. She would work on her mending while she and Sarah talked.

The wagon swayed and creaked as the angry wind tore at the canvas top, and bursts of rain gusted in past the flapping curtain behind the driver's box. Abby leaned past a heavy trunk, struggling to retie one of the curtain's string fasteners when a mighty blast of wind blew in from behind her. When she turned to attend to that problem, however, she let out a small, startled cry. It was not a loose flapping curtain that had allowed the storm in, but Tanner McKnight's unexpected entrance.

For a long, silent moment she stared at him, wishing he had not come here, yet absurdly pleased that he had. Beneath the dripping brim of his hat the ends of his hair were wet. His slicker shed rivulets of water onto the floor as well. He looked wild and dangerous, and she could not tear her eyes away.

She rubbed her shaking hands up and down the folds of her slicker before she found her voice. "You shouldn't be here."

He took his hat off and speared his fingers through his dark hair. "You shouldn't either." His midnight-blue eyes ran over her, and though she was completely covered by the shapeless slicker, the weight of his scrutiny lifted goose bumps all over her. How would it be if he'd actually touched her?

"You shouldn't be here either," he repeated. "Let me take you back to Chicago, where you belong now."

Abby stiffened. Of course. He'd come because he had his job to do. His reward to earn. Knowing she was absurd to feel so disappointed, she half turned from him, finished gathering her sewing materials, and stuffed them in the pocket of her apron.

"I don't belong in Chicago," she countered. "Besides, what you are proposing is quite impossible," she added, striving to sound casual and offhand. "Dexter plans to build a church in Oregon, and I plan to be at his side." *And perhaps one day I will learn to crave his touch as I so foolishly crave yours.*

"You don't really want to do that, Abby."

She looked sharply at him. "You don't know anything about what I want. You don't know anything about me!"

Her stinging accusation hung in the air between them. A raindrop fell through the canvas to plop on the bed, then another. Abby automatically moved a pot to catch them, and in the close quarters the metallic sound of the drops seemed to tick away the seconds. The minutes.

"I know you're far too passionate for the likes of Dexter Harrison."

Abby swallowed hard. When he spoke to her of passion in such low, moving tones, he seemed to strike some chord in her that left all her nerves thrumming. "Dexter . . . Dexter and I, we shall get on very well."

He smiled at that, a taut smile that seemed at once both sympathetic and somehow pained. "You would make the best of it, I'm certain of that. But I hardly think a preacher would let his wife publish stories about a pair of little mice and all their adventures." He paused, watching her. Letting his words sink in. If they didn't echo so closely Abby's own fears, she would have been better able to ignore them.

"Don't you pretend to care a bit about me or my stories. All you want is the money this man—"

"Your grandfather," he interrupted.

She glared at him. "The money this man has promised to pay you."

One side of his mouth curved down ever so slightly. "I do care about what happens to you, Abby."

Why did he have to say that? He didn't mean the words the way she wanted him to mean them, yet her foolish heart insisted on beating faster till she thought she could not breathe.

"Just leave me alone, Tanner McKnight. Go back to your employer and tell him . . . tell him that my mother and father loved each other very much. For whatever reason he objected to my father as a son-in-law, my father made my mother happy. Now they're at peace together—" She broke off and fought down the hard rush of emotion that rose to choke her. "They are at peace together despite his interference. I don't intend to let him interfere in my life any more than they did."

He nodded once as if he understood and maybe even agreed. But then he said, "Do you love Harrison?"

Abby didn't answer.

He didn't give her time to, she tried to rationalize a few minutes later as she picked her way across the mud-slick that was their campsite, heading toward the Lewis wagon. He'd turned around and left before she had time to say that her father hadn't loved her mother right away either. He'd come to love her, just as she would come to love Dexter.

Only she feared that in her case it would never happen. She'd already lost her heart to an undeserving rogue who didn't value it in the least.

The day remained gloomy and wet. Even Sarah's ebullient revelation that she thought she was in the family way couldn't completely dispel Abby's mood. One person died and another soul came to take its place. It was the way of the world, and that at least restored some of her equanimity. Perhaps she'd name her own first son Robert, after his grandfather. If Dexter would agree.

Dexter. Suddenly the realization that every decision for the rest of her life would be made only with his approval depressed her enormously.

She tucked her needle into a corner of the blouse she was repairing. "I think I'd best be going." She smiled gratefully at Sarah and Victor. "Congratulations on your good news."

They didn't protest when she left, and Abby suspected Victor was happy to have his little wife all to himself. They were so obviously in love with each other.

Dusk had seemed to come early due to the low-hanging clouds. As she picked her way through the drizzle that still lingered, she saw Doris Crenshaw struggling to build a fire from her hoarded chips and kindling. Rebecca Godwin was with her, chattering with Doris's daughter. Rebecca was healing from the trauma she'd endured, and so would she as well, Abby supposed.

But once Abby climbed into her lonely wagon, what little flare of optimism she'd had died. Her father's tobacco pouch hung down on a peg near the front of the wagon. His prayer book lay on a trunk.

She should have buried him with that book, she realized with a guilty twinge. Or with the big family Bible. No, not the Bible. She needed to hold on to their family Bible and pass it on to her own children.

At that thought she began to cry, only this time it was not for her father, or even for herself. She cried for her children, hers and Dexter's. How happy a home could she possibly hope to make for her children if she so deeply dreaded their father's husbandly attentions?

Abby sat on the bed, hugging the big leather-bound volume to her chest as she wept. Only when a man's voice hailed her did she look up.

"Miss Morgan?"

"Yes?"

Captain Peters opened the back curtain just enough to peer in. "I just wanted to express my condolences to you and to say that Cracker here has offered to help you with your team if you need assistance."

He pulled the curtain farther aside so that she could see Cracker O'Hara standing beside him. Abby tried to look grateful, but she knew she failed. "That won't be necessary," she answered. "I'm to marry Reverend Harrison tomorrow. He'll be seeing to the stock."

"Well, that's good news, miss. Mighty good news." He smiled, clearly relieved not to have a young, unattached female traveling alone in his wagon company. "I wish you both the best."

After they left, Abby just sat there, staring at the wet canvas curtain as it ebbed and bellowed in the never-ending wind. Captain Peters was relieved to see her care shifted onto some man's shoulders. Any man's. But that was the way of the world, after all. No matter her dissatisfaction with the limitations placed on women—they must be wed; they could not possibly have careers of their own—that was the way things were. And she was going along with it.

But why? she asked herself. Why marry a man she didn't love, and feared she never could? For possibly the only time in her entire life no one could force her to do anything she didn't want to do. So why was she fleeing from that freedom into the constraints of a marriage she didn't really want?

Abby sat a long time in the wagon just thinking. She'd promised her father, and she'd been raised to honor her promises. But what about her father? a rebellious part of her demanded. Why had he hidden the truth from her?

The meager light faded to a gray twilight and then to a wet darkness, broken only by the sputtering of a few campfires. But she sat unmoving, angry with her father and mother. Angry with the world.

In the end, though, she was reduced to wondering if she could manage on her own. And if she could find the right words to let Dexter down easily. Best to tell him tonight, she realized, pushing herself wearily to her feet, though facing him and his disappointment was not something she relished. But it had to be done, and the sooner the better, she resolved.

Her bonnet was still damp, so she wrapped a blue

knitted shawl around her head and shoulders and climbed down into the churned-up mud outside her wagon. Most people had already bedded down for the night, and snores of varying volumes wafted on the wet breeze. But she found Dexter still awake, sitting at the Godwin fire, leaning forward, his face intent as he expounded to Rebecca and her father.

"That broad appeal is what makes the Bible the miracle it is. For the simplest souls it says, 'Do unto others as you would have them do unto you.' For those souls who would search deeper, however, there are passages that, when studied, can illuminate and guide us the full length of our lives. And for those who would delve even deeper, they have only to— Why, Abigail." He broke off when he spied her. "Are you looking for me?"

Abby sent Rebecca and her father an apologetic smile. "I'm sorry to interrupt. But might I have a few words with Reverend Harrison?"

Rebecca looked disappointed, but Mr. Godwin only stifled a yawn. " 'Tis past time to turn in anyway. We'll say a good night to you, Reverend. And to you, Miss Morgan. Uh . . . should I stay up and walk you back to your wagon?" he added.

"It's all right. I'll see Miss Abigail home," Dexter answered for her, placing a proprietorial hand on Abby's waist. "Since we're to wed in the morning, there's no threat to her reputation."

That remained to be seen, Abby thought. But she refrained from expressing herself until they were a little distance from any of the wagons.

"What is it?" he finally asked when it seemed she would lead them completely out of sight of the wagons. "Abigail, what is it?"

She turned to face him, hardly able to make out his features in the moonless night. "The thing is," she began, nervously clutching the shawl to her throat. "I . . . I don't think we should be married tomorrow."

He was quiet a moment, and she began to wonder if he'd heard her at all. "I said, I don't think—"

"It's all right, Abigail." He reached out and took her hands between his. "It will be all right. You're just nervous now. But once we're married—"

"No." Abby jerked back, and her shawl slipped from her head to her shoulders. "You don't understand. It's not nervousness. The truth is—" She took a sharp breath, willing herself to be calm and to be kind, though she feared there was no kind way to decline a man's proposal of marriage. "The truth is, I don't love you, Dexter. I like you. I respect you. But I do not love you and I know I never will."

"Now, Abigail. You can't be certain of that. And anyway mutual respect—"

"I just don't think mutual respect is enough for me."

"If you would give it time. Think about it more."

"But I have thought about it, Dexter. I have. And I . . . I just don't think I'm the right sort of woman for you. You'll find someone far better suited to the role of minister's wife than I could ever be."

"It's him, isn't it? McKnight. He's turned your head, just like everyone says."

Abby's heart sank. He was right of course. At least partially. And by turning Dexter's marriage offer down, she would appear to be confirming the gossip Martha had obviously started. But what else could she do? When she didn't answer his charges, Dexter sighed and his shoulders slumped.

"Well, if that's how you want it," he mumbled.

She left him then and with a determined stride made her way back toward the wagons. She was free now. Truly free to choose her own path in the world. Yet she found it impossible to exult. She was free, yes. But she was also alone, and though it had not been her choice to lose her parents, she had made tonight's decision of her own free will.

The mud sucked at her heavy working boots and

dragged at the ends of her shortened skirt as a sudden sense of loneliness dragged at her soul. Today she had turned down a perfectly good offer of marriage, as well as the dangling promise of a wealthy grandfather's attention—if Tanner McKnight was to be believed. But though the rest of the world would surely think her mad, she knew she was right. Like her little Tillie, she could not settle for a life that did not truly fit her.

The trouble was, just like Tillie, she had no idea what sort of life *would* fit her. She didn't know what tomorrow might bring, nor which way its winds might blow her.

She hugged her shawl tight around her arms, not caring that her hair came free and lifted on the vagaries of the night breezes. For now she didn't have to worry, she reassured herself. The next few months would be spent heading west. She had nothing to do but keep putting one foot before the other.

After she reached Oregon and claimed her land, well, then she'd decide what to do next with her life.

17

Abby came rudely awake when a large hand clamped over her mouth. Fear erupted through her, but before she could do more than try to twist away from her unknown intruder, a heavy body descended onto hers, pinning her to the bed.

No! she wanted to cry. But the callused palm that pressed her head into the pillow prevented her from even taking the breath needed to speak. She bucked hard and tried to free her hands to strike at him. But one of her arms was caught between them, and the other was trapped beneath the tangled sheets.

This could not be happening to her.

And yet it was, she understood as panic took over her reason. It was happening to her just as it had happened to Rebecca.

Abby bared her teeth and tried to bite the unyielding palm. She tried to knee him in the groin as Doris Crenshaw had advised the other women should they ever be subject to an attack. But the brute seemed to anticipate her every move.

"Just relax, dammit. I'm not going to hurt you."

Abby went stock-still, but not because his words so reassured her. No. Rather it was his voice. Tanner's voice.

Her heart sank, though her fear did not ease one whit. Was *he* the one who'd hurt that innocent child?

He shifted slightly, raising himself up on one elbow,

though his hand remained firmly in place on her mouth. "That's better. I know you're not going to like this, Abby, but I can't let you marry that preacher."

Abby's eyes widened and she stared up at the vague shadow of his face. Her heart thundered like a herd of buffalo in her chest, but now she dared hope. He didn't want her to marry Dexter? Did that mean that he . . .

"I'm loosening my hand now, but don't yell. Understand?"

Abby nodded. As if she would yell and thereby alert the entire camp that she had Tanner McKnight in her bed. When his hand slid away, she took one deep gulp of air, then another.

To her acute embarrassment, however, those deep breaths caused her breasts to flatten against his chest. He must have felt it too, for he shifted again, and his chest moved up an inch or two. She could breathe more easily now, true. But this new position only pressed their lower extremities closer together. She could feel the outline of his belt buckle against her stomach. And something else as well.

"Get off me," she bit out, trying to cover her mortification with anger.

One of his fingers pressed against her lips. "Be quiet, Abby," he murmured in warning.

She jerked her head to the side, appallingly affected by the touch of his fingertip to her sensitive lips. Why did he have to be so infuriating—and so obscenely appealing? She should be outraged at his unforgivable behavior, yet she was overwhelmed by her own physical response to him. When he lay upon her full-length this way, and touched her lips . . .

The fact was, if he would just have kissed her, she could have died then and there a truly happy woman.

But he didn't kiss her. He seemed more interested in talking, and Abby had to struggle with the sinful feelings that beset her as best she could.

"I can't let you marry him, so we're going to leave here tonight."

"Leave here?" Abby stared up at him, seeing the whites of his eyes, the flash of his teeth as he spoke.

"I'm taking you to Chicago," he explained as if she should have known as much. "Your grandfather's not just paying me to find you. He's paying me to bring you back to him. And it's time for us to get going."

Maybe she was just slow, but it took several long seconds for Abby to fully comprehend what he'd said. He was taking her back to Chicago. *That* was what this was all about. Not that he couldn't bear to see her marry Dexter. Not that he wanted to marry her himself.

He was taking her back to Chicago to collect the reward her grandfather had offered.

"You *bastard*—"

He blocked the rest of her furious tirade with his hand, and once more Abby felt the full press of his weight on her. He was bigger, he was stronger. But she was by far the angrier. She managed to free one of her hands and struck the left side of his head as hard as she could.

"Son of a—" He broke off when she twisted sharply to the right and nearly brought one knee up between his legs. But before she could do any real damage, he rolled off her, then jerked her over and pushed her facedown into the feather mattress. No matter how much she struggled, he held her down, straddling her hips and pinning her legs down with his booted ones. With astonishing swiftness he bound her mouth with a bandanna, then tied her hands behind her back the same way. Only then did he flip her over again.

Abby tried to kick him, but he just sat on her legs and stared at her.

"I'm doing this for your own good," he growled, rubbing his ear gingerly and breathing almost as hard as she was.

Her own good! Abby wanted to scream her rage at

him, and her frustration. He didn't have her good in mind at all, only his own.

She tried her best to get her feet free, but he just grabbed her ankles and bound them as well, using her own shawl to do the deed. When he finished, he moved off her legs, but he kept one of his hands on her calf.

"You're making this harder than it has to be."

She glared at him, wishing more than anything that she could shoot him with his own gun. But she was forced by the way he'd trussed her up simply to endure his ill treatment. Harder than it had to be? She scoffed inwardly. He didn't know just how hard she planned to make it on him. He couldn't keep her tied up forever, she silently fumed. And once she was free, she'd make him sorry he'd ever laid a hand on her.

His hand moved on her leg, just the slightest slide of his fingers and palm against the fullness of her calf. But it was enough to throw her angry thoughts of revenge into sudden turmoil. She hated him. But his touch was turning her insides into melted butter. Against the dusty bandanna she let out a faint groan. Why must she react so violently to this most inappropriate of men? Why couldn't she have been happy with Dexter?

Why hadn't she married Dexter immediately as he'd wanted her to, instead of making him wait till tomorrow?

Then she remembered. She'd turned Dexter down completely tonight. Only Tanner didn't know that. He was kidnapping her, when there was no need.

"Lft mr gw!" she demanded through the muffling gag that choked her.

But he ignored her. With the frightening efficiency of a man who knew precisely what he was doing, he grabbed a carpet bag and dumped its contents out. Then he began rooting through her belongings, stuffing random clothing and other items into the bag until it would hold no more.

He turned toward her then, and though Abby tried to shrink back into the bed, her old familiar bed that she'd slept in for as long as she could remember, she could not escape. He tore the sheet from her and after a moment's pause, when his eyes raked her from head to toe, tugged her nightgown down to cover her thighs and knees. When he grabbed her boots, though, and started to force them onto her feet, she fought him with every bit of strength she possessed.

She would not go with him. She refused to go!

In the end, however, she went. He laced her boots up, wrapped her in her rain slicker, and after tying her bag of possessions onto his horse, he gathered her in his arms and stood her upright on the tailgate of the wagon. Then he mounted his big horse Mac and pulled her in front of him.

Swathed as she was within the voluminous folds of the slicker, Abby could hardly see what was happening to her. But she knew anyway. He was taking her to Chicago. Everything she owned in the entire world, what little she had that mattered at all to her was being left behind. The wagon train would take her oxen, divide up her food and other provisions, and leave the rest behind. Other travelers might pick over the remains, or perhaps Indians might, but everything else would be left to rot.

Tears crowded the backs of her eyes, but she willed them away. She could barely breathe as it was. If she were to cry, she'd probably drown in her own tears. Instead she concentrated on the fact that someone was bound to search for her. They'd miss her first thing in the morning, and a search party would hunt Tanner down and set her free.

She clung to that hope until their heavily burdened horse headed down an incline, then began to splash through water. They were crossing the river. Instinctively she shrank back against Tanner. If he were to drop her, tied as she was, she would immediately sink and drown.

Tanner seemed to sense her fears, for he reined the horse to a walk and pulled her slicker away from her face.

"I'm going to free your hands—just while we're in the river. But if you give me any trouble at all, I'll tie you over Tulip's back like a canvas pack. You understand what I'm saying?"

If she hadn't been so afraid of the water flowing between Mac's legs, Abby would have ignored his words completely. But more than anything she wanted her hands free. And once her hands were free, perhaps she might be able to loosen the awful gag. To breathe freely —and to scream for help.

She nodded, and in a matter of seconds her hands were free. As she rubbed the chafed places on her wrists, however, and flexed her stiff shoulders, the last thing Abby felt toward Tanner was gratitude. When he urged Mac forward into the river, she leaned as far over the animal's neck as she could, hoping to minimize contact with her captor.

If he noticed her pointed avoidance of him, she couldn't tell. His complete concentration seemed to be focused on the placid-looking river. But Abby was conscious of him. Every tensing of his arms. Every shifting of his thighs. He and his horse functioned in concert, and when the animal floundered in a sudden deep spot, Abby was inordinately relieved by the unity of thought between the man and the horse. For Tanner kicked free of the stirrups and floated just behind the horse, holding Abby in place but taking his weight off the animal as it swam.

In a few seconds Mac found his footing and Tanner regained his seat behind Abby, but they were both soaking wet now, and Abby was more miserable than ever. He'd brought them across the Platte to the Mormon Trail. If they headed east now, there'd be fewer people who'd even heard of Captain Peters's company.

But there *would* be people. If she could just call out to someone. Raise an alarm.

Once more Tanner anticipated her move, for he

caught her hand as it inched up toward the bandanna gag.

"I'll remove the gag when we're farther away from the trail, Abby. Till then you'll just have to endure it."

So saying, he grabbed both her wrists in one of his hands and took out a short length of cording.

"Nwr!" Abby fought to free her hands and to loosen the bandanna. But as much as she flailed and wriggled, he managed to stop her every bid to reach her gag.

"Be still, dammit to hell!" he muttered against her ear as he wound one steely arm around her, effectively clamping her arms against her sides. "Be still, or I swear I'll tie you over Tulip's back with your pretty little fanny pointing up to the sky."

Though he tied her hands in front of her this time, the bindings were tighter, and Abby could do nothing but subside into helpless fury. She heard his weary sigh of relief. Then he urged Mac up the muddy bank of the river and into a ground-eating canter, rocking her back against his chest.

Just behind them she heard the wet sound of Tulip's uneven gait. Tulip still limped, she realized. She hadn't completely healed, poor thing. But that also meant Tanner's threat to tie Abby like so much baggage over the mare's back was just that, a threat he couldn't actually carry out. Although she was relieved to figure that out, it nonetheless meant that she would have to ride before him on Mac all the time. And that was surely the worst torture of all.

As they made their way in the darkness along a muddy track that, she supposed, paralleled the north bank of the Platte, Abby tried to make out her surroundings. Though Tanner kept one hand on her bound wrists to prevent her from raising her hands to remove her gag, he didn't stop her from tugging at the wet slicker. Once her face was free of the stiff, confining cloth, she stared about.

Dawn was still hours away. One lantern burned in the

distance—someone sitting up with their sick, Abby supposed. Across the wide river two or three flashes of light signaled more of the same. God hope they sat up for birthings rather than deaths. But the deadly tide of cholera had been on the rise of late. Her father was not the last soul who would be taken by that terrible disease.

And she would never lay eyes on his grave again.

That realization, though not a new one, for she'd accepted as much already, nevertheless depressed her on an entirely new level. What was her life anymore but a series of disasters that propelled her first one way, then another? She had no say in any of it.

The wind blew harder from off to the left, and she caught the milling sound that was unique to a stock impoundment. Though she shivered from where the wind crept beneath the loose slicker to her wet skin, she ignored the cold. Instead she strained her eyes in the darkness, looking for one of the night watch who guarded every wagon train's stock.

"Forget it." Tanner abruptly shifted her in the saddle so that she faced the blackness that was the river. He pulled the slicker high around her shoulders, blocking her view despite her bucking protests, and kept an iron grip on her two wrists.

Abby wanted to scream her frustration, but even that was denied her by the now-wet gag. She trembled as much from anger as from the cold. But, covering her wrists, his hand was warm. Hot even.

What else should she expect from an earthly manifestation of the devil himself?

They rode along the trail, following the river for hours, it seemed. Abby lost track of the time, for there was no moon nor any stars to be seen beyond the rain-swollen clouds. The first sign of impending dawn was a pale gray shadow on the horizon before them, for they rode steadily east of course. Back to the States, toward Missouri and Lebanon and home. But it wasn't home anymore, and anyway he wasn't taking her to Lebanon.

He was taking her to Chicago and her mother's father. A man her kind-hearted mother had never spoken a word of. How horrible a monster must he be to deserve such from his own child.

Beset by her dour thoughts and weary beyond description, Abby stared blindly ahead as the landscape slowly unfurled before them. A dull mud-gray world covered by a grim sky, everything was wet and sullen looking. By now her body heat had dried the bodice of her flannel nightgown. But the skirt was still damp, and the shawl that bound her ankles still dripped a watery trail.

Too bad she couldn't leave a trail the way Hansel and Gretel had. But their bread markings had been absorbed into their environment just as her own trail of droplets would be. Besides, their story was just a made-up tale. Her nightmare was unfortunate reality.

Up ahead she could just make out a cluster of white canvas-topped wagons, and a glimmer of hope fanned to life in her chest. If she could only attract someone's attention.

But once again Tanner dashed her hopes. With a flick of his wrist and a slight lean to the left, he headed Mac in a new direction, away from the river, at an angle that would steer them well clear of the still circled-up wagons.

It was all too much. With a sharp movement of her arms she elbowed Tanner as hard as she could in his stomach. Then she kicked wildly, not caring if she hit him or Mac with her heels. She simply had to do something or else explode.

Mac shied to the left, although to Tanner's credit he prevented the horse from bolting. But while he was distracted by his flustered mount, Abby managed to grab the gag. With a rough jerk she yanked it down, unmindful of how it pulled at her sorely dried lower lip.

"Help!" she screamed, though it came out more a croak. "Someone, please help me—"

He silenced her with one hard palm crushed over her

mouth, then before she could react, flipped her facedown, sprawled over his lap.

"I warned you," she heard him mutter roughly. But she could not answer. She was too terrified by the view that presented itself to her. Large, flashing hooves, moving faster and faster as Tanner urged the unsettled Mac into a jarring gallop. The ground tearing before her at a dizzying speed. The wet grasses whipping at her face and catching in her streaming hair.

She lay on her stomach over his legs, and her breasts jounced with painful regularity into his rock-muscled thigh. Panic-stricken, she clutched at his booted calf with her tied hands, holding on for dear life. But it was his hold that kept her from tumbling beneath those lethal hooves, she knew. His unyielding hand spanning her waist, resting partly on her derriere. Worse, the very impersonality of his hold on her, in that most intimate of locations made her ordeal even more obscene. She was just so much baggage to him—troublesome baggage at that. While she . . . She'd actually been foolish enough to think herself in love with him.

Her upside-down ride seemed interminable. When Tanner brought Mac to a standstill, then yanked Abby upright, however, she knew they'd not traveled very far. The sky had barely lightened at all.

He held her with one arm, for which she supposed she should be glad, for her head spun and the horizon seemed to tilt as she scanned their surroundings for anyone who might help her. But there was no sign of anyone. They'd come over a low hill, and now they were completely alone.

He swung one leg over the saddle, then dismounted, still keeping a firm grip on her. When her feet touched the ground, she swayed unsteadily. But he made her sit down. Then he walked a short distance away from her and stared off somewhere to the north.

Abby eyed him balefully, wishing him drowned in the river or some other equally violent finish. Even in her furious state, however, she recognized the tension in his stance. It showed in his stiffness when he removed his damp wide-brimmed hat and raked his hair back with one hand.

Now what? she wondered with sinking heart when he still did not turn toward her. But she wasted no time. As her head cleared, she realized that her bound ankles were finally within reach of her hands.

Her shawl was ruined, the wool yarn stretched and misshapened, and her frantic tugging to release the soaked knot only made it worse. But she was succeeding, though she bent a fingernail painfully back in the process. She was succeeding, when Tanner jammed his hat back on his head and turned to face her.

For a moment she froze, caught like a mouse in the stare of a big predatory cat. When he didn't move, though, and only continued to stare at her, her numbed fingers jerked back into action. She tore a wet end of the shawl from the knot, then kicked first her left leg free, then her right.

The blood rushed to her feet with the excruciating sharpness of a thousand needles pricking the soles of her feet. She wriggled her legs, urging them back to full functioning, but all the while she warily watched him.

Then he smiled—that easy, confident smile she'd once thought so beautiful yet recognized was wicked as well—and her heart began a hard hammering in her chest. She scrambled to her feet, shrugging her disheveled hair over her shoulder and holding her still-tied hands before her as if to ward him off—futile gesture that it was.

"Don't stop on my account," he said in a voice so reasonable that it made her want to laugh at the insanity of the situation. "You've taken off your shawl." He closed the distance between them one slow step at a time. "Now take off the rest of your clothes."

18

"No." She backed up as Tanner advanced, her steps matching his one for one. But his were longer, and slowly he closed the gap. "Get away from me, Tanner McKnight," she warned in a voice that shook. "Just . . . just get away before—"

"Before what?" he cut her off. But then he stopped and his grin faded. What in the hell was he trying to prove, tormenting her this way? He had the right girl and all the evidence he needed. Why this insane urge to prove something to her?

Tanner stared at Abby, uncomfortably aware of the fear in her eyes. But he also saw the wild tangles of her loosened hair, the oversized rain slicker threatening to slip from her shoulders, and the plain blue flannel gown, still wet and clinging to her breasts and thighs. He swallowed once and fought down the hot rush of blood to his head—and other places as well. She looked like a pagan offering to some ancient god. An earthly Venus, soft and all female.

And scared to death.

Not the way he wanted a woman to look at him. Especially not her.

He took a step back. "You're wet. I just meant for you to put some dry clothes on." He sidled toward Tulip, then rummaged in the bag he'd packed full of her things. He turned his head to peer into the bag. She'd need a skirt and blouse—and she'd worn no undergarments beneath her night rail as she'd slept. He'd noticed that right away.

Before he could find everything she'd need, though, Tulip shied hard away from him. A clod of mud—meant for him, no doubt, had struck the animal in the rump. The next one hit him squarely in the back.

"Dammit, woman—" He spun around, then ducked when she flung a rock at him.

It was almost funny the way she had to throw her pitiful weapon with both hands bound together. She nearly fell each time. If she hadn't had such a murderous expression on her face, he would have laughed. But that would have hurt her pride even more than it had already been hurt. For some insane reason he didn't want to do that to her.

Still he didn't want to be pelted with rocks, either, so with a quick feint to the left he spun around, then, half running, half leaping, he caught her around the waist and bore them both down onto the wet, squishy earth.

He didn't want to hurt her so her sharp cry of pain sent a renewed spurt of guilt through him. He scrambled to get his weight off her and was rewarded by a pair of muddy fists slammed against his head.

"By God!" Would he have to hog-tie her all the way to Chicago?

With one hand he captured her flailing fists and forced them high above her head. With his other he thrust the bunched up the slicker away from her face. Though she fought and twisted beneath him, cursing him with her limited repertoire and trying desperately to inflict damage on his body, his weight and the careful placement of his legs prevented her from succeeding.

When she subsided all at once, however, he was undeniably relieved. He didn't want to hurt her, though he knew she'd never believe that. Still, he had to take a stab at convincing her.

"Abby, just listen for a minute. Just hear me out." He smoothed a thick wet knot of hair back from her brow, only to be met by a glowering stare. Her eyes were more green than hazel when she was angry. Green as jade. Then she blinked, and he sternly brought himself back to the matter at hand.

"I'm not going to ravish you," he stated, wanting to reassure her as much as remind himself that she was off-limits to him. "You can hate me for taking you away from the wagon train and dragging you to Chicago. But you don't have to be afraid of me. I'm not going to hurt you."

He saw her swallow and felt the twin pressure of her breasts against his chest as she took a shaky breath. Of relief? It bothered him to admit that it was. Then her lashes lowered, and he could no longer read the emotions in her expressive eyes.

"Get off me," she muttered, tugging against the hold he had on her hands.

His body wanted to stay right where it was and even to deepen the contact. But when that wayward desire manifested itself in a swiftly rising arousal, he practically leaped away from her. He swore silently, viciously, at his own perversity. If she'd noticed the hard bulge in his pants, she'd never believe what he'd said about not ravishing her. And he couldn't really blame her.

He sat next to her, his knees bent and his arms draped over them while she lay still a moment. Finally she pushed herself to a sitting position beside and a little behind him.

Tanner blew out a long, weary breath. Against his bowed neck the unrelenting drizzle felt cool and welcome for a change, helping to wash away both the mud and his ardor. "There's clean clothes for you in a bag on Tulip—"

He broke off and with lightning reaction grabbed for his gun—the gun she was trying to jerk from his holster. "Dammit!"

With a roar the gun exploded between them, and with a sharp cry she fell backward.

"Abby. Abby!" He shoved the gun back into his holster, unaware that he even did so. Where was she hit? How bad was it? And then, how could he have been so careless?

She lay on her back, her eyes wide and staring. Green as spring grass, one part of his mind noted. He quickly scanned her body. No telltale spurt of blood showed past the mud that now covered her clothes. He scrambled to her side.

"Abby! Are you hurt? Talk to me, sweetheart." He reached a hand to her face, almost afraid to touch her, but needing to find out if she was hurt.

But when his fingers grazed her cheek, she jerked back in fear. "I hate you," she cried, her voice filled with loathing, her face tight with anger. "I hate you and I wish you were . . . you were dead!" she spat out the rest.

She was unharmed. Tanner's emotions careened from a panicked fear to absolute relief. And then to flat-out fury.

"You stupid little bitch!"

He yanked her to her feet, ignoring her gasp of fear and her frantic attempts to resist. "Don't you ever try an idiotic stunt like that again. Do you understand?" He shook her hard for emphasis. "You could have been shot —or the wet powder could have made the gun misfire. If you'd been hurt or even killed, what good would that have done you?"

"At least I'd be away from you!" she screamed back at him.

It was the last straw. If she didn't shut up, he was going to do something violent. So he did the one thing that always shut a woman up. What he'd been wanting to do all along anyway.

He kissed her.

She struggled for only a moment, just a shocked stiffening of her body and a startled attempt to turn her face away. But he easily thwarted her, for her arms were still tied and caught between them, while one of his arms wound firmly around her slender waist, and his other hand tangled in her hair.

She tasted like the sweetest honey—tempered with a bit of mud. But as Tanner pressed his mouth to hers, probing for entrance, licking along the seam of her lips, sucking her pouty lower lip, he didn't mind the mud. She was a Venus, a woman made for love. Warm. Willing.

He slid his hand down from her waist to cup her buttocks and press her more intimately against him. God, but she felt so good.

When she gasped at his boldness, he took unashamed advantage and deepened the kiss, sliding his tongue within the heated confines of her mouth, tasting and wanting more of her with every velvet thrust.

If only her arms weren't in the way of a full-length embrace.

Tanner pulled just far enough away that he could fit his hand between their damp bodies. Then he ducked his head and with one quick move, looped her tied hands around his neck. In the same instant he did that, however, unpleasant reality intruded. The heady feeling of losing himself in the soft warmth of her sweet kiss dissolved when she opened her eyes and their gazes met.

He hadn't stolen her away from the wagon train for this—no matter how appealing the idea was. Yet there was no pretending he hadn't—at least for one insane moment—planned to continue kissing her. And more.

She leaned back, alarm but also chagrin dawning in her expressive eyes. But tied together as they now were, there was no easy way for them to separate.

Tanner raised her arms and extricated himself from their suddenly awkward embrace, then took a muddy step backward. "That won't happen again," he muttered, though he knew it hardly sounded like an apology. "It won't happen again," he repeated, but with more conviction as anger rose in his chest. "Unless you try another harebrained stunt like that. Then I won't be held responsible for what I do."

He gave her a dark scowl before striding off to retrieve the two horses who had shied away at the sound of the gunshot but now grazed peacefully just a little beyond them. Abby, however, was not in the least concerned by Tanner's furious expression. She watched as his long legs carried him to Mac, then to Tulip, and all the while she simply stood where he'd left her, too confused to seek escape, too stunned even to be angry.

He'd kissed her as if . . . as if he meant it.

A part of her knew that made no sense. Of course he'd *meant* it. He'd probably kissed any number of women that way and meant it. But he'd broken it off, and that, as ridiculous as it seemed, meant even more than the kiss. He'd stopped their kiss—just like the other time —before it could go too far. He did not mean to trifle with her, and that knowledge warmed her heart despite her previous outrage about what he was doing.

The unanswered question, however, was why he was restraining himself when it was so apparent that she would not restrain him. She practically melted every time he touched her; he couldn't have mistaken that obvious fact.

She pushed a hopelessly matted lock of muddy hair back from her cheek, then shivered in the damp morning wind. He might be restraining himself on account of the reward. If she were to accuse him of having had his way with her, it might be awkward for him to claim a reward from this man who was supposedly her grandfather.

Abby grimaced. What was wrong with her that with one kiss her anger dissolved and logic fled her mind? Was she so far gone that she could forget that he'd kidnapped her? That she'd lost everything in the world she owned because of him? Why couldn't she accept the cold, hard fact that he was everything her father had said, and worse? A bounty hunter. A man of violence who got his way no matter who tried to stop him.

Leading Tulip, he rode up on Mac and dismounted without a word. She watched as he retrieved clean

clothes for her. Then he turned toward her and gave her
a cold, scrutinizing look.

"I'll untie you while you change. I'll even turn my
back to give you some privacy. But don't even think
about trying anything stupid," he added caustically.

Abby lifted her chin and glared back at him. She had
already done—and thought—enough stupid things
where he was concerned. And imagining that this hard-
hearted man could ever have been honestly interested in
her was undoubtedly the stupidest of all. She was a reward to him, that was the sum total of it.

Best to remember that. And to remember that the
reward money made them adversaries.

"What do you mean, we're not going to search for her?"
Victor Lewis demanded, his face a study in disbelief. Behind him Sarah wrung her hands together, worried sick
over her friend's absence.

Captain Peters raised his callused hands placatingly.
"The good reverend has just given me a little news that
puts a different slant on things."

All eyes turned toward the gangly reverend, and he
swallowed and colored slightly. "Well, the thing is, Miss
Morgan—I mean, Miss Bliss—she informed me yesterday that she . . ." He paused and swallowed again before straightening to his full height. "That we would not
be wed today after all. Or ever," he added in clipped
tones.

Doris Crenshaw's eyebrows raised almost to her hair-
line. Victor frowned. But Sarah looked thoughtful. "Did
she say why?"

"No." The reverend looked indignant at the question. But then his wounded pride got the best of him. "It
wouldn't surprise me a bit, however, if she took off with
that man. That McKnight."

A number of knowing murmurs buzzed in the small
group that clustered outside the abandoned Morgan
wagon.

"McKnight's missing too," Captain Peters confirmed. "Is there anyone who has reason to believe there was something between those two? Something intimate?"

Victor glanced at Sarah, who nodded. He cleared his throat. "He was interested in her, all right."

"And she had eyes for him," Sarah added, a small smile showing on her lips.

"She was always panting after him," another caustic voice threw in.

Everyone turned to look as Martha McCurdle elbowed her way into the circle, and the frowsy blonde puffed up under all the attention. "She acted all pure and pious around everyone else, but I saw how she was around him. Like a cat in heat—"

"That's not true!" Sarah shouted, pushing past Victor to confront the malicious Martha.

"Are you saying she *didn't* share an attraction with McKnight?" Captain Peters interjected before the women's disagreement could escalate into something unpleasant.

Sarah looked up at him. "They shared an attraction, yes," she admitted. "But she was never less than a complete lady around him."

"He slept in her wagon," Martha taunted.

"Her father was there," Sarah shot right back.

"Yes, but now he's gone."

At that undeniable fact the others nodded once more, and many a knowing glance was shared.

"It appears they packed food and clothes. And even her family Bible is gone. I think it's pretty clear that she went with him willingly," Captain Peters said with an air of finality. "Now, I've made some decisions about how the rest of her goods will be divided up—and who's to get the oxen."

As people drifted away—some gossiping about the morals of certain women, others debating about the captain's apportionment of the Morgan/Bliss household goods—one man only appeared well pleased with the day's proceedings.

Captain Peters might bemoan the delay this caused. The Bliss girl's friends might worry about her well-being. But Cracker O'Hara was elated.

At last things were under way. No more riding herd on the stock at midnight. No more sleeping in a wet bedroll and doing without either whiskey or women. Time for him to get going. He'd pick up Bud and they'd track down McKnight and the girl. Within a month he planned to be holed up in some fancy hotel in Chicago with a sweet young thing to pass the time and plenty of money to pay her with.

19

She was dry, but in no other way was Abby any more comfortable than before. She still rode in front of Tanner, though at least she was decently clothed. But he'd insisted she ride astride, so her bottom nestled in the most obscene manner against the vee formed by his thighs.

She'd fought the idea of course. Not that it had done a bit of good. To her horrified objections that it wasn't seemly, that her legs would be bared all the way up to her knees, he had just scoffed.

"There's no one to see your knees where we're going," he'd laughed, though he had sounded more grim than amused. Then he'd lifted her onto Mac's withers as if her weight were a small thing indeed, and mounted behind her before she could formulate a plan to escape.

Now they rode a steady direction northeast, so far as she could tell from the watery dawn that lit the world before them. She was outraged by his easy manhandling of her, exhausted from lack of sleep, and starving. Yet he seemed unaffected by any of it. He just sat behind her, stiff and erect, his chest not quite touching her back.

As if his rigid posture could negate the way their hips nestled together.

"I'm hungry," she muttered through gritted teeth. "And my hands have gone numb."

He didn't respond to her first statement. But at the

second he covered her hands, which were clasped around the saddle horn, and began to massage her knuckles.

"I'll untie you," he began—reluctantly, it sounded to her. "But only if you promise not to fight me."

Abby closed her eyes in utter frustration. Why must he touch her this way, stroking life back into her fingers and feeling into her suddenly sensitive skin? The fact was she wanted her hands free. She couldn't bear the helpless feeling being tied up gave her. At the same time, though, she still needed to fight him, for that, perversely, was the only way she could prevent herself from succumbing physically to him.

Not that he *wanted* her to succumb, she reminded herself in painful honesty. He wanted the reward. So why was she still so pulled toward him?

"Well?" he prodded, leaning forward ever so slightly, just enough so that his breath tickled her right ear. "Will you promise to be peaceful—not to pelt me with mud and rocks—if I untie your hands? Not to steal my gun? Not to try to escape?"

Abby nodded, though it was as much to avoid the disturbing warmth of his breath as to agree to his demands. His unreasonable demands.

He reached around to the bandanna that bound her hands, and after a few moments the bindings came free. Blood rushed to her fingers, stinging and welcome. But she was even more aware of his chest pressed against her back and the sudden, quickened pace of her pounding heart.

Only when he straightened in the saddle again did she remember to let loose the breath she'd unconsciously held. Yet the removal of his broad chest from against her back served only to emphasize the close proximity of their hips. Once again Abby's fingers tightened on the saddle horn, only this time she fought the distressing rise of heat inside her, rather than physical bindings. The former bound far tighter than the latter, she recognized obliquely as the last remnants of good sense fled her mind.

She shifted uncomfortably, then froze when he let out a low but extremely pointed oath.

"Sorry," she whispered, hunching forward in mortification, even though she knew she owed him no apology at all.

Tanner, too, must have recognized the irony in her word, for he laughed, albeit without much mirth. "Not as sorry as I am," he replied.

"I rather doubt that," Abby snapped back, restored to anger by his arrogance. "If you were truly sorry, you'd let me go. Right now," she added.

"I'm sorry you won't go with me to Chicago willingly," he retorted. "I'm sorry your father died and your life is not turning out as you expected."

"But not sorry enough to leave me alone."

They rode in silence a moment, through grasses that brushed at the stirrups, following no trail through the undulating plains but the one Tanner had set in his mind.

"You should thank me for saving you from marrying Harrison."

She rose furiously to that smug comment. "For your information I had already informed Dexter that I could not wed him."

She felt him tense in the saddle behind her and she knew she'd surprised him. But her triumph was ruined by the unwarranted shiver of awareness that coursed through her when his denim-clad thighs rubbed against her derriere. The several layers of muslin and calico she wore were no buffer at all against the heated feelings his slight movement roused in her.

"Why did you do that—break off with him?"

Abby swallowed. The low rumble of his voice so very near her ear caused the most unseemly fireworks to set off inside her. Why had she broken off with Dexter? Because she longed for someone else. It was that simple.

But she could never tell him that.

"Not that it's any of your business, but despite outward indications to the contrary, Dexter and I were not truly suited to be man and wife."

He snorted derisively at her pompous explanation. "I could have told you that."

She refused to respond to his comment, even though his perceptiveness irritated her. Perhaps if she'd not succumbed to her father's pressuring—if she'd never accepted Dexter's suit in the first place—she would not now be in this awkward position.

"Since I have no intentions of marrying Dexter Harrison any longer, I don't see why you shouldn't return me to the wagon company."

"Harrison has nothing to do with it."

"But you just said—"

"I said I saved you from marrying him. But even if I'd known you had already called the wedding off, I still would have had to take you back with me."

"Oh, yes. Of course. For the reward," she sneered, hating the truth of her words. "How much is he paying you, anyway? What do grandchildren go for these days?"

He didn't answer, but then Abby hadn't truly expected him to. For a while they rode in silence toward the thin white glow on the horizon that was the sun's best efforts this morning. No glorious display of heavenly color. No breathtaking view of rolling hills, green and verdant. As they topped one low rise and ambled downhill and toward the next roll of land, Abby saw just more of the same. A dull, green world, wet and dreary, that stretched away until forever.

And not another soul in sight.

"Do you even know where we're going?" she finally asked, unable to hide the peevish note in her voice.

"Burlington."

"Burlington, Illinois? But . . . But that's halfway across the Nebraska Territory."

"The railroad has opened up that far. We'll take the train from there to Chicago."

Abby tightened her jaw, restraining another fruitless outburst. He'd obviously had the whole thing planned out from the beginning. "What if you'd never found me? What would you have done then?"

He shrugged out of his slicker before answering and laid it behind him over his saddlebags. "Why, I guess I would just have found some poor motherless little girl and passed her off as you."

Abby twisted around and stared at him in horror. "You would actually have done that? Kidnapped some-one's child?"

His eyes lost their mocking glow. "There's lots of orphans who'd jump at the chance to be a rich man's only grandchild. Those two little kids whose parents died yesterday, for instance. I bet they'd be grateful as hell to have someone want them. Want to do things for them and look out for them."

Abby turned away from his pointed stare. Put that way, she almost felt guilty for her blanket rejection of her mother's father. Almost.

"If he's so rich, he ought to spend his money helping orphans, then. They need his help. I don't."

"The hell you don't."

"The hell I do!" she snapped right back at him. But what was the use of arguing with him? It was hopeless. *He* was hopeless. Suddenly she wanted to be as far away from him as she could get. Being so near him—nestled in his embrace—was too frustrating to bear when they were so vastly apart in thoughts and beliefs and attitudes.

"Let me down. I want to walk awhile. Stretch my legs," she added sarcastically.

She hadn't actually expected him to agree, so Abby was mightily surprised when he pulled Mac to an abrupt stop. "Don't try to run," he warned. Then before she could reply with some appropriately scathing retort, he lifted her by the waist and without ceremony lowered her to the ground.

Arrogant clod, she fumed as she started forward, paralleling Mac's ambling direction.

Smart-mouthed brat, he seethed as he stared straight ahead, yet kept her within his peripheral vision. But as much as her wish to be rid of him stung his pride, he also knew that he'd never make it to Burlington if she had to ride before him the entire time.

Or rather, *she'd* never make it to Burlington, at least not as an unspoiled virgin.

Damn it to hell, but he'd really screwed himself this time. If only she was a kid. Or some whey-faced little mouse he didn't feel the least attraction toward. Or a bitch.

That almost made him smile. He glanced sidelong at her, noting her ramrod-stiff posture, her determined stride and jutting jaw. She was stubborn, sarcastic, argumentative, and willing to shoot him, given half a chance. If that didn't qualify her for being a bitch, he wasn't sure what did.

But she'd had plenty of provocation, and that knowledge forced him to consider her more brave than bitchy. She was brave even when she was scared to death. She was beautiful even when she was dirty and bedraggled.

The fact was, she was a hell of a woman, and he wanted her so bad, it hurt.

They stopped in a willow grove beside a rain-swollen creek somewhere around midmorning. The lower portion of Abby's skirt was wet and dirty from her walk, her feet were wet and aching, and she was drooping from exhaustion. But she absolutely refused to reveal that to Tanner. As he dismounted and saw to the two animals, she just stood to the side, making a point of not looking at him but nevertheless conscious of every move he made.

The sun had broken through the remnants of the storm clouds that had dogged their trail for days, and now it heated the wet earth until it seemed almost to steam. Abby was hot, hungry, and sticky. She eyed the narrow rushing creek with longing but did not make a move toward it.

"Go on and rest a while," Tanner ordered. "We can't have a fire, but I've got biscuits, jerky, and some cold beans."

Abby lifted her chin a fraction higher. "I'd like some coffee. Why can't we have a fire?"

She thought he meant to ignore her, he took so long to respond. "Someone might try to follow us. I wouldn't want to make it too easy for them."

She turned to face him. "Follow us? You mean . . . Dexter?" she asked, her voice rising hopefully.

He hunched over one of his packs, pulling out two tin cups and several bundles of food. It was quite clear he had no intentions of hiding the amusement her words roused. "Dexter Harrison?" He shook his head. "No, I'm not too worried about your suitor, especially now that I know he's a *spurned* suitor. As big as he is, he still couldn't find Independence Rock unless he walked straight into it. The man has got other good qualities," he conceded in faint deference to her stormy stare. "He's just not a plainsman. No, if anybody follows us, it'll be Captain Peters or someone he sends. Maybe Lewis."

"Victor Lewis?" Abby had stiffened at Tanner's belittlement of Dexter. But now she knew a sudden fear for Sarah's husband. "You wouldn't hurt him, would you? I mean, he's done nothing to you—"

"If he tries to take you away from me, I'll do whatever it takes to stop him."

He stared at her, the flat, deadly stare of a predator, and Abby swallowed in sick comprehension. Her father's warning came swiftly to mind. Tanner was a man of violence who lived by his gun. All the rest—the charming side of him, the brief glimpses of gallantry, the sensual aura that drew her so powerfully—they were all peripheral to the central truth of him. He was a man who hired himself out at the best price he could get to hunt people down. And he would let nothing and no one stand in the way of his reward.

"Don't hurt him," she whispered, unaware she'd done more than think the words. "Don't hurt Victor or anyone else on account of me."

A bird called down from the tree behind him. The water rushed willy-nilly on its long way south, and another bird answered with a shrill whistle that could have been either reassurance or warning. Tanner straightened to his full height and faced her across the dappled shade of the willows. "As long as you cooperate with me, we won't have any problems with someone trailing us."

He waited for her response, though she sensed he already knew how she would answer. How she *must* answer.

"I'll cooperate," she said after a long, awful hesitation. "But if you hurt anyone—anyone at all," she added in a voice gone low and venomous, "I'll fight you every way I can. And one way or another I'll make you pay."

After that they didn't talk. She helped herself to one stale biscuit and a few mouthfuls of beans, although her appetite was suddenly gone. She stuck several strips of jerky into her pocket and filled her cup several times from the stream. The water was cold and refreshing, though gritty with silt and other run-off debris. But Abby really didn't care.

She washed her face and neck, her hands and her arms as far up as she could push her sleeves. She waded into the cold water almost up to her knees to refresh her aching feet. But she didn't speak to Tanner again. Nor did she even look over at him.

All she could think was that she was truly the daughter of Eve. A woman beguiled by the serpent, intrigued by his dazzling appearance and glib tongue. She'd been warned by her father, but she'd been so certain that she knew better.

Yet in the end he was still the devil, though in a pretty disguise. He would do or say whatever was necessary in order to get what he wanted. And what he wanted was the money her grandfather offered. If anyone tried to get in his way . . .

As they prepared to leave, Abby knew that despite any other feelings she had for Tanner, she must let her fear of his potential violence toward others dominate everything she did. She must aid him, even in their escape. But revenge flickered to life deep in her heart. The bitter need for revenge took the place of the softer emotions she'd harbored for him. Eventually they'd get to Chicago. Eventually she'd be a wealthy, respected woman, if what he'd said of her grandfather was to be believed. And when that happened . . .

When that happened she'd find a way to avenge herself on this man who had no heart in his chest. No soul in him at all.

She crossed to Tulip, suddenly eager to reach their destination. "I can ride on my own now."

"No."

Abby frowned and glared at him. "I have no intention of trying to escape," she stated in her most scathing tone.

But he only grinned, a slanted mocking expression that drew her hands up into fists. "Tulip's not strong enough to hold a person's weight."

"But her pack—"

"Is half your weight." He arched one brow. "You'll have to ride on Mac. With me."

Abby swallowed hard, burying her resentment and a burning sort of panic beneath a show of icy calm. "I'd rather walk."

He tossed out the remnants in his cup and tucked it in his pack. "Too bad. I've given you all the time I can to work off your temper. We've got to put more distance between us and the overland trails. In case someone's following us. I'd hate for us to have to confront anyone," he added. "Wouldn't you?"

She hated him. She absolutely hated him, Abby fumed as she perched before him once more, as stiff as an iron gate post. He was cruel, unfeeling, and quite the vilest person she'd ever had the displeasure to meet.

But as they rode steadily east, her hatred was small comfort. She would spend untold hours in his company during the coming weeks. She would ride with him during the days and make camp with him at night. Undoubtedly she would prepare their meals and then, when night came, lie down at the same fire to sleep.

Her heart began to race at the idea of such intimate proximity to him, and though she forced herself to count all the various ways she might seek her revenge while he slept, she couldn't quite erase the one perverse thought that dominated all the others: they would be alone together. All night. Every night.

In desperation she began to pray. "Oh, my God, I am heartily sorry, for I have sinned—"

"You? Sinned? What could you possibly have done that would be considered a sin?" Tanner asked.

Abby hadn't been aware she'd said the words out loud, so Tanner's question caught her a little off guard. "Mind your own business," she muttered ungraciously.

Maybe that was good advice, Tanner decided as she bent her head to resume her prayers, albeit silently this time. But he knew already that it would be damned hard advice for him to take.

She was just a job for him, just a nice fat reward for a relatively easy delivery. Or at least she should be.

He guided Mac effortlessly while his mind stayed focused on the woman that rode before him. The dark glints in her long hair. The faint smell of her—sweaty, sweet. Womanly. The firm press of her nicely rounded bottom against his crotch. How in the hell was a man supposed to think straight with such a ripe young body pressed this close to him?

But he feared it was more than her very appealing female form. Abigail Bliss was an unexpected mixture of purity and passion. Though she fought that passion—even now her prayers were probably directed toward keeping that passion in check—it was there and was made all the more tempting by the innocence that veiled it.

It would take very little to push past that veil.

She moved slightly, probably to find a more comfortable position. But Tanner's thoughts made her movement pure torture for him. "Sit still, dammit," he growled in a barely controlled voice.

She froze in a hunched-forward position, probably as uncomfortable as hell, he suspected. But though he regretted his temper, he didn't know what else to do. She was there; he wanted her; and damn her, she wanted him too. With one kiss, one caress, he could ignite the simmering fire that burned inside her. They could lose themselves in the flames of desire, and maybe, just maybe, he could get his wayward feelings back under control.

But then what?

The wind blew a single lock of her hair across his cheek, and it was almost his undoing.

"Get your hair out of my face," he bit out, though he cursed himself for the unfeeling way it came out. It was better this way, he told himself as she tucked the wind-blown curl back in with the others. Let her hate him. Let her think she was only a reward to him, that their few kisses had meant nothing to him.

After all, it was true. She meant nothing to him because nothing could come of it. Even if she could be his kind of woman, he was not her kind of man. they'd been born of different worlds, and they were headed in different directions.

Willard Hogan would be the first to remind him of that fact.

20

Cracker O'Hara squinted, trying to see the two of them. They had camped beside a narrow creek, under a high, clear sky. The creek was little more than a swale, collecting rainwater from the surrounding low hills. In drier weather it would simply be a bed of sandy ground winding through the rolling terrain. But it was flowing now, and it was deep enough to drown a woman in.

McKnight had forgone a fire. *Still cautious*, Cracker smirked. But his caution had all been pointless, because Cracker had known who he was all along. Who he was, what he was up to, and now where he was headed with the girl. McKnight had done the hard part for him, tracking her down. The easy part would be killing them both.

At the moment, they were sitting down, hidden from view in the tall prairie grass. But they were there all right, and once they fell asleep, he and Bud would make swift work of them.

"I ain't killin' no kid," Bud Foley had said. It was the same puling song he'd been singing all day, and Cracker ignored it. The man was as soft as McKnight—a fact Cracker intended to use to good advantage.

They would have to wait until the pair below were well asleep. From his perch downwind Cracker could see the two horses quietly grazing, two dark silhouettes against an already dark landscape. A sliver of moon cast just enough light to see by, yet not enough to be sure of what you saw—unless of course you were focused on your quarry. And Cracker was completely focused.

"Make sure he's dead this time," he ordered Bud when they finally began their descent toward the sleeping pair.

"I guess I know what I'm doin'," Bud snapped back. Cracker only smiled to himself. *Maybe. Maybe not.*

Abby lay on a doubled-over blanket with her shawl clutched over her like a shield. Tanner lay but five feet away from her, and she knew he was not asleep.

They'd passed a long, silent afternoon, sticking to the lowest land, meandering between the gentle swells of the endless prairie west. At one point they'd followed a narrow streambed for an hour to hide their tracks, though he still seemed edgy and watchful. Given how flat and open this part of the Nebraska Territory was, it seemed futile to hide, yet Abby was nonetheless impressed with his precautions.

Still she'd not spoken a word to him—at least not willingly. She'd responded to his curt orders with equally curt replies. Now, however, as they lay so near each other beneath a spectacularly brilliant display of starlight, it seemed awkward for them not to speak. But she absolutely refused to initiate such a discourse. And so she lay there, her mind filled with too many thoughts to keep straight: her abandoned past, her uncertain future. Her unsettling present.

When he finally did speak, she nearly jumped in alarm.

"Get over here."

The lively silence of the vast plains roared like a storm in her ears. "No."

She heard him moving—the dry rustle of the tall grasses, a disgusted sigh as he sat up.

"I'm trying to protect you, not hurt you. Now, come over here, Abby."

Abby swallowed hard and clasped her poor shawl all

the tighter. She'd feared all along that he would tie her up so that she couldn't escape while he slept. When he hadn't, she'd been relieved almost to the point of gratitude. Now, however, it appeared he'd reconsidered.

"Why should I come over there? And why should I believe even one word out of your deceitful mouth?"

"Because I want to keep you safe. Because I'm good at what I do—"

"And proud of it too," she angrily interrupted him. "You're quite the expert at kidnapping unwilling women, and proud of your talent."

Even through the darkness she felt the heat of his gaze on her. "Perhaps you'd care to define the term *unwilling women*," he drawled. "Or in this case, *unwilling woman*. I haven't noticed that you've been particularly unwilling with me up to now."

The husky intimation in his voice sent a hot shiver through her. But it was followed just as quickly by denial. She'd not been all *that* willing then, at least not in the way he was implying. And she certainly wasn't willing now. Without stopping to consider her action, she threw her battered ankle boot at him. It was a wild throw, missing him by a mile, and that fueled her outrage even further.

"You arrogant bastard," she accused, her voice rising in volume as she sat up. "If I gave any indication that I was . . . that I was kindly disposed toward you, it was only because I was unaware that any man could be so completely lacking in moral fiber as you are!"

Almost before she had the words out, he was at her side and had grabbed her by both arms. "Keep quiet, dammit! Sound carries out here—"

"I don't care—"

"Well, you'd damned well better care. I told you before, I won't have the least bit of mercy on anyone who comes after you."

Her heart sank at his reminder, but still she could not let the matter drop. "So you admit I do need rescuing!"

His hands tightened on her upper arms, making Abby distressingly aware of their intimate position. She knelt on her paltry bed while he crouched in front of her, holding her still before him. They were but inches apart. If either of them was to lean the least bit forward . . .

Abby immediately made herself lean back, as far as his implacable grip allowed. Yet still she was much too near him for comfort. It was true, she knew. All of it was true. She was willing where he was concerned, no matter how hard she struggled not to be. But she would hide it from him if it killed her.

She heard his harsh breathing, as if he were as angry as she. But what did *he* have to be angry about?

"Perhaps, Abby, you'd be better off considering that your grandfather—and by extension myself—is rescuing you from a dangerous trek you no longer have any reason to make."

"I could have made it," she contended.

She felt his shrug. "Probably. But what's the point of struggling for years when your grandfather can lay the world at your feet?"

"He can't give me back my parents," Abby accused in a bitter tone.

"No."

"If he hadn't hounded my father . . ." She trailed off as misery overwhelmed her.

"Your father didn't have to head west," Tanner said more quietly, his voice low and soothing. "He could just have told you the truth and let you make up your own mind about your grandfather."

Abby winced inside. She'd thought as much herself. Her father could simply have trusted her with the truth. He could have treated her as an adult instead of a child that needed to be protected from unpleasantness. But to agree with Tanner seemed too disloyal to her father, who had, after all, only meant the best for her.

"How easy it is for you to criticize my father. He at least acted out of concern for me. While you . . ." She trailed off contemptuously. "And anyway, now that I know the truth, why don't you and my grandfather trust me to make up my mind about him, as you put it?"

"That's exactly what we're doing. You can't make up your mind about him until you meet him."

Abby didn't want to admit it, but there was an unwelcome truth in his words. Still, if her mother had rejected the man . . .

"Come over here by me. But leave your bedroll. And don't stand up."

Abby glared at the dark shadow of him, seeing only his movements and the flash of his teeth when he spoke. "I am tired unto death," she snapped. "Isn't it enough—"

He cut her off by grabbing her hand and nearly toppling her over with a sharp tug. "Just shut up and crawl," he ordered tersely.

He was absolutely the most contrary and difficult man in all of God's creation. But he was bigger and stronger, and in the end Abby crawled as he directed. Her skirt hampered her every move. Her palms became grimy and her hair hung down in her eyes.

But then what difference did that make, she wondered with ironic humor. She'd been dirty since the beginning of her westward trek; her hands had become so tough and callused that a few rocks and twigs were nothing at all. As for her hair in her face, it was dark and she couldn't see anyway. She was reminded of mice creeping through the grass, of Tillie and Snitch. If she hadn't been so tired and so furious with Tanner, she might have laughed at how ludicrous the whole situation was.

They stopped some distance from where their bedrolls lay, almost to where the horses grazed. Tanner bid her stop with a hand on her shoulder, then, to her surprise, pressed one finger to her lips, signaling her to silence.

Much as she needed to contradict every order he gave her, there was an odd tension about him that prevented her. They sat that way a long while, with only the night sighs of the wind in the tall grass to break the huge silence. Then he drew his long-bladed knife from its sheath and released the guard on his side gun. Abby shrank back into a frightened huddle, just watching him with wide eyes and a sinking heart.

Someone must be coming. She hadn't heard anything odd. The horses hadn't even looked up—at least not that she recalled. But something had alerted Tanner.

He gave her a hard warning look. It was difficult to make out in the darkness, but she felt it anyway. Be still and maybe they'll go away. Keep quiet and maybe no one will get hurt.

They stayed like that for what felt like forever. The moon inched its way across the velvet-black sky, a cold, silent witness to the activities going on so far below. That same moon shone over the wagon company. It shone as well over her old home and her grandfather in Chicago. It shone down on her parents' graves.

Then, as weariness slowly over took her anger and tension, she heard it.

Just a shiver of sound on the wind. A rustle that could have been a rabbit or a mouse. Or a snake. She drew her feet closer to her body, remembering her previous run-in with those rattlesnakes. But a sharp shake of Tanner's head warned her to be still. She stared at him, sensing that he was gathering himself, getting ready to react. And she knew then that the sound was of people approaching. Her rescuers stumbling into Tanner's trap.

"Don't," she breathed the word, pleading with her eyes for him to relent.

He only frowned and removed his hat, preparing to strike. But Abby persisted.

"I'll tell them you're not taking me against my will," she promised in a whisper, though she nearly choked on the words. "I'll tell them I *want* you to take me to Chicago."

That caught his attention, for his brows arched up in surprise, then lowered again as he studied her.

But before he could respond, all hell seemed to break loose. A triumphant whoop, the crashing sound of bodies through the grass, and two barks of gunfire.

Abby's heart thundered in horror. Tulip and Mac shied away, snorting and kicking, though their hobbles prevented them from moving too quickly.

"Shit! They ain't here!" someone yelled in the blackness.

"Shut up and find 'em!" came an angry retort.

One of the voices sounded familiar, though Abby couldn't quite place it. Someone from the wagon company, no doubt. But why the gunshots? Did they mean to kill Tanner?

A new fear joined all her others. She didn't want Tanner to hurt anyone on her account, but neither did she want to see him hurt.

There was only one solution.

"I'm all right," she cried desperately into the night. "Don't hurt Tanner. Please, I . . . I'm going with him willingly."

"Stand up, Miss Morgan—ah, Miss Bliss," someone called out after just a second's hesitation.

"No." Tanner's harsh command and even harsher grip on her shoulder stopped her from standing above the shelter of the grasses.

"I don't want anyone hurt," she whispered furiously at him. "This way they can leave peacefully, and you"— she spat the words—"you can get that filthy reward you so covet."

"I'll tie you up and gag you, woman," he threatened, his voice as hard as the steel barrel of his deadly weapon. "So help me, God, I will unless you swear to shut up and stay put. You don't want me to be forced to kill them, do you?"

It was that which convinced her, for more than anything she feared having their deaths on her conscience.

"I swear," she muttered. "But don't you dare hurt them in any way," she added, her eyes flashing with fury.

He didn't answer. Instead he melted into the thick grasses, blending in with their rustling as the wind pushed them in an endless ebb and flow.

She heard the erratic movement of the other men, closer now than before. Drawn by her voice, no doubt. One was just beyond her, the other farther back and to the right. But she didn't make a sound. She just pulled her knees up against her chest and curled her arms around her legs, holding on for dear life as her ears strained to decipher the noises around her.

"Where's he at?" the one farther from her growled, though Abby detected a fearful quiver in his voice. This one's voice was not familiar at all. For some reason Abby didn't think he was from the wagon train, and that sent a niggling shiver of fear up her spine. Who were these men?

The other man didn't reply to his friend, but Abby heard his stealthy movement just to her right. He was coming her way. But where was Tanner? Her heart began to race in rising panic. Something was terribly wrong here.

Then the other man gave a startled cry, and she nearly jumped out of her skin. In the moonless night the ominous sound of struggle lifted the hairs on the back of her neck. Tanner had found one of them! Her breath caught in her throat and she strained desperately to see and hear. But only grunts and curses resounded and the muffled thuds of two bodies colliding. Dear God, they were killing each other!

Without thinking she cried out, "Don't kill him!" though she meant Tanner now, not the man he fought.

But before she could take a follow-up breath, she was grasped from behind by a pair of beefy hands and hauled to her feet. She knew before he said a word—something in his cruel grip, in his very smell—and her heart plummeted in awful realization.

"Howdy-do, Miss Bliss," Cracker O'Hara chuckled in her ear. "You and me, we're sure gonna have a blissful time of it tonight." He laughed at his own coarse humor.

She must have screamed, though she didn't remember consciously doing so. O'Hara had her in a crushing hold, her back pressed against him, his thick arm tight around her throat. It wasn't the grasp of a rescuer, she noted dimly as she struggled to breathe. Her fingers clawed his arm, seeking frantically to loosen his grip. But he only yanked harder at her.

"Settle down, little girl. Once McKnight's gone, you and me will have more time to get acquainted."

His taunt chased away the last of her hopes that he had come to rescue her. She didn't know why he'd want to hurt her, but she was sickeningly sure he did. A fear far worse than anything she'd ever felt froze her awkwardly against him.

In the darkness beyond them the other two men still grappled, and it was an awful thing to hear. For life or death they fought, cursing, gasping for breath. Then an unearthly shriek ended abruptly in a gurgling sound that subsided into horrifying silence.

One of them was dead. Bile rose in her throat and she fought a wave of dizziness. One of them had just gone to meet his maker. *Please, God, don't let it be Tanner.*

"Bud?" O'Hara's arm tightened as he called out to his cohort. Abby's head began to spin from lack of air, but she struggled to stay sensible. *Don't panic. Just breathe. Slowly. Steadily.*

"Bud?" he called again, angry this time. "Goddammit," he muttered when there was no response. She felt his burly chest fill rhythmically with air, breathing hard and heavy as he waited in the hollow prairie darkness. But all Abby could think was that Tanner was alive. He must be!

O'Hara apparently thought the same thing. "Well, well, well. Now, what are we gonna do about this, McKnight? I've got that little ol' prize you was looking for.

That sweet little reward you was chasin'. Speak up, little girl." He directed this last at her. "Tell our pretty boy who's got his hands all over you."

"I'm fine, Tanner," she said, though she was anything but.

No response came, however, except for the distant cry of a coyote and the night call of some predatory bird. Abby's heart thundered painfully in her chest. Where was he? Where was he! But despite her own overpowering fear, she sensed Cracker O'Hara's as well. He stood stiff with tension, poised to react. But a muscle twitched in his left arm, twitched like the tail of an agitated cat. His gun pointed over her right shoulder into the darkness beyond them while he held her unyieldingly with the other.

What could she do to help Tanner? she wondered as the man's grip on her throat loosened ever so slightly. If she suddenly became a dead weight in his arms . . .

Something moved to their left, and O'Hara spun, firing wildly. Abby lost her footing—and very nearly her hearing. But she scrambled for balance, too terrified to do anything else. Another noise behind them. Then one to the left. Abby could feel the violent slamming of O'Hara's heart against her back as he jerked them around to face each new sound.

He was as scared as she was, she realized. Somehow that helped.

"Show yourself, you fuckin' coward!" O'Hara screamed at his invisible foe. "Show yourself, or I'll blow her head clean off her shoulders—"

Before he could finish the threat—before he could lower the barrel of the gun to her head—another gunshot sounded. Like a giant puppet pulled by invisible strings, O'Hara jerked forward at the deafening sound, and they fell. Abby landed hard with her captor's crushing weight on top of her. The breath exploded out of her lungs, and she lay half stunned, wondering for a long painful and dazed moment if she was dead yet. She couldn't cry out. She couldn't catch her breath for the pressure on her back. Then she heard Tanner's voice, and with a harsh rush she sucked in great lungfuls of air.

"Abby? Abby! Talk to me!"

The weight was abruptly removed from her—Cracker O'Hara's inert form, the awful realization hit her. Then she was rolled over, and Tanner's face loomed, shadowed and worried just above her own. "Abby. Sweetheart . . . Are you hurt? Are you hurt?"

"Tanner—" She croaked out his name, but for the life of her could manage no more.

"Are you hurt?" he repeated in an urgent tone. But he didn't wait for her response. As she lay, gasping for breath, grappling with the reality of what had just happened—and what had almost happened—he ran his hands carefully over her, efficiently checking her for wounds. When he slid his fingers down her side, however, it tickled, and to her vast dismay she released the most inappropriate giggle.

"Abby?"

"You're . . . you're tickling me," she said, her voice caught somewhere between another obscene chuckle and a hiccup. Then a violent shudder wracked her, head to toe, and panic began to set in. "Is he . . . is he . . ." She couldn't finish the thought.

"He's dead," Tanner stated flatly and without the least show of emotion. "The other one too."

Abby squeezed her eyes closed against the horror, but hot tears leaked between her lashes. "I . . . I don't understand. They weren't trying to rescue me."

"No," he answered. "They weren't. And the other one—Foley—I'm pretty sure he tried to kill me back at Fort Kearney."

"Kill you?" she gasped in renewed horror.

He seemed to realize then that he'd spoken out loud. "It doesn't matter anymore. They're both dead. They can't hurt you now."

Abby pushed herself up onto one elbow, shivering

from both her shock and the cold. "Yes. They're dead," she repeated. Then she reached out a hand to touch his arm. "None of this makes any sense," she admitted, unable to hide either the wavering of her voice or the tears that spilled past the edges of her eyes. "None of it. But I know you saved my life. Thank you."

He let out a slow sigh, then stood up and took a step back. "If you're all right, let's get out of here. There could be more where these two came from." He didn't acknowledge her words of thanks. He neither took credit nor accepted the blame, Abby realized while he quickly retrieved the two horses, stuffed their bedrolls into the packs, and saddled the pair. He acted as if nothing of any particular consequence had taken place in this open, lonely place, somewhere in the vastness that was the Nebraska Territory.

Perhaps he was leaving that part of the task to her. He fought and killed so that they might survive; her role was to worry and moralize and regret anything and everything she might have done to contribute to this horror. That Tanner had kidnapped her and thereby precipitated the pursuit was undeniable. But this had been no rescue attempt. If they'd meant to harm her here, the intent had no doubt existed long before now.

Then she thought of the attack on young Rebecca Godwin, and the hideousness of this night trebled. These men preyed on defenseless women. Eventually they would have caught her unprepared. Eventually they would have plotted some way. It sickened her even to think of it.

Thank God Tanner had been with her. And yet it seemed one of them had tried to kill him too. Was any of this connected?

She didn't realize how still she'd been, how small and slight and buffeted by the restless night wind she appeared. Tanner paused before her. "We've got to go, Abby."

"Yes." She nodded, still struggling with her fear. "But shouldn't we do something? Bury them . . . ?"

She saw him remove his hat and rake one long-fingered hand through his midnight-dark hair. The faint starlight glinted in those long ebony strands. Like stray bits of goodness gleaming bright from within an otherwise frighteningly dark soul.

"Do you think they would have buried us?" his harsh reply came. "They can rot here, for all I care. The buzzards and coyotes can pick them over. It's no more than the bastards deserve."

She accepted what he said, for it so accurately reflected how she felt. Terrified. Vengeful. Yet once mounted before him, encircled by the strength of his arms, held gently and securely by the same man who only minutes before had engaged in—and won—a violent struggle for life or death, she was less sure. Her old values surfaced. Someone must have cared for those men, horrible as they were. Someone must wonder when they never returned.

"They were awful," she said, whispering in the night as Mac's rolling canter carried them away from the nightmarish scene. "But everyone deserves a proper burial."

"Not everyone," he bit back in a angry voice. "Not them."

When she didn't reply, Tanner felt an undeniable relief. He didn't want to argue with her. He didn't want to defend his beliefs or justify his actions. He just wasn't up to it.

He'd killed before, and though he didn't relish the idea of taking another man's life, he'd always had good cause. It had always tempered any feelings of guilt he might feel.

But tonight . . . It wasn't that he felt guilt for killing. He'd do it again. He wished he *could* do it again and that he could prolong the bastards' agony and make them suffer more for what they'd tried to do.

That was what scared him.

What he felt wasn't as simple as self-preservation or rage, or even righteousness. His arms tightened without conscious awareness around Abby. Those men had wanted to hurt *her*. They'd wanted to hurt the purest, most perfect woman he'd ever known. His need to protect her had sprung with astonishing strength from out of nowhere.

He hadn't denied to himself that he was attracted to her. He knew she favored him too—or at least she had before she'd found out the truth about what he was up to. But this was more. This need to protect her went deeper than mere physical attraction. It was stronger than just the value she had in reward money. He'd fight for her against anyone, no matter the odds, and that scared the hell out of him.

He took a slow, steadying breath, catching the womanly scent of her, mingled now with dirt and fear and sweat.

He'd fight anyone on earth to keep her safe. Trouble was, there was someone out there—someone he didn't know—who wanted her dead. O'Hara had called her Tanner's prize. He'd known there was a reward for her return, only it was obvious he hadn't meant to take her to Chicago.

That could only mean that someone was paying to make sure she *didn't* return.

21

They rode through the now ominous night for an indeterminate distance before stopping again. This time they camped beside a year-round creek, between a pair of ancient cottonwood trees that twisted in gray-barked torment beside a scoured-out section of the streambank. They'd ridden in silence, for Abby had been too drained even to speak, and anyway Tanner had been so remote, she dared not try. But he held her tighter than before and she'd slumped gratefully against his sturdy chest.

It could not precisely be called clinging, yet when he dismounted, Abby felt as if that was exactly what she'd been doing. She needed the strong, reassuring touch of him, and she let out an unwitting cry of disappointment when it was removed.

The coldness that had gripped her ever since the confrontation with those men sent an uncontrollable shudder through her. Seeing it, he reached up to help her down. But that only made it worse, for the touch of his hands on her waist, so strong and warm and alive, sent new tremors through her, and this time they were hot.

Too many confusing feelings. Too much death. And yet so much life.

Abby drew a breath, fighting even for the air to breathe, it now seemed. But Tanner's blazing stare fed her the air and life and reassurance she needed.

"Tanner," she whispered, not meaning to impart such

a wealth of emotion in that solitary word. "Tanner," she pleaded with him, unaware she even did so.

"Don't do this," he replied, the words low and guttural. Pained even. "Don't, Abby."

But it was too late. Even had she known how to stop —or what to stop—she would have been unable. In the midst of chaos Tanner stood rock hard. Firm. In the midst of terror he brought salvation. In the midst of death he was life itself.

She leaned toward him, just a fraction of an inch, the merest shifting of her weight in his direction. He drew her the rest of the way, lifting her free of the saddle and sliding her down along his rigid length, down until they were locked together, chest to breast, belly to loins, thigh to thigh. Tanner's arm encircled her, crushing her, pressing her to him in an almost desperate embrace. Abby clung to his neck, her arms fastened around him, her fingers caught in his shoulder-length hair.

And their lips met.

Amid all the trappings of hell on earth, Abby found heaven in their kiss. It quenched a thirst that was parched for relief. It fed a hunger that consumed her soul. It filled every crack and crevice and ache in her heart. Just that clinging together, that meeting in mutual longing and need, made all that was wrong disappear. It made everything right.

But if she was starving for this—this affirmation of life, this need to affirm it only with him—he was positively ravenous. He took possession of her mouth with his lips and then with his tongue. Not tentative. Not gentle. But needy and demanding. It was what Abby wanted above all things.

His mouth slanted across hers, fitting them closer as his tongue slid between her sensitive lips in the most provocative manner. In and out he boldly stroked, causing her entire body to react each time he dipped deep, then seductively drew away. Like the telegraph lines she'd heard of, his kiss sent an urgent message skittering up and down her spine, making her skin heat, her breasts tingle, and something warm turn over deep inside her, someplace way down low.

Then he slid one of his hands down her back and over her derriere to cup her bottom and press her close, and her legs nearly melted beneath her. Fire erupted inside her, a brilliant, life-giving fire, and Tanner was at its source.

Abby gasped at the yearning pleasure of it. His long fingers curved very near the apex of her thighs. He gloried in her thighs, the blasphemous thought came to her. Like the bridegroom in Solomon's Song, he gloried in her thighs. And she gloried as well.

She clutched his head between her hands, reveling in every new sensation. The rake of his stubbled cheeks against her palms. The smell of sweat and mud and leather—and man—that was him and him alone. The firm contours of his mouth.

Emboldened, she used her tongue to explore his mouth as he'd done to her, rubbing back and forth between his lips, gasping when he sucked her tongue farther into his mouth. Back and forth, tongues and lips, they danced the ritual dance, and the fire that had seemed so hot inside her only grew with each new step.

When at last they drew a little apart, each of them gasping for breath, each of them overtaken by passion, his head fell to her shoulder and his lips found her neck and ear. He trailed hot kisses along the overly sensitive skin there, then nibbled and tugged at her ear until she was squirming against him. He thrust his hips forward in response, and it was then Abby realized that he was as affected as she—*aroused* was the term, she knew. For against her belly, hard and insistent, she felt the proof of it.

It should have frightened her, but it didn't. Instead she was filled with a heady sense of power, purely feminine and wholly new. He desired her every bit as much as she desired him. No, she desired him *and* loved him, the unbidden thought came as she reveled in the crushing pleasure of being caught between his hard arousal and his possessive hand. She loved him, but did he love her?

"Tell me to stop." The words were a hot, urgent demand in her ear. A plea, almost. "Tell me to stop before it's too late."

It is too late. She turned her head and kissed him, rubbing the entire length of herself against him in shameful repudiation of his demand. Her nipples, hard and alive as they'd never been, felt the nuances of his shirt and vest and even the ridges of his chest muscles. The soft place between her hipbones pressed against the thickness of him, pillowing his thrusting need. And her mouth demanded that he kiss her back.

Still he struggled to reason with her. "You don't know —you don't know what you're doing, Abby."

But she did. Or at least she was fairly certain she did. When he capitulated, however—a low curse and a sudden crushing embrace that lifted her off her feet and swung her around and around until she was dizzy and giddy and no longer aware of up or down, right or wrong —she wasn't certain of anything at all.

For a few moments she'd been in control, and it had been incredible. Now he took over, setting her down in a bed of sedge and foxtail barley, tossing aside his hat and stripping off his holster, vest, and shirt. Abby lay there, bereft of his warmth, scared of what she might have unleashed, yet still desperate to finally know the answer to all those secrets between a man and a woman. And to know them through Tanner.

In a moment he spread a blanket for them. Then he extended a hand to her, and in that instant she knew that the decision could still be hers. She could turn away and he still retained enough self-control to let her do so. Despite the dark of the prairie night she nevertheless could see that much in his eyes. He wanted her. His harsh breathing and smoldering gaze left her in no doubt on that score. But he wouldn't force her.

As those other men would have.

For an awful second that horror intruded. Then she reached her hand to him, and all else faded away. Tanner was a hard man. He could be violent and cruel. But he would never force her to this act. She would have to come willingly.

As he met her hand and took it into his own strong grip, she was willing.

They lay down on the blanket together beneath the two cottonwoods. The ancient pair formed an enclosure for them, a private bower that excluded the rest of the world. The wind sighed for them, cool and refreshing. Some night-hunting bird offered its mournful solitary song for them. A mosquito buzzed but then disappeared, so that for Abby there was only Tanner.

He knelt at her feet and unlaced her boots—so ordinary a task, yet made intimate beyond all understanding because he did it for her. He rolled her stockings down and then left her skirt bunched at her thighs as he lightly caressed her ankles and calves and knees.

Abby's heart pounded so violently, she feared it must surely burst right then and there. With every touch, every gentle stroke, he pitched her anticipation to new and impossible heights. A low moan came—hers? Her breathing quickened to a fast, shallow panting. She needed to breathe deep.

She couldn't breathe at all.

Then his hands disappeared beneath her skirt, slipping up along her thighs, and Abby thought she would surely faint. It was so exquisite to have him touch her there. She felt the toughness of those limber hands, and every callus on his fingers and palms as they caressed the soft, secret flesh beneath her skirts. She'd imagined these things in her private, dark wonderings. But the tiny thrills she'd felt then were nothing like this. Nothing at all.

Her eyes came open when he stopped—when had they fallen closed? As she watched, he removed his own boots and socks. Then, never taking his eyes from her, he peeled his dusty trousers down.

In the sparse light of the crescent moon and watching stars, he stood, clad only in his long drawers. Drawers much like what her father had worn. Like every man wore, she supposed. But though she'd seen such garment hanging from many a clothesline and indeed had washed her father's often enough, she'd never seen them on a man. Against the soft fabric his maleness strained, almost like something alive and apart from him, a separate something that was necessarily a mystery to all females. But she had ever been a curious student, and she was mightily curious now.

No, more than curious. She *needed* to know about such things. She needed to know or else she would surely expire from the tumultuous feelings inside her.

He freed the two buttons at the waist and with one swift movement removed the last of his clothes. Then he stood, proud and motionless at her feet, while she quite simply stared.

At the sight of his masculine nakedness Abby was positively unsettled. He was so unlike her—so unlike any woman—as to make him seem part of some other species. He was hard and lean, his body sculpted in planes and hollows that bore no resemblance to hers. Ripples of muscles patterned his stomach where she was soft and smooth. Hair made dark designs on him—dark at the chest, narrowing down his stomach. Then at his groin that bold, jutting flesh that was meant to fit within her.

Something warm and wet stirred between her legs, and she shifted restlessly. She lifted her eyes back to his shadowed face. "Shall I . . . shall I remove my dress?"

He shook his head. "Allow me."

With that simple declaration, words that a gentleman might say on any number of occasions to a lady, the most exquisite sort of torture Abby could ever imagine began. He joined her on the blanket and once more kissed her, long, slow, mind-drugging kisses that had her clutching him to her. But whenever she tried to get too near, he held her off.

"Slow down, sweetheart. Let me show you how."

With great effort she did so, lying back, breathing hard, and trying not to imagine how he'd learned what he meant to show her now. That he'd done this with another woman—or other women—didn't bear thinking about.

But Tanner swiftly drove those thoughts out of her mind, for once more his hand wandered up beneath her skirts even as his mouth trailed kisses down her neck and throat. Then his lips moved along her collarbone to her chest and the upper swells of her breasts, and Abby stopped breathing again. When had the small buttons of her blouse come undone? When had he opened her bodice to expose her chemise to his view?

Those questions, however, needed no answers, for truly she did not care. Her left arm curved around his head; her fingers tangled in his hair as his mouth moved in devastating kisses to the loosened edge of her lace-trimmed chemise. Just as surely as he roused her nipples into hard, yearning crests, anticipating the first touch of his clever lips to their aching need, so did his fingers wend their way, amid several fiery side forays, to the damp place at the juncture of her legs.

Then both goals were simultaneously attained, and Abby cried out both in relief and in a greater need. His lips caught her left nipple through the soft cotton fabric, wetting, sucking, destroying her very sanity, just as his fingers dipped inside her. She nearly came off the blanket, as if lightning had flashed from the sky to strike her, to jolt her to the absolute depths of her being. To scar her and leave her forever changed, forever marked by this one moment in time.

He sucked her breasts, evoking soft cries that Abby didn't even know she made. His fingers dipped deeper, slipping rhythmically as his tongue had done in her mouth, stroking with unbearable accuracy, burning with its heat any shred of decency that should demand that she make him stop. He stroked in a slowly building pulse, alternating the attentions of his mouth from one of her breasts to the other, and Abby began to pant in an uneven panic.

"Something . . . something . . ."

Her hands twisted the blanket into knots. Her heels dug in as she rose to meet the unholy rhythm he'd created. Then his fingers slid up to a new place and she nearly swooned with a new form of agony. His head lifted from her breasts and he watched her face with an avidity that embarrassed her.

"No," she whispered, turning her face so that he could not see. It was somehow wrong if he could see what he did to her. How he made her so wanton. How me made her so willing.

"You want me to stop?" His hand stilled, though his breathing still came fast and hard, almost as if it hurt him to breathe.

"No," Abby answered without even thinking. She looked back at him, fearful, needy. Confused.

He stroked her again, a long, sensuous slide of his finger within the damp folds of her most private place. It wrenched a hoarse groan from her throat.

"Do you like this, Abby?" he asked, low and urgent as he started up the rhythm once more. "Do you?"

She was breathing so hard, she could barely answer. But his dark, unrelenting gaze forced her to. "Don't watch me," she pleaded, knowing she bared everything to him now. "Don't . . ."

"But that's the best part," he answered, an odd note in his voice. Then his tone grew huskier still. "I want to watch you shatter under my hand."

He dipped his finger inside her, then began to rub the same place again, the place she'd not even known she possessed. "I want to watch as you find that ultimate pleasure."

That ultimate pleasure. Could there be even more

than this? Abby wondered as she met his intent gaze.
Then all rational thought shut down and she gave herself
over to him.

He kissed her, taking absolute possession of her
mouth and thrusting his tongue in and out, mirroring the
action of his hand. There *was* more. There was, she realized dimly as her body lifted and strained—and then suddenly peaked.

Like a visceral bolt of lightning, a jagged burst of
heavenly energy, it tore through her, scaring her—killing
her with its very intensity.

Abby was stunned almost senseless, blind to all but
this piercing inner turmoil, deaf to anything but the rush
of her own blood in her ears. But before she could recover, before her world stopped spinning, Tanner covered her with his body.

Her clothing somehow was gone. Where her skirt
had been his powerful thighs now lay. Where her blouse
and chemise had rested his chest now pressed. He parted
her thighs with his own, even as he once more slid his
finger inside her.

Abby stared up at him in wonder. There was more to
come? Then his freed hand curved around her cheek,
holding her for his kiss while his other hand guided the
heated length of him to where he'd touched her before.

Slowly he pushed in, stretching her, filling her until
she thought he would tear her apart. She wanted to make
him stop. He was too big. She couldn't do this.

But his kiss kept her still. His tongue delighted and
distracted her, and with every stroke of his tongue he
also stroked a little deeper into her down there. Then his
hand slid between their two sweat-slicked bodies to tease
and please that other secret place as he'd done before,
and she felt a shameful rush of moisture low inside her.
Only then was he able to slide fully inside her.

It hurt, but just a little. He lifted his face and cupped
her head with both hands now, simply resting inside her
for a long moment. It was the most intense emotional

connection that she'd ever experienced. They were physically joined together, as God intended man and woman to be joined. But Abby had never figured on the purity of such a connection. The bone-deep rightness of it.

Their gazes met and clung. He smoothed a bit of hair back from her brow as his eyes searched her face. Then he moved ever so slightly, just the merest shifting of his hips, and Abby moaned in involuntary pleasure.

"Oh, Tanner . . ."

"Tell me, Abby," he whispered as he moved again, just a little more than before. "Tell me. Do you like this?"

She nodded, scarcely able to breathe as he did it again.

"Slower? Faster?" He ran his thumb over her bottom lip, then dipped it into her mouth, wet it, and rubbed her moisture over her own lips.

"Both," she breathed, unable to be logical under such a sensual assault. She ran her hands down his side, tracing the bone and hard muscle with fleeting touches. When her hands reached his buttocks, she hesitated only a moment before sliding them there too.

At once his thrusts grew harder, and she gasped in blind pleasure. It was as if their passions each fed upon the other. She touched him and he responded, then that forced her to some new level of excitement, which in turn drew from him an even more urgent response, until it seemed they were gripped in a race. Thundering together in a great, heaving effort. Coming stroke upon stroke. Until once more that wild peak raised before her. Wilder. Higher. She could never make it—

But then she did in a frenzied burst, their sweaty bodies doing together what they could not do alone. Into a fiery heaven they leaped together. Her body shook in violent tremors. His heart thundered against hers. His big body plunged again, then once more, but less forceful.

The energy left them both, fled as fast as it had come,

leaving in its stead an incredible weakness and warmth. But it was good, too, perfect in its own right.

Tanner's head rested in the curve of her neck and shoulder. His body shuddered from his effort as he sucked in great gasps of air.

Abby's hand slid along his back, feeling the dampness, measuring in her dreamy state every breath he took. So this was what the joys of the marriage bed were. She smiled to herself as the wonder of it sank home.

No wonder they hid this truth from unmarried maidens.

22

She'd overslept.

Abby's mind came awake abruptly. The sun was well into its climb across the sky. The fire hissed low and steady, a sign it had burned awhile. Why hadn't anyone awakened her?

When she stretched, she had her answer. She was naked beneath a well-worn woolen blanket. Under her was another blanket of the same vintage, and then a bed of grass and earth. A small gasp of realization caught in her throat, and her heart quickened in panic—or was it remembered passion? She was naked. Her hair fell loose and tangled; she'd not even braided it for bed.

She closed her eyes and fought the urge to pull the blanket over her head. Bother her braid. She'd lain with a man last night in the way a woman lies only with her husband. Only he was not her husband.

She took a fortifying breath and felt the odd sensation of the coarse blanket pulling across her bare skin. Dear God, she'd truly done it now.

Only where was Tanner?

It took all her courage to open her eyes and warily glance about. She lay below the outstretched branches of two monstrous cottonwood trees. The welcome smell of coffee wafted to her from the nearby fire. Tanner had been busy, it seemed. But where was he? Then again perhaps she should consider his absence a blessing.

Acting on that thought, she sat bolt upright, snatched

up her chemise and petticoat, which lay forgotten in the grass beside her and in an instant donned them. Her blouse was next, though it sported dried wisps of last year's grasses and the silver threads of a spider's web. She had only one arm in the sleeve of that rumpled garment, however, when Tanner suddenly came into view. Upon spying him she froze in place.

He froze, too, or rather he paused for one long moment. Then with a carefully blank expression on his face he continued toward the fire, carrying water in two tin cups.

Abby could have died of humiliation. She would willingly have sunk down into the ground—all the way to China, as he'd teased her the very first time she'd met him, when he'd plucked her out of the mud. The Song of Solomon had not forewarned her. How did one handle this most awkward of moments on the morning after?

Tanner set the cups down slowly, keeping his face averted. Giving her time to dress, she belatedly realized. She jammed her other arm into the second sleeve, then hastily stepped into her skirt and pulled it up. But even her garments seemed to conspire against her, for the skirt twisted backward, and the unbuttoned ends of the blouse would not cooperate when she tried to tuck them in. Her fingers trembled to the point of complete clumsiness and her cheeks burned hot with shame.

It took forever. Eventually, however, she managed to get herself decently covered, though *decent* was a relative term, she understood when she finally looked up at him. He was decently covered too. His denim trousers and chambray shirt were just as they should be. But he was different to her now. She knew about the warm skin beneath that well-mended shirt. She'd felt the hairs on his chest against her own smoother flesh and the bunched power of his buttocks as he'd moved over her.

Her skin burned with heat to remember such things, yet Abby could not look away from him. She knew him now, in the biblical sense. And he knew her. So how were they supposed to behave toward each other?

It was the same question that had bedeviled Tanner since he'd risen at dawn.

How was he to behave toward Abby now that he'd taken her innocence? For all the women he'd bedded in the fifteen years since that very first time, not one had been a virgin. Not one had been a schoolteacher, either, he realized. Nor had any of them been churchgoers. Certainly none of them had been the sought-after daughter of the richest man in Illinois.

But when he'd awakened with her beside him, sweet and warm, fast asleep between his two blankets, he'd been hard-pressed to think of all the reasons why she should not be there. He'd remembered instead that for all her innocence, she'd been a surprisingly passionate lover.

No, not so surprising. He'd seen flashes of it before. In their brief kisses. In her temper. She'd been innocent of a man's touch, true. But she'd been more than ripe for it. But now that he'd touched—and tasted, and more— how was he supposed to treat her?

She fancied she was falling in love with him. He knew it and in too many ways he'd encouraged her. But the fact was she'd turned to him in fear last night. She'd needed comfort and he'd wanted to give it. In the light of day, however, when cool heads could prevail, their differences had never seemed greater. He was a hired killer. Women like her had no future with men like him. He knew it. Her father had known it. And Willard Hogan would know it too.

"There's coffee," he said, more curtly than he needed to.

She swallowed. He watched the convulsive workings of her smooth throat and the rapid rise and fall of her chest, all the while damning himself for a fool. First he bedded her. Now he treated her as if it had meant nothing to him.

But then, it *didn't* mean anything to him, he reminded himself. It couldn't. And it shouldn't mean anything to her either.

He gestured to the dark enameled pot propped up in the fire. "Better wash up and get something to eat. We've got to get going."

He watched her draw herself up, as if it were a painful act just to take a deep breath and straighten her back. Then she blinked and turned abruptly away from him.

Tanner nearly went after her. He was hurting her, when that was the last thing in the world he wanted to do. But going after her would only make it worse than it already was; he knew it even though he hated it. He spun away, not able to bear the stiffness in her slender back, the jerky stride as she made her way toward the stream. He strode past the fire, then slammed his fist into the trunk of one of the trees.

The sharp pain that shot from his knuckles up his arm helped. A little. Pain at least helped him face reality. Pain was a constant in everyone's life. You learned to live with it or you died.

Every woman he'd ever slept with had been a survivor. Most of them used their bodies to bargain their way through life, and if it pained them to do it, well, at least they were alive. By contrast Abby had lived a painless existence. Loved and sheltered by her parents, it wasn't until her mother had died that she'd known any pain at all. Then her father had died—just two days ago. And now she'd lost her innocence to the wrong man. He stole a glance at her. She was in pain now, but it was for the best, he told himself. She'd better get strong now, or she wouldn't survive later.

It was as simple as that.

Abby walked on bare feet to the edge of the rain-swollen creek, then followed it upstream until the scoured-out bank hid Tanner from her view. Only then did she allow a pent-up sob to escape—and then it was repressed and very small. Last night he'd made her feel

. . . *cherished* was the only word that came to mind. He'd protected her from those horrible men, then made love to her in the most thrilling and yet tender fashion imaginable. She'd known he didn't love her. But cherish her? Yes, that was it.

Now, though, he acted as if he didn't give a damn about her.

Yet what did she truly expect? He'd been manipulating her from the very first. Lying to her—or at the very least misleading her. Using her. Last night he'd just used her again.

But even she couldn't blame last night's events entirely on him. She had wanted him desperately. She still did. Oh, but she was a fool.

With steely resolve she quelled any further hint of tears. Instead she lifted her bedraggled skirts and waded straight out into the narrow, rushing stream.

The shock of the ice-cold water on her flushed skin brought a sharp gasp to her lips. But she lifted her skirts higher still, past her knees, and waded in farther.

As cold as the surging waters were, Abby was suddenly obsessed with the idea of a bath. All the warm feelings she'd felt for Tanner now seemed a bad joke. Now she just felt dirty and abandoned. And stupid. What was wrong with her that he always managed to make her behave so stupidly?

A jolt of anger prodded her to action, and with a yank she pulled her skirts over her head and tore them free. Her blouse came next, minus a button or two. But she didn't care. With one furious movement she threw both garments to the shore, then, without a second's thought, sank up to her chin in the torrent.

For a day that promised to be blisteringly hot, the water was frigid beyond all expectations. Yet Abby didn't care. She took a few short breaths, trying to get used to the freezing cold, then dunked her head.

By the time she'd scrubbed her hair, her face, and her entire body with the ragged end of her chemise, Abby was no longer so cold. Her self-esteem was marginally restored as well—or so she thought as she wrung out the drenched length of her hair. But as she sat on the grassy bank, clad only in the wet chemise, finger-combing her hair as best she could, Tanner appeared. Whatever composure she'd recovered fled at his first glance.

He held her comb and brush in one hand and a cup of coffee in the other. When he spied her, however, he stopped so fast, the coffee sloshed over the rim and onto his hand.

Abby glared at him. What difference did it make if he saw her now? she asked herself. He'd seen more. He'd seen everything—she'd made certain of that, fool that she was. She lifted her chin and gave him her coldest, most condemning stare. What further did she have to lose?

Tanner gaped for a moment, then lowered his eyes to his hand. He'd scalded his fingers with the steaming coffee. *Good*, she thought uncharitably.

"I . . . I'll leave your . . . your things here," he muttered. Before Abby could wonder why he'd followed her—and why he'd bothered to bring her hairbrush and comb from her wagon in the first place—he set everything down, spun on his heel, and strode away.

At once Abby's resolution dissolved. What in heaven's name was he trying to do to her? How could he be so charming and yet deceive her about his true purposes? How could he seduce her so passionately, then freeze her out the next morning? And now to be so thoughtful of her needs . . .

But then, that had always been his way, hadn't it? He'd kept her in a constant state of turmoil, luring her closer, then pushing her away. Then last night . . . last night she'd gotten way too close.

"Dear Father in heaven," she whispered the prayer. Then she realized what she'd said, and all her misery seemed to become compounded. God the Father was in heaven, but so was her own dear father. To whom did she make her desperate plea, her tearful confession?

Her father had warned her about Tanner, but she'd been too smart, too sassy and sure of herself, to listen. "I'm sorry, Papa," she murmured, her head bowed in desolation. Slow, hot tears leaked from beneath her eyelashes to splash on her tightly clenched fists. "I'm so sorry."

She sat that way a long while, praying. Apologizing. Resolving to learn from this terrible mistake. By the time she squared her shoulders and looked about, the trailing ends of her hair were drying, lifting in the slowly heating breeze. Her chemise, too, was dry on her shoulders and the upper swells of her breasts.

Half the morning was gone. She wouldn't have expected Tanner to allow her so much time alone.

It was probably guilt that kept him away, she decided before she could attribute any softer emotion to him. She scrambled to her knees, shook off her damp chemise as best she could, then snatched up the comb and brush. The coffee was cold by the time she had most of the knots out of her hair. But then she'd had so much cold coffee on this journey west that it almost didn't matter anymore. She drank it quickly, then braided her hair over one shoulder. Finally, her wet skirt and blouse held before her like a shield, she started back toward their meager camp. Toward Tanner.

To her surprise clean clothes were laid out for her on a blanket at the campsite. Her shoes were aligned just beside the clothes, and a plate of beans, biscuits, and jerky was perched on a flat stone. But all other signs of the camp had already been obliterated. Even the firepit had been swept away and sprinkled with dirt and dried weeds. A little way beyond her, Mac and Tulip grazed, fully loaded for travel. But where was Tanner?

He didn't make his appearance until she was fully clothed, a coincidence that gave her the uncomfortable feeling that he'd been watching her all along. But then, so what? she decided with a belligerent jut to her chin. Let him look. Looking was the closest he'd ever get to her again.

She laced up her second worn calfskin boot, refusing even to glance at him, though she was vitally aware of his every move. He led the horses nearer, then busied himself checking their girth straps while she consumed her hasty meal.

"You can drape your wet things over Tulip's pack."

Abby chewed the dry biscuit, afraid she'd never be able to swallow for the lump that rose in her throat. Why must he suddenly act so conciliatory when they both knew it was all a farce?

"I want to ride Tulip today. If her leg is strong enough," she added as an afterthought.

"It's not."

Abby stood up and threw the remainder of her biscuit on the ground. "Then I'll walk."

Finally they were looking at each other, standing ten feet apart, Abby glaring, Tanner frowning.

"You can't walk, Abby. We need to move fast today. In case someone else is following us."

She shook her head, buying time until she was sure her voice would remain steady. Both fury and utter despair battled within her, neither of which she wished to reveal to him. "If you think someone's following us, why have we lingered here so long?"

She took small satisfaction that his jaw clenched and his gaze flickered momentarily away from hers. But it quickly returned. "We shouldn't have delayed this long," he muttered. "I just thought you . . . that you might need a little extra time."

"Oh?" She lifted her chin even higher. "And when did *you* suddenly become so thoughtful?"

With a gesture she'd come to recognize, he removed his hat and whacked it against his thigh, raising a cloud of dust. "Look, Abby. I know you're mad. And you have every right to be. I know last night was a mistake. But if you're afraid to ride with me because of that—"

He broke off when she whirled away from him. She hadn't meant to react so strongly. But having him confirm his feelings was simply too much.

"I'm a fast walker," she choked out, clinging to their initial subject.

He didn't respond, and for a moment there was only the prairie quiet, wind and insects and the distant bark of a fox. Then he exhaled slowly. "You ride with me," he bit out as though he dreaded it too.

He took her wet clothes and draped them over Tulip's pack. Then he led the horses toward Abby. "Don't fight me on this," he warned.

Abby swallowed hard, then responded with a reluctant nod. In a moment his strong hands were on her waist, then he lifted her so that she could straddle Mac's wide back. Their eyes met briefly, just a furtive glance. Yet it fanned to life what had become her two greatest fears: that she could succumb to him again on the flimsiest of pretexts and, perversely, that he would never give her the chance to.

They rode until sunset with only one stop in the early afternoon. At first Abby held herself stiffly erect, trying to minimize the contact between their bodies. It was of course a hopelessly doomed task. His thighs snugged up around her derriere and upper legs. His knees bumped into the back of her legs.

She held his chest and arms at bay a little better. But every time Mac changed direction, every time they went up a low hill or down an incline, her back moved up against his chest, and his arms necessarily slid along hers.

But he didn't show by either word or action that he was the least bit perturbed by their enforced proximity, while she . . . she was dying from it. Still, when he pulled Mac to a halt beside the confluence of two muddy rivulets, he pushed himself away from her and slid down Mac's rump as if he'd been counting down the seconds to do so. He didn't even linger to help her down, though Abby was relieved at that. She was fully capable of dismounting on her own. It was facing him—meeting his piercing blue gaze—that she wasn't certain she could handle.

She swung her leg over the patient Mac's back, then held on for dear life once her feet hit the ground. She was a fast walker but an inexperienced rider. With her inner thighs burning from the unfamiliar friction and her muscles stretched in new ways, her legs were almost too weak to sustain her.

Or was it a different friction and a different sort of stretching that affected her so?

Abby pressed her lips together, stilling their sudden trembling. And she had thought Martha a hussy. Here *she* was, utterly fallen from grace, and yet still unsure whether she loved or hated the man responsible.

She pushed herself away from Mac and squared her shoulders. What was she doing, feeling sorry for herself all the time? She'd never been this way before.

She'd never lost both her parents—and her heart—before either, a forlorn little voice reminded her.

And yet she was a grown woman, not like those little children who'd lost both parents to cholera. Now, *they* had reason to feel sorry for themselves.

She retucked the front of her blouse into her waistband, then smoothed the flyaway tendrils of hair back from her brow. She was headed to Chicago with a man who saw her as no more than a bounty to be reaped—in more ways than one, it appeared. Now that he'd won the physical pursuit, however, he seemed to be regretting it, for it was bound to make their forced proximity extremely uncomfortable. The most she could do was hurry their trip along and be rid of him as soon as possible. It would be horrible while it lasted, but eventually it would end.

As for what she would find in Chicago, she would simply face that when she got there.

When Tanner returned from his heated walk—anything to distance himself from the torture of Abby's too-accessible presence all day—he found that she had started a fire, unpacked the cooking utensils, and unsaddled Mac. Her sleeves were unrolled and she had an apron on.

"Fetch water," she ordered him without even bothering to glance at him. "While I start dinner, you can tend the horses."

When he only stood there, puzzled and staring, she sent him a fulminating glare. "How many days till we get to Chicago?"

"A couple of weeks," Tanner answered automatically. A couple of long, torturous weeks of being with her every minute of the day and night.

"A couple of weeks," she repeated as if the thought was too daunting to comprehend. She picked up a length of willow wood and placed it in the fire. "Well, the sooner we get started each day, the sooner we'll get there."

It was a fact neither of them knew whether to celebrate or mourn.

23

Once before—a lifetime ago, it seemed—Abby had remarked on the routine of life on the trail. The numbing sameness. The one saving grace of that sameness had been that it had freed her imagination to soar. The dullness of her own daily tasks had allowed Tillie's adventures to unfold with many a twist and turn. Abby's little mouse had met prairie dogs and rattlesnakes, survived a buffalo stampede and ridden one wild and stormy night in an Indian brave's arrow sheath. Poor Snitch had been worn ragged keeping up with the irresponsible Tillie.

Now, however, Tillie had changed. Though Abby tried by day to imagine her furry heroine in all sorts of exciting situations—a flood, a wounded rabbit friend, a snowstorm in the Rocky Mountains—it wasn't working. Riding in front of Tanner all day, her mind imagined all sorts of things, but none of it pertained in the least to mice.

At night, across the fire from him but studiously ignoring him, Abby's mind was invariably blank. She had nothing whatsoever to write down in her paper tablet about her mouse characters.

It still confused her that Tanner would even have thought to pack her notes and paper and pencils. In fact he'd packed a surprisingly complete array of belongings for her. Personal items. Precious items.

She bent back to her tablet now, frowning at the

empty page in a vain attempt to drive Tanner and his inexplicable behavior from her mind.

Snitch. She would work on Snitch. What did Snitch want from life anyway? What were his goals and his most secret longings?

He wanted Tillie to love him of course.

Abby sighed and looked up at the horizon where the last streaks of a vivid red and gold sunset faded into the cool gray-violet of night. He wanted Tillie to love him yet he did nothing to profess his own love.

Well, did *he* love her?

Would he follow her to the ends of the earth, rescuing her whenever it proved necessary, reining in her unfettered enthusiasm for life when it threatened to turn dangerous? Of course he loved her. He just didn't know how to say the words.

So, when would Tillie ever figure it out on her own?

Sooner than Tanner ever would.

As ever, Abby's thoughts turned back toward Tanner and she practically groaned in denial. She didn't love him. She couldn't possibly.

The point of her pencil gave with a snap and the pencil tore a jagged hole in the paper.

"Need a knife to sharpen that?"

Abby peered uneasily over at him. Could he tell what she'd been thinking? Did he know just how thoroughly he'd managed to get to her?

"No," she muttered. Then after a moment's hesitation, "Well, yes."

Instead of just tossing her the bone-handled knife he wore in a sheath on the opposite leg from his handgun, Tanner stepped past the fire and squatted on his heels beside her. If he noticed that she leaned a little away from him when he reached for the pencil, he didn't indicate it. Instead, with a few deft strokes he whittled the pencil to a fine point, then handed it back to her.

But he didn't move away. He only stared at the

scarred page of her tablet as if waiting to see what she might create.

"I can't write with you watching me," she snapped, hoping her irritated tone did not betray the extreme attack of nerves his nearness had generated. They'd been in even closer proximity all day on horseback of course. For three days now. But that was a necessity, more or less. This was different.

"You writing another story about your little mouse?" he asked as if she hadn't spoken.

"I'm trying to," she replied with excessive hauteur.

He didn't respond, and for what seemed an endless time they just sat there, side by side, not speaking, though Abby felt as if his body was speaking directly—and clearly—to hers. Was he doing this on purpose?

"Look, Abby," he finally began, a note of strain evident in his low tones. "I'm sorry about . . . before."

"Before?" she asked, her mind accountably slow to comprehend. "You mean about making me go back to the States?"

He cleared his throat. "I mean about the other night."

Her face turned a hot and vivid shade of scarlet. She slammed the tablet closed. Before she could get her feet under her to rise and get away from him, however, he caught her by the arm.

"Hear me out, Abby."

If anything worse than this could happen to her, Abby could not imagine what it could be. She was trapped face-to-face with the man she was falling in love with and he was apologizing to her for ever having touched her. It was utterly humiliating and she didn't want to hear any more.

And she *wasn't* in love with him!

"I'm sorry about it, too," she muttered, trying frantically to free her arm from his hold. But he didn't relent.

"It wasn't what I intended to happen."

"Me either," she answered, though it hardly sounded

like the dismissive reply she'd hoped for. She lifted her tormented eyes to meet his serious gaze. Even in the waning light his eyes were a shade of blue she'd never be able to forget. "We don't have to talk about it," she finished in a whisper.

"You're wrong about that. What if you, well, wind up in the family way?"

It was the very last thing she'd expected him to say and somehow it made things even worse than they were. "The family way?" she repeated like a dumb child who simply did not understand. Only she feared she understood all too well. If she were pregnant, how would he ever explain this to her grandfather? If she were pregnant, would he still get his reward?

Tanner frowned. "I take full responsibility of course. I should never have let . . . things get so out of control."

Abby couldn't bear to hear another word. With a sharp cry she tore her arm from his hold, then scrambled to her feet. She was unmindful of her pencils or tablets or that her skirt caught and then tore on a spiky stalk of soapweed.

"You can just . . . just go to hell, Tanner McKnight!" she shouted as she backed away from him. "Just go straight to hell!"

"Dammit, I'm trying to apologize, Abby." He stood up and started slowly toward her. "I didn't set out to . . . seduce you."

"Oh, no?" She grabbed at the chance to blame it all on him. It made it easier than acknowledging her own role in this mess.

He stopped three paces away and just stared at her. The fire gilded his left side in red and gold. The other side lay in darkness. He seemed taller than ever, and more dangerous, too. With his expression lost in the contrast she had nothing to go on but her own confused emotions—her yearning for him and her terror that he'd been using her all along.

"I didn't know you were the one I was looking for. In

the beginning . . . in the beginning I was attracted to you. If I misled you, well, I'm sorry. But once I found out you were who you are, I kept my distance. Or at least I tried."

Abby raised her chin and tried to breathe slowly, regularly. He was attracted to her until he found out her true identity. Could this be true? Could she trust him?

"If that's so," she began in a carefully controlled voice, "why should things be any different now that you know my real name?"

It was Tanner's turn to look uncomfortable. "You're Willard Hogan's granddaughter," he replied as if that should explain everything.

"That doesn't mean a thing to me."

"Well, it should. And it will once you meet him."

"He's not going to run my life," Abby countered. "I've had enough of other people trying to run my life. My father. You."

He nodded slightly, almost apologetically, then took a step nearer her. "If I could have convinced you to go back without kidnapping you, I would have."

Around them the twilight gathered, soft and cool. Abby stared at Tanner. He was just an arm's length away, close enough to touch. When he spoke so directly to her, so honestly, it seemed the connection between them could grow stronger and stronger. If he would just let it.

"Tanner." His name came out like a sigh, like a fervent wish, although she did not realize it.

He responded with a frown. "Don't, Abby. Don't make things worse than they already are. You don't realize how different your life in Chicago is going to be."

"I don't want to live in Chicago."

"You don't know what kind of man I am, then."

Abby pressed her lips together, not sure how her anger had turned around so swiftly—not sure she wasn't trying to seduce him. Oh, when had she abandoned her moral upbringing?

"I *do* know what kind of man you are. You saved my life—not once, but twice."

He laughed, a short, unpleasant sound that held no hint of mirth. "I was protecting my investment, Abby. Nothing more."

"Not the first time. Not when Carl and I were surrounded by those snakes."

He looked away from her and she saw his chest rise then fall in a slow sigh. "I was trying to impress a pretty woman. Nothing more, nothing less."

He was being deliberately evasive, and Abby couldn't bear it. "Why are you doing this?" she cried in complete frustration.

He swore fluently. "Because somebody's got to be sensible, and you're sure as hell not doing it!" His fists clenched, then relaxed, and he ran both hands through his hair.

"Listen, Abby. You're making me into some kind of hero. But I'm not. I'm a bounty hunter. I hunt down people for money. I'm not educated like you and I never read the classics."

"But you knew about Venus," Abby countered, not wanting the things he said to be true.

"A story I heard during the two years I more or less went to school. I use it as a line with women. It always works," he added pointedly. When her face fell in disappointment, he pressed on. "My mother was a prostitute, Abby. A whore. I grew up watching a stream of men go in and out of her bed. But it gets better," he said, advancing on her as he warmed to his story. "One of them killed her when I was fourteen. So I killed *him*. And I've killed other men too."

He smiled, a cold grimace that made him a stranger to her, a man she didn't know and shouldn't want to. "Your father was right about me all along. You should have listened to him while you had the chance."

He reached out a hand to tilt her chin up, and Abby flinched at the gesture. His smile changed then, and for an instant she was certain she saw regret—and sorrow. He didn't want her to be afraid of him, even though he was doing everything he could to scare some sense into her.

That realization, coupled with the power of his simple, seemingly impersonal touch, chased away all that fear and uncertainty. In that moment she knew he was afraid of his feelings, too, and uncertain about her.

Without weighing the consequences she stepped inside the curve of his arm and pressed up against him. Her arms slipped around his waist and she stared straight up into his shocked and wary eyes.

For one long second he went completely still. His hand had slid to her cheek when she'd moved near, and he cupped her face now with surprising tenderness. Then he let out a pained groan, and any tenderness was swept away by the violence of his embrace. He crushed her against him like a wild man, clutching at her, devouring her with his hands and then with his mouth. Their lips came together in a crescendo of emotions, and Abby let herself be swept along in the overwhelming tide. It was terrifying and wonderful, desperate and thrilling. He forced her mouth open, then took swift possession with his tongue, searing her inner lips with his bold thrust, demanding that she grant him every right, every privilege.

But Abby wanted as much from him. She accepted his need to dominate her in that moment, yet found a way to conquer him by her very submission. She coaxed him to greater liberties, to a hotter fire. She curled her fingers in his hair and held him remorselessly. Then she rubbed her breasts against him, meeting the urgent pressure of his loins with her own softness.

When they broke apart, gasping for breath, she knew a sweet victory, a delicious sense of power that made being a woman the most glorious thing she could ever hope to be.

But her victory was short-lived. Their eyes met in

complete concert, then in a blink he seemed to come awake. As if he'd let himself dream for an instant, then abruptly come back to reality.

"Son of a bitch!"

He thrust her back from him, holding her a stiff, unyielding arm's length away. He struggled for breath and for words. "Don't ever do that again, woman. Do you understand me? Never!"

Abby shook her head, not willing to back down when she was so close to breaking through to him. "I want you, Tanner McKnight. And you want me, too."

He let go of her as if she were on fire, and backed up with a haste that would have been laughable if it weren't so heartbreakingly sad.

"Forget it, Abby. You and me—" He broke off, shaking his head vehemently. "Christ, what an ass I've been."

Abby hugged her arms across her chest. She was taking a huge chance, assuming Tanner could care for her as she cared for him. But if she didn't try, she'd never know. Still, she was charting new territory, lost in a strange landscape with love as her new and perhaps unreliable guide.

Ignoring her galloping heartbeat, she took a shaky breath. "The thing is, I love you."

The night seemed to rise up around them in the silent aftermath of her words. The dark seeped up like a fog overtaking the land, chilling the world. And as the silence lengthened, it chilled her too.

"You don't love me," he countered in a flat tone that revealed nothing. His eyes, too, hid whatever he really felt. "You've felt a passion for me. Desire. But neither of those has anything to do with love." Then he turned away, and that more than what he'd said struck her as cruelly as a mortal blow.

"Perhaps you feel that way. Perhaps you can do what . . . what we did with any woman who makes herself available to you. But I couldn't. I could never make love with a man I did not love."

He turned his head, just enough to see her, to see all her emotions laid open for him to examine and weigh and reject. The last of her pride was stripped from her. The last of her self-respect. Yet she clung still to the touch of his eyes on her in the hope—the desperate hope —that he would take back everything he'd said and profess his love, just as she had done.

His jaw flexed once, then again beneath the shadow of two days' stubble of beard. "You don't love me, Abby. Once you're in Chicago, you'll realize it's true. It wasn't love at all, just lust."

24

"You ride on Tulip."

It was the first words he'd spoken to her since their disastrous confrontation the night before, and it fell like one more lethal blow to her heart. But you couldn't kill something—or someone—that was already dead, Abby decided grimly.

She didn't respond to him, just swiftly finished plaiting her hair, then jammed her battered straw hat on her head. Her stomach knotted, then turned over. He hadn't protested when she'd not prepared breakfast. He'd eaten a handful of crackers, stuffed a length of jerky into one of his pockets, and drank two cups of cold coffee. But Abby had been unable to eat. Now she watched as he reapportioned their supplies between the two patient animals. Though she was relieved that she would not have to ride with him any longer, she was nonetheless infuriated to be once again rejected.

She refused to help him in any aspect of this forced journey. On principle. But she kept a close eye on him, and once he finished with Tulip and turned toward Mac, she shoved her comb and brush into her small carpetbag and slung it over the saddle horn. Then without waiting for his assistance, she half jumped, half dragged herself up onto the saddle and fumbled to fit her feet into the stirrups.

She'd never ridden much, at least not until the past couple of days. But between her newly acquired experi-

ence and her determination to show Tanner up, there
was no room left for fear. With reins in hand she gave
Tulip an experimental kick, and they were suddenly under way.

"What the hell—"

She heard Tanner's irritated oath with a certain satisfaction and she leaned forward more confidently. What
did he have to be irritated about anyway? She was heading east, wasn't she? It wasn't as if she were fleeing back
to the wagon train on his horse. Not that she wouldn't be
justified in doing so. But there no longer seemed any
reason for her to head for Oregon. She was going to
Chicago. She would hear what her mother's father had to
say. But from now on she was going to chart her own
course. Be her own woman. She would become a writer
and follow her own muse no matter what anyone else
wanted her to do.

Tulip headed down the long slope of a hill, ambling
with hardly any limp through a sea of dock and sedge
grass. Behind her, Abby could hear Mac's snort, then the
thud of the bigger animal following at a canter.

She had decided during the long, sleepless night that
the sooner she got to Chicago, the sooner she'd be rid of
Tanner—and the constant reminder of what a fool she'd
made of herself. She'd wept copious tears of self-pity,
then plotted myriad vengeful plans to get even with him.
In the end, however, she'd had to admit, if only to herself, that the loss of her virginity and the breaking of her
heart were both, in their own perverse ways, rather liber-
ating events. What did she have to fear now? She was
ruined both for marriage and for love.

"Don't ride off without me again."

Abby ignored his angry order when he drew up beside
her. She planned to ignore him all the way to Chicago.
But she didn't intend to let him ignore her. Oh, no. Let
him rant and rave and order her about all he wanted. She
would make him very sorry he'd ever thrown her love for

him back in her face. She wasn't sure quite how she was going to do it yet. But she knew she would.

They made good time, keeping a steady pace through the morning until the sun was a hot, hazy ball standing straight overhead. A constant breeze out of the northwest kept them reasonably cool, and at least here, away from the well-traveled trail, there was no dust. Even her legs were not as tired as they had been the past two days. Tulip was a smaller horse than Mac and easier for Abby to ride astride.

Still she was more than ready for a break when they spied the green outline of trees snaking through the otherwise treeless sea of tall grasses. A sure sign of water and shade.

She urged Tulip ahead, though the little mare was more than eager once she scented water. By the time Tanner rode into the dappled copse of box elder and ash, Abby had dismounted and was removing her heavy pegged boots. She flung her hat aside, rolled her sleeves up, then boldly hitched the back of her calico skirt up between her legs and tucked it securely into the front of her waistband. Then still ignoring Tanner, she waded up to her knees in the shallow waters of the lively creek.

It felt divine. If she could have stripped down to nothing and plunged fully into the refreshing water, she would gladly have done so.

And how would Tanner react to that, she wondered bitterly. She sent him a sidelong glance, then froze when she found his gaze fastened intently upon her. She looked away at once, but goose bumps rose up on her arms and legs. From the chill of the stream, she preferred to believe, but she could not wholly convince herself.

Nonetheless she was heartened to know that desire at least still burned in him. That one night had not exhausted it for him either. It scared her to think of the consequences should she try further to entice him. But then, what precisely did she have to lose?

As if totally unaware of his proximity, she lifted her

skirt above one of her knees and with her other hand cupped water to trickle on the warm flesh she'd just exposed. She did the same with the other leg, boldly displaying her anatomy in the most shameful yet exhilarating manner imaginable. She was both refreshed and overheated by what she did. But how was Tanner reacting to it?

She dared a peek at him when she bent down to splash her arms, only to be frustrated anew. He'd turned away. In the same way he'd ignored her all day, he acted as if she were not even there.

She sent his broad back a venomous glare, but he was unaffected. He only lifted one set of saddlebags from Mac, then squatted down to remove a tin of crackers from the bag.

"Jerusalem," she swore, then nearly lost her footing in the uncertain creek bottom.

Tanner heard her softly muttered curse, but it hardly eased his mind. It only meant that the seductive pose she'd struck wasn't an accident. She'd meant to draw his eye with the exposure of her legs and knees. She'd meant to arouse his lust. And dammit, the little minx had succeeded.

Hell, but he'd opened up a hornet's next when he'd seduced the very prim Miss Abigail Bliss. A Pandora's box, he decided, remembering another of those mythological stories he'd listened to so avidly all those years ago. He'd opened the closed door to her natural sensuality and now he was going to have to pay the price. Almost two weeks of travel ahead of them and he would need to be on his guard the entire time.

He shut his eyes and took a long, cooling breath. God help him, but he would stay away from her if it killed him.

Unable to prevent himself from looking at her, however, he stole a sidelong peek. She was standing now, shaking her hands dry as she clambered up the sloping streambank. Water had trickled down her throat and upper chest to dampen her bodice and her breasts thrust high and firm against the cloth. The skirt, wet at the ends, hung heavy, showing the gently rounded shape of her hips and thighs.

He closed his eyes in utter frustration and barely stifled a groan. This was going to be the longest two weeks of his life.

Without a doubt this had been the longest two weeks of Abby's life. And definitely the most frustrating. Tanner McKnight was just as her father had said, a cold, hard man who was motivated only by greed. In this case monetary greed. He was also amazingly adept with his weapons, which figured since that was how he made his way in the world. He picked off rabbits with an ease that even she recognized, and they'd eaten fairly well. No doubt that was one of the first requirements of being a bounty hunter: hunting game just as well as you hunted your human quarry.

Despite her bitter analysis of him, however, she was honest enough to admit that he was also the same man who'd charmed her with his references to Venus and his interest in Tillie and Snitch. Though he'd been working hard to keep that side of himself hidden lately, it still surfaced every now and again.

She looked over at him from her perch on one of the saddles that lay now on one side of the fire. She could make out only his silhouette against the fading western sky. Every night while she loosened her hair, combed it out, and rebraided it for sleep, he tended the horses, checking their feet and untangling their manes and tails. And he always sang to them.

Actually he hummed to them, or whistled softly between his teeth. Whatever, it was unexpected and intriguing and utterly beguiling. She didn't think he even realized he did it, though, so she was careful not to comment on it for fear he would stop.

Some evenings the songs were slow and somber.

Mournful. Other times he preferred jaunty little melodies with no words but that were nevertheless memorable.

Tonight he seemed more animated than usual. Ever since they'd topped a low hill and descended into this valley, he'd seemed different—almost excited—as if this place was a destination and not just one more camping spot. But that was probably just because they were nearing their ultimate destination.

Abby frowned at the thought. By tomorrow evening they'd reach the Mississippi River. Once they crossed into Illinois, they'd be but another day to Chicago. The train lines were complete, Tanner had informed her in one of their typically abbreviated conversations. He planned to board his horses in Burlington while he completed his task and delivered her to her grandfather.

Then he'd disappear from her life forever.

She blinked back the sudden sting of tears. How long would she sustain this foolish hope that she could make him change?

"You're in an awfully good mood," she muttered, just loud enough for him to hear. The whistling stopped at once, but that only made her feel worse. Why was she being so dense about him? Why couldn't she accept him for what he was and go on with her life?

"It's a nice night," his noncommittal reply came back through the shadows. "And this is a nice little valley," he added, an odd note in his voice.

Once more Abby was struck by his optimistic, almost hopeful mood. She swallowed a sad sigh and with it, her ill temper. "It's as pretty a spot as I've ever seen," she conceded, for it was. The treeless plains of the Nebraska Territory had slowly given way to the gentle hills and more varied terrain of Iowa. He'd decided to stop earlier than usual today, not that she minded. They'd camped in this delightful valley beside a wide, shallow stream. Oaks and hickory and maple trees dotted the open meadows.

Birds sang and she'd spied squirrels, rabbits, and even deer.

"Yes, it is a pretty spot," Tanner echoed. "It'll make a nice home for some family someday."

"It makes me wonder why people want to emigrate to Oregon when such beautiful land is available," she answered, wanting to continue their conversation. And it was true. Though she was no farmer's daughter, she still knew enough to recognize fine land. Whether a person chose to farm or raise stock, this valley would provide well for anyone willing to work.

"The Donation Act is what draws people to the Oregon Territory," Tanner replied. "In Missouri and Iowa land like this costs money."

Abby stared in his direction, aware that while she could hardly make him out, she was probably visible to him in the last of the campfire's light. Was he even looking at her? Did he know—or care—that she could forgive him everything. She would go anywhere with him, live anyplace he wanted if he would just—

Just what?

Without pausing to think, she rose to her feet, unaware that she clutched the hairbrush as if it gave her strength. She picked her way barefoot through the soft grass and moss growing beneath the canopy of trees and stopped at Tulip's head. The mare bumped Abby's arm in a friendly fashion. They'd become fast friends on the trail. But though Abby obligingly scratched Tulip's chin, she had eyes only for Tanner. He, however, concentrated on the horse.

Abby forced herself to speak. "What will you do after? After you leave Chicago?"

He shifted slightly and smoothed a hand along the slope of Tulip's back and side. "That's hard to say."

She bit the inside of her cheek. "Will you take another job? You know, go find somebody else?"

"You mean hunt them down for the bounty of their head?"

Abby cringed at the ugliness of his description. Once again he was being truthful and she hated it.

"Yes," she snapped. "Are you going to hunt someone else down? Maybe even for my grandfather?"

He moved to the other side of Tulip. "No. I don't think so."

She didn't know whether his answer should please her or not. "Should I assume that the reward on my head is so high that you won't need any more money?" she asked sarcastically.

He looked straight at her then. "Listen, Abby. You can't hold this against your grandfather. You can't blame him for using his money to find you. You're the only family he has left."

"I *don't* hold it against him!" she burst out. "I hold it against *you!*"

The air suddenly seemed charged with tension. Anger, resentment, fear. Yearning. Abby didn't know which emotion was the worst.

Even Tanner was not able to completely hide the quick surprise that painted his features. Then his brows lowered, and whatever he felt was hidden by his slight frown. "That's probably for the best."

"I'm not asking for your blessing!" she shouted as the last of her self-control shredded.

"Then what the hell *do* you want?" he snapped.

For one long, horrible second they glared at each other. What did she want? For him to love her and want a future with her. But even as the answer formed in her head, he seemed to sense it. With a sharp motion of his hand he silenced her before she could speak.

"There's only one thing between us, Abby. I was a fool before and I'm sorry. But if you're with child . . ."

He let the words trail off, but she knew what he was offering. If she were with child, he'd own up to it. Take responsibility for it. Probably even marry her, if she wanted it and her grandfather approved.

It was one way to keep him, she realized. But not the way she wanted.

She spun on her heel, swallowing a sob though it threatened to choke her. But Tanner ducked around the horse and caught Abby by the arm.

"Is there a chance you could be?" he asked, the words low and urgent.

She tried to shrug off his grasp to no avail.

"Answer me."

"I don't know," she muttered, struggling to keep the misery out of her voice.

His taut grip loosened a little at that, and she took swift advantage of it. But putting some distance between them didn't really help her at all. What if she *was* carrying his child? During the long weeks of travel her monthly cycle had become irregular—not an uncommon occurrence, she'd been given to understand by some of the other women. Was that all it was? Or could it be more?

She knelt down on the bedroll she'd already spread out. As always, Tanner's lay on the opposite side of the fire. But though she tried to find solace in the comforting routine of prayer, it was a futile effort. What was she to pray for? To be pregnant or not? To be well rid of Tanner, or to have a way to cling to him?

She shouldn't pray for anything, she told herself. She should just beg God's guidance and ask that he lead her to the right path.

But Abby was fresh out of prayers. She lay down on the soft blanket, tucking her feet beneath a fold as she stared up into the night. Like the hero of a book she'd once read, she knew she was tilting at windmills, chasing after something she could never have.

Above her the arcing leaves of a hickory tree swayed in the night breeze. An owl hooted, and somewhere beyond her head some small creature scuttled about, seeking a safe hiding place from the night-hunting owl, she supposed.

Snitch hated owls almost as much as he hated cats. Tillie would like this place, though. She'd be happy to live in a house built in a little valley just like this. Abby would be content here, too, she admitted to herself. If Tanner were here as well.

She closed her eyes and curled onto her side. Why did she persist in torturing herself this way? Her destiny lay in Chicago now, not in a valley out in the middle of nowhere.

Tanner sat a long time at the dying fire, staring across the starlit meadow, down toward the stream. What had ever possessed him to bring Abby here? He'd worked long and hard to get the money to buy this land. His land now. With a lot more work he'd eventually fill it with the finest horseflesh available. He'd build a little house—and a big barn. Those were dreams that had sustained him for years.

But now that he'd brought Abby here . . . Now those dreams fell flat. He'd never be able to come here without remembering her. Without imagining her as part of his dream.

And the thing of it was, if he asked her, he knew she'd stay. She'd be happy to be a rancher's wife in some un-named valley. Only he couldn't do that to her.

Abby was going to be rich soon, so rich that she could buy and sell a hundred valleys like this one. A thousand. It wouldn't be right to let her make the wrong decision now.

He drew a long, weary breath and tossed a twist of grass into the wind. No, Abby wasn't a part of his dream. Never was, never could be. Better to accept that truth, bitter though it might be, than to torture himself with what might be, but never would.

25

They crossed the Mississippi River on an ungainly-looking ferry. It floated so low in the water that Abby was certain it would founder. Tanner stayed with the horses, reassuring them during the crossing, while they rolled their eyes at the unsteady footing and the rushing water.

Abby needed reassuring, too, though not because of the water. If they should sink, she could swim. It was her future that she feared. But Tanner was hardly the one to set her mind at ease. So she stood alone at the stern, staring back at the shrinking Iowa shoreline.

Perhaps she should have gone on to Oregon after all. Then she shook her head. Tanner would have stopped her. And anyway going west had not been her goal but her father's. The truth was, she'd never really had any goals to speak of—other than to become a writer. Where she would write hadn't mattered to her; she'd never even thought about the possibility of leaving Lebanon. Now, however, she was heading toward Chicago, one of the fastest-growing cities in the country. And all she could do was stare back to the west.

The ferry edged toward a rickety-looking dock. The skinny ferryman tossed a rope deftly to someone waiting on the dock, then extended a plank walk to bridge the short space. Before she was ready, Tanner approached, leading the horses and urging her on as well.

"We'll get hotel rooms," he told her. "You can relax

there—take a bath or whatever—while I board the animals."

That was pretty much the sum total of their conversation for the next hour. No elaboration. No indication how he felt about their journey nearing its end. He checked them into a three-story wood-frame hotel that was so recently completed, it still smelled new. But the whole town looked like that. Construction went on everywhere. All due to the new railroad line, she understood. The railroad that connected Burlington to Chicago.

"Lock the door while I'm gone," Tanner said as he sat her bag on a table in the sparsely furnished room. "I'll only be gone a short while."

"Where's your room?" She didn't look at him but at the plump bed with its iron and brass fittings.

"Here." He opened a door that connected to another room very like her own. After tossing his saddlebags on the floor in there he turned to face her.

"When I get back we need to go shopping. Get you some new clothes. A hat." He fingered the brim of his own hat, which dangled from his hands. "You'll want to dress up some to meet your grandfather tomorrow."

Abby sent him a bitter look. "Why? So he won't notice my broken nails and sunburned cheeks?" She laughed at the irony. "If he wanted a lily-white debutante, perhaps you should have brought someone else back to him. I'm not lily-white anymore." *In more ways than one*, she silently added.

Tanner took a step nearer, crossing the threshold from his room into hers. "Your grandfather isn't going to be put off by your sunburn, or by the condition of your fingernails, Abby. Believe me. He doesn't care about anything except finding you. You're a beautiful woman. Beautiful," he added more quietly. Then he cleared his throat. "But that has nothing to do with anything. He won't care how you look, so long as you're with him."

The pulse had started to race in Abby's throat and she

could feel color creeping into her cheeks. He thought she was beautiful. "Why . . . why do you want me to get a new dress, then?"

He shrugged. "I thought you might like it."

There it was again, that considerate side of him that got to her every time. But before she could respond, he shut the door to his room and strode over to the hall door.

"Don't open this to anyone but me. There're a lot of rough characters in town, though this hotel should be pretty safe. I'll be back within the hour."

Then he was gone, and Abby was left more unsettled than ever. She wanted to hate him. It would be so much easier if she did. But he made it impossible. Just one generous gesture, just one compliment—even a grudging one—and she was dissolving in emotions she knew she'd later regret.

"Jerusalem," she muttered as she unlatched her battered carpetbag and drew out her clothes. And what a tattered lot they were. Two blouses, two skirts, stockings that should have been thrown away long ago. An extra petticoat that would never be white again.

What was the point of cleaning up if this was all she had to wear?

Yet clean up she did. She bathed using the water in the pitcher and bowl provided, and brushed her hair out. She took more care than she had in a long time to put it up. Yet once she was finished and awaiting Tanner's return, she knew she only looked like a shabby emigrant woman with a rather elaborate coiffure, given the poor condition of the rest of her outfit.

Still, what did it really matter? She wasn't trying to impress anyone—especially not Tanner and her grandfather. Yet when she heard Tanner's footsteps in the adjacent room, she knew that wasn't entirely true. She'd do anything to impress Tanner, to draw him to her. To keep him. Only she had no idea how to accomplish that.

He knocked, then entered at her subdued response.

"Ready?"

Abby nodded but didn't face him. Instead she stared into the dresser mirror and positioned the only bonnet she had left, tying the slightly frayed ribbons beneath her chin. She picked up her reticule and moved toward the door. Easier not to talk. Easier simply to get this entire venture over with.

Burlington had two dressmakers' shops, but Tanner led her to a large general store instead. Abby had never bought a ready-made dress. She and her mother had sewn all their own clothes. Only their shoes had come ready-made. Being faced now with so many choices was a little daunting.

"This brown and white calico is very practical," the shopkeeper's wife said, urging Abby to feel the skirt. "It's sturdy fabric and very well made."

"She needs something finer," Tanner put in before Abby could reply. "We're heading for Chicago."

"Oh. A city dress. Well, why didn't you say so?" The little woman's brows lifted and she deftly steered them down the narrow aisle. "Here. You'll find these far more appropriate for town."

When she held out a beautiful apple-green-and-cream outfit, Abby couldn't help giving Tanner a doubtful glance. "They're awfully dear," she murmured for his ears only when she spied the price. Twelve dollars! She could buy fabric for half a dozen dresses for that price. But the woman overheard her remark.

"We have others not quite so costly. This pretty pink dress. This mauve-sprigged walking dress."

"I like the first one," Tanner said, fingering the rich sateen of the green dress. He studied Abby a moment. "It's the same color as your eyes."

The woman agreed enthusiastically, but Abby swiftly looked away. She knew her cheeks already flooded with color. Why must he say things like that? Why had he come in with her at all? He could just as easily have claimed one of the chairs out front on the boardwalk and waited for her to shop.

"Shall you try it on, madam?"

Abby squared her shoulders, then faced the expectant woman. "Yes, that will be fine."

"And bring her whatever accessories she might need. A hat. Gloves. And the rest." Thankfully Tanner did not go into further detail, or Abby would have been completely mortified. Bad enough that she was shopping with a man unrelated to her. Discussing undergarments would be unthinkable.

"Your wife is going to look breathtaking in this," the shopkeeper assured Tanner as she bustled off to assemble the rest of what was needed. "Simply breathtaking."

His wife. Inside, Abby cringed, but if Tanner was concerned by the woman's mistake, he didn't give any indication. To cover her own nervousness, Abby whispered, "I can't afford all this."

"I can," came his whispered reply.

"No. I don't want—"

"Your grandfather will reimburse me." He took her arm and steered her toward the back of the store, where the woman awaited them. "And his money will soon be your money," he added more curtly. "The fact is, Abby, you can afford to buy anything you want. This whole damn store, if you take a notion to it."

He waited outside while the shopkeeper helped Abby change. Abby went through the motions: donning the featherlight chemise; holding her arms out while the woman tightened the latest style of corsets around her; stepping into the several layers of petticoats, then lifting her arms to allow the dress to be slipped over her head. She twisted and turned as instructed, but all the while she worried over Tanner's last remark.

He was angry at her, that much was obvious. He was angry, and she figured it was because her grandfather was wealthy and therefore she soon would be wealthy too.

But that wasn't her fault. If anything, it was Tanner's

fault. He was the one who'd tracked her down and then dragged her off against her will. What right had *he* to be angry with her?

"Don't you like it, madam?"

Abby glanced at the waiting woman and, when she spied her concerned expression, realized that she must have been scowling. Pasting on a more pleasant expression, she swiftly turned her gaze toward the tall tailor's mirror in the corner, then couldn't disguise her shock. She looked . . . she looked better than she'd ever looked before. Something about the bright green color, one she'd never worn.

The shopkeeper must have sensed Abby's changed mood, for she stepped forward, beaming proudly. She tugged at the left side of the skirt and straightened a ruffle on one of the wrists. "A fine choice, if I do say so myself. Your husband will surely be pleased when he sees you."

Would he? Abby wondered, ignoring the fact that he wasn't her husband at all. Would Tanner be pleased by what he saw? "Yes, a very fine choice," she agreed.

Abby walked out of the store wearing the green dress. She was as heartsore as ever, but she certainly felt a lot more self-confidence than before. Tanner followed after settling the bill. Her other purchases—a traveling costume, a nightgown, a pair of kid-leather shoes, two pairs of stockings, and more—and a trunk to hold them all would be delivered to the hotel later. Meanwhile they were to have dinner, and she would test her newfound confidence upon his wary defenses.

His eyes had widened when she'd first walked out of the dressing room into the crowded store. His eyes had widened, and for one long, wonderful moment all his emotions had been laid bare for her to see. He'd actually been struck dumb. He'd stared without saying a word, just looking at her—drinking her in, it had felt to her. Only the shopkeeper's smug interruption had brought him back in focus. The woman had boasted about the quality and the value and the stylishness of the goods Abby had purchased, and he'd turned abruptly away from Abby.

But that was all right, she thought now, taking in a deep breath of warm evening air. That was all right. He'd been impressed by how she had looked, and that was all she needed to know. It occurred to her that they had the rest of the evening to spend together, then the train ride to Chicago. Did she dare try one more time to break through his damnable control?

The fact that she was actually plotting to seduce him should have shocked her more. But Abby was past that. She was not the same girl who'd left Lebanon just a few short months ago. She was on her own now. The direction of her life was in *her* hands—no matter *what* her grandfather and Tanner thought. It was up to her to get what she wanted, and whether it was foolish or not, she wanted Tanner.

They moved down the boardwalk side by side, not touching. When they neared a group of men outside a saloon, however, he took her elbow, guiding her—claiming her, she preferred to think when several of the men turned to look at her and tipped their hats.

"The restaurant's just a little farther," Tanner murmured once they were past the cluster of men. But he kept his hand on her arm, and Abby felt a surge of hope. If he was affected by their slight touch only half as much as she, her plan was well on its way to working, for she found herself hardly able to breathe.

At the entrance to McDowell's Restaurant he moved his hand to her waist, and for a moment a wave of light-headedness washed over her. Nothing she'd ever read in any novel had prepared her for the impact of even the lightest and most impersonal of Tanner's touches. The fanciful thought occurred to her that if she could but impart this giddy feeling in words to readers, she could assure herself a place in literary history. Not a woman alive would be able to resist this delicious, sinking feeling.

Tanner's thoughts were not very unlike Abby's as he seated her at a corner table. If he made it through this evening in one piece, it would be a miracle. He ordered a whiskey even before the waiter could point out the menu on the chalkboard near the door. But Tanner had no interest in food. He needed a drink and he needed to get Abby locked into her own room—with a damned strong door between the two of them.

"I'm famished," she said, smiling across the small table at him. "How about you?"

He hung his hat on a brass two-prong hook just above his head. "I can eat," he retorted, staring intently at the chalkboard menu.

"I hope you're not in a big rush," she continued, her voice soft and musical. "It's been so long since I could linger over a meal—a meal I didn't have to prepare," she added, smiling straight into his eyes.

Tanner swallowed and shifted his gaze to the fork and knife that lay before him. Gone were her remoteness and anger. One shopping trip and already she was smiling and happy. She pulled off the wrist-length butter-soft gloves she'd purchased, and despite himself he watched every movement of her hands. She was the most desirable woman he'd ever known, and now in that green dress she was only more so.

His eyes reluctantly returned to her face. Her eyes sparkled, warm and inviting. Her cheeks glowed with healthy color. Her dark hair glinted with golden lights in the lamplight, and in that moment he would have given every penny of his reward, and then some, for the chance to let that thick, shining mass of hair down. To slowly, slowly strip that silky green dress off her shoulders and slide it down past her hips—

The waiter placed the whiskey before him, and without thinking Tanner lifted the glass and downed it in one stinging gulp. The waiter raised his brows slightly, but he swiftly went back for a refill when Tanner wordlessly thrust the empty glass back at him.

Abby, to her credit, pretended not to notice. She was, after all, raised to be a lady, he reminded himself. Not like all the other women he'd known in his life.

He took a slow breath, then exhaled, willing himself to be calm, willing the whiskey to deaden the feelings she aroused in him. God help that waiter if he didn't get here fast with that refill.

"What time does the train depart tomorrow?" Abby asked.

"Six-thirty."

"And how long will the trip take?" she prompted when he did not elaborate.

"We should arrive about five-fifteen in the evening."

He drummed his fingers restlessly on the table. Maybe she would get mad once she realized this wasn't going to be a chatty meal. If she would just keep quiet, he could get himself under control.

But Abby seemed determined to talk, for she leaned forward, just enough for him to notice the thrust of her firm young breasts against the shimmering fabric of her bodice. "Does my grandfather know we're arriving tomorrow?"

Tanner stared at her breasts and felt his body begin to react. Son of a bitch! Why had he bought her that dress?

"I wired him before I boarded the horses," he muttered in a strained voice.

"I see." She stared down at the table and ran one of her fingers back and forth along the edge of the striped cotton tablecloth. "Did he . . . did he have any message for me?"

Senseless as it was, that one hesitant question got to him more than anything else could have. Willard Hogan hadn't sent a message to his only grandchild. His office had received the message and wired back a message that Tanner knew Hogan ordered: IT'S ABOUT TIME. But noth-

ing in the way of welcome for a frightened young
woman.

He cleared his throat. "He said, 'Welcome to the
family,' and that he was looking forward to meeting
you.'"

The waiter returned then, and while Abby ordered,
Tanner downed the second whiskey, albeit a little more
discreetly than the first. He shouldn't have to cover up
for the other man's thoughtlessness, yet Tanner was glad
he'd done it, for a faint but undeniable expression of
relief had flitted across her face before she'd turned to
the waiter.

She was scared, pure and simple. As much as Hogan
had to offer Abby, he was still a stranger to her. And
given the hard-bitten businessman's curt manners and
abrupt style, it was unlikely his welcome would be a
warm one. At least not warm in the way Abby needed it
to be.

Leaving Abby in Chicago was going to be hard, he
admitted. Then another thought occurred to him.
They'd been followed before by men who knew she was
Tanner's "prize." Whoever had sent those men to stop
them from reaching Chicago was still around. And he
was bound to try the same thing again. Tanner would
have to talk to Hogan. Make sure he protected Abby
adequately. But he didn't want Abby to know about it or
to worry.

He ordered a steak and potatoes—and another whiskey—then leaned forward, frowning slightly. "Chicago
may be a little overwhelming at first."

"Will you be there?" she asked, also leaning forward.
A hint of lilacs floated around him. Intriguing. Enticing.
Had she put a little perfume on too? "I'd feel better if
you stayed for a while," she continued. "At least till I get
settled."

Tanner sat back. She needed someone to watch out
for her, all right. But he wasn't the right person. The
third whiskey arrived, and he grabbed for it as if it would

somehow save him from the crazy feelings that were gripping him. His eyes stung from the bite of the drink. "If Hogan needs me to stick around, I will. Assuming he and I can come to terms."

It was her turn to sit back in her chair. She didn't like being reminded that it all came down to money for him, he realized. That was the surest way to rile her up. The surest way to make her stop going soft over him when she should know as well as he that they were a mismatched pair. It would never work. He continued, "If I can get a few more weeks' work out of him, I'll be sitting real pretty."

Her jaw tightened, but she managed to keep her voice relatively civil. But it was costing her, he thought with an inner smirk. "And what is it you intend to do with all your newfound riches?"

"Buy a stud horse," he said, trying to make it sound as vulgar as possible. "Yeah, a stud horse and a dozen or so brood mares."

Instead of being put off, however, she got a speculative look in her jade-green eyes. "You're going to raise horses?"

He nodded, but warily. This wasn't going as he'd expected.

"Have you already got a farm or ranch for them?"

"No." He practically shouted the word when he realized where she was leading. A farm. A home. A wife and family.

She looked at him suspiciously. "Don't tell me you're going to drag all those horses around with you while you hunt down people. It'll be awfully hard sneaking up on them."

He cleared his throat and slid the empty whiskey glass back and forth between his two hands. Why had he admitted he was buying horses? What had he been thinking?

The problem was the whiskey had caught up with him, he realized. Three drinks on an empty stomach and all of a sudden his mouth was saying things before his brain could stop it.

"Well?" she persisted, looking like a cat waiting to strike. An adorable kitten ready to pounce.

"I have some land," he admitted, thinking back to his valley, the one he'd foolishly wanted her to see. "There's nothing there but grass and trees, though. No house. Not even a barn."

"But you intend to build them." She sat back, looking much the contented feline.

Tanner cast about desperately for a reply. "I'll probably just build a sod house. That's all I really need." He stared at her, forcing himself to look unconcerned about her and her interest in his future plans. He even yawned, or faked a yawn. He saw the shadow of doubt that crept over her face and then the confusion she tried to hide. When the waiter finally brought their meal, he suspected that she was almost as relieved as he.

They ate their meal in relative silence. At a table near theirs a couple with two young children ate, and the barely restrained antics of the young girl and her even younger brother were welcome distractions.

The man wore a three-piece suit of gray wool with crisp white cuffs and his watch chain showing. The woman was small and round, her hair a wispy blond. They looked nothing at all like him and Abby. Yet when the man helped his daughter place her napkin on her lap and the mother cut her son's meat for him, Tanner's whiskey-influenced imagination too easily made the connection.

Abby would make a wonderful mother. She was good with children; he already knew that. And she could teach them so much.

He, on the other hand, couldn't teach them a damn thing, except maybe how to hunt down men for a living.

He pushed his plate away, suddenly unable to choke down another bite. He signaled the waiter for their bill.

"Bring me a bottle of whiskey too," he muttered to the man. "A fresh one."

It had been a long time since he'd felt the need to get blind drunk. On the trail it was too dangerous—he needed his wits about him. The same was usually true in town too. But tonight . . .

Tonight drinking himself into a stupor was the only thing that would stop him from making a mistake that would ruin Abby's life forever.

26

Abby closed the door to her room and locked it, just as Tanner had instructed. Then she turned, leaned heavily against it, and stared at the other door, the one that led to Tanner's room. She heard him enter from his hall door, heard the dull thud of the bottle he'd bought hit the wood dresser, then the fall of each of his boots to the floor.

One thin door, six panels of golden oak with handsome brass fixtures. All she had to do was open it.

Tanner had told her to lock it, too, as if he needed that extra barrier between them. But Abby just stared at it, wondering if he meant to lock his side.

He was the stubbornest man alive, she thought, shoving herself upright. She began to pace, ripping off first one glove, then the other, and tossing them on the dresser. The bonnet was next. Then she stopped and, breathing hard, studied herself critically in the beveled-glass mirror.

Perhaps she was no beauty, at least not in the flashy way some men preferred. But she wasn't ugly either. And the fact was Tanner had been attracted to her from the first. At least he'd acted like he was. Now, though, he seemed determined to keep her at arm's length.

Was it because she'd already given in to him once?

Abby turned away from the mirror in dismay. She didn't think that was the reason. More than likely it was that she was Willard Hogan's grandchild. He'd started acting cool toward her once he'd determined she was the one he was searching for. She was Willard Hogan's lost grandchild, the only heir to the man's wealth, if Tanner was to be believed. How rich could one man be anyway?

She unfastened the row of tiny buttons down the front of her bodice and removed the lovely garment with care. The skirt was next, and the tied-on dress improver. As she reached around to untie the tapes for the top petticoat, however, the most scandalous idea took root in her head. She caught her breath in a rush as she considered just what the ramifications of such behavior would be.

Had her mother ever plotted in just such a fashion to capture her father's attention?

Abby didn't stop to consider. Instead she removed several of the pins that helped hold up her hair, then leaned toward the mirror to pinch her cheeks. But she didn't need to use any artificial means to brighten her face. Just the thought of what she planned to do was enough to bring a rosy blush to her cheeks and darken her eyes.

Tanner McKnight had better watch out, she bravely reassured herself. Then before she could turn coward, she moved to the door that separated their rooms, took hold of the knob, and opened it.

Tanner sat on the edge of the bed, his head in his hands and an opened bottle of Monongahela whiskey on the floor between his bare feet. He looked up at her entrance and stiffened. "I told you to lock that damned door." He grabbed the whiskey bottle by the neck and took a swift gulp. "What do you want?"

Abby could not have been more nervous. Her knees shook and her palms were damp with perspiration. "My . . . my corset. I need help to unlace it."

He looked at her, as dumbfounded as if she'd just announced the hotel was on fire. No, he would have reacted better if she'd told him that. He looked as if he couldn't believe what she'd just said. "Son of a bitch!"

Abby quaked at the vehemence of his tone, but she didn't retreat when he stood up. "It laces up the back," she murmured. "The lady at the shop—"

"Shouldn't have sold you such a stupid thing. Clothes that you can't take off without help. Damn," he added furiously.

"She thought I would have help," Abby snapped right back at him. "She thought you were my husband."

"Well, why didn't you correct her?"

"Why didn't you?"

By now they were facing each other, practically shouting. He stood with his legs spread, his fists on his hips in a belligerent, blatantly masculine stance. Abby placed her fists on her hips, too, and lifted her chin challengingly. The heavy knot of her hair slipped lower on her neck, and one hairpin landed on the wooden floor with a faint plunk.

Tanner looked down at the pin as if puzzled. Then slowly he returned his gaze to her. He seemed to gather his strength before he spoke. "Turn around."

"I have to remove this corset cover first."

She accomplished that task fairly quickly, considering that her fingers were trembling so bad, she could hardly control them. Once she shrugged the delicate linen garment from her shoulders, however, the rest of her hair tumbled loose, thick and silken about her shoulders and back. His eyes turned almost black at the sight, and though Abby knew it was what she wanted, she became even more rattled.

"It has two sets of laces," she whispered, knowing her voice must give away every one of her emotions. "They both lace from the middle."

She turned around then, away from that devouring gaze and the frown that drew his brows together and tightened his jaw. He seemed all at the same time to want her and to want her to leave.

It was torture, knowing he would eventually touch

her and yet not knowing if it would be efficient and impersonal or seductive and very, very personal.

Then she felt him, just his nearness. The warmth that seemed to emanate from him. His breath stirring her hair ever so slightly.

"Why are you doing this, Abby?" One of his hands stroked slowly down the length of her hair, but so lightly that she might only be imagining it. "Why?"

Abby didn't answer. How could she? But in truth he seemed not to expect an answer from her. Once again his hand moved along her hair, but this time he took its weight into his hand, and she heard him inhale, slow and deep.

"You're making this harder than it has to be," he muttered. But he didn't release her hair. If anything, he drew her nearer with his reverent handling of it.

Abby's eyes had fallen closed. It was heaven to be desired by him, for she knew now that he still did desire her. But she wanted him to love her. Until he did, she must suffer the perverse torture of loving alone.

He let her hair fall free and put his hands on her shoulders instead. "You'd better get out of here, little girl. Before it's too late."

But Abby only shook her head a little. "I need help with my corset," she repeated breathlessly.

His fingers tightened a long moment, then with a sigh, as if in resignation, he parted her hair so that he could find the corset laces. Abby bent her head forward, allowing him freer access to the restrictive garment. With two pulls he released the bow ties. Then he tugged the crisscrossed lacings loose. With every tug, however, his fingers moved along her spine, along the warm flesh, covered now only by her new lawn chemise. By the time the corset was loose enough to be removed, her breath came fast and her heart sounded like a drumroll in her own ears.

She caught the corset with her hands but continued to stand there, waiting for him to make the next move, yet worried that maybe she should do it. Then his knuckles skimmed along the length of her back, from her neck down to the curve at her waist and the swell of her derriere. She stopped breathing; her heart seemed to halt as well.

"Tanner . . ." His name slipped out, filled with all the love and longing that she felt for him.

"Hell's bells," he muttered. Then before she could wonder if his reply was good or bad, he kissed the nape of her neck.

Abby sucked in a sharp breath at the first touch of his warm mouth to her sensitive skin. His hands moved back to her shoulders as he again kissed her in the same spot, tasting and exploring. His tongue stroked the gentle protuberance of bones there before he moved the kiss along her shoulder and to the side of her neck.

Abby wanted to hold him close, to catch him fast in her arms and keep him there forever. But what he was doing with just those nibbling little kisses was far too wonderful for her to give up. So she contented herself with covering his strong hands with her own smaller ones and relaxed her weight against him.

Tanner groaned, then nuzzled past her hair to find her right ear. "I don't want to hurt you," he murmured, the words sounding too angry, given the delicious way he tormented her.

"You won't." She tilted her head sideways so he could strengthen the kiss. At once his hands moved down her arms, then under them to her waist. He hauled her abruptly against his loins, and she felt most clearly the press of his arousal against her derriere.

"You're a fool," he muttered, again sounding angry. His hands slipped around to her stomach. One slid down to flatten against her belly and start the most alarming sensations deep inside her there. The other moved up to cup one of her breasts, and with that Abby thought she would actually faint.

"Tanner," she moaned, leaning her head back against his shoulder.

He answered with a short oath—an oath of capitulation, she realized even in the fog of desire that gripped her. For his kiss changed with that oath, as did his hold on her. He sucked at her neck; his teeth bit down on her earlobe, just enough to hurt, yet not enough to kill the fire that burned full force between them. His hand at her belly slid down even farther, so that his fingers curved despite her linen petticoat into the dark space between her legs.

At her gasp of surprise he whispered hoarsely, "Are you sure you want this, Abby? Are you sure? Because this time there'll be no holding back. Not by me or by you."

She answered him by moving her hand to his denim-covered thigh and then sliding it between his legs to touch the hard maleness that raged there.

It was all the answer he needed. With a groan that was part triumph and part surrender, he scooped her up in his arms. Forgotten was the poor corset. Ignored was the bottle of expensive Monongahela. He headed for the big bed, and when she wound her arms around his neck, he followed her down upon it.

Having Tanner's magnificent body, so hard and heavy, weighing her down into the thick feather bed was truly the most marvelous sensation Abby could imagine. Yet even as that fuzzy thought took form in her mind, one of his knees parted her legs, and the pressure of his rough-clad thigh between her delicately covered ones only intensified the feelings.

Her hands slid wonderingly along his shoulders and then down the rigid muscles of his arms. When he propped himself up on his elbows, she met his burning gaze, searching out every emotion he hid inside, wanting to know if what they contemplated meant as much to him as it did to her. And for a moment she was sure it did. For a moment some light sparked in his eyes, something more than just the heated gleam of passion.

Then he lowered his head and captured her mouth in a harsh, demanding kiss, and every other thought was driven from her mind. The man she loved was in her arms, making love to her, and nothing else mattered.

Nothing else mattered to Tanner either. All his moralizations—about the sort of woman she was and the kind of man he wasn't—meant nothing once he took possession of her mouth. Abby was his, at least for the moment. And there was nothing in the world he wanted more.

His lips parted hers and his tongue delved deep, exploring her sweet mouth, staking a claim. Branding her as his. The touch of her hands was light and yet demanding as she stroked his arms and up along his shoulders and neck, urging him on though he needed no urging. If anything, he was careening out of control too fast. Way too fast.

"Slow down, sweetheart. Slow down." He broke their kiss by only the most stringent exercise of control. When he saw the clear desire burning in her eyes, however— the dark heat there—he nearly lost that control all over again. Here was a woman who would match him in passion, who would meet him in total honesty. Total love—

He broke off before he could finish that thought. If they were different people, maybe. But they were who they were.

He slid down on the bed, until his face was just above her breasts. Her hands stopped when she anticipated what he was about, but Tanner deliberately prolonged the moment. The single oil lamp on the dresser cast a golden glow over her, a soft, surreal quality that suited her perfectly, he realized. His sweet, serious Abby, who nonetheless wove tales of mice and their adventures. Her face was flushed with desire, her body tense with longing. Ah, but she was like no other woman he'd ever known. Despite the whiskey that dulled his senses, he knew he would never find another like her. But that just intensified what he felt. He would make this memorable for her.

He would make her swoon with passion, faint with the pure physical pleasure of their joining.

And he'd make sure she never, ever forgot him.

With a sense of resolve he lowered his head to rest the side of his face against her breasts. Soft and warm, yet the tightened peaks of her nipples revealed her excitement to him. She shifted restlessly beneath him, and one of her hands slipped beneath the collar of his shirt.

"Tanner?" she whispered, husky and needy.

In answer he rubbed his bristly cheek along the crest of her breasts. He heard her labored breathing, and her other hand tangled in his hair.

Damn, but he was already about to explode!

With a groan he cupped her breasts in his hands, then took first one, then the other in his mouth, kissing, sucking, tugging until she was squirming and panting beneath him. The thin fabric of her chemise was no barrier to his pleasure or to hers, it seemed.

Still, he wanted to taste her flesh, to feel the precise texture and particular flavor that was his Abby. With a single tug he opened her chemise.

"Sorry," he murmured as he ruined the brand-new garment. But he wasn't really sorry, and she knew it, for she gave him a tremulous smile.

"I don't care," she answered, meeting his bold stare.

Incited by her answering boldness, he rid her of her petticoats with just one sweep of his shaking hands, so that she lay naked and oh so inviting before him. His eyes ran over her, marking everything as his, committing it all to memory. She was exquisite, and for tonight at least she was his. Suppressing an overwhelming need to state that possessive thought out loud, he kissed her belly instead and then tasted the indentation at her navel. But he needed more, he knew. He was so hard for her, he hurt.

With an effort he pushed himself to his knees, though he still straddled her long, pale legs. No man but he had ever seen those sweetly shaped limbs. No man but he had ever felt their supple strength wrapped around his hips.

But someday some other man would.

He drove that unbearable thought away, tearing off his shirt as he did so. When Abby reached for his belt buckle, however, he stilled his impatience, though his chest heaved from the effort. He'd meant to prolong her enjoyment, to tease and torture her and make certain her pleasure was complete. But as she unfastened the silver buckle, all the while holding his gaze with her own wide green stare, he realized the tables had turned. Her fingers worked slowly, promising him all sorts of rewards with every button undone. One of her hands slid tentatively along the loosened waistband of his denim trousers, caressing skin he'd never thought particularly sensitive and certainly not erotic. Yet when she touched him there . . .

"Where have you learned . . ." He trailed off when her nails raked low, very near his groin. "How do you know what— Hell's bells!" He grabbed her hand before she pushed him right over the edge.

She smiled, clearly pleased with the effect she was having on him. "I'm a fast learner," she replied without a hint of coyness in her voice. Somehow that lack of artifice made her sexier still. "And I've always had a vivid imagination."

She tried to free her hand from his, but he tightened his grasp. "It would be better if you saved your imagination for your books," he muttered, fighting desperately to regain some semblance of control.

But the sudden gleam in her eyes, followed by a faint, knowing smile warned him it was a futile effort. "Perhaps this is only research for my books," she mused, reaching her other hand up to lightly trace the tensed muscles of his stomach. "Maybe Tillie and Snitch shall someday fall —make love," she amended with only the slightly change of expression. "Snitch is so unwilling," she continued in an even huskier tone. "I fear Tillie will need to convince him. To seduce him . . ."

He was lost. Tanner released his death grip on her hand, then groaned out loud when she used both her hands to explore his waist and hips. His trousers parted beneath her curious fingers, while the rest of him—muscle, skin, and other parts—grew painfully taut. He was going to embarrass himself here and now, before he'd given her even the least semblance of the pleasure he'd intended.

"Dammit, Abby!" In a trifling he jerked away from her touch and the unimaginable feelings she roused in him. He peeled off his trousers and drawers, then without giving her a change to spur him on farther, flung himself full-length over her. Her sweet flesh was hot and firm, yet soft and yielding too. Was it the whiskey that had him so drunk or simply her intoxicating presence?

"You think you know so much," he growled, catching her roving hands in his and pinned them above her head. "You read your damned Song of Solomon and make up your pretty little stories. Then one time—one time!— you join with a man, and you think you know so much."

He opened her legs wide with his knees and pressed the hard proof of his raging need against her belly. "But you're so innocent," he accused, angry even though he knew it made no sense. "You're so damned pure and innocent."

Then as if denying the words he'd just muttered, he raised his hips and without preamble thrust himself fully within her.

He heard her gasp, and gritted his teeth against the all-consuming pleasure he found in her. "Did I hurt you?"

"No." For emphasis she moved her hips against his greater weight, gasping again. "No," she breathed the word, managing to impart an impossible amount of emotion in that single syllable.

It was all he needed to hear. Like the dark tide of a

buffalo herd thundering across the plains, devouring everything in its path, his lust overwhelmed him. He could be neither subtle nor gentle with her. She'd pushed him too far.

Damn her for dominating his every thought, day and night. Damn her for being so irresistibly sexy behind that prim facade she wore. Damn her for being too good for the likes of him.

"Damn you," he swore as he thrust with frantic need into her warm, accepting depths over and over again. "Damn you. Damn you. Damn you."

27

They were on the train by six-twenty, sitting opposite each other in the half-filled passenger car, each of them pointedly avoiding the other's gaze. How much easier it would be if she could sleep, Abby thought wistfully. Just to sleep and then wake up in Chicago and thereby ignore everything that had happened between her and Tanner. And everything that never would.

But Abby was unfortunately completely wide-eyed, despite the fact that she'd slept at most an hour or two—and that in snatches between their torrid rounds of love-making.

A telling wave of scarlet rose in her cheeks and she swiftly averted her face. In the dark of the night, in the heat of the moment, it had all seemed so right, so absolutely essential. Yet now . . . Now he avoided her gaze and had said no more than ten words to her the entire morning. Was he so sickened by her wanton display last night? He even looked ill, if the pasty color beneath his tan was any indication.

He'd cursed her even as he'd made wild and furious love to her. Now she wanted to curse him.

But she had no true reason to, and that made things so much worse. She'd started it last night. She'd started it, knowing they would end up in bed together. Wanting them to end up in bed. Only she'd thought it might bring him around and force him to reveal deeper feelings for her.

Foolish, foolish hope, she now knew.

Yet everything he'd done . . .

She leaned her head against the padded headrest, keeping her eyes quite deliberately closed. The train let out a piercing whistle, two long blasts. Steam billowed with a rushing sound from the side of the engine, and Abby heard the snap of the iron steps as the conductor folded them up. The whistle sounded again, then with a series of lurches the heavy train got under way.

She should have been excited about such a trip. After all, she'd never before ridden on a train. She should have been nervous, too, for by evening she would meet her grandfather, her mother's father and her only living relative, so far as she knew.

But Abby's thoughts circled around and around one thought only: she had lost Tanner.

Not that she'd ever truly had him. Still, she'd been so convinced that they were good for each other. Right for each other. And after last night . . .

She shifted restlessly as erotic memories of last night flooded through her. He'd made love to her like a man possessed, and she'd responded in kind. A complete wanton had taken the place of the prim schoolteacher she used to be, but with Tanner it had felt so perfect. It had been so easy.

The train picked up steam as it left the bustling town of Burlington behind. Tanner stood up, and she heard the tread of his boot heels moving down the wooden floor of the train car's center aisle. But Abby didn't open her eyes. She was consumed with a need to understand where she'd gone wrong, what mistake she'd made. What she could have done differently, and perhaps still could.

They'd made love with utter abandon. He'd possessed her almost violently, pinning her to the big bed with his hands and the weight of his powerful body. And with the force of his thrusting, she added, swallowing hard. He'd plunged in and out of her with such ferocity, she would expect to have been torn completely apart.

But she hadn't been. She'd been filled with joy, a total joy like nothing she'd ever known. Of the heart and the body and the soul. He'd driven into her in a blind passion that had seemed somehow needy, and she'd accepted every thrust with a need of her own that only grew greater and greater. He'd touched some rare part of her soul with that swift and desperate coupling. She trembled now to even recall the resulting explosion.

She'd cried out, she knew. She'd probably revealed her love for him again, for the excruciating intensity of it had pushed her beyond conscious thought.

Maybe that was what had turned him away from her, some inadvertent profession of love. She opened her eyes and stared unseeingly at the green countryside, the fields rushing by, the stands of beech and maple trees. He'd told her once that what she felt was not love, but lust. He'd also said that he was not looking for a wife. Perhaps he'd interpreted something she'd said to mean she wanted them to marry.

But then, that was exactly what she did want. She wanted to see him every day and to make love with him every night. And to give him strong sons and graceful daughters.

With a sigh Abby withdrew her hat pin, carefully removed her new bonnet, and set it on the empty seat beside her. Tanner wanted a lover, not a wife. He'd made love to her so cleverly, so thoroughly, that she could not doubt his experience. He'd had any number of lovers before her—and no doubt intended to have many more after her.

But she never would, she vowed as anguish threatened to overcome the feeble remnants of her self-control. How could she? No one could possibly take Tanner's place. No one's touch could ever thrill her so perfectly as did his.

A heated knot seemed to unfurl deep inside her, sending disturbing tendrils of lingering passion up and down her spine. Oh, but he did thrill her, she thought with despair. His fingers along her ribs and waist. His hand cupping her sensitive breasts. His mouth ever exploring and tasting her. His lips . . . his tongue . . .

She shuddered with latent passion, then cautiously peeped about. Did anyone notice? Could anyone guess?

But the other passengers were too preoccupied. Most of them stared out at the fast-moving countryside, enthralled by the speed of this new form of travel. Abby should have been just as enthralled too. They'd probably already traveled as far in an hour or so as the wagon and oxen could manage in a day. But today she simply did not care.

Tanner had done things to her with his lips and tongue, things she should be horrified by. Yet she remembered them not with horror but with a melting sense of completeness. He'd forced her to grip the bed's iron headboard with both hands while he laid siege to her body the second time—or was that the third? She couldn't remember the details, only the searing, soaring pleasure.

One time he'd made slow, almost reverent love to her. He'd worshiped her with his hand and his mouth. With words and with tender caresses.

But that other time . . . She'd held tight to the bed, though she'd arched and bucked beneath his rough lovemaking. His words still rang in her ears. "You're mine, Abby. Mine to do with as I please. And I plan to do everything—"

He'd teased her unmercifully, torturing her almost to the point of tears. He'd brought her so near, over and over again. And every time she'd released the bed frame to touch him, he'd punished her as only he could do.

"You'll pay a dear price for that, sweetheart," he'd whispered once, turning her onto her stomach and clasping her fingers around the ironwork headboard.

Once more she shuddered, remembering the heated

stroke of his tongue down her spine, reliving the sensuous assault of his hands on her derriere. He'd raised her up on her knees then and entered that way, like a stallion mounting a mare, and she had nearly swooned. Even now her heart raced to remember it.

He'd stroked deeper and harder, more fiercely than ever, until she'd erupted in violent shudders. But he hadn't stopped even then. He'd pushed her farther, drawing out the heart-stopping spasms until she was utterly spent. Only when her legs were collapsing beneath her did he turn her over.

For one long, timeless moment their eyes had held. It had been dark, with neither candle nor lamp to cast a light on his features. But she'd seen something in his eyes. The light of love, she'd thought then, though now she was not so sure. He'd kissed her deep and long, possessing her mouth with an urgency that stirred her now just to recall it. Then he'd entered her once more and swiftly found his own peak.

She remembered him hoarsely calling her name, but beyond that nothing. She'd plummeted like one felled by a blow into the oblivion of sleep.

Abby blinked hard and reached for the handkerchief in her reticule. That had been her fatal mistake, she realized. At the moment when he'd been the most susceptible to an emotional confrontation, she'd gone to sleep. Sweet Jerusalem, but she was an utter fool.

She rode a long time staring beyond the glass window to the Illinois countryside. It grew warm, but she didn't slide the window up. She wondered where Tanner might have disappeared to, but she knew better than to seek him out. One by one she'd lost everything she'd ever loved: her mother, her home. Her father.

She sighed and closed her eyes. Her corset chafed the skin under her right arm. A bead of sweat trickled down the valley between her breasts. But she hardly noticed those discomforts, for her thoughts sank her into the dark morass of dejection. She'd lost her old life through no cause of her own, though that fact did nothing to assuage the pain of those losses. But Tanner . . . Tanner she'd managed to lose quite on her own.

When the conductor announced Galesburg, Abby forced herself to straighten in her seat. From Galesburg they would go to Mendota and Aurora and eventually Chicago. At what point in their all-day journey would Tanner seek her out? At what point would they say their final good-bye?

Abby didn't see him until she was hurrying back from a trip to the Galesburg station's private facilities. Tanner was pacing back and forth along the short raised walkway beside the passenger car. When he spied her, he halted, then flung the remnants of his cheroot between the twin rails of the track.

"Where the hell have you been?"

Abby sent him an incredulous look. Where the hell had *he* been? was more appropriate. She jerked at the gray striped peplum of her traveling costume and drew herself up. "I doubt you actually wish to hear all the details. Suffice it to say, I was attending to a private matter."

She would have marched past him and mounted the step to the train car. The conductor was there waiting to help her up, and even as she started forward, the whistle sounded, loud and impatient. But Tanner caught her arm when she would have stormed past him. "Don't go anywhere again without telling me first."

She glared at him, not believing what she was hearing. "I had no idea you cared so much," she snapped sarcastically. It was enough to give him pause, and she took advantage of it. She hurriedly mounted the nearest steps in a flurry of skirts and petticoats, relieved to be away from him. Who did he think he was, ordering her about? And after abandoning her these past two hours!

Yet even in her anger Abby recognized the fact that her fury was just a shield she hid behind. Easier to be angry at his unreasonable attitude and high-handedness than to face the fact of his rejection.

Unfortunately in her haste to flee him Abby had entered the wrong passenger car, and by the time she realized it, the train had resumed its lumbering progress. She had no choice but to make her way, muttering in annoyance now, to the door at the far end of the car. To her dismay, however, Tanner waited for her on the small swaying platform outside.

"If you'll excuse me," she said in a polite tone calculated to freeze him out.

"Just a minute, Abby. I think we'd better talk."

She tilted her chin up to a pugnacious angle. "Do you, now?"

"Yes, I do." Beneath the shaded brim of his hat his brows met in a frown. "I have good reason for keeping an eye on you."

"Oh, yes. Your reward. How *could* I forget?"

His jaw tensed at her flippant reply. "Have you also forgotten our two nighttime visitors back in the Nebraska Territory?"

Abby couldn't help flinching at his harsh reminder. Those awful men. Still, they were dead now. He'd seen to that most efficiently.

"I haven't forgotten anything," she conceded. "But since they're not likely to follow us from the Great Beyond—"

"They were sent by someone else. They were paid to find you."

"So were you!"

"But they were willing to bring you back dead."

Abby turned and gripped the iron rail of the swaying platform with both hands. She shook her head, trying to deny his words, trying to make sense of too many conflicting facts. "But that would gain them nothing."

"Obviously it would gain somebody something," he stated in a tone gone so cold, she peered over her shoulder at him. He removed his hat and raked his long fingers through his hair, all the while staring intently at her. "The way I see it, someone doesn't want Willard Hogan's granddaughter showing up after all these years."

It was ludicrous. Yet even as Abby dismissed his conjecture as the product of a too-suspicious nature, she nevertheless could not ignore the basic logic of his argument. Those men, whom she'd initially thought meant to rescue her, had made no secret about their true intentions. One had even ordered Tanner to give up his "prize." At the time she'd taken it to be a general sort of reference to her. But could the man have known all about the reward Tanner would receive from her grandfather? Could they have been pursuing a reward of their own, though with a completely opposite outcome, at least for her?

If Tanner was right . . .

The acrid scent from the locomotive's wood-burning engine filled the air, and a shiver snaked its way down her spine. "You're just trying to frighten me," she accused, desperately wanting it to be just that.

Tanner jammed his hat back on his head. "Just stay close to me and you won't have anything to worry about."

The irony of that statement almost made her laugh. "You left *me* this morning. Remember? And anyway once we reach Chicago, you'll be rid of me and any responsibility for my well-being."

She was giving away too much with her eyes, she knew. Though her words were meant to be matter-of-fact and completely uncaring, she feared they fell far short of the mark. As if in confirmation, Tanner stepped nearer. She was neatly sandwiched between the unyielding iron railing and his towering form, with the world flashing past at a dizzying rate. Abby was suddenly gripped by an insane urge to make everything stop. Their conversation. The train. The world even.

He caught the ribbon of her bonnet as it fluttered in

the breeze created by the train's headlong pace. "I'll keep you safe for as long as necessary."

Abby swallowed the lump that formed in her throat. Dare she read anything into his quiet avowal? She leaned toward him—blame it on the train's movement, she thought, though she knew that wasn't the case. She leaned toward him, and when he caught her shoulders in his hands, she let out a slow, involuntary sigh. Why did this feel so right?

But before their bodies could come together—before they could meet in the embrace she needed so badly—his fingers tightened and his arms grew tense. "I'm staying for one reason only, Abby. So don't get the wrong idea." He thrust himself away, then let out a string of oaths that should have left her ears burning.

But she was too stung by his abrupt rejection to care about his language. "Why do you do that? Why do you act as if you care, then push me away?"

Embarrassing tears burned behind her eyes, but she didn't care about them either. "How can you make love to me one night and then have it mean nothing the very next day?"

"No. No, Abby, you've got it all wrong," he began. "I don't want you to think it meant nothing—"

"But it didn't, did it?" she interrupted him raggedly. "It meant nothing to you. *I* mean nothing to you."

She wanted him to deny it. Sweet God in heaven, but she needed him to say it wasn't true. None of it.

But he didn't.

He shoved his fists into his pockets then stepped back the meager width of the passenger car's rear platform. "It was fun while it lasted," he said slowly, distinctly. "But that's all." He paused. "You'd better get inside now, before your new clothes get covered with soot."

After a long, disbelieving moment Abby did as he suggested. She stepped over to the next car's platform, then opened the narrow doorway and entered. She closed the portal behind her and sought out her seat.

Once there, she removed her hat and peeled off her gloves.

But though she performed those tasks with the outward semblance of normalcy, inside something had died. Her heart bled. Her soul grieved. Her last hope had been dashed. All that was left was the unknown that was Chicago, and the endless, empty years that stretched out beyond then.

Endless, empty years. Tanner's grim thoughts echoed Abby's as he watched her retreat. With every fiber of his being he wanted to call her back, to tell her how he really felt. She made him want things he'd never thought he'd want: a family, the love of one good woman . . . But the fact was he could not escape his past any more than she could escape the future that awaited her.

No doubt her grandfather would find the right sort of man for her to marry. And maybe he'd find the right sort of woman, too, once he forgot about her.

But somehow he didn't think so.

28

Willard Hogan was precisely what she should have expected. After all, the coach he'd sent for her and Tanner was the most brilliant shade of maroon, trimmed in black with gold braid and tassels in every imaginable spot. The vehicle was pulled not by two but by four high-stepping horses, perfectly matched white steeds with braided manes and tails.

Then there was the house.

After winding down a driveway of crushed gravel, bordered by one landscaping vignette after another—a Japanese garden with a pagoda, a miniature castle complete with a moat, a tropical village beside an actual waterfall—they had just pulled up before a structure Abby could only describe as astounding. If a house could be considered both sprawling and towering, this one most certainly was. The rusticated granite facade rose three stories, with wall dormers above, almost like the crenellations of a medieval castle. The front doors soared the height of at least two men, she estimated as she stared out the coach window. Had it not been for the absolute profusion of flowering plants that surrounded the harsh stone edifice, she would have thought it more likely a government building—a prison even—than a home. But it was a home. Hers now. And the flamboyantly dressed man standing alone before a bevy of other onlookers must be her grandfather.

The coach door opened, and the step was folded

down by a man in royal-blue livery. A red carpet lay waiting just beneath the step, and Abby had everything she could do to stifle the hysterical need to laugh. Tanner had not exaggerated. The man must be as rich as King Midas. But if he meant to impress her with this gaudy show of his wealth, he was falling far short of the mark.

Gathering her skirts as well as her scattered wits, she took the hand of the waiting servant and stepped down. She didn't look for Tanner. He'd ridden with the driver and no doubt stood somewhere behind her, watching the cozy little reunion he'd arranged. Instead she focused on the balding man with the huge muttonchop whiskers who bore down on her now, like a peacock in full regalia.

To her enormous relief, he stopped short an arm's length from her. She wasn't in the mood for pretending an affection she did not feel. But it was equally hard to withstand his undisguised scrutiny.

"I expected a younger girl."

"Then perhaps your bounty hunter should take me back and find you one," she snapped before she could stop herself.

As one, the collected servants and other onlookers seemed to catch their breath at her tart reply. Hogan, too, drew back, his thick, graying brows arched in shock.

Then he surprised her, and everyone else, it was clear, by breaking into booming peals of laughter. "Aye, she must be the right one, for she's got her mother's lovely coloring, her father's stiff neck, and my own quick wit and glib tongue." Before Abby could stop him, he enfolded her in a crushing embrace of welcome.

In the complete chaos that followed, she had only one enduring impression. She met myriad servants, was shown through innumerable rooms, and was given a rundown on the activities planned for the coming week. But it all faded into a muddy babble she couldn't quite sort out except for one thing: he smelled of tobacco and peppermint.

She could have remained aloof and separate from all

the frantic activity but for that. Her mother had loved peppermint above all flavors. Perhaps a carryover from her own father? And Abby's father had smoked a pipe. The two scents combined together in this man—this stranger—managed to affect her as nothing else could have. She didn't care a fig for his grand house and endless wealth. But he was a connection to her parents. He was the last of her family.

Abby took a ragged breath. "I need to be alone," she murmured to the housekeeper who shadowed her left elbow just as her grandfather shadowed her right.

"Yes, miss." The woman, whose name Abby had promptly forgotten, steered her adroitly into the first empty room they passed.

"Mrs. Strickland? Mrs. Strickland!" Abby's grandfather protested, wheeling around to follow them. "I wanted to show my granddaughter the ballroom, since we shall entertain the cream of Chicago society—"

"She is nigh on to fainting from exhaustion," the wiry little woman whispered, closing the door firmly and shutting everyone else out. "A fine introduction that would be."

Though fainting was something Abby had never done, at the moment it was as good an excuse as any. She pressed the back of her fingers to her brow, then sat down abruptly on a gilded bench carved with dolphins and upholstered with embroidered lilies.

"Oh. Well." Her grandfather bit his lip in indecision as he studied Abby. Mrs. Strickland's birdlike gaze darted back and forth between Abby and her employer, but finally rested on Willard Hogan with an expression Abby could only describe as amazement. It occurred to Abby that this man probably never evinced any sign of indecisiveness. That was the source of his housekeeper's surprise. Judging by his house and his personal bearing, he had definite opinions about everything. Was that what her mother had been fleeing all those years ago?

Of course her own father had also held very strong

opinions on just about every subject imaginable. Abby
had often chafed under his strictures, but she'd nonetheless remained an obedient daughter—at least until the
last few months. When he'd become so melancholy,
she'd had to take up the slack. She was not about to
relinquish her newly found freedom to this man, grandfather or not.

"I don't believe I'll be available for any social engage-
ments this week," she stated, watching for his reaction.
"If I could be shown to my room now? Please?" she
added when his brows pulled together as if he were about
to protest.

"This way, miss," the housekeeper said, gesturing to
a different door from the one they'd entered through.
Abby stood up and murmured a quiet good night to her
now slack-jawed grandfather. Then she planted a shy kiss
on his whiskery cheek.

She was almost out the door when she heard him call
in a wondering voice, "Good night, my dear."

When Tanner was ushered into Willard Hogan's presence, the old man was sunk deep in thought, his brow
lowered until his entire face seemed shadowed in thick
gray hair. It was unlike the aggressive Hogan to meet
with anyone in a room so frivolous and bright as the
morning room. Tanner knew the massive study, lined as
it was in framed newspaper articles about each and every
one of Hogan's myriad business coups was the man's
preferred meeting room. It properly cowed anyone who
thought they might pull a fast one on the wily Willard
Hogan.

But he didn't look so wily now, Tanner thought. No
doubt Abby had disconcerted her grandfather almost as
thoroughly as she'd disconcerted him.

"Have a shot," Hogan directed, indicating a tray with
a decanter and two glasses.

Tanner declined. He knew from past dealings with
the man that Hogan served the finest Irish whiskey. But

Tanner had only just now recovered from his excesses of the previous night—and look where that had gotten him. No, he needed to keep his wits about him.

"Someone tried to kill Abby."

Hogan's whole body jerked to awareness. "Kill her? When? Why?"

After relating all the details of Cracker O'Hara and his cohort, Tanner asked, "How many people knew about Abby? About you hiring me to find her?"

Hogan frowned. "Once you left, I didn't keep it a secret, at least not here in my office. Talk gets out, though. I s'pose it wouldn't have been hard for anyone to find out."

Tanner leaned forward in the hard leather chair, his elbows resting on his knees. "All right, so anyone could have known. Who would benefit most if Abby had never shown up? Who would inherit if you died?"

"I'm sure not going any time soon!" Hogan harrumphed, but his brow creased in thought. "I don't have a will. Don't believe in them."

"Surely you've thought about who would manage your businesses."

"I've got a passel of managers. But I s'pose if I had to pick one, well, it would be Patrick. Patrick Brady, my godson. He takes care of my East Coast and European interests. But you're barking up the wrong tree, McKnight. I take good care of my people. It's my competition we ought to be worrying about. My enemies."

"That was my next question," Tanner replied. "I need to know if you have any enemies."

Hogan snorted. "Enemies? Me? Considering that I've bamboozled just about every businessman between Ohio and the Mississippi River at some time or another, that's gonna be a mighty long list. There's Mad Jack Horton—he's the one I beat out for the railroad franchise. And Amos Phillips—I bought out his bank in Springfield. He's been nursing that grudge for the past five years. Hell, it could be anybody."

"I'll need all their names—and all their reasons."

The older man's jocularity faded at Tanner's terseness. "All right, then." He ran his hand through his hair restlessly, then his eyes narrowed assessingly. "Seems to me you didn't exactly want to take this job a few months back. I had to offer you a king's ransom to get you to agree. How come you're not just asking for your money?" He pointed to the thick cream-colored envelope that lay on the bamboo tray beside him. "How come you're worrying about any of this when all you have to do is take the money and go?"

Tanner had known that question would come up and he was prepared. "I plan to charge you another king's ransom to keep her safe—just until I track down whoever's behind this. I can buy an awful lot of breeding stock with another king's ransom."

It was the kind of explanation a man like Hogan understood. To him money was the most powerful motivator there was, and a short time ago Tanner would have agreed. Now, though, there was another, even stronger motivator: love. Though he'd fought the idea with every logical argument he had, ever since they'd camped in his valley, he'd been unable to pretend otherwise. He'd fallen in love with Abigail Bliss.

He was a twice-cursed fool, he knew. But there was no denying the truth—nor the futility of the situation. So he'd decided to take Hogan's money, just to throw the man off the truth. But he meant to ferret out the person behind this murderous scheme, whether he was paid for it or not. He'd see Abby safe, then he'd get out of her life. It was the best thing he could do for her now.

Abby lay awake though night had descended long ago. The huge house seemed as still as a tomb—and nearly as dark. She should be passed out from weariness, and in truth she felt very near doing so. Her exhaustion went beyond bone deep to the absolute depths of her soul. Yet in the huge canopy bed, in the biggest bedroom she'd ever seen, she lay wide-eyed, every nerve on edge.

She could handle her grandfather, she decided. He might bluster and he might bellow, but he'd spent a fortune to find her and it was not likely he'd abandon her just because she behaved in a manner contrary to his expectations. But what was she to do about Tanner?

He was going to stay—to guard her, he'd said. Did she dare continue her wanton pursuit of him? Would it ever gain her what she ultimately wanted—his love? Was it even possible for him to love at all? He'd lived a very hard life, it seemed. He'd referred once to his mother—a prostitute, he'd admitted. While still a boy he'd tracked down and killed the man responsible for his mother's death.

An enormous wave of sadness washed over her. The poor boy. That boy had grown up to be a hard man, and she knew he had a will of iron.

But he did have his moments.

An inappropriate warmth curled in her stomach, a delicious memory of how he'd touched her and kissed her. And made wild, wonderful love to her. Was it only last night?

"Oh!" She rolled over onto her stomach seeking a cooler spot on the smooth satin bed linens. But it was useless. The room was magnificent—if a little ostentatious for her tastes. The bed was truly phenomenal. But it was far too big for one.

In the end she abandoned the bed in favor of a pink chintz overstuffed settee. She would save the bed for when Tanner could join her in it, she vowed, throwing the coverlet onto the floor as she sought to cool her overheated body and overstimulated mind. Until she could win Tanner's love she would sleep on the settee.

29

Her first morning at Hogan Hall, as she learned her grandfather had named his excessively showy home, was hardly better than the first evening had been. She was awakened when Mrs. Strickland knocked, bustled in, drew back the richly figured damask curtains, and let the morning sun spill in through the tall bank of windows. Abby pushed herself up on one elbow, groggy and disoriented at first. But when Mrs. Strickland took a silver tray from the maid accompanying her and set it down on the table next to the settee, everything came back to her. Her grandfather. This house.

"And why aren't you in the bed?" the birdlike housekeeper asked.

"It's too big," Abby muttered. She shoved her braid over her shoulder, swiveled to sit upright, and reached gratefully for the cup of chocolate on the tray.

"If you'd like a smaller bed moved in, I'll inform Mr. Hogan—"

"That won't be necessary," Abby broke in.

"As you wish," the woman said. "A tub is being prepared in the adjoining bathing chamber. Your grandfather wanted to have breakfast with you, but I told him you were probably exhausted and needed to sleep in. So he canceled a very important luncheon just so that he could lunch with you."

Abby took a careful sip of the steaming chocolate. It was delicious. Too bad she couldn't just drink it, get back under the covers, and forget her grandfather even existed. "What time is it?" she asked ungraciously.

"Just past ten. I've taken the liberty of laying out your clothes. The carriage will come around at eleven forty-five sharp."

At high noon Abby was sitting at a magnificently laid-out table in what she guessed had to be the finest restaurant Chicago had to offer. Everyone had stared when she'd been swept in by her grandfather—with Tanner following like a shadow behind her, scowling all the way. Now she sat alone at the table, aware that everyone in the place was discussing her, while Tanner and her grandfather spoke privately in the courtyard beyond the window.

Actually they appeared to be arguing, for even without being able to see Tanner's face, she could tell that he was furious. He'd tried to forbid her from going, but she'd ignored him, just to be contrary. Now he was obviously haranguing her grandfather, and from the progression of expressions that crossed the older man's face—anger, frustration, then chagrin—Tanner was just as successful at bullying the grandfather as he was the granddaughter. It was enough to bring a half smile to her lips.

When her grandfather finally joined her, he was much subdued.

"Is something the matter?" she asked, using her sweetest tone.

But her grandfather only frowned. "Don't you give me a hard time, too, missy. You'd think he was your father, the way he's acting so protective of you."

Her father. That chased her humor away. "Yes. I've noticed that Mr. McKnight is very diligent about his work. How much do you pay him, anyway?"

"Now, just never you mind about that. You don't ever have to worry about money again, Abigail. Not ever. In fact I want you to call in dressmakers, milliners—whatever you and Mrs. Strickland think is necessary—and order twice as much as you think you'll need. Three times as much," he added, gesturing expansively with his hands.

It was to become the order of the day—of all her days. Buy whatever she wanted. Order whatever caught her fancy. When she asked for drawing materials, he ordered enough to supply an entire artists' colony with paper and charcoal and pastels. When she mentioned that she liked to ride, he bought her three exquisite steeds: a palomino mare, an Appaloosa gelding, and a chestnut hunter.

But for all his excessive generosity, they were still awkward together. It was her fault, she knew, for she was still angry about everything: his absence all these years, then his high-handedness in having her kidnapped. Even though she knew her father was as much to blame as her grandfather, her grandfather was the only one available to vent her anger on. Him and Tanner.

Tanner, however, seemed somehow able to avoid her. He was there all the time of course. Shadowing her every move. Following her. Guarding her, he called it—as if someone were going to jump out at her any moment. But she felt as if he were torturing her, not guarding her. He was always so near and yet so remote.

For ten days she'd tried to provoke him into a confrontation, but there was always someone else around. They were never alone. Today, however, she'd hit upon a plan. It was so simple! Now, as she made her way across the foyer, determined to escape the house, it seemed she was finally going to get her way, for Tanner appeared as if on cue.

"No more shopping." He barred her way, his arms crossed over his chest, his legs spread in a posture that was at once both outrageously masculine and infuriatingly condescending.

"Since my accounts at all the shops are in perfectly good standing, I can think of absolutely no reason not to shop," she replied, giving him her sweetest, most innocent smile. She even batted her eyelashes at him, something that she'd learned just yesterday made him decidedly uncomfortable. She took a step nearer him, all the while gazing steadily up into his glowering blue eyes. "Or if you're tired of accompanying me to the dressmakers' and milliners' establishments, perhaps you'd prefer if we went riding, say, out along the lake? I can be changed in just a minute."

Tanner gave way to her deliberately provocative assault. It almost made her smile to see his throat flex convulsively as he struggled for control. But for every step he took backward, she took one forward. She was not about to let him off easily. More than anything she wanted him to take her riding on one of her new mounts. She was sick to death of shopping, though she would never let him know it.

"Well, riding in the open countryside *would* be safer than shopping in town. Until we find out who—"

He broke off at the clicking sound of footsteps on the marble floor of the immense foyer. When Abby looked around, she wasn't sure whether to be pleased or not. Her grandfather's right-hand man, Patrick Brady, dapper as ever, strode briskly toward them. She'd already discovered that flirting with Patrick was a sure way to irritate Tanner. But now, when it appeared she'd almost convinced Tanner to take her riding, Patrick's timing couldn't have been worse.

"Good morning, Abigail. McKnight," he added a little more coolly. He turned his bright brown gaze on her, effectively dismissing Tanner's presence entirely. "It just so happens, my dear, that I have just concluded a meeting with your grandfather and am free now for the rest of the day. It would be my pleasure to accompany you shopping."

He took her arm with one of his perfectly manicured hands and deftly steered her toward the door. "I'll see to Miss Abigail's personal safety," he threw back at Tanner as he drew her outside to his waiting carriage.

Abby had all she could do not to protest. She would

just have to make the most of a bad situation, she realized. At least Patrick's offer had made Tanner mad, if his thunderous expression was any indication. But Patrick's warm grasp on her arm and his intimate smile warned her that there were two sides to this situation she'd created. It had never been her intention to lead Patrick on.

"He's quite the overbearing bodyguard," Patrick murmured as he herded her up into the small drop-front phaeton he drove himself.

"I'm afraid I'm so accustomed to dealing with overbearing men .that I hardly even notice," Abby retorted, more crisply than perhaps she ought.

He laughed, either missing or deliberately ignoring the possibility that he might be included among that group. "Willard can be, well, rather a bully at times. If I may give you a bit of advice"—he leaned toward her conspiratorially—"if you'll simply smile and nod and give every outward indication of agreeing with him, he's really just a pussycat."

A pussycat. If his roar was any indication, he was more an aging lion than anything else. He seemed incapable most of the time of speaking in anything less than a bellow. He shouted at the household help. He shouted at his army of secretaries and other office underlings. She'd heard him yelling at Patrick just this morning.

But her grandfather hadn't once raised his voice to her. At least not yet. If he did, however, she was prepared. She planned to treat him just as she would a difficult schoolboy: deprive him of something he really valued until he understood that such behavior was unacceptable. For schoolboys it was usually recess. For her grandfather it would be the company of his only grandchild: herself.

". . . for Joshua Hamilton's dinner, party," Patrick was saying when she returned her attention to him. "After all, you've been here a week and a half. It's time you met the cream of Chicago society—such as it is," he added with that condescending tone she found so aggravating.

Patrick handled her grandfather's foreign interests and spent most of his time in their New York office. He made no bones about the fact that he found Chicago a rowdy, uncouth town by eastern standards.

"I'm looking forward to it," she murmured, dreading the coming hours with him.

"And shall your hulking shadow attend as well?" he asked, referring to Tanner, who rode a rangy blood bay gelding just beyond the phaeton, at the corner of Abby's peripheral vision.

"If Grandfather wishes," she replied. And he would, she knew. This business of someone wanting to hurt him through her was silly in the extreme. Though she didn't discount the seriousness of that horrible attack on the trail, here in Chicago such behavior seemed highly unlikely. Besides, those men were dead now. Tanner had seen to that, she recalled with a shudder. Though Tanner believed—and had convinced her grandfather—that someone else had been behind that failed attempt, there'd been no indication since then that he might be right. Besides, it just made no sense.

She made it through the shopping trip only by the hardest exercise of good manners. It was bad enough to be somewhere you didn't want to be, with someone you didn't want to be with, but it became even worse when she spied a pair of women trailing two nannies and five youngsters. The children were too young for school, but not too young to enjoy stories, she thought as she stared longingly at them. What she wouldn't give to spend a peaceful afternoon telling stories to a group of round-eyed little children like that.

When Patrick offered to buy her lunch, she declined, pleading a headache. It wasn't exactly a lie: her face *did* hurt—from keeping a smile so firmly in place. Once home, however, she swiftly changed out of her apple-green gown and into the simple riding outfit she'd had made up in a rush order. If she couldn't tell stories of Tillie and Snitch to children, she could at least work on ideas for some new stories. She gathered up her writing instruments. Then, after wrapping two apples, a couple of fresh dinner rolls, and a thick slice of cheese in a linen napkin, she made her way toward the stables. Just as she'd hoped, Tanner was quickly onto her plan.

"Where do you think you're going?" he demanded, falling into step with her as she strode across the manicured rear lawn.

"How do you do that—anticipate my every move? Where were you, anyway?"

"I have my ways. And I was with Hogan. Now, answer my question. What are you up to?"

She chose her words carefully. "I've been thinking of that ride along the lake ever since this morning. I'm sick to death of shopping and being dressed up like a china doll all the time. I suppose the prairie must have gotten to me," she confessed. "I've been feeling awfully cooped up lately. And I thought I'd do a little writing while I was out."

She knew he'd agree. How could he not? He was feeling cooped up these days also. She could tell by the restlessness in his eyes and the small crease between his eyebrows that seemed to be a permanent part of his expression lately. Besides, he'd always been amazingly understanding about her storytelling. Most of all, though, she hoped he would want to be alone with her, for she most desperately needed to be alone with him.

A delicious shiver of anticipation curled up from her stomach. When he held the stable door open for her, however, and their eyes met in a lingering moment of understanding, the shiver turned into the most wicked surge of pure, undeniable longing. Sweet heavens, but he was making her life a living torture!

"All right," he conceded. "We can ride."

* * *

From his temporary office on the second floor of the Hogan mansion, Patrick Brady watched the pair ride off. Even he, with his meticulous eye for color, balance, and proportion, had to admit that they made a handsome couple. McKnight had that brooding, dangerous look about him, while Abigail fairly bubbled over with life and curiosity. She'd spent weeks in the man's company— alone in his company. And according to Hogan, the man had saved her from sure death at the hands of two thugs somewhere in the Nebraska Territory.

The bumbling fools!

He let the curtain fall, smoothing the creases so that the burgundy brocade once more hung in rich, graceful folds, and turned to face the massive library that served as his temporary office whenever he was in Chicago. If those idiots had just eliminated her as he'd ordered, his position in his godfather's business hierarchy would be secure once more. This time he'd handle things himself.

Only he had a better plan, just as effective and far more pleasurable. For besides being her grandfather's obvious heir, Abigail Bliss was also an exquisitely beautiful woman. She was slender, and yet lush, with glorious hair and a mouth that made him hard every time he stared at it. How he longed to teach her all the things she could do to him with that lovely pair of curving lips.

Yes, Abigail would make a striking partner to his own blond handsomeness. Once he'd wooed and married Hogan's new heir, his position would be assured once and for all. He would inherit all of Hogan's wealth and power through Abigail. And he'd also have the delectable Abigail completely to himself.

There was still McKnight to deal with, however. If there was something between them, it would have to be stopped. Patrick fingered the diamond and jet ring on his little finger. It would have to be stopped.

Abby rode a sweet-mannered palomino mare named Lizzie, a pleasant creature who reminded her unaccountably of Tulip. Abby had learned to ride on Tulip during those long days on the trail, and now she wondered who was taking care of the funny-looking mare. Mac too. If Tanner hadn't looked so forbidding, she would have asked him. But he rode far enough to one side of her to make conversation awkward, and besides, his hat was pulled low over his eyes and he stared straight ahead as he rode. It was plain he didn't want to talk.

Still, why should that stop her? Would Tillie pander to every one of Snitch's moods? Lately her fictional little mouse had become quite outspoken and aggressive—at least in Abby's daydreams. Today she planned to commit those daydreams to paper. She might as well also act upon them in her dealings with the difficult men in her own life.

"Will you be shadowing my every move at the Hamiltons' dinner party?" she called out to Tanner as they walked the horses along a hard-packed road that led north.

She was rewarded with an irritated glance. "That depends on whether you go, now, doesn't it?"

Insufferable, ill-tempered oaf! But instead of giving voice to the peevishness he so easily roused in her, she leaned forward over her responsive mount and abruptly goaded her into a rolling canter. When Tanner shouted at her to stop, she only hunched lower over the animal's whipping mane, until the canter became a full-fledged gallop.

Tanner caught up to her in a matter of moments. But then Abby had known he would. As he pulled alongside her, though, she sent him a challenging smile, then veered somewhat to the right. At least now she had his attention.

"Dammit, woman!" This time he caught hold of the mare's bridle, forcing her to slow down. Though Abby slapped at Tanner with the ends of the reins, it was a futile effort.

"You're such a spoilsport."

"And you're behaving like a spoiled child."

"I know how to ride. You forced me to learn, remember?"

The horses had stopped now, and as they jostled, Abby's knee nudged against his. At once he released her reins and edged a good foot away from her.

So he was as moved by that accidental touch as she was. Abby didn't try to fight the wave of color that rose in her cheeks. "I know how to ride, Tanner." She took a steadying breath but kept her eyes fastened upon him. "You taught me that. You taught me to do a lot of things I'd never done before."

"Dammit!" he muttered, low and vehemently under his breath.

But Abby exulted at his unexpected reaction, for she knew the direction his mind was taking. "You taught me how to care for a horse. How to hobble them, how to pack them." She stifled the grin that so wanted to break free in the face of his mounting frustration.

"Now I want to teach you something," she said as inspiration struck her.

He eyed her suspiciously. "Teach *me* something? What?"

The horses were on their own, ambling down the overgrown trail that led to Lake Michigan's long shoreline while the two riders focused all their attention on each other. Abby watched Tanner carefully. "I'm going to teach you to dance."

He frowned and broke the hold of her eyes. "No. You're not."

"Then you're going to look awfully dull and boring, standing against the wall at the Hamilton party. Everyone else will be dancing, while you . . ." She paused. "While you shall probably just stand around and glower in that unpleasant manner you so often adopt."

She was getting to him, that was obvious to Abby. But he was a hard nut to crack, as his deliberate silence proved. They rode on without speaking, but Abby was determined to goad him quite beyond his ability to remain aloof. How she despised that remote look and forced calm he affected whenever she got under his skin.

So she began to hum. She'd never been the best member of her church choir, but she could carry a tune credibly enough. What she lacked in finesse she overcame with enthusiasm. Today, however, was not a day for hymns, but for a catchy foot-tapping tune, and after a while she added a few snatches of the lyrics to the melody she'd hit upon.

> *". . . for with this dance I'll take your hand*
> *And turn you 'round the ballroom floor.*
> *And maybe then I'll find my chance*
> *To win your heart forevermore."*

Tanner recognized the tune. He knew the words well enough and he knew what she was up to. She was as transparent as glass. He must remind her never to take up cards or any other games that required hiding her feelings behind a sober expression. She wore her heart on her sleeve, and it was getting harder and harder to inure himself to it.

Why shouldn't he have a chance with a woman like her? Why couldn't he take what she was so eager to offer? Just being around her made him want things he'd always relegated to the future, to someday. A wife. A home. A family.

"This way," he barked, wanting her to stop that singing before it broke down the resolve he was fighting to maintain. Hogan would never let his grandchild marry a no-account bounty hunter, no matter how good a job Tanner did for him. And besides that, Abby deserved better. She deserved a more learned man than him. A more cultured one.

"Does Patrick dance very well?" Abby asked from just behind him.

"How the hell should I know?" he snapped. But inside, his heart sank. Patrick Brady was exactly the kind of man she deserved. But the thought of that smooth bastard laying one of his lily-white hands on her made Tanner's blood boil.

"He probably does," she remarked. "If you won't let me teach you to dance today, perhaps you can watch Patrick tonight. No doubt he had a dancing master as a boy. He seems the type, don't you think?" she added with a giggle.

Tanner drew his handsome mount to a halt beneath a wind-bent elm tree. Patrick had probably had a dance master, all right. And tutors and the grand tour and every other luxury his wealthy godfather could provide. He was as close to a son as Hogan had, and the perfect match for Abby.

If Tanner was even half a man, he'd step aside and let their romance blossom. But something stopped him. He'd kill any man who tried to steal one of his horses, and he felt the same way about this man who had made his interest in Abby clear. Abby was not Tanner's to claim, so his possessive feelings for her were asinine. But logic didn't change the way he felt.

He eyed the rippling surface of the lake that spread before them, as wide and reaching as the ocean was purported to be. He needed a cold dunking, an icy bath to chill both his desire for the woman who sat watching him and his insane need to throttle Patrick Brady.

Instead he dismounted and turned to stare at Abby. Her smooth cheeks were rosy with color, and the sparkle in her wide eyes was as clear as emerald. Good God, but she was the most desirable woman he'd ever laid eyes on.

He loosened his horse's reins and tossed his hat carelessly to the ground. The brisk wind off the lake caught it, and it rolled in reckless circles before coming to a rest against a tuft of grass. "So, come teach me to dance," he said, watching the startled look that came over her expressive face. He held out his arms. "Do you know how to waltz?"

She did. Not that she'd ever danced it before. Her

father would never have approved. But she'd seen it done and she'd occasionally practiced the steps alone, imagining some tall, handsome man sweeping her around and around in his arms. Up to now the closest she'd come had been dancing the polka with Gustav van der Haar after the Hoffmans' barn raising. That rousing dance had left her breathless with her heart racing. But that was nothing compared to how Tanner's invitation affected her now. Every one of her senses raised to new levels of awareness. Her skin tingled, her muscles tensed. Her heart might even have stopped as she crossed the short space that separated them. Certainly she did not remember to breathe.

"Your hands need to go here," she said breathlessly. "And here." He obliged so that one of his arms encircled her and his hand rested lightly at her waist, while the other hand, big and strong, grasped her damp palm. Then he urged her nearer. "Sing us a waltz," he murmured in that low, husky tone that always turned her insides to butter.

Abby stared up at him. All she could think was that they were close enough to kiss. If he wanted to . . . If she wanted to . . .

"Sing," he ordered.

She couldn't sing, for she couldn't manage words. But she could hum, and once she found an appropriate three-quarter-time melody, they began to dance, right there on the open banks of Lake Michigan, with no one to see them but the circling gulls and several scuttling crabs. They danced stiffly at first, for Abby was in a state of shock. She'd never truly expected to make this much headway with him today. But his touch warmed her, and the rhythmic movement of their bodies soon began to have the most heated effect on her. It was clear he already knew how to dance, but she didn't want to think about that, about whom he'd danced with before. For now he was with her.

Their eyes locked. The wind ruffled his raven-dark

hair and lifted tendrils of hers about them both. If she were to die, this would be her idea of heaven.

But in Tanner's gaze there was a disturbing glitter, some intrusive something that should have warned her that heaven was not a place easily attained. He cleared his throat. "I guess it might be too soon to tell—and that you don't want to hear this. But I need to know if you're in the family way."

The tune died on her lips. Her skirt caught on some spiky dark-green plant and she stumbled to a halt. This again. Was that what this was all about—this ride, their dancing—so that he could ask her? And what if she was to lie? What if she pretended her monthly courses hadn't finally come the day after they arrived in Chicago? What would he do then?

"Abby?" His fingers tightened around hers and she felt his other hand splay open at the small of her back.

She shook her head, unable to lie even to hold on to him.

He frowned. "Does that mean no, you're not, or no, you're not certain?"

"No, I'm not."

"You're sure?"

"I'm sure, damn you!" she exclaimed. Then her eyes narrowed belligerently. "But what would you do if I was?"

He let go of her then and took a step back. "Since you're not, it hardly matters."

"It matters to me," Abby countered, though a part of her wished she could just drop it. She was bound to hate his response.

A muscle tensed in his jaw as he stared at her. She saw him take a slow breath. "I'm a bastard. My mother didn't have any idea who my father was." He shook his head as if he wanted to deny the ugly truth of his words. "I wouldn't want any child of mine born a bastard."

Abby wrapped her arms around her waist, though what she really wanted to wrap them around Tanner. He looked so vulnerable at that moment, despite his forbidding posture and remote expression. So scarred inside. Yet those scars were the source of his odd code of honor.

"We could have children," she whispered in a shaky tone. "They wouldn't have to be bastards."

"Son of a bitch," he muttered. "You just don't get it, do you? We're good in bed, Abby. I'll never deny that. But that's not reason enough to marry a person."

Abby swallowed hard. Well, she had her answer, cold and blunt and honest. "I see."

"No, I don't think you see at all. But tonight at that party you will. You're Willard Hogan's granddaughter, and after tonight you'll be the toast of Chicago society. I'm just some bastard gunslinger he hired to find you. I don't fit in."

"But you could," she pleaded, grasping at the only hope left to her. "You could."

He sighed, and his hands fell to his sides. "No, I couldn't. I don't want to."

"Then I'll give it all up. I never wanted to be rich anyway," she persisted. "I never wanted to come here. We could leave together—"

"No! No, dammit. It's not going to work, Abby. You'd end up hating me eventually. We're just too far apart."

Abby stared at him, at his face set in such stern lines, and his eyes so shuttered that they appeared black, and clutched her arms around her waist. She truly thought she would be ill. That was it. This was the moment she'd thought she could avoid by tempting him with her new dresses and her coquettish ways. By flirting with other men and wearing French perfumes. But for all the lures she'd thrown his way, Tanner wasn't biting. Once again his streak of honor was keeping them apart. That and her damnable *position* in society.

She looked down at her feet, at the brightly polished toes of her new riding boots peeking from beneath the fine Pekin of her ankle-length skirt. At that moment she knew she had truly lost everything that mattered to her. She was only a well-dressed mannequin with no heart left inside to keep her alive.

The breath caught in her throat when she tried to speak. "Under . . . under the circumstances . . . it might be better if you give up your position working with my grandfather," she managed to get out, mustering the last reserves of her bravado.

"Someone's got to protect you from whoever it is that—"

"The only protection I need is from you!" she burst out in a strangled voice. "The only one who's hurting me is you!"

Then, unable to bear the sight of him, so tall, so appealing—so distant—she turned and fled toward the horses. She left pencils and tablet behind her as she mounted and forced the startled mare into a reckless gallop. What did it matter about her mice or her writing?

What did anything matter anymore?

30

Willard Hogan toasted his lovely granddaughter and her return to the bosom of her family. Patrick Brady, paired with her as her dinner partner, toasted her beauty and her wit. Joshua Hamilton, president of Chicago's largest bank and a major stockholder in several of Hogan's business ventures, and his wife, Eulalie Hamilton, widely acknowledged as queen of Chicago society, toasted their guest as a welcome addition to the city's community of business and social elite.

Abby did not drink at any of the toasts. That would have been a social faux pas of rather large proportions. But between toasts she surreptitiously emptied the delicate crystal stem of its contents, then nodded when the white-garbed table server appeared to refill it. She needed something to deaden the pain that threatened at any moment to overwhelm her. She must remain calm. She couldn't make any sort of scene, not here. Not now. It wasn't the fault of these people. No, nor even her grandfather. They didn't deserve being forced to witness her complete emotional collapse.

Besides, Tanner would see, and he would know why.

She gulped another glass of the pleasantly bubbling beverage. Champagne was every bit as good as she'd heard. After the first startling sip it had gone down easier with each subsequent glass. But it was no miracle worker, she knew. Tanner still waited just beyond the entrance to the Hamiltons' ostentatious dining room.

She had protested to her grandfather that she hardly needed a guard to accompany her, especially with him and Patrick there. But though he'd made her promise to stay close to Patrick, he'd still ignored her request to leave Tanner behind. Gordon Jenkins was to be there, he'd explained. And Benny Finks. They were particular competitors of his, and though he didn't think them likely to resort to violence, he and Tanner were not about to take any chances. Now, as she identified the two businessmen far down the table, Abby wanted to laugh. Did he and Tanner honestly expect one of those old men to jump out and murder her in the midst of this esteemed company? Though she did not know why Cracker O'Hara and his cohort had attacked her and Tanner back there on the prairie, she was more and more certain that their deaths had been the end of it.

She caught the waiter's eye again. It wasn't hard, for he seemed ever to be staring at her. All the men seemed to be catering to her tonight. Especially Patrick. She grimaced to herself. She supposed the daring décolletage of her salmon-colored taffeta dinner gown had something to do with it. At the time she'd ordered it, she'd thought to capture Tanner's eye. But though he'd watched her closely when she'd come down the stairs tonight, his expression had remained stony and his eyes shuttered.

"Be careful, my dear." Willard patted her hand, then held it still beneath his big bear paw, preventing her from taking up her glass once more. "Overimbibing is not the answer."

Abby stared wide-eyed at her grandfather. Did he know what a fool she'd made of herself over the man he'd hired to find and then protect her?

"I know this evening is difficult for you. I remember my first few dinner parties." He chuckled. "I was like a fish out of water. Didn't even know which fork to use. Almost drank from the finger bowl. But you'll get used to it," he assured her.

Abby returned his earnest look with a tight smile. Her mother—his daughter—had taught Abby the subtleties of proper society. But she was not about to enlighten him about his misconception. Still she hoped he was right and that she would get used to this hollow feeling inside her. This sense of utter hopelessness.

Patrick leaned toward her, and his elbow brushed her arm. "Are you feeling unwell?" he murmured for her ears only. "For if you wish to plead a headache, I'm quite willing to see you home."

"No." She glanced only briefly at him before averting her eyes. *If you were Tanner, I'd leap at the chance. But you're not Tanner. And he'd never ask.* "No," she repeated. "I'm fine."

She concentrated on her food for a while, but when Mrs. Hamilton rose to lead the ladies into the drawing room for coffee while the men had their after-dinner smoke in the library, Abby was inordinately relieved.

Once shed of the men's company, however, the other women turned their avid attention to Abby, the newest addition to their elite company. Instead of toasts there was now more overt curiosity. One matron, decked out in purple sateen and black ostrich plumes, did not even pretend to hide her inquisitiveness.

"We all know our Patrick is a stickler for the proprieties. So tell me, is he holding that unchaperoned journey of yours against you?"

"Patrick?" Unsettled by the dozens of pairs of eyes turned upon her, Abby plucked at the ribs of the fan tied to her wrist. "I'm sure Patrick is far too polite to express his opinion about my . . . my adventure, one way or the other."

"Pish-posh," Mrs. Hamilton snorted, a most inelegant sound for a woman swathed in silk from just beneath her triple chin to the ruched and scalloped hem of her emerald-green gown. "Patrick may be a stickler for the proprieties, but he's hardly above expressing his opinion. Even if he doesn't say so in words, I trust I am a good enough judge in these matters to say that he does *not* concern himself with the recent and unfortunate circumstances that our dear Abigail found herself in. I think"—and here she paused so that even Abby leaned forward just a little in anticipation of her coming pronouncement—"I think he is so smitten with her that he may seek to secure his position with Mr. Hogan by marrying Abigail."

Abby's mouth dropped open. Marry Patrick! Her? No, she did not think so. But amid the chatter that had sprung up at Mrs. Hamilton's pronouncement, one voice carried more piercingly than the others.

"Well, she may have Patrick Brady. Just so long as she introduces me to Willard's new bodyguard."

"Why, Rita Gadsdon!"

"My word!"

But for as many women who appeared shocked by the woman's bold words, just as many of the others laughed. An unaccountable spurt of jealousy forced Abby to seek her out, to identify the woman who had so swiftly recognized Tanner and the pure masculine vitality he exuded.

She was a small woman with nonetheless a rather lush and well-formed figure. She arched one of her precisely shaped brows and gave Abby a self-deprecating grin. "You'd have to be dead not to notice him. And I'm far from dead."

"Though your poor Clarence is not so fortunate," Mrs. Hamilton proclaimed huffily.

"My dear aging husband is well tended to by his nurse, so never you mind, Eulalie. Anyway, I've been considering hiring a bodyguard for myself lately—this town is so rough, you know." She turned toward Abby. "Do tell, dear girl, who is he and how much does your grandfather pay him? I'm certain I can more than match it."

Abby was already a trifle dizzy from the champagne. Being hemmed in by the brazen Mrs. Gadsdon on one side and the matchmaking Mrs. Hamilton on the other was enough to make her head spin. It occurred to her that her mother would not approve of the tart words that bubbled to her lips. But it was quite beyond her to prevent them from spilling forth.

"Mr. McKnight is quite the most capable bodyguard," she began, her eyes glittering with the light of battle. "He's saved my life on two separate occasions. Once from a bed of poisonous snakes." She heard the women's gasps of surprise, but her eyes remained locked on Mrs. Gadsdon. "The second time from two despicable creatures, who had more than merely murder on their minds.

"He dispatched them both rather handily. And without even the faintest show of emotion. He is quite the hardest and coldest man I've ever met," she finished. At least in some ways, she thought, her heart aching.

But if Abby had thought to frighten off the lush Mrs. Gadsdon, she realized at once that she'd seriously misjudged the older woman. While Mrs. Hamilton and the other women clucked in appropriate tones of both fascination and repulsion, Rita Gadsdon only smiled.

"A hard man, you say. He sounds more and more interesting all the time."

"Now, Rita, stop that," Mrs. Hamilton interrupted. "You are going to give our dear Abigail quite the worst impression of your character with our teasing. Come, dear." She directed this last to Abby, at the same time steering her to sit upon a delicate settee covered in blue damask. "We want to cast our society in a good light this evening and perhaps interest you in some of the charitable works we engage in."

When they rejoined the men later in the parlor, there was music, coffee, and more wine, and an endless, circuitous shifting of people from one intimate group to another. She met everyone; her grandfather saw to that. If it hadn't been for Mrs. Hamilton's automatic pairing of her with Patrick, she would have been relieved when he stole her from her grandfather's side. But instead of easing her tension, Patrick's constant hovering only added to it. It was enough to drive her quite mad and she was able to be little more than civil to several of the more admiring men she met.

To make it worse, Tanner was nowhere to be seen, and she thought at one point that she would actually be sick. Her grandfather would blame the champagne, no doubt. Mrs. Hamilton would probably harangue her cook. But Abby knew it was jealousy—jealousy of the gut-deep, stomach-churning variety—that made her insides roll and her head throb so unmercifully.

When they finally took their leave, she was inordinately thankful that Patrick had come in his own vehicle. At least she would not have to suffer his presence on the ride home. In the foyer she searched again for a glimpse of Tanner, and when she did not see him, tall and forbidding as usual, she almost panicked. But he was outside on the front landing, she realized a moment later, searching the shadows in the elaborate shrubbery that set off the front entrance of the mansion. Her panic swiftly gave way to relief and then to the more comfortable emotion of anger. Should that shameless woman offer him her favors, no doubt he'd welcome the chance.

"Did you check the coach?"

Tanner nodded in answer to Willard's question. "Keep the shades down, though."

Tanner didn't so much as glance at Rita Gadsdon, who stood on the lowest step, awaiting her own carriage and not hiding in the least the seductive glances she sent his way. Abby enjoyed a smug feeling of triumph over the lovely Mrs. Gadsdon. But it was a short-lived pleasure, for Tanner ignored her almost as thoroughly as he did the other woman. Had he absolutely no feelings whatsoever? she fumed.

Her grandfather handed her up into his elaborate coach, then followed her in. Once the coach lurched to a start, he leaned back and patted his generous girth in a satisfied manner. "Well, Abigail. What do you think of Chicago society?"

With no outlet for her inner turmoil but her grandfather, she succumbed to her need to express her frustration, or else explode.

"It's very like society everywhere, and at every level," she began, though her stomach churned and her head had begun to pound once more. "It has far too many vain peacocks and posturing fools for comfort."

He turned to face her, straightening in his seat. "Vain peacocks? Posturing fools? I'll have you know—"

"Oh, and I left out overdressed strumpets."

At that he began to laugh, much to her self-righteous surprise. "I had hoped you would have inherited less of your father's humorless disposition and more of your mother's tractability."

"My mother's tractability!" she exclaimed, rounding on him. She'd been spoiling for a fight ever since Rita Gadsdon's little display and suppressing her anger at her grandfather ever since she'd met him. But it seemed she could suppress nothing tonight.

"My mother was sweet as could be, but she had a core of steel," Abby snapped. "She softened my father and brought out his good humor. And it's clear she stood up to you. After all, she left here, didn't she?"

She'd succeeded in silencing him with that. But she'd hurt him, too, she realized. Even in the dark of the well-sprung coach she saw his expression change. His head drew down between his hunched-over shoulders.

"She didn't have to run off that way. It was that damned Bliss who lured her away."

"He told me once that he wasn't even interested in her at first. That she pursued him," Abby persisted, knowing that every word twisted a knife into the old man's heart. "She preferred his 'humorless disposition,' as you put it, to your . . . to your . . ."

She trailed off, unable in the face of his sudden vulnerability to add to his misery. The coach rolled along, swaying, rumbling. But inside, the silence was deafening.

Abby closed her eyes and for a moment she thought she would be ill. Her mother would never approve of such a display of cruelty. Her father, yes, for he believed in a God of anger and wrath and punishment. But her mother had believed in love and forgiveness. And so, Abby had always thought, did she. Hot shame filled her, and she tore back the shade and pushed her face near the window to breathe deeply of the cool night air. Unfortunately Tanner rode astride a tall gray gelding just beyond the coach. When he turned toward her, she forgot to feel ill any longer. For one long second she saw concern in his expression, and all the other feelings he usually kept so well hidden. Then a shadow fell over his face and he was once more his normal, somber self.

The last remnants of her anger fled, replaced by the heavy press of sorrow. She let the curtain fall and leaned back into the plush upholstered seat, taking slow, deep breaths.

"I'm sorry."

"What?" Willard Hogan shifted on the leather seat across from her.

"I'm sorry. For being so ugly and ill mannered. My mother didn't raise me to behave so."

He shrugged and sat up a little straighter. "No, you're right. You can't make a silk purse out of a sow's ear, as they say. And that's what I am—and Hamilton too. And all the rest of us vain peacocks and overdressed strumpets. Just upstarts. We've got shitloads of money— Ah, damn. There it is. That rough side of me sticking out again."

Abby shook her head. "If you're a sow's ear, well, so am I."

To Abby's complete surprise Willard leaned forward and reached out to take her hand. "We *are* family," he stated. "The only family either of us has got."

Despite all the unsettled matters that lay between

them, Abby could not deny that truth. She returned his grasp. "The thing is, I don't understand what happened between you and Mama. How could the two of you turn your backs on each other so completely?"

"Ah, Abby girl. It all seems so foolish now."

Abby smiled into the darkness. "My father used to call me that. Abby girl."

"Did he, now? Well, I suppose there must have been some warmth inside him after all. For you. For my Margaret. But back then . . . All I could see was a fire-and-damnation would-be preacherman. He saw my money as the devil's pay and my ambition as some sort of sin that damned me to hell. And he turned my little girl against me."

"Mama did love him," Abby countered, though gently, for she sensed the pain beneath his gruff words. "I just don't understand why she had to choose between you both." Yet even as she said the words, a flash of insight came to her. Her father had been a rigid and unyielding man. So, obviously, was her grandfather. Her mother had chosen to love a man very like her own father, though neither of the men could ever have recognized that fact. Perhaps Margaret hadn't realized it either. But Abby did, and she couldn't help wondering now if she had done the very same thing with Tanner. He was rigid and unyielding, too, fixed in his ideas and resistant to letting a woman disrupt the life he'd chosen for himself. Her mother had been forced to choose between her father and her husband. Would she, too, be forced to make the same sort of choice, Abby wondered. Would she even be given the chance to make the choice?

The sharp report of a gun split into her thoughts, like lightning from a clear night sky, and at once chaos broke out. The coach lurched. From somewhere outside she heard Tanner bark out an angry order. Another shot. Then two more.

What was happening? Was Tanner in danger?

Her grandfather jerked her away from the window and pushed her roughly to the floor.

"Get down, dammit!"

Even from her ignominious position on the floor, surrounded as she was by foams of taffeta and lawn and Belgian lace, Abby could nonetheless see the gun her grandfather had drawn. It was a small, gleaming weapon, nothing like Tanner's heavy sidearm. But it looked every bit as lethal.

What in the name of heaven was going on?

Like a stampeding herd of buffalo the coach careened through the suddenly threatening Chicago night. The vehicle might have been a living creature, panicked and in full flight. Abby only knew that she was hurled from side to side, bruised and scraped as she sought to keep herself upright. But none of that mattered in the least to her. Where was Tanner? Was he all right?

The rumbling of the coach precluded her hearing any other sounds. It wasn't until they swerved wildly to the left, then came to a bone-jarring halt that she heard the nervous dancing of a horse outside the coach.

Tanner!

"Get her into the house! I'm going after them!"

"No!"

But Abby's fearful cry was lost as her grandfather scrambled to his feet. Before she could right herself, Tanner was off in a thunder of hoofbeats. She was hustled into the house and the door was barred, and all the while her grandfather bellowed at the top of his lungs.

"Get up! Man the doors and windows! Send around for the law! And get Abigail into the vault!"

In the vault, sitting with Mrs. Strickland, Abby's heart slowly eased from its frantic pulse. But as she waited in the small room, deaf to all the outside sounds, she nevertheless could not completely relax. If Tanner were hurt . . .

She threw off her cream-colored lace shawl and elbow-length gloves as she paced, and removed the diamond earbobs her grandfather had given her.

"Be still, child. Mr. Hogan will see to everything."

Abby glanced at Mrs. Strickland, who sat on a wooden crate. Filled with money? she wondered half hysterically. "Yes, he's good at that, isn't he? Seeing to everything."

The woman's eyebrows only raised a very little despite Abby's sarcastic tone. "Why, yes, you might say he is. It's how he's come to rise so far from his humble beginnings."

There was no real reproof in Mrs. Strickland's tone, but her words nonetheless hit their mark. Abby slumped back against the heavy door, facing her grandfather's housekeeper. "I sound ungrateful, I know. But if it weren't for his wealth, no one would give a fig about me. No one would be chasing me. Hunting me down."

"Mr. McKnight was only doing his job."

Abby threw her hands up in utter frustration. "I didn't mean *him*. I meant . . ." Her voice fell. "I meant whoever shot at us tonight. Whoever tried to kill us back in Nebraska." Despite her wish to remain strong and calm, a faint tremor crept into her voice. "Why is all of this happening?"

"Now, child. It will all come to rights. You'll see. Mr. Hogan, why, he'll fix things."

But it wasn't Mr. Hogan Abby was worried about. Her grandfather wasn't the one taking his chances against the desperadoes out there. It was his hired men. It was Tanner.

By the time the two women were allowed to vacate the vault, the house had filled with people. The sheriff trailed a half-dozen deputies. All the house servants, the gardening staff, and the stable workers milled around as well. A man from the newspaper took notes while her grandfather's bellows rang out over all the other excited murmurs.

But she didn't see Tanner anywhere.

Abby hurried through the huge foyer, dodging people in her panic-driven need to find Tanner. The reporter dashed after her.

"Miss Hogan, Miss Hogan," he called, confusing her name with that of her grandfather. One of the liveried servants caught the man by the arm when he would have followed her into her grandfather's private office.

It was there she found Tanner. His coat was flung over a chair. His shirt lay abandoned on the floor, stained with scarlet blotches. But Abby only had eyes for him— for the broad expanse of his bare shoulders and the stark white bandage that bound his left arm above the elbow.

"Dear God in heaven!"

Tanner's head jerked around at her horrified whisper, and the sight of his frowning face worked perversely like a balm to her fears. He was all right. If he could frown at her in so frustrated a fashion, he must be all right.

She drew in a sharp breath. "What happened?" she said, managing somehow to keep her voice calm.

"More nocturnal visitors," he answered. But his sarcasm did not make it all the way to his eyes. What she saw there for the brief moment he held her gaze was a depth of caring she'd only dreamed about. He would protect her with his very life if circumstances demanded it. She knew that, for he'd repeatedly shown her so. But it was was more than just for the money. It had to be.

If only they could get away from this place.

"Why, Abigail, my dear." Patrick's smooth tones cut jarringly into her thoughts. With a firm hand on her arm he turned her away from Tanner, then steered her out of the room. "What a positively dreadful introduction to Chicago society—but not altogether a shocking one, considering the sort of people drawn to the place. Why has Mrs. Strickland allowed you to be exposed to this tawdry mess?" he added.

"Mrs. Strickland has no say in the matter. Besides, I'm fine. Really I am," she insisted, trying to twist free of his too-solicitous hold.

But he wouldn't release her. "Your grandfather asked me to bring you to him," he stated as if he'd heard the words of God in Willard Hogan's demand and must obey at all costs. Ignoring her foot-dragging reluctance, he ushered her through the throng in the foyer, past all the staring eyes, and toward the library. Once there, he closed the double doors with a decisive thud.

Abby finally managed to throw off Patrick's presumptuous grip. But before she could take him and her grandfather to task, she stopped.

Willard Hogan, usually such a dandy, was a mess. His cravat hung loose and drooping. His gray hair stood out at odd angles from around his balding pate, and both his waistcoat and his vest gaped open around his massive girth. Yet disheveled as he appeared, he seemed nonetheless more real to her in that moment, with his society veneer stripped away, than at any other time she'd been with him.

She might actually be able someday to grow fond of the man, Abby realized.

"Off with you, Patrick," he barked, dismissing his godson with a flick of his hand. "You. Come here, Abigail. I have something to discuss with you."

Abby heard Patrick leave. The muted uproar from the lobby seeped in as he opened the door, then disappeared when he closed it. In the resulting quiet of the library, insulated by books, most of which looked as if their spines had never once been cracked open, Abby crossed warily to stand before her grandfather. Despite his rumpled appearance Abby detected a gravity in his bearing. A determination she wasn't certain she liked.

"I've made a decision," he began after she perched on the edge of a high-backed leather library chair opposite him. "Until we can ferret out this rat who seeks to hurt me by hurting you, it's not safe for you to be in Chicago."

"But—"

"Hear me out," he interrupted her with a scowl.

"Patrick has made a suggestion—a very good suggestion. Or perhaps it would be better termed an offer. In any case it's a sound solution to what might have been a bit of a business dilemma for me one day. It solves both my short-term problem and the long-term ones."

Abby listened with a sinking heart. In his own way he sounded very like her own father. Though that one had always spouted Bible verses, the curt business jargon her grandfather used reflected the same sort of unemotional decision making. Robert Bliss had always used the Bible to validate his decision. Willard Hogan obviously used the bottom line.

"What long-term problems?" Abby ventured to ask.

"Why, about your inheritance of course. Who will manage it when I'm gone?"

Abby stared down at her hands. "Don't talk that way," she pleaded, surprising herself with the sincerity of her words. "I've dealt with enough death. Enough loss." She raised her eyes back up to him, really seeing him for once. The nose so like her mother's. The eyes that were the same changeable hazel green as her own. "Please, don't talk as if you're about to die. We've only just found each other."

He smiled then, the warm smile of a loving grandfather. It sent her burrowing into his arms.

"Ah, Abby girl. It's lucky I am to have you. To have this second chance," he admitted more quietly. For a few moments he simply stroked her hair, which had spilled free across his lap. "But I can't sit idly by while someone threatens to rob me of my heart's dearest possession. No." He set her firmly away from him and stared into her eyes as she knelt before him. "Patrick has a capital idea. I should have thought of it myself. He wishes to marry you and take you on an extended tour of Europe."

Abby gaped at him, not believing things could have progressed this far, this fast. Patrick wished to marry her? But that was out of the question. She started to protest, but he raised a hand, forestalling her words.

"Don't you see? You'll be safe in Europe with Patrick. And while you're gone, I'll have time to discover who it is that plots against me. Plus the management of all my businesses can remain in Patrick's capable hands. It's a perfect solution, don't you think?"

31

"Absolutely not."

Abby flung the silver-gray moire gown on the floor of her dressing room as if it were of no more value than a cleaning rag. "He will not bribe me with either gowns or jewels. Or with grand tours of Europe!" she added scathingly.

Mrs. Strickland only raised her thin eyebrows, then signaled the wide-eyed serving girl to collect the fabulous gown and hang it up again. "Mr. Hogan only wants you to be safe."

"But not happy," Abby retorted.

"Ah, child. He wants you to be happy. Of course he does."

"Then how can he propose such an unlikely match?"

The woman shrugged. "Patrick Brady is considered by many to be quite a catch as a husband."

Abby ignored that. No doubt it was true. He was handsome. Well mannered. He certainly had excellent prospects. But he was not for her. It was just that simple.

She opened the chinoiserie armoire and pulled out a pair of low-heeled leather shoes and a simple mauve-striped gown. "I'm not ready to marry," she stated, using the same words she had used—to no avail, it seemed—with her grandfather. Mrs. Strickland, at least, did not explode with anger as Willard Hogan had done. She only pursed her lips and narrowed her gaze.

"I suppose you would have had this same reaction to

whomever he might have suggested. Even Mr. Mc-Knight."

Abby's head jerked up at that and her hands fumbled at their task of lacing on her shoes. "I'm not ready to marry. Anyone," she insisted. "I have other plans."

"Oh?"

But Abby was not about to enlighten her grandfather's housekeeper. Mrs. Strickland might turn a deaf ear to most of Willard Hogan's bellowing and run his enormous household staff the way *she* saw fit. But she obviously thought the world of the man. It was clear where the woman's loyalties lay.

Abby stepped into the mauve dress with the silent young maid's help, then found a light shawl and straw bonnet to match. Finally she glanced at the disapproving Mrs. Strickland. "Would you see to it that a carriage is brought around?"

Abby might as well have instructed the woman to fetch Tanner, for he was already waiting in the foyer when she descended. Maybe that was what she had wanted, Abby mused as she nearly missed a step. All night she'd worried about him and what terrible damage that white bandage covered. It did her heart good to know he was up and on the job as always.

As she drew nearer him, however, she noticed that he was a trifle pale underneath his tan. She hurried down the last few steps, the state of his health her overriding concern.

"You're not stepping one foot out of this house."

She came to a skidding halt on the polished marble floor before him. If he was well enough to order her around this way, she supposed she should take it as a good sign.

"You cannot make me a prisoner here."

"I can. And your grandfather agrees with me."

"Oh! Men are so thick-headed. How can you be so sure I am the one this person was after last night? It could have been my grandfather. It could even have been you."

"Well, I'm not taking any chances." He caught her arm with his right hand and steered her away from the door.

"And what am I to do with myself all day?" she protested as he marched her toward the east-facing morning room.

"Write your stories. Finish that book about your mice."

"I was going to do just that. But I need an audience. For inspiration," she added when he finally released her arm.

At their entrance the one maid in the plant-filled room melted quickly away, closing the door behind her. The muffled click of the brass hardware sent an unexpected thrill of awareness up Abby's back. They were alone. But there was still the matter of her confinement to the house.

"I want to visit the orphanages here," she stated, turning away from his disturbing gaze to restlessly wander the room. She plucked a yellowing frond from a maidenhair fern and tested the soil beneath the dense foliage of a Chinese palm for moisture. "I'm a teacher at heart, Tanner. The stories spring from there. I love teaching and being around children, and I miss it so. Is that such a terrible thing? Is it so very hard for you to understand that I need to be surrounded by children again?"

She heard him sigh, and when she looked over her shoulder, she caught him rubbing his left arm gingerly. He shouldn't be up today, but he was. For her.

Guilt surged through her at the realization. And now she was making things even harder on him.

"Sit down," she ordered, turning to face him. "Don't worry, I won't dash off," she added with an exasperated grimace. She sank onto a gilded chair, carved to look as if it were made of bamboo. "Look. I'm sitting too."

He sat on a yellow brocade slipper chair—an incongruous sight that brought a wry smile to her lips. The chair was delicate, designed for a lady and made in such a way as to accommodate voluminous skirts. His broad shoulders and long legs were far too large for the piece of furniture. Despite that, however, he managed, as he always did, to project the most disconcerting air of being both totally relaxed and conversely ready to spring into action at the least provocation. Like a tiger at rest, he was made no less intimidating by his nonchalant pose.

"Now," she said, bargaining for time to get her unsettled nerves under control. "I want to teach again and I think the local orphanage is a worthy place to do so. Don't you?"

He nodded once, but the stern expression on his face didn't change one bit. "Your intentions are commendable, Abby. But until we find the person behind these attacks, I can't let you go. Don't worry, the orphanage will still be there when this is over."

"But in the meantime I shall go quite out of my mind with boredom!" She jumped to her feet and began once more to pace. "This house is huge, but it completely lacks any sense of vitality. My grandfather bellows and everyone jumps."

"Everyone but you, it seems."

That quietly worded statement slowed her steps. What precisely was he referring to? Did he know about Patrick's offer—and that she'd turned him down? "What do you mean?" she asked, though she longed to ask him other things. Far more personal things.

"I mean you refused to—" He broke off, and his slate-blue gaze veered away from hers. "I mean you refuse to listen to reason. You're just as hot-headed as ever."

"Hot-headed! If I were truly hot-headed, I'd jump at his plan to flee this mausoleum, and devil take the consequences."

"The consequences being Brady?"

Was Tanner jealous? Abby caught her breath. Should she be honest about the finality of her refusal or let him wonder whether she might eventually accept Patrick's suit? Oh, how she hated this uncertainty. Why must Tanner be so pig-headed?

"If I could be assured that he would be as good a lover as . . ." she trailed off, refusing to feel the least bit of shame for provoking him this way. And her bold words did most obviously provoke him, for his expression grew black as thunder.

"That sort of talk will ruin your reputation," he bit out.

"Really? Well, a certain Mrs. Gadsdon was even more bold than that last night, and it doesn't seem to harm her standing in Chicago's esteemed society."

"She's already married—"

"And that makes it all right? Does that mean you would not care if your wife sought—" She broke off, searching her mind for the right word. "Sought dalliances with other men?"

He stood up, tall and forbidding in his gray trousers and black vest. Though he wore neither coat nor neck cloth, the casualness of his attire did not lessen the aura of leashed power that emanated from him. He looked as if he were more than ready to throttle her. "Marriage is a sacred union," he stated, his voice dark and low.

"Sacred?" Though she agreed totally, Abby was nevertheless gratified to know his view mirrored her own. She wanted to explore the subject further, but he cut her off.

"If you don't intend to take up Brady's offer, then you'll have to find other ways to occupy your time— here, in this house."

Abby could think of one particularly pleasant way to pass the time, though she was not quite bold enough to suggest it. Especially given the temper she'd already roused him to. She stifled an impatient oath and whirled on her heel to pace once more.

"No riding, I suppose."

"And no shopping."

She sent him a furious glare. "Perhaps I shall have the merchants bring their goods to me, then," she snapped, though shopping was the last pastime she actually desired.

As quickly as she said the words, however, a far better idea occurred to her. She didn't want to shop; she never had. It was just a diversion. What she wanted was to teach again, to tell stories to little children. If she could not go to them, why, there was no reason why she could not bring them to her.

A smile crept onto her face, filled with the sudden hopefulness she felt. "Oh, Tanner." She moved toward him and without thinking laid a hand on his arm. "I could bring the children from the orphanage here. There are so many rooms. And the grounds too. I could have a classroom, and we could give them a good dinner every day."

To her surprise he capitulated without argument. No, to be honest, she was not truly surprised, for she'd come to the conclusion that there were two Tanner McKnights. The one hunted down people for the money it gained him. He was hard and without emotion. Trained to kill without hesitation and without remorse.

But the other Tanner gave his horses fanciful names and never mocked her desire to write stories about mice. He rescued foolish young women from mud and snakes and desperadoes. And for all his professions not to care for children like young Carl, she suspected otherwise.

"Thank you, Tanner," she murmured, made suddenly shy by their harmony on this subject.

"I only said I wouldn't oppose the idea. You're still on your own when it comes to convincing Hogan."

"A passel of kids! Here?" Willard Hogan shouted from across the immense desk in his office. Three secretaries stared at Abby as if to see how she dealt with his frequent outbursts.

"You don't have to shout." Abby crossed her arms and stood her ground.

He cleared his throat and glanced uneasily around. "Get out of here," he growled to his staff. Once they'd scurried off, he met Abby's stubborn gaze. "If you want me to make a donation to the orphanage, I will."

"Why, what a splendid and generous idea, Grandfather." She gave him her sweetest smile, but her determination didn't falter in the least. "Between your donation and my instruction those poor unfortunate little children shall surely prosper." Before his sputtering could form into a new protest, she added, "You know, Mama always said a person's soul was shaped in childhood. Give them love and hope—and a good education—and there is no limit to what they can accomplish in life."

Up to now they had stepped lightly about the subject of her mother—his daughter. Abby suspected it was because he saw Margaret's abdication as one of the few failures of his life. Bringing her mother into this matter was a bit of a gamble. But Abby saw from the convulsive workings of his beefy throat that she'd hit the mark this time. He slid one thick finger back and forth along the edge of his desk pad.

"There is no guarantee they will ever thank you for it."

Abby paused at the bitterness in his tone. All at once it seemed more important to deal with the past than with the present. "My mother loved my father. So much—" She broke off, for emotion clogged her throat. For the first time she really understood how much her mother had loved Robert Bliss. Enough to give up her family and the comfortable future awaiting her. Abby understood because she would do the same for Tanner. The difference, however, was that Robert Bliss had wanted Margaret to give it up. He'd placed very little value on money and the things it could buy. He'd expected her to give it up and follow him. But Tanner was not like that. He needed to make his own fortune, and that perversely would not allow him to cost Abby her inheritance. Though Abby could willingly give it up for love, just as her mother had done, Tanner would not hear of it.

Her grandfather swiveled in his high-backed leather desk chair and stared out the window onto the grounds that stretched green and well tended down toward the road that led into town. "She loved him so much it seemed that she had no room left in her heart for me."

An abandoned little boy could not have torn at her heart more than her aging grandfather did at that moment.

"Would you ever have accepted my father as her husband?"

He tensed, then just as quickly slumped back into the chair. "If he hadn't been such a stiff-necked bastard, I might have. But he . . . he . . ." He trailed off under her steady gaze.

"You and my father are so much alike—"

"Like hell we are!"

"So much alike that I understand completely why my mother was drawn to him."

He grumbled beneath his breath, but Abby ignored it. "My mother was loved all her life. First by her father, then by her husband. She had a good education and made certain I had one as well. And she was the most optimistic and hopeful person I ever knew. I think it's only right that I pass on those gifts she passed on to me. That's why I want to bring children from the orphanage here. There's no reason why you should say no."

"Tell me one thing, first. Tell me why in all those years she never wrote me. Tell me why she never told you anything about me."

In truth Abby had wondered about that very thing. "My father . . . He was a man of strong opinions."

"Inflexible is what you mean."

Abby sighed and wove her fingers restlessly together.

"I suppose he was. Just as you are," she added. "Anyway Mama never openly opposed him. I suppose she thought it best to keep the peace. And perhaps she thought you wouldn't have anything to do with her anymore anyway." She bit her lip anxiously. "Did she have any reason to think that might be the case?"

Her grandfather let his head sag against the chair back and stared up at the high coffered ceiling of his office. Carved cross beams with classical egg-and-dart detailing and with a different scene of heaven painted in each recess gave testament to the vast riches he commanded. Not many kings lived as well as did he. But Abby knew such wealth could not substitute for the love of a family. And she suspected he realized it as well.

"I told her . . ." He faltered, then blinked as he cleared his throat. "The last time I saw her, I said . . . that if she married Bliss, she would no longer be my daughter."

Abby sucked in a harsh breath. So there it was. Words spoken in anger—though he'd later repented of them— had sent them off in opposite directions forever. Her mother should have realized he would eventually regret them and written him. But no doubt Abby's father had forbidden it. Dear Lord, Abby wondered. What had been the use of all that foolish pride?

On impulse she came around the desk and knelt before her grandfather. He looked down at her when she took his two hands in hers, and she saw all the pain and sorrow he'd hidden up to now.

"Let's not repeat the mistakes of the past, Grandfather."

He caught her fingers between his own and held on tight. "No, let's not." He managed a smile. "I suppose that means I should abandon any hope that you might still agree to marry Patrick."

She nodded.

He shifted in his seat but kept hold of her hands. "All right. But you must abide by my wishes and stay on the grounds until we've determined who it is that seeks to hurt you."

"And the children from the orphanage? Can I bring them here?"

He shook his head in exasperation. "If you want those children underfoot here—just during the day, mind you —then I suppose it's all right." Then his faint smile faded and he looked every one of his sixty-odd years. "It's glad I am to have you home, Abby girl."

She smiled up at him. It was the first time she'd truly been glad to be home too.

32

" . . . Snitch stared around him, not at all certain about this place that Tillie's curiosity had brought them to. Bits of dust and dried roots sprinkled down upon his head as they inched along through the low tunnel, and he wondered why any creature would choose to live beneath the surface of the earth." Abby paused and stared at the rapt faces of the children spread out on the morning-room floor. "Can anyone tell me why prairie dogs build their homes—whole cities even—underground?"

"I know! I know!"

"To hide from wolves and coyotes and foxes!"

" 'Cause there's no trees to climb!"

Strictly speaking it was not the most organized way to run a classroom. But Abby couldn't help smiling at her enthusiastic young charges. Sometimes order and discipline got in the way of true teaching. How much easier it was to teach geography by way of her two traveling mice. How much more readily her students learned and responded. Their interest in a subject normally considered dry and dull was obvious.

In the week since she'd begun her school for the orphans, her whole life had turned upside down. From the moment her eyes opened in the morning until the time she dropped into exhausted slumber, she was on the go. She'd had rooms to convert, transportation to arrange, meals to plan and lessons to prepare. Only the youngest students came each day, for the older students had lessons at the orphanage in the mornings and worked at a variety of small jobs in the afternoons. But the fourteen little ones she taught were handful enough. Most of them had never even seen a book or a slate. Other than "please" and "thank you," they were abominably lacking in manners, and from their chewed fingernails to their scraggly hair, they were all poorly groomed.

But Tillie and her fastidious manners were a great aid to Abby, and so the storytelling had become a twice-daily part of her teaching program.

So had Tanner's visits.

She knew when fourteen pairs of eyes shifted toward the doorway now that he was here.

"It's playtime," a towheaded rapscallion named Cliff shouted, leaping to his feet. "Let's go dig for prairie dogs!"

"That's so mean," fussed Rosemary, a serious little girl with huge brown eyes.

Cliff made a face at her. "I'm not gonna hurt them. I just wanna see them up close." He ran to take Tanner's hand. "Can you find some prairie dogs for us to see?"

From order and quiet to rowdy excitement, Abby's classroom had disintegrated. Yet she didn't have it in her to object. If anything, Tanner's visits threw her more off kilter than her students. Or maybe the children sensed her befuddled state whenever Tanner came around and simply took advantage of it. At any rate she tried to compose her features and still the nervous trembling of her hands as she rose to face him.

For just a second their eyes met, just one tiny moment stolen from the rest of the day's time. Yet that moment meant more to Abby than any portion of the rest of her day. Tanner stood tall and oh so masculine in the midst of the swarming children. As always he dressed austerely. Dark trousers, a collarless white shirt. A black leather vest. But the same appearance that might intimidate adults worked somehow to beckon Abby's students. If she was the storyteller who drew them into adventurous worlds peopled by all sorts of odd little creatures, then he was the adventure come vividly to life, someone who encouraged them to act out those adventures on the well-tended lawns that surrounded the house.

He would make a wonderful father, she thought, not for the first time.

"Aren't you coming, Miss Abigail?"

Abby glanced toward the terrace door at Dorothy's question. She was a delicate little girl, but that fragile exterior hid a will of iron, as Abby had soon discovered. Each of her students dealt with their orphaned state quite differently, and Dorothy had attached herself to Abby with a determination that was almost frightening. The child stood in the open door, clutching Tanner with one hand and reaching out to Abby with the other. "Come on, we're waiting."

So Abby went, though awkwardly. She didn't know how to act around Tanner anymore. She didn't know why he came every day. Though she wanted it to be for the sake of her company, and not just to check on her as part of his job, she feared he came mainly for the children. He would very likely never admit it, but she knew he enjoyed their company as much as they enjoyed his. From what little he'd revealed of his past, she knew his childhood had been sorely lacking in family. No father. A mother who had died when he was still young. The way Tanner responded to these children was proof to her that they were as good for him as he was good for them.

As they made their way down the terrace and out to the lawn, Dorothy holding on tight to the pair of them, Abby decided not to let her wistful yearning get the better of her. She would just enjoy Tanner's presence and not long for anything further. Besides, she had an idea and she knew she'd have to get his approval first.

"I'm gonna be a prairie dog!" a sturdy fellow named Alfred shouted. He glanced over at Dorothy. "Come on, Dottie. You can be a prairie dog too."

"I want to be Tillie," she called back.

"But I want to be Tillie," Rosemary protested.

"I'm Snitch," Cliff stated, jumping up and down while he turned around in circles.

"You can be the prairie-dog girl," Abby said, trying to head off an argument. "Priscilla the prairie dog."

Dorothy ran off, happy with that, and caught up with Alfred. How dear they all were, Abby thought, hugging her arms around herself. If only she could get other people to see this side of them, she would have no trouble finding them homes. That brought her back to her idea. But first she must get Tanner to agree.

She turned to him, ready with the words she'd practiced last night in bed: it would be perfectly safe; he could oversee any safety precautions he wished.

But those words died on her lips when she met his eyes. He was staring at her as if he were baffled, as if she completely confused him.

"What?" she whispered, surprised she even had the voice to speak.

At once his expression changed. "Ah, you have something . . . something in your hair." His fingers brushed lightly at her temple. Just a feather-light touch. But it threw Abby into a dither.

She looked away. "I . . . I have an idea. Something very important to me. For the children," she added, moving forward again, though her direction had become aimless. She plucked a glossy green leaf from a boxwood plant sculpted into the shape of several stacked spheres.

"Be careful, you'll destroy the symmetry," Tanner warned, his voice mocking.

"If I do, I'm sure my grandfather will simply buy another plant to take its place," she answered, adopting his tone. It was easier to be sarcastic than sincere. Less risky. "He certainly enjoys spending the money he makes."

"And you don't?"

She turned to face him. "There are other, more important things in life. Such as these children."

"For you he'll build them a whole new orphanage. You only have to ask him."

"The finest orphanage in the world could never be as nice as homes for each of the children."

He studied her, then sighed and gazed out at the frolicking children. "Yeah, I guess that's true."

"I have an idea how to do just that."

That drew his attention back to her. "Don't get your hopes up too high, Abby. Most people don't give a damn about kids like these. They're the leftovers of society. When they're twelve or so, someone might take them in, in return for their free labor. But little ones like these?" He shook his head, lost, it seemed, in memories of his own past. For all his appearance of invincibility, there was a sad, neglected child still somewhere inside him. It made her want to take him into her arms and kiss away his pain.

With an effort she stepped back a pace and concentrated instead on the subject at hand. "What if I organized an afternoon reception—any pretext will do. And what if the children from the orphanage provided the entertainment? They could sing. Maybe put on a play. I could write one, you know. If they were all clean and well dressed with their hair cut and combed, and their manners drilled into them," she added, breathless with her rising enthusiasm. "If we invited not just my grandfather's society friends but others as well. Shopkeepers and boatbuilders and doctors and . . . and everybody. Especially people who don't have any children of their own." Her smile faded, however, when his face closed in a disbelieving frown.

"You want to invite half of Chicago here when someone's trying to kill you? Absolutely not!"

"You don't know they're really after me," she protested, refusing to let him sabotage her project before it could even get under way. "You're the one who hunts down all sorts of people. It's much more likely that someone has a grudge against you, revenge for something you did to him in the past. There's just no reason for someone to want to hurt me."

"Maybe. But until we know for sure, there's no way you're opening these grounds to so many people."

"All right, then," Abby conceded, casting about for an idea more acceptable to him. "What if we do a series of these receptions and limit the number of people? You could have a complete guest list in advance—like you do for the meeting my grandfather is hosting here for the stockholders. In fact," she continued, getting excited about the possibilities, "I could tell him to have the stockholders bring their wives along. The children could sing—"

A loud wail broke into her determined sales pitch. At the far end of the lawn near a half-hidden pergola, a group of children crowded around a slight form crumpled upon the grass.

By the time Tanner and Abby rushed over, the child, Rosemary, was sitting up—a good sign. But the little girl pressed one hand to her left eye, all the time howling that Cliff had poked it out with a stick. Abby knelt beside Dorothy, who was trying to console the other child. Dorothy looked up at Abby, her worried eyes brimming with tears.

"Rosie would feel lots better if her mother was here."

Immediately Rosemary took up the lament. "I want my mama. I want my mama!"

Abby swept the child into her arms, reassured that the physical injury was slight. But the little girl had been wounded deep in her soul—as had all of these children. Abby still longed for the unconditional love and guidance her mother had always offered. How much worse for these children—these babies.

Her own eyes stung with tears, but she sternly held them back. When she looked over at Tanner, however, she nearly lost that hard-won control. He crouched on his heels just across from her, with Cliff in the circle of his arms and three other little ones draped over him.

What had started as curiosity and mild concern on the part of the other youngsters for Rosemary's injury had turned without warning into a mournful yearning on all their parts for what they no longer had. Rosemary voiced the need they all felt: they wanted their mothers, their fathers. A family to love them. They clung to any adult who showed them the least sign of affection.

Abby watched as Tanner's hand slid comfortingly up and down Cliff's thin arm. Beneath his creased brow, however, Abby knew Tanner saw the same desperate need in these children that she saw. His eyes had never appeared bluer than at that moment, and she knew before he formed the words just what he would say.

"All right," he began, reluctant and slow. "All right. We'll have your receptions. But only if you follow all my precautions."

She could have kissed him right then and there, in the middle of her grandfather's grandiose landscape and surrounded by over a dozen sniffling children. But Rosemary was in Abby's lap, and Cliff occupied Tanner's. So Abby contented herself by kissing the little girl on her forehead and smoothing back the thick curls that were damp now, both from tears and from the midsummer heat.

"Thank you," she murmured, not even trying to hide the love that shone in her eyes for Tanner. "Thank you."

Abby stood in the driveway, waving at the coach full of children until it was lost behind a tall hedge of strictly pruned hornbeam. Perhaps, with any luck, she would find families for at least some of them. She continued to stare down the gravel drive, her mind spinning with plans and ideas. Teaching was rewarding. Writing her stories was stimulating and fun. But finding a happy home for even one of these children . . .

She trailed off with a sigh, then turned, eager to find Tanner and put her plan into motion. But it was Patrick who came down the wide granite steps toward her. It was all she could do to hide her disappointment behind a pleasant expression.

"Oh, hello, Patrick. How are you?"

When his only reply was a wry smile and a long, steady perusal of her, she shifted from one foot to the other. "I, ah . . . I hope the children's games didn't disturb you in the library."

"No, Abigail. For my own part I hardly noticed they were here. But for your sake—" He stepped closer and took her two hands in his. "I worry that you overtax yourself with them. All day. Every day. I have a suggestion, though. Why don't you allow me to take you into town this evening? There is actually a rather notable theater company in town performing vignettes from *Hamlet, Othello,* and *Macbeth.*"

Tragedies. Her least favorite literary form. But Abby smiled. "You are more than kind to offer."

"But it's more than an offer, my dear." He smiled warmly, but his hands tightened determinedly about hers. "I vow I shall not allow you to say no. Your grandfather agrees with me that you bury yourself among those children and neglect the rest of society."

"It's *his* idea that I be confined to the grounds. Not mine."

He pursed his lips ruefully, looking smooth and very handsome. Rather tempting if she'd been in the least inclined toward him. "Yes, he has confined you. I know. I also know how limiting that must be for you. But he'll be away this evening. He'll never have to know. And I will guard you with my very life," he finished.

Though Abby chafed under the limitations her grandfather and Tanner had set, at the moment she was grateful for them. She pulled her hands free of Patrick's with no small effort. "Your offer is very thoughtful, but I could not possibly go along with such a duplicitous plan."

Patrick didn't bother to disguise his absolute fury as he watched Abby walk away. The conniving little bitch!

Between Willard's fawning eagerness to keep her happy and McKnight's menacing presence as her guard dog, she now thought every man must dance to her tune. If she went too far, however, he would be forced to pull the rug out from under her.

The attack on the coach the night of the Hamiltons' party had been meant to rid himself of McKnight once and for all. With him out of the picture Patrick would have stepped in and with Willard's support would ultimately have succeeded in coercing her into marriage. He would have finally had the entire Hogan dynasty under his control—and Abigail's sweet little body as an added treat. But the fools he'd hired had botched it.

That was twice now. Twice that his hirelings had failed. Twice that McKnight had been the one to foil his plans.

But the third time would be the charm. She'd turned down his offer of the theater tonight. He'd thought to get her tipsy and then let things get out of hand. He was certain she would never be able to fend off his amorous attentions once her guard was weakened by strong drink. One quick indiscretion followed by his heartfelt confession to Willard with an offer to make things right by marrying her. However it occurred, it would accomplish the same end results. Only now he'd have to manage the seduction here, in her own home.

With deliberate precision he relaxed his clenched jaw, then shook out the tense fists he'd made. Time to go courting.

And if she proved too wily to be caught? Well, maybe the person seeking to hurt her would have to make another attempt. Only this time Patrick had no intention of leaving it to some bumbling fool. This time he'd have to find a way to get rid of her himself.

If it came to that.

Abby schooled her face into a more pleasant expression as she hurried into the house. She should not let Patrick's overly friendly attention bother her so. After all, today's invitation could simply be his way of saying he held no hard feelings after her refusal to consider his offer of marriage.

But the way he'd held on to her hands. She shook her head, trying to drive the unsettling thought away. The fact was, she would be very glad when business demanded that he return to his New York office.

"What was that all about?"

Abby whirled around, and her hand flew to her throat in surprise. Tanner stood just inside the morning-room door. Waiting for her? She hoped so as she sought to regain her composure. Or was he just watching over her as he was paid to do?

She tucked a stray lock of hair behind her ear. "You mean Patrick?" She affected a careless attitude. "He was kind enough to offer to take me to the theater. Sadly I had to remind him that I am confined to the house." She sent him a curious look. "Would you have let me go?"

He shut the door behind her. "No."

"Even if you'd come along to protect me?"

"He wouldn't have agreed to that."

Abby weighed his words carefully. "Does that mean you would have let me go alone with him?"

"I already said no."

"But if my grandfather had agreed, if Patrick and I had gone anyway. What would you have done then?"

She was goading him. It was clear to her and probably to him as well. But Abby didn't care. She stepped closer, gazing up into the unsmiling face of the one man she wanted but who for his own perverse reasons held her off. "Would you have followed us anyway?"

"That doesn't really matter since you already turned him down. You're not going."

His words were curt, but she saw his throat flex in a swallow.

"Maybe I'll change my mind," she whispered breathlessly.

He shook his head and frowned, but she saw him swallow again, and it was that solitary indication that there might be a chink in the wall of his resistance to her that made her bold. Without thinking about what she did or considering the consequences of it, she placed her hand upon his chest.

Just one touch. Just the simple press of her palm to the leather vest that covered his shirt and chest. Yet she felt the warmth of his body and the heavy thud of his heart beneath her fingers, and those two completely ordinary facets of his existence seemed to reach down into the most vital part of her. It was physical; it was emotional. It connected her to him so completely that she knew it must affect him just as much.

"Dammit, Abby—"

She silenced his muttered protest with a kiss. Even balanced on her toes she could barely reach his mouth with hers. But once the fleeting contact of their lips was made, everything changed.

Like a dam cracking beneath the pressure of a mighty flood, that hesitant kiss gave way in an instant to a crushing embrace. Tanner's arm came around her in a grip that was at once both desperate and angry, it seemed to Abby. His mouth devoured hers with a violence that might have been meant to frighten her, or even punish her. But she met it with an answering fervor.

It was what Abby had craved for weeks, she realized with only dim awareness. It was what she would crave forever.

Tanner's arms tightened, tilting her back as he deepened the kiss. Abby was off balance in his arms, dependent upon him to keep her from falling. But Tanner was there for her, in this as in all things, she knew. In surrendering that part of herself to him—in trusting him completely—she always found her greatest joy. And it was then that he always responded from the truest part of himself.

A delirious sort of happiness swept through her, and

she opened eagerly to the demanding thrust of his tongue within the sensitive recesses of her mouth. Wanton images of them together in every way possible turned her blood to fire, and she pressed herself passionately to him. Against her belly she felt the rigid outline of his quick arousal. There was something so glorious in the knowledge, the absolute proof, that he needed her as badly as she needed him.

"Jesus, Abby," he muttered when they broke apart for a breath.

But Abby put a finger to his lips. "No, don't you dare try to deny this or make it less than it really is. You love me, Tanner McKnight." She stared deep into his eyes, past the dark curtain he struggled to keep up, and into the clear blue emotions that lay beyond. "You love me," she whispered. "Just as much as I love you."

He shut his eyes and groaned. Then, as if he sought to silence the words he didn't want to hear, he kissed her again. But Abby tasted the truth on his lips. Though she had initiated the kiss, he had been swift to take full possession of her mouth. Now, though she was the first to reveal her love, he nonetheless made her understand what he felt in return. For reasons that would probably never make complete sense to her, he did not want to love her. But she knew he did. She knew.

Abby could willingly have drowned in the voluptuous pleasure that overwhelmed her. As hard and dangerous a man as Tanner was, there remained a hidden place in him, a soft spot in his heart that was gentle and generous and vulnerable. He'd kept it secret a very long time, but she'd found it out. And now that she knew, now that she had all the proof she needed, she meant never to let him go.

One of his hands slid down her back, past the stiff corset she wore, to where her flesh was soft. Even through the several layers of skirt and petticoats and chemise she wore, her skin thrilled to his rough caress.

"God, what am I going to do with you?" he muttered

between pressing a devastating line of kisses down her neck to her collarbone, then up again to her earlobe. It was as if he knew where her most sensitive spots were, where to touch and kiss so that her entire body responded, quivering with erotic anticipation.

"I know what I would like to do with you," she whispered, shocking herself with her bold honesty. She pressed her kisses along his jawline, reveling in the faint scratchiness that gave way to the smoother skin of his throat.

He met her searching lips with a heart-stopping kiss and moved one of his hands lower to cup her derriere. Abby writhed beneath his possessive touch. How she wanted to possess him back!

Once more he groaned, an almost pained sound. "How can you quote Scriptures and still be so—" He broke off when she pulled his head down and thrust boldly with her own tongue. She didn't want to talk. She wanted to make love with the man she loved. Now. This very minute. Right on the morning-room floor, if necessary.

"Not here," he murmured as if he'd read her mind. His arms tightened for a moment and his fingers curved intimately into the space between her legs. Abby knew without a doubt that she would die right then and there if he did not relieve her of the terrible tension building inside her. The wonderful tension.

"Yes, here," she countered, sliding one hand down his back and over his hard buttocks. If it worked on her, it would probably work on him, she reasoned.

And it did. He muttered something harsh and indecipherable. Something that sounded as if it might be obscene, she guessed; but then, that was certainly appropriate. Then he lifted her off her feet and, backing up to an armless chair, sat down on it.

To Abby's shock—and delight—she found herself straddling Tanner's lap. With only a few swift tugs he forced her bunched-up skirts aside so that her bare bottom was suddenly pressed right over his bulging manhood. It was a position that promised all sorts of interesting possibilities, and a new wave of heat and dampness swept through her.

Equally promising was the proximity of her aching breasts to his hands and mouth.

Her breath came shallow and fast as they faced each other that way. He stared at her breasts, which strained against the cotton muslin that covered them, then raised his eyes to hers. "You are the most incredible, unlikely woman—" He broke off and let his hands do the talking instead. One of his palms slid up her bare thigh until his thumb just brushed her damp curls. With his other hand he stroked her breasts, running his knuckles down the upper slope then back and forth, ever so slightly across the peaked and aching tips.

Abby's senses reeled as the exquisite torturing went on. She needed to be rid of all this fabric. His trousers. Her blouse and chemise and corset cover.

"I love you so much," she breathed, taking his head between her hands and kissing him. Once more she felt his resistance to those words. But he kissed her back, and his thumb slid back and forth across the swollen little bud that guarded the entrance to her feminine core. "I love you," she breathed as passion welled up so strong that it hurt. "Marry me, Tanner. Marry me and we can have this forever."

His thumb paused. Only an instant, but it was enough for Abby to know, even in her inflamed state, that she'd said too much. But then the erotic rubbing started again and his other hand moved more aggressively on her breasts. With both thumbs and his tongue he initiated a rhythm that pushed her farther than ever before. She clutched at his straining shoulders and writhed in utter abandon. His tongue filled her mouth while his thumbs drove her to madness.

Then it came, that lightning striking from within, and she cried out in the most exquisite agony. It came and came, driven by the things he did to her, until she sagged against him, limp and useless, completely without artifice.

"I love you," she breathed urgently against the side of his neck. "Please . . . say you love me too."

With his hands at her waist now, he pressed her down against the bulge that yet remained in his trousers. "This is all I can give you," he retorted in a harsh, strangled growl.

She raised her head and captured his gaze. "That's not true," she whispered. "We could marry—"

"Dammit, no!"

He stood up so fast, she nearly fell backward. He steadied her briefly and yanked her skirt down on one side. But once she was upright and fully covered, he turned away. "We're not getting married, so drop the subject."

Abby drew herself up, hurt and yet loving him just the same. "You won't marry me, but you'll do this with me. What if I offered to be your mistress? Would you agree to that?"

"No!" He turned to face her, his expression a mask of utter frustration. "You can't be some man's mistress."

"Not some other man's. Yours," she insisted, just as frustrated by his stubbornness, yet wanting to drive her point home. "Just yours." She deliberately let her gaze fall to the prominent bulge in his trousers. She knew he wanted her, and yet he wanted to deny it. But he couldn't have it both ways.

And want her he did. At her bold glance Tanner stormed out of the room. *Fled* would have been a more apt description, he knew. How could he have let things get so out of hand? She'd become a little tyrant, one who'd swiftly learned how to pull all his strings. And now she wanted them to marry.

He strode across the lawn to the stables. A hard ride on a fast horse was no substitute for the ride he wanted to take with Abby, but it would have to do. If he'd stayed another minute, he'd have given in to her every demand. Made love to her in the morning room, where anyone could have walked in on them. Agreed to marry her.

Willard Hogan would have his balls before he'd let some lowlife bounty hunter marry his only grandchild.

But it wasn't really that, Tanner admitted as he yanked a blanket and saddle from the tack room and flung them on a rangy gelding that reminded him of Mac. The fact was, she deserved better than the likes of him. She'd been well educated and went to church on Sundays. She'd been raised to be a proper lady, and to top that off, now she moved in high-society circles. What could *he* ever offer her beyond a good time in bed?

Tanner mounted, then urged the horse out the wide stable opening and into a full-fledged gallop. He leaned low over the animal's powerful neck, moving at one with the horse when what he really wanted was to move at one with Abby. But he was going to raise horses in Iowa, and Abby would become a grand-society matron. The two were worlds apart. Yet despite that, whenever they were together, they sparked off each other like flint and steel.

He kicked the horse to an ever faster pace as he fought the knowledge of what he must do.

It was time for him to leave. He'd deluded himself long enough about why he was hanging around. She was like a sickness in him, something he couldn't seem to shake off. But he had to. He had to get away from her because he couldn't control himself anymore. Despite what she thought, he wasn't right for her.

From now on he had to keep his distance from her. He would get rid of the threat against her first. But then, like it or not, he'd get the hell out of her life.

33

Everything was perfect. Abby surveyed the manicured front lawn, which for this occasion had been converted into a country fair. There were booths with all sorts of games of skill—ring toss, darts, balls and hoops—manned by the older children from the orphanage. Other food booths providing sausages, fried chicken, and pies, as well as lemonade, tea, and beer, were staffed by the household help.

Her grandfather had supported the idea wholeheartedly, which shouldn't have surprised her. After all, her fair appeared to be just one more of his elaborate landscaping vignettes.

The younger children ran gleefully about, shouting and happy, exactly as all children should behave, she thought, rather pleased with herself. Most importantly, however, were Abby's special guests, who meandered amid the pleasant bedlam: every childless couple of any consequence in Chicago society or trade. None of the children knew what she was up to. She hadn't wanted any of them to get their hopes up that they might find a new home today. But Abby couldn't help feeling hopeful, for almost everyone she'd invited was here. The guest list had ended up being longer than her grandfather had originally approved, but she'd eventually talked him into agreeing. It was Tanner who'd been harder to convince.

Tanner. Everything was perfect this afternoon, she amended, except for Tanner.

Abby twirled the green-and-white gingham parasol on her shoulder restlessly. She'd dressed just for Tanner today, wearing green because he seemed to like her in that color, selecting a casual style in keeping with her theme of a country fair. She did not want to appear the society belle today, yet with all her guests bedecked in their finest summer garments, it was hard to pretend otherwise. She was gushed over by the women and admired for her cunningly planned entertainment. She was eyed surreptitiously by any number of the men, though to his credit Patrick diverted them from her with the most expert sense of timing. He'd been helpful all afternoon, pressing drinks into her hand and bringing her a plate of food, though she was far too wound up to eat or drink a thing. He'd shared host duties with her grandfather and behaved politely yet not too familiarly with her.

But it was Tanner she longed for in the role of host beside her. Patrick could never take the place of Tanner. But Tanner was nowhere to be seen.

"Alice Corsan seems very taken with one of your little children," Patrick whispered, leaning near enough that his shoulder brushed her own. Abby's gaze followed the direction he indicated, though she pulled slightly away from him. Just as he'd said, Alice Corsan appeared involved in earnest conversation with little Rosemary. Daniel Corsan came up with beverages for them, and judging by his smile, Abby suspected that he and his wife were of the same mind.

Abby clutched both hands around the bone grip of the parasol. Rosemary even resembled Alice, with her wealth of heavy auburn hair. *Please, Lord, let them decide to make her theirs*, Abby prayed. She looked around, automatically searching for Tanner, wanting to share her hopefulness with him. But it was Patrick who was there.

"What a splendid idea this has been," he beamed, gazing deeply into her eyes. "It's clear you shall set Chicago on its ear, my dear. I predict a new standard for society now that you're here."

"I'm sure you exaggerate—"

"No, I don't think I do. Come along," he drew her forward with a hand on her arm. "Shall we visit with the Corsans?"

Abby went along with him. This was, after all, precisely what she had hoped for from this afternoon's reception. All across the close-cut lawn couples chatted and strolled, as often with children as with other adults. They helped the younger ones compete at the games and accepted refreshments from the freshly scrubbed older ones.

If even one child found a home today, it would be well worth the effort, Abby decided as she accompanied Patrick. But she nonetheless needed somehow to discourage him. His renewed attentions today might be no more than simple friendliness, but her instincts told her it was more. She needed to stifle any romantic notions he might have about her still, and the sooner the better.

"Oh, Abigail." Alice Corsan smiled when Abby and Patrick walked up. "This sweet child was telling us that they'll be entertaining us with several songs."

"Yes, they will. And I might add that Rosemary sings beautifully."

"Do you play as well?" Alice asked the child.

"Play? You mean like games?" Rosemary replied with a puzzled look on her piquant face.

"No, the piano. Do you play the piano?"

"Rosemary hasn't had a piano available to her," Abby interjected. "I suspect, though, that she has a musical talent that is just waiting to be fostered."

When they took their leave of the Corsans, Patrick patted Abby's arm. "Well done. Well done indeed."

"You don't think I was too obvious?" she worried, peering back at the threesome. "I wasn't too transparent?"

Patrick steered her around the trunk of a huge maple tree. "You were perfect," he said. Then before she could prevent it, he kissed her directly upon the lips.

Abby gasped and pulled away. She should have known he'd try something like this; she'd had an inkling all afternoon. To her relief, however, he didn't press her further, at least not physically. But it was clear now that he hadn't given up on his pursuit of her after all.

"And now." He smiled at her. "You must tell me, my dear Abigail. Am I being too forward in expressing my feelings for you? Though I have tried to honor your earlier refusal of my suit, I find myself unable to stop thinking of you. I don't ask for an answer now," he said, forestalling her words by laying a finger against her mouth. He moved the digit across her lower lip, then trailed it down her cheek and along the side of her throat. "Just tell me you'll think about it."

Perhaps if he hadn't kissed her, if he hadn't touched her in that intimate caress, she might have found it in her to be noncommittal. He was trying so hard to be kind and patient with her, and he was a handsome and prosperous suitor. Besides, Tanner had repeatedly put her off. Maybe she should reconsider Patrick's offer.

But Patrick's touch did nothing to her. No warm thrill. No shivers of anticipation. If it had been Tanner instead of Patrick touching her so, she would be melting at his feet and flinging herself into his arms. To give Patrick even the faintest encouragement when she could never feel that way about him would be cruel and selfish.

"I'm sorry, Patrick," she began, her brow creased in concern. "It's just that you . . . that I . . ." She shook her head as she searched for the right words. She'd done this once before with Dexter Harrison, but she'd not become the least bit better at it. "I can't," she mumbled, feeling awful as his smile faded and his lips thinned. "It wouldn't be right."

"It wouldn't be right?" He stepped back from her and swept her with a gaze that had abruptly gone cold. "What isn't right is the way you ignore me and yet fling yourself so shamefully at your grandfather's employees. A bodyguard," he added contemptuously.

Abby's emotions veered from humiliation at his far too accurate description of her behavior toward Tanner to outrage at his condescending dismissal of Tanner's suitability. "As I recall, you, too, are one of my grandfather's employees," she retorted, her voice quivering with fury. "I suppose I should thank you for having lowered yourself so far as to offer for me, for overlooking my shameless behavior. But it's clear that that flaw in my character would always have bothered you. Under the circumstances I believe it's quite for the best that we remain only acquaintances," she finished in an icy tone.

Above his elaborately knotted cravat Abby saw his throat flex. But she realized it was anger he fought down, not chagrin. Absolute fury. She stepped back from the venom in his stare, fearful for a moment that he might even go so far as to strike her. But to his credit he kept his emotions under control. He gave her a sharp, abbreviated bow. "If that's how you want it." Then he turned on his heel and stalked away.

Abby sagged back against the maple, grateful for the support it offered, for she was not quite sure she could stand on her own. From the heights of hopefulness about one of the children to this distressing scene. The day that had seemed so perfect was now shadowed and grim.

"Abby? Abigail! Where are you, girl?"

She straightened with a start when she heard her grandfather's impatient call. "Here," she managed to get out, stepping out from behind the massive tree trunk.

"What in the world are you doing back here?" he demanded, hurrying toward her with surprising agility, given his age and girth. "You're supposed to be circulating among our guests. Oh, and Dan Corsan and his wife are looking for you."

Little Cliff appeared from behind Willard. "They're gonna take Rosemary away from me. I know that's what they want to do. But you can stop them, Miss Abby. You can stop them, can't you?"

"Don't be silly, boy." Willard frowned, waving the

fair-haired youngster away. "What d'ye think this is all about anyway? To try to get all you children new homes."

"Grandfather!" But Abby had no time to waste on her grandfather, for the frightened little boy needed her more. He stood there, pale beneath his summer tan, fighting back the tears he'd so often been told a big boy never shed.

Abby gathered him in her arms, grateful when he began to cry. Better to let those awful feelings out than to bottle them up. She would gladly have succumbed to a bout of tears herself had she not needed to be strong for Cliff.

"What's gonna happen to me?" he wailed. "What if nobody wants *me*?" He buried his head against her neck. "I want my own mama back. And my papa."

"It'll be all right, sweetheart. It will. You're going to be fine," Abby murmured, trying to soothe his six-year-old panic. But she shot her grandfather a speaking look over the child's tousled head.

"It's not as if they all wouldn't have figured it out," Willard said in self-defense.

That was true, Abby supposed. But she'd hoped to spare the feelings of those children not adopted right away.

Willard cleared his throat. "You know, maybe we could use a boy around here," he offered tentatively.

Abby wasn't certain whether he meant to placate her or the sobbing child in her arms. But whomever his words were intended for, their reactions were identical.

"*You're* willing to take in a child?"

"You want a boy like *me*?"

Willard shifted from one foot to the other. "Well . . . Well, yes, dammit. Yes, as a matter of fact I do. Girls are a hell of a lot of trouble. I don't understand 'em at all. But a boy . . ." He trailed off, but he was smiling, and it lit an answering smile on Cliff's face.

"You want *me*?" he asked again as if he had to be sure.

"I want you."

Cliff pulled out of Abby's embrace and wiped his damp eyes on his sleeve. "Okay," he agreed, suddenly all business. "Only I want to play with Rosemary sometimes."

"I can arrange that." Willard stuck out his palm. "Deal?"

Cliff took the old man's gnarled hand with his own sun-browned one. They shook, or Abby supposed they did. Her eyes had filled with too many tears for her to clearly see. But when her grandfather extended his other arm to her, she could see well enough to fling her arms around his waist and snuggle into his embrace.

"Thank you," she whispered against the stiff brocade of his waistcoat. "Thank you, Grandfather."

"Ah, my little Abby girl. I made so many mistakes with your ma. And with you, too, I s'pose. Maybe I can get it right with . . . with . . ."

"Cliff," the boy supplied his name from the other side of Willard's ample frame. "My name is Cliff."

"Your name is Cliff *Hogan*," Willard corrected proudly.

There were more pairings being made, Abby realized when the three of them rejoined their party. Dorothy sat with Jacob and Mildred Walliford. He was headmaster of the Illinois Academy, a school for boys. But they had no children of their own. Alfred was tossing a leather ball to Philip Miller, of Miller Mercantile, while his wife looked on, beaming.

Oh, but life was good to her, Abby thought. She'd found her grandfather today—really found him—after weeks of being in his household but not really a part of it. But from now on they'd be a family, and so would these other newly forming families.

Her gaze swept the lawn, taking in the peaceful scene spread across the green shadows of the late afternoon. Then she spied Tanner, and the rest of it all faded away. He stood apart from everyone else, separate. Watchful.

Did he choose not to mingle because he felt he could never fit in? Or was he merely being the bodyguard, cautious and suspicious?

Abby's heart was so full of love and hopefulness at that moment that despite their last disastrous conversation, over a week earlier, she knew she had to try to reach him one more time. She took hasty leave of her grandfather and Cliff, both of whom wore equally wide grins. Willard Hogan had just struck the best deal of his life, though he might not yet know it. She was determined to do just as well.

Patrick watched Abby thread her way across the lawn, making brief conversation with their guests. But it was more than clear to him where she was headed. He nursed his gin sling, only paying token attention to Mrs. Hess's meandering description of her idyllic childhood in Pennsylvania. Abigail had thrown *him* over—Patrick Brady, vice president of a worldwide enterprise—for a no-account bounty hunter. The little slut had no shame. She should be grateful that Patrick had been willing to make an honest woman of her. But no, she was like a bitch in heat for McKnight.

But there was no way Patrick could allow her to marry McKnight and put her fortune—the fortune that rightfully should come to him—in the hands of a shiftless bum who had only his skill with a handgun to commend him.

He tossed back the contents of his glass, then coughed at its bitter sting. "If you'll excuse me," he interrupted Mrs. Hess's monologue. Without further explanation he turned and hurried into the house. It would have to be now. With all this confusion and so many people, suspicion would never fall on him. He'd have to kill McKnight, too, though how he'd love to let him live to take the blame for not protecting Abigail as he'd been paid to do. Patrick laughed out loud. Willard would want to kill McKnight himself, but Patrick wasn't taking any chances this time. He'd have to kill McKnight himself.

In his grief Willard would undoubtedly turn to his godchild for support. Patrick smiled at the thought. As always he intended to be there for the man.

"If you don't come with me right now, I vow I shall go directly to the stables, saddle a horse, and gallop off all alone." Abby glared at Tanner, matching his forbidding expression with one she hoped was equally determined. "You'll have to follow me because that's what you're paid to do. So why not just come with me now and save us both a lot of aggravation?"

"We can talk here."

"No, we can't. I need more privacy."

A muscle jumped in his cheek, a tense, rhythmic pulse that was the only sign that he might be even the least bit unsettled by her demand. She stepped nearer. "This can't wait, Tanner." She stared up into his eyes, so dark, so blue. So closed off from her and yet glittering now with a hungry sort of light.

"Let it alone, Abby. Why in the hell can't you just let it alone?"

The flatness of his tone, the weariness in his voice, almost made her do as he asked. Stop pursuing him. Accept the fact that they were entirely mismatched. But she couldn't. She started for the stables, head held high, though she fought back tears with every step. Before she'd gone even half the distance, he caught up with her.

"You're being an idiot." He grabbed her by one arm and spun her around to face him. "And a spoiled brat."

"And you're a coward."

That drew him up, and in that moment she leaped on the offensive. "You're afraid of me, aren't you? You're afraid of the feelings *I* arouse in *you*—and I don't mean the physical ones. I mean the ones in here." She pressed her free hand against his chest.

Beneath the wool jacket and striped waistcoat he'd donned for the occasion, under the crisp linen shirt, the warm flesh and hard muscle, his heartbeat felt strong and steady. It was a heart she wished to take into her tender keeping just as she longed to give him hers.

"Son of a bitch!" He thrust her away from him, then swore again, a fluent string of curse words made no less vehement by the low pitch of his voice. "Maybe you deserve to get just what you're asking for. A man with no prospects beyond what he can scrape up out of the dirt. A man without a decent job to speak of or even a house to bring you to. A man who's got nothing to offer you. Nothing!"

Despite his seething anger Abby had never seen him so vulnerable, and it made her love him all the more. "You have everything I need, Tanner. Can't you see that? None of the rest matters. Certainly not money or things," she stated quietly. "I love you—who you are inside. Together we can overcome all the rest."

Her eyes held fast with his, demanding that he believe her. Pleading with him to take a chance, to open up to her. Then something flickered deep in his eyes, something changed, and the breath stilled in Abby's chest.

"Dammit, woman," he muttered. But she heard capitulation in his voice, and her heart soared with rising joy. "You're making a foolish mistake. The worst mistake of your life."

"No, I'm not," she countered, love shining in her eyes.

"Ah, Abby," he groaned. Then he lifted his hand and stroked one of his fingers down the curve of her cheek. "I never believed I could feel about a woman—love a woman—the way I love you."

"Tanner," she breathed, stepping into the curve of his hand.

"How utterly touching."

At that unexpected and sarcastic comment, both Abby and Tanner whirled around.

"Come here," Patrick ordered from a partially hidden position behind one of her grandfather's many fancifully pruned boxwood hedges. He spared only a brief, contemptuous glance for Abby before focusing both his attention and the shiny pistol he held on Tanner. "I suggest you cooperate, dear Abigail, or the virile object of your vulgar affections shall be no more than a bleeding mess on the ground. As for you, McKnight. Kindly divest yourself of the weapon beneath your coat."

Abby's fearful gaze sought Tanner. This was her fault. She'd turned Patrick down, though she'd never suspected his emotions to be this intensely involved. Now he seemed intent on killing Tanner, and all because she was foolish enough to state her feelings where anyone might overhear.

"Do as he says, Abby." Tanner's voice was low and evenly pitched. No hint of fear at all, though Abby was frightened enough for them both. But he kept his stare steady on Patrick, menacing despite the clear advantage the other man held.

"Toss it over here," Patrick ordered, a faint smile curving his mouth. "That's it," he said when Tanner complied. He swiftly pocketed Tanner's weapon, then gestured toward a Japanese pergola half hidden in a shroud of ginger plants and English ivy.

Tanner guided Abby forward, though she realized he kept himself squarely between her and the gun Patrick held.

Dear God, don't let Tanner try to prove his love by protecting me with his body. It should be the other way around. She'd rather tell him good-bye forever than see him hurt in any way.

"Patrick, please. You don't understand. I . . . I've thrown myself at Tanner, true. But he . . . he's always turned me down."

"Always? I don't think he's *always* turned you down. You're rather too fetching for any man to resist for long. Especially when he's riffraff and you're the one doing the pursuing."

"And especially when she's so rich. Right, Brady?"

Patrick's smile turned ugly at Tanner's mocking remark. "It doesn't hurt," he replied. "But then all I wanted was to keep what I already had. Now, get inside."

Abby stepped up into the shaded pergola, frowning as she tried to make sense of Patrick's words. "But you didn't have me. You never *had* me."

"He means your inheritance, Abby. He was the logical beneficiary of your grandfather's will—before *you* came on the scene."

Abby gasped and stumbled, but Tanner caught her and bent to free her heel from her trailing skirt.

"Get away from her!" Patrick screamed.

To Abby's surprise Tanner complied at once. He circled to the opposite side of the pergola so that Patrick, standing in the single entrance, had to shift his attention back and forth from one of them to the other.

"I killed the two thugs you sent after her on the trail," Tanner said, soft yet boasting too. "They were a pair of inept fools."

Patrick pursed his mouth. "They may have been, but I'm not. And now I intend to kill you."

"And Abby? You plan to kill her too?"

"Oh, not me." Patrick answered, smiling again. How even and evil that smile now appeared. "Her death and yours will both be blamed on Hogan's damnable enemy. You know, the one who attacked his coach and caused us to employ so many bodyguards. You shall go to your death defending her." He rocked back on his heels. "I shall berate Hogan for not hiring Pinkertons as I originally suggested. With any luck, guilt and grief shall send him to a premature grave."

"I doubt he'll mourn me for long," Abby stated, determined to wipe the smug look off his face. "He's just decided today to adopt a child. A boy, this time. One he can mold into his own likeness and train to take over his business interests." It was her turn to smile, though her knees shook beneath her skirts. "I'm afraid you shall lose out all over again, Patrick. This hideous plan of yours has all been for naught."

The color drained from his face, and for a long moment he simply stared at her, wild-eyed. She'd meant to rattle him, and so she had. But she feared now that she would be shot for her efforts for he shifted the gun toward her, and his knuckles turned white, he gripped the weapon so tightly.

"You're lying," he growled. "You're a lying bitch. A slut—"

With a deafening roar the gun exploded. Abby fell back, certain she was shot. But Patrick went down, too, felled when Tanner launched himself at the man. Wood splintered as they crashed against a delicately wrought bench. The gun went off again, and this time she screamed. But she wasn't shot, she realized as she scrambled frantically to her feet.

"Run, Abby!" Tanner's order came out as a harsh grunt.

But there was no way she would leave him. This was *their* fight, not just his.

While the two flailed about, struggling for the gun, her searching eyes spied a length of wood—a leg from the bench. With a cry of triumph she grabbed it, then whirled to help Tanner.

Her knees nearly folded at the sight of them. The two fought wildly on the floor, but across one part of Tanner's jacket a glistening stain spread, dark and insidious. Blood. He'd been shot!

Even as she watched, horrified, Patrick struck his fist against Tanner's bloodied shoulder. With a cry of pain Tanner's fingers loosened from around the weapon they fought for. Patrick wrested the gun free, then shoved the muzzle against Tanner's head.

The rest seemed to occur in slow motion. Patrick's finger squeezed. The skin over his knuckle thinned and went pale with the pressure he put on the slender metal trigger. At the same time Tanner's knee came up. Patrick screamed in excruciating pain. Once again the gun exploded, but Tanner's blow to Patrick's groin had jarred the weapon just enough to send the bullet crashing into the latticework instead of Tanner's skull.

Then someone screamed again, a high-pitched cry that subsided abruptly into a weak gurgling sound. It was unlike anything she'd ever heard before.

But that wasn't true. Visions of Tanner's fight that night in the prairie made her legs go weak. She'd heard that sound before!

From off in the distance she heard raised voices and anxious cries. Of course. The gunshots had raised an alarm. But if it was too late . . .

She stumbled over to Tanner, who had collapsed on top of Patrick. They both lay so still. . . .

"Tanner. Tanner," she repeated his name over and over again in a desperate whisper. She fell to her knees beside him. Should she turn him over? Would that only make things worse?

Dear God, don't let him die. I'll do anything. . . .

She eased him over with one hand on his side and the other cradling his head. When he groaned in pain, she wanted to die. Yet she also rejoiced, for that groan meant he was alive.

As he rolled off his adversary, however, it was obvious that Patrick was dead. The carved hilt of Tanner's hunting knife projected sharply from a spot just below Patrick's breastbone. Though the stain of blood on his finely tailored waistcoat was not nearly so large as Tanner's, Abby feared she knew the reason. The stab wound had killed him almost instantly. He didn't bleed because his heart no longer beat.

She stifled a shudder of horror, then focused back on Tanner. Though his eyes were closed, he gripped his upper arm, trying in vain, it seemed, to stop the blood that seeped from the gunshot wound.

"Oh, my love," she whispered, wadding the hem of her skirt to press against the wound. "Oh, Tanner—"

"Is he dead?"

She nodded, unable to speak.

At that moment her grandfather burst into the pergola, now a shamble of broken wood and broken bodies. "What in God's name—Abby! Abby girl, are you all right?"

"I'm fine. Fine. But Tanner—"

"Oh, my God. Patrick!"

"Patrick tried to kill us. Both of us," Abby managed in a strangled tone. "Get a doctor for Tanner. Hurry! He's bleeding to death!"

In the crush of people beyond the pergola the cry went up for a doctor. Willard crouched beside her, his face ashen and confused.

"But why would Patrick . . . ?" He trailed off.

"Because he was your heir before Abby came along," Tanner said. "Or at least he expected to be. He was the one behind the attacks."

"But that's preposterous. He's rich in his own right. I've seen to that. And he wanted to marry her," Willard protested. "He meant to take her to Europe to keep her safe."

"As my husband he would have controlled my inheritance," Abby stated, anger slowly taking the place of horror. "That's all he ever wanted. While I . . . I've never wanted it at all."

"Let me through. I'm a doctor." A man pushed through the crowd.

"It's not as bad as it looks," Tanner protested as Abby and the doctor helped him to a sitting position. "It's only a flesh wound."

Abby watched as one of their guests, a Dr. O'Shaunessey, cut off Tanner's coat and blood-soaked shirt, but she held on to his hand all the while.

Tanner suffered the man's ministrations in grim-faced silence. Once cleaned, the wound was revealed as only a small round hole—or rather two small round holes in the fleshy part of Tanner's upper arm. But Abby never once broke the connection to him as the doctor applied an ointment, then bandaged him securely.

Someone covered Patrick, then had him carried away, while her grandfather's other servants kept curious onlookers at bay. But Abby cared only for Tanner's well-being, and when the doctor closed his bag and departed, leaving her, Tanner, and her grandfather alone in the wrecked pergola, she knew what she had to do.

"I'm marrying Tanner," she stated flatly, though whether her challenging words were directed more at Tanner or at Willard was hard to determine. "I'm marrying him and going off to live with him. You have Cliff now." She turned to face her grandfather. "And with any luck we shall provide you with a houseful of great-grand-children. Isn't that right, Tanner?" She turned back to him.

For all Abby's confident words, as she stared into Tanner's face, she was more frightened than she'd ever been before. Not Cracker O'Hara nor even Patrick Brady inspired so much terror in her as did the thought of Tanner turning her down.

He'd said he loved her. Or at least he'd started to. But he hadn't agreed to marry her. A lady wouldn't force the issue this way, she knew. But she didn't care about being a lady. She only cared about being Tanner's wife.

She waited for Tanner's response. She waited for a nod, or a smile, or some word of consent. God forbid that he should frown. Then his hand tightened on hers, and she knew.

If he smiled or nodded after that, she didn't know, for tears of happiness clouded her eyes.

"Well, I'll be a son of a bitch," she heard her grandfather mutter. But there was a wondering sort of acceptance in his tone.

Tanner brought her hand to his lips for a kiss, and with a gasp that was half sob and half laugh, Abby wiped her tears away. She met the dark stare of the man she loved, the intense blue gaze that was unclouded now, no longer shuttered, but clear and shining with the love she'd always hoped to see there. Then he shifted his eyes to her grandfather.

"Sir, I know this comes as a surprise, but I love your granddaughter and she loves me." He looked back at Abby, a smile on his dear, handsome face. "I want to marry her and care for her every day of the rest of our lives. I'll work my tail off to give her everything she wants. I hope you'll give us your approval and your blessing."

Willard Hogan ran a hand across his brow, quite at a loss for words as he stared at the hopeful faces of his granddaughter and the man she loved. Once more his plans were falling apart.

He blinked when Abby's face blurred and her mother's face—his dear Margaret's face—appeared instead.

Perhaps you *could* make a silk purse out of a sow's ear, he realized. Perhaps he'd already done it and never recognized it, first with his lovely Margaret and now with Abby. She was beautiful, cultured, well educated. Everything a lady could hope to be. Marriage to a certain sort of man couldn't improve her; she was already perfect.

Slowly he pushed to his feet. "My approval *and* my blessing?" He studied them both a moment, then smiled. "You have it. But only if you let me throw you the biggest, grandest, most spectacular wedding this town's ever seen."

They agreed. But then he'd known they would.

EPILOGUE

The McKnight Horse Farm
Iowa
1859

Abby's toe pushed at the earth, and the wooden swing began its slow, lazy rhythm. Tanner paused at the corner of the house and for a long moment he just stared at her. Little Will was dozing off against her side. Every now and again his big blue eyes would open. But Abby's singsong telling of another of her Tillie and Snitch tales was drawing the three-year-old off into peaceful story dreams of his own.

Abby lay the latest of her published books down on her lap, then ran her fingers through Will's dark curls. She smiled—the most beautiful smile in the world, Tanner thought. And as he had done a million times, he marveled that she could actually be his. His wife. His lover. The mother of his child.

As if she sensed his presence, she lifted her head and met his devouring gaze. Her smile changed then, becoming no less tender and loving, but adding a certain womanly awareness, an appreciation and an invitation.

Fighting down an urge to make love to her right then and there, he moved forward.

"Would you carry Will upstairs for his nap?" she whispered.

He bent down to kiss her, and the swing's pattern altered. "Sure." He started to pull away, but her hand curved around his neck and tangled in his hair.

"Hurry back," she pleaded. She kissed him, then darted her tongue against his lips. Tanner deepened the kiss until Will squirmed between them. When he drew back, his breath was coming faster.

"Your grandfather and young Cliff are due in sometime this afternoon," he reminded her.

She smiled in that sweetly wicked way she had. "Then you'd better hurry, hadn't you? I'll be in the barn."

Tanner hurried all right. He carried his precious young son into the child's bedroom and tucked the boy beneath fresh-smelling sheets. He ran his hand once over the tousled curls and down the faintly flushed cheek. *His* child in *his* house. And *his* wife was waiting in his barn for him.

As he took the stairs three at a time and strode impatiently across the yard to the barn, he thought, not for the first time, that he was the luckiest man in the world, and the happiest.

The barn was dim and cool, and the smell of horses and straw was familiar and yet erotic. He and Abby had played this game before, and he knew all her favorite hiding places. As he searched, growing more and more eager for her, he heard a muffled laugh.

In a moment he had her, soft and warm and firm beneath him. They lost track of time in the barn and were oblivious to anything but each other. Horses nickered in the corral outside. The wind sighed in the maple tree just beyond the barn door, and somewhere a mockingbird trilled. But Abby and Tanner were oblivious to it all.

Above them, scampering across one of the barn's hand-hewn beams, two mice paused and stared down at

the people embracing in the haystack. But the mice had
other things on their mind, things much more pressing
than the goings-on between humans. For there was that
little pile of corn set out for them each day, which had to
be brought back to the nest for their young ones. And
there were other adventures to be had: an old wagon
covered with a tarp that must be explored, an abandoned
rabbit hole in the yard. The cat to tease.

Ah, but life was good.